Peggy & Mrs. Whelan

Haslemere
1958

THE LIGHTHEARTED QUEST

THE
LIGHTHEARTED
QUEST

by
Ann Bridge

THE REPRINT SOCIETY
LONDON

FIRST PUBLISHED 1956
THIS EDITION PUBLISHED BY THE REPRINT SOCIETY LTD
BY ARRANGEMENT WITH CHATTO AND WINDUS LTD 1958

PRINTED IN GREAT BRITAIN BY
BUTLER AND TANNER LTD
FROME AND LONDON

This novel is pure fiction. Real places are
mentioned, but none of the characters
introduced is intended to bear any relation to an actual person, living or dead.

ANN BRIDGE

Chapter 1

"I SIMPLY can't think how to get hold of him," said Mrs. Monro dolefully, leaning forward in her chair to poke unskilfully at the fire of rather damp logs, which hummed and sizzled faintly in the wrong sort of grate for wood.

"Have you advertised?" asked Mrs. Hathaway. As she spoke she picked up the tongs, arranged the logs better, and pushed some bits of bark from the log-basket in between them; then kneeling down she began to ply the bellows.

"Yes," said Mrs. Monro, with a sort of weak pride. "In *The Times*, and the *Telegraph*, and the *Continental Daily Mail*—Edina said I ought to try that."

"Quite right. And how long ago was that?" asked Mrs. Hathaway, continuing to blow the fire, in which the bark now began to burn rather more hopefully.

"Three weeks the Continental one, and five the others, and there's still not a word. But now that his Uncle's dead, Colin simply *must* come home—I can't run this great place alone."

This was at least the eleventh time in the course of a single conversation that Mrs. Monro had said that her son Colin must return to run the property in Argyll, which would be, and indeed effectively now was, his. Since her husband's death her brother-in-law, Colonel Monro, had taken charge of it for his young nephew, but when he took pneumonia and died the crisis had arisen; and Mrs. Monro, as usual when a crisis arose, had sent for Mrs. Hathaway.

"When did Colin write last?" Mrs. Hathaway asked.

"Oh, *ages* ago; at least nine months. He is so naughty and unkind; it's really *wrong*," said Colin's mother.

Mrs. Hathaway in her heart agreed, but she kept to the main issue.

"Where did he write from, then?"

7

"Let me think—was it Tangier, or Casablanca, or Cadiz? —or that place with the funny name? Wait—I'll look," said Mrs. Monro, getting up and walking across the worn and faded carpet, with its hideous pattern of bunches of roses tied with ribbon on a black ground, to her cluttered Victorian escritoire, where papers bulged untidily from all the pigeonholes and lay piled in heaps, obstructing the drawers. She poked and pulled and peered ineffectually, while Mrs. Hathaway looked on with the mixture of pity and irritation which her friend always aroused in her.

"No, I can't find it. How tiresome," said Mrs. Monro, stuffing papers back into quite different orifices from those whence she had removed them. She opened a drawer, muttering "This is only bills. Oh, no, here it is," she exclaimed in triumph, and returned to her chair. "Look, it *is* from the place with the funny name—Cuter, I should call it, but Edina says it's pronounced Theeoota." She handed the letter over.

Mrs. Hathaway read it with attention. It was short, and uninformative to a degree which to her suggested some form of deliberate concealment. The boat was all right, though they had had a spot of engine trouble; business had been fairly good; one of his partners had gone home—none of them was mentioned by name, Mrs. Hathaway noticed—but he and the others were well; the weather was splendid, and he was her loving son, Colin.

"Tell me again what exactly the 'business' is," Mrs. Hathaway said, folding up this unsatisfactory missive and handing it back.

"Selling oranges, or bananas," said Mrs. Monro. "They go in and buy them in one place, and then sail off and sell them in another. I remember he said about eighteen months ago that they had done very well in Marseilles; that was what made Edina think of the *Continental Daily Mail*, because it's published in Paris."

Mrs. Hathaway passed over this characteristic *non sequitur*.

8

"I shouldn't have thought there was much profit to be made out of selling oranges round all those Mediterranean ports," she said. "They grow them in Africa as well as in Spain, and even in that extreme south-west corner of France, I believe. And if he was going to pick up bananas he'd have to go right out to the Canaries. How big is the boat?—big enough for that?"

Of course Mrs. Monro had no idea how big the boat was. Edina might know, she said; but Edina was out seeing about draining those fields on McNeil's farm, that poor John had been so keen on—"It was standing over those wretched drainers, in the East wind, that made him ill and killed him," said Mrs. Monro, beginning to dab at her eyes.

"Does Colin ever ask you for money now?" Mrs. Hathaway asked, ignoring her friend's all-too-easy emotion.

"*No*," said Mrs. Monro, perking up and putting away her handkerchief. "That's the extraordinary thing. He did ask for three hundred pounds to help to buy the boat, right at the beginning—but since then he's never asked for a penny. So you see there *must* be money in selling oranges, Mary, whatever you say." Mrs. Monro quite often caught the drift of more that was said than her friends ever expected her to, Mrs. Hathaway knew. She considered this last item in silence. For Colin not to ask for money for at least three years was, as his mother said, extraordinary; but nevertheless this business of orange—or banana—selling sounded strangely unconvincing.

"May I see the letter again?" she said, and having looked at it—"Does he never give any sort of address?" she asked. "This just says 'Ceuta'."

"No—that's all he ever says and I write '*Poste Restante*, Cadiz,' or whatever it is."

"And he never says where he's going next, so that you could catch him with a telegram?"

"No. He really is very naughty and unkind," said Mrs. Monro, beginning to sniff and fumbling for her handkerchief

9

again. "He used to at first, now I come to think of it; but he hasn't now, for a long while."

A gong boomed through the house, announcing lunch; the two ladies went downstairs, past windows on which rain beat violently, borne on a westerly gale. The fire in the dining-room was worse than that in the sitting-room upstairs, and the deaf and immensely aged butler who crept round on flat feet, handing rather surprisingly good food, somehow added to the general sense of depression—obviously, Mrs. Hathaway thought, it would be useless to try to make him get up a good fire.

"What is this cook you have?" she asked, as a flaked pastry *vol-au-vent*, full of some meat heavily flavoured with garlic, succeeded a delicious omelette.

"Oh, isn't she awful? She's a Spaniard, and one can't say a word to her," said Mrs. Monro. "She *will* put all these flavourings in, and I can't stop her, because she can't understand."

"I think her food is frightfully good," said Mrs. Hathaway. "May I have some more of this?" She got up, the aged butler having retired.

"Oh, yes, do, if you can bear it. Forbes hates her food—he makes her grill him a chop every day."

"Forbes always was a silly old ass," said Mrs. Hathaway, tucking into her second helping of garlic. "You're frightfully lucky, Ellen, to get food like this. But why on earth does she stay up here?—your cook? I should have thought a Spaniard would have frozen to death."

"Oh, she likes having the Macdonald's chapel just next door; she goes to Mass there every single morning. Ronan Macdonald talks a little Spanish too, and she likes that—but he won't translate for *me*," said Mrs. Monro resentfully.

There was a sound of dogs scuffling and being rebuked in the hall outside; after a pause the door opened and Edina Monro came in, a tall girl with very dark straight hair cut close to her head, grey eyes, and a dead-white skin—she wore cream-coloured corduroy slacks and a blue seaman's jersey.

"Is there some lunch for me? I had to come in, it's too wet for the men to go on," she began—"Oh, Mrs. Hathaway, it's nice to see you. Did you have an awful trip?"

"It was a bit rough coming round Ardlamont Point, but I don't mind that," said Mrs. Hathaway, getting up, with the manners of her generation, to shake hands with the girl. "How are you, Edina? You look well."

Miss Monro in fact did look well; there was nothing unhealthy about her intensely white skin, to which not even hours out of doors in a howling gale gave the faintest tinge of colour.

"Thank you; yes, I am very well," said Edina, as she spoke going over and pressing the bell after a brief inspection of the food on the side-table. "Plenty, I see," she muttered, "thank God for Olimpia.—Yes, this revolting climate is in fact incredibly healthy," she said to their guest, pulling up a chair and sitting down beside her. "Forbes, get me a very *hot* plate, and then come and lay me a place," she said, as the butler appeared at the door, a resentful expression on his old face. "And tell Olimpia that we shall want coffee."

"Dear, we don't need coffee after lunch," said Mrs. Monro.

"Oh, yes, we do—I see you hadn't ordered it, even for your poor friend after her long journey! Really, Mother, you are barbarous."

"I'm sure Forbes doesn't like the way you speak to him," said Mrs. Monro, changing her ground.

"No, why should he? But he does what I tell him, which is more than he does for you," her daughter replied tranquilly —"Spoilt, lazy old bastard." Mrs. Hathaway could not restrain a tiny laugh; she liked Edina very much.

"Well, he is, you know," the girl said, encouraged by the laugh. "But at least one doesn't have to carry in trays, or wash up, thank God."

A *crème brûlé*, faultlessly made, followed the *vol-au-vent*; Mrs. Hathaway, accustomed to the mutton-and-milk-pudding rigours which normally prevailed at Glentoran, mentally echoed Edina's thanks to her Creator for the Spanish cook. Over the coffee, which the girl made Forbes bring up to the sitting-room, the subject of finding Colin again arose.

"Mother, you'd better go and rest; it's past your time," said Edina, after Mrs. Monro had recapitulated at some length most of what she had said to her guest before lunch—"I made you late, I know, but off you go. You'll be wretched this evening if you don't have it." And with a sort of kindly firmness she hustled her parent off, finding her book and spectacles for her.

"There—now we can talk," the girl said with satisfaction, returning to the fire, on which she placed two or three more logs. "It is good of you to come up," she said. "Poor Mother is in a frightful state."

"That's very understandable," said Mrs. Hathaway. "But Edina, tell me one thing—how much good would Colin be at running this place, even if you could get him back?"

"Oh, you know, I think he might manage all right. He didn't do too badly at Cambridge, or at Cirencester. He's capable enough; it's just that he likes changing—he doesn't seem to care about sticking to one thing."

"He would have to stick to this," said Mrs. Hathaway. "The land is one thing that can't be left to itself."

"Well, he might, now. There wasn't much point in his sticking up here while Uncle John was running it perfectly, and loving doing it."

Mrs. Hathaway meditated.

"You wouldn't take it on yourself, Edina?" she presently asked. "Robertson was singing your praises all the way from the pier: 'Miss Edina gets a grup on things,' he said," she added smiling.

"Oh, yes, I get a 'grup' all right," said Edina cheerfully,

"but it's not really the sort of thing I care to do, nor what I was educated for, at vast expense. And I'm not sure that we can afford it, really."

"How do you mean?"

"Well, there's not much more than a living for two to be got off this place, and in London I'm making fifteen hundred a year. I give Mother *her* dress-allowance these days," said Edina, with a grin.

"Good Heavens! Fifteen hundred a year!" Mrs. Hathaway was startled. She knew that Edina had taken a good degree in Modern Greats at Oxford, and that she was working at some job in London, but she had never imagined that her young friend was making a living on that scale. "What do you do?" she asked, with interest.

"Oh, I'm in advertising—the new high-powered sort. In its rather phoney way it's really very interesting, and now that we're beginning to get into T.V. it's going to be more interesting still, and better paid."

"*Better* paid? Gracious."

"Oh, yes, I'm due for a rise to two thousand pounds in June, unless my coming off up here bitches it," said Edina. "They gave me three months' leave, when I said I had to have it, without a murmur, so I dare say it will be all right. But I want to get back as soon as I can, rise or no rise; there are some rather tricky things coming up soon that I specialise in, and I don't want anyone else to handle them and probably rot them up—and nor do my bosses," she added.

Mrs. Hathaway observed, with slight surprise, that there was nothing objectionable about Edina's complete self-confidence; it was entirely objective.

"Yes," she said after a pause. "I see that you really oughtn't to be held up here. But have you any ideas as to how to get hold of Colin?"

"No—that's what so tiresome. Maddening boy! Have you, Mrs. H.?"

"Well, I've been thinking about it, since your Mother told me what she knows—which is little enough," said Mrs. Hathaway. "And I have got the impression that there is something rather funny about the whole thing."

"Funny or phoney?"

"Well, both, really. Anyhow, writing is no good, since his last address is nine months old; and advertising is no good, because either he doesn't see the papers, or if he does he doesn't choose to answer. I think someone will have to go and find him."

This time it was Edina who was startled. She opened her grey eyes very wide.

"That's a thought! But I don't see quite how anyone would set about it. You mean go and enquire at all these film-scenario ports?"

"Yes. And the boat must be registered—what's her name, by the way?"

"Oh, that damnable child has never even told us that!" Edina exploded. "He really is *too* tedious."

"Well, all the more reason for on-the-spot enquiries," said Mrs. Hathaway. "Three or four young Englishmen, cruising about and selling oranges or bananas or whatever they *do* sell —I don't really much believe in the orange part, myself— ought to be tolerably identifiable."

"You know, I believe you really have got something there," said Edina. "But who's to do it? Would *you* go?"

"Oh, no, I should be useless at badgering consulates and accosting harbour-masters, or whatever one does to find missing yachts—it would have to be someone young and enterprising.'

"Anyone in mind?" Edina enquired, eyeing Mrs. Hathaway rather suspiciously.

"Yes. Julia, I thought," that lady replied.

"Julia? Do you think she'd be any good? Well, yes, I suppose she might—she's not really half as stupid as she looks," said

Edina. "But would she go? She has oodles of money of course—but one's only allowed a hundred pounds, and I should think all this foraging around in Tangier and places would cost a lot."

"That's why I think Julia would be so suitable. She's a journalist, and they can get extra foreign allowances for trips."

"She's a pretty half-baked journalist; only this free-lancing for weeklies, and the *Yorkshire Post* now and then," Edina objected.

"Oh, my dear child, I'm sure that doesn't matter a bit. I know a woman who writes for most terrible magazines, things you've never even heard the names of, and she is always rushing off to Cannes and St. Moritz and so on to write up the film-stars and their clothes and all that—she gets colossal foreign currency allowances, I know."

"I see. Yes, well then Julia is quite a thought. She could get away all right, I expect. I don't suppose her papers would mind," said Edina, rather cattily.

Mrs. Hathaway laughed.

"All right—let's ring her up tonight," Edina went on. "The sooner we find him the better, for me as well as for Mother. Only I still wonder if Julia is up to it."

"Oh, don't underestimate Julia. You don't really know her much, do you?"

"Well, no. One has one's own friends, somehow. Do you know her well?"

"Yes—her mother was a friend of mine," said Mrs. Hathaway, rather slowly. It flicked into Edina's mind, belatedly, that she had heard that after Mrs. Probyn's death and Major Probyn's re-marriage, Mrs. Hathaway had befriended Julia, their only child. Colin and Edina were not very closely related to her. Julia's mother had been their father's first cousin, and had often brought her to Glentoran when they were all children; but after Mrs. Probyn's death all that had ceased—the Monros had never greatly cared for Major Probyn, and liked his second wife even less. Julia had been left a considerable fortune by her grandmother, so that she was able to lead a quite independent life, not shackled to her father and step-mother; she worked as a journalist because it amused her, not because she was in any need of earning her living, and she had been abroad a good deal, as Edina, feeling rather exculpa-tory, now pointed out to Mrs. Hathaway—one didn't see so much of people if one never knew whether they were there or not, she explained.

"Yes, of course," said Mrs. Hathaway pleasantly. "I don't blame you for not knowing Julia, Edina—I'm only pin-pointing the fact that you don't! *C'est une constatation*, as the French say."

Edina laughed, relieved. How sensible and *nice* Mrs. Hathaway was.

"I wonder if she would go," she went on. "Shall we put it all up to her on the telephone, or try to get her to come up? It's rather a long business to explain."

"We'll see how she reacts," said Mrs. Hathaway. "It would be better if she came, I think, if she can get away at once. Another reason why she would be a good person to go," she pursued, "is that she's a very fair linguist; her French is excellent, and she speaks quite tolerable Spanish too."

"Oh, well then, do let's get her to come up," said Edina, "to brace up Olimpia. She cooks quite differently after Ronan's been talking to her, though I believe he only knows about twenty-eight words."

"He must have been talking to her this morning," said Mrs. Hathaway. "That *lovely* lunch."

Julia, when telephoned to, made no difficulties at all about coming up. Mrs. Hathaway, who by common consent did the talking, merely said that they were all in trouble about Colin, who couldn't be got hold of just now; they thought Julia might be able to help, perhaps, and was there any chance of her coming up to talk it over? "To be much good," said Mrs. Hathaway, with her customary clarity, "it ought to be *soon*."

"Oh, yes, I'll come at once. If I take a sleeper tomorrow

16

night—no, that means two days. I'll fly to Renfrew tomorrow, the first flight I can get, and wire for a car to bring me on; that will save a day. Unless I ring up, if I *can't* get a seat, I'll see you about tea-time tomorrow. It will be lovely to be at Glentoran again. How's Aunt Ellen?"

"As easy at that," said Mrs. Hathaway, having retailed these plans to the other two.

"Well, it must be nice to be able to splash money about like that," said Edina.

"Yes—and sensible, too. Julia is rather good about knowing what to spend on," said Mrs. Hathaway. She turned to Edina with a small smile. "Bottle up your prejudice till she comes— you are far too sensible yourself to let my approval of Julia put you against her," she said—and Edina, who had been doing exactly that, did cause her vague hostility to subside.

"I still don't see how Julia is to find him, Mary," said Mrs. Monro.

"One finds very little without looking for it, Ellen," replied Mrs. Hathaway. "Do you mind if I go to bed? I feel rather like it, after the journey."

Julia Probyn arrived next day, not at tea-time, but as they were sitting down to lunch—a scrunch of car wheels on the gravel outside the dining-room windows announced the advent of a huge Chrysler, driven by a smart chauffeur.

"I'll go, Forbes," said Edina to the old butler, who was bumbling round with dishes with his usual maddening slowness; "lay another place"—and she went out. A moment later she returned, ushering in her young relation.

"Dear Aunt Ellen, I do apologise for being so early," said Julia, kissing her aunt affectionately. "I rang up the air-line last night and got a cancellation for the first flight, such luck —so I told them to tell Renfrew to have a car ready, and here I am." She turned to kiss Mrs. Hathaway with even more warmth. "How blessed to see you. And Aunt Ellen, can my driver-man have some lunch?"

17

"Of course," said Edina, answering for her parent. "Just come and mutter some of your Spanish to our cook, and she'll be your slave."

"Really, Edina—" Mrs. Munro began in protest; but her daughter ruthlessly led the guest out across the hall and through the red baize door to the back regions. Julia, smothering mirth, spoke solemnly in elegant Castilian to Olimpia, whose haughty features relaxed at the familiar accents in which she was asked to provide food for the chauffeur—bowing, smiling, she expressed her desire to do everything she could.

"*Le agradeço mucho su amabildad,*" said Julia, eyeing her sternly, and returned to the dining-room, telling her driver on the way to wait in the hall till Forbes should summon him to his meal. "Don't smoke," she added casually, earning Edina's silent approbation.

Julia was tall, and built on full if graceful lines; her large smooth oval face usually held very little expression; this mattered less because of her perfect, faintly tawny complexion, as lightly flushed with colour as a nearly-ripe apricot, the exquisite level line of her mouth, and above all her immense grey-blue eyes, which somehow seemed to promise all sorts of delightful expressions, though entirely without her volition. (Her friends called them doves' eyes, her enemies likened them to the eyes of cows.) Her hair was a sort of tawny blonde, a most peculiar shade; she wore it drawn back plainly from her shapely forehead, to hang, a deplorable length, half-way down her shoulders, where it ended in flowing curls, like liquid treacle. To complete this exotic appearance she was beautifully dressed, and had long perfect legs. During lunch Edina studied her, fascinated. She usually spoke very slowly, without actually drawling, and her deep voice was as devoid of expression as her face. Except that her fairness had this curious tawny quality she was, Edina thought, the arch-type of the dumb blonde.

The other exception to the type was the fact that she was nothing like as dumb as she looked; this emerged during the discussion of her mission, which took place after lunch, when Mrs. Monro had again been despatched to rest by her daughter. Mrs. Hathaway and Edina had no need to stress the urgency of Colin's return, since Mrs. Monro had dealt with that aspect with wearisome thoroughness during lunch, and indeed until she retired; they concentrated on telling the little they knew— about the boat or yacht, the friends, the orange or banana-selling, and the ports at which he was known to have touched during the past three years. Julia listened, largely in silence— at last she said—

"In fact you really haven't a clue as to where he may be now?"

"No, not the faintest."

"Detection!" said Julia, delighted, a gleam of interest at last showing in her face. "Pure detection! What a frolic! Yes, of course I'll go; I'd love to escape this hellish winter. And Colin used to be such a darling—I'd adore to find him. I expect I shall."

"How shall you begin?" enquired Mrs. Hathaway.

"Could we look at a map?" said Julia. "I'm rather vague about where all these places are, and how to get to them."

Edina brought an atlas, in which Julia underlined various ports with a rose-tipped finger—"Casablanca, Tangier with Gib. almost opposite," she murmured; "Ceuta, yes, and Malaga up round the corner—and then Oran and Algiers and all those places. *I* see."

"We never heard of his going to Oran or Algiers," said Edina; "it was more Malaga and Gib. and Cadiz, and Tangier and Casablanca—down that end."

Julia lit a cigarette, slowly as she did everything, and blew out smoke.

"I shall begin with Africa, I think," she pronounced.

"Why?"

19

"Well, Morocco and Algiers are news just now, with all these assassinations and bomb-throwings and skirmishes and things, and I shall have to get the papers lined up in order to get an extra currency allocation." Edina nodded approvingly —they had not yet raised this point with Julia; obviously there had been no need to.

"*Ebb and Flow* and *The Onlooker* can't run to special correspondents out there, but they would be sure to love articles and call them 'from our correspondent in Morocco' without paying a farthing extra," she pursued, a slow smile making her beautiful mouth even more beguiling. "So they would give me the right chits to push across the counter to those elderly virgins in the Bank of England."

Edina laughed.

"I can do Spain later," Julia pursued, "if I draw a blank on the coasts of High Barbary."

"How shall you go?—fly?" Mrs. Hathaway enquired. She was delighted, secretly, that Julia was showing up so well.

"Oh, no, I think not. Some boat—if I'm going to look for a boat, I'd rather start on a boat, to get the feel of the thing, if you follow me. I'll ring up some of the lines later—if you'll let me?" she said to Edina, who registered suddenly how agreeable these pretty manners were; she knew that Julia would pay for her calls, but the question was graceful. "Of course," she said.

Julia got up and went over again to the atlas, and gazed at it.

"The Lynches are in Casablanca," she said. "They might know something. He's in some bank, and banks know a lot."

"I shouldn't have thought Colin used a bank much, except to wheedle the manager into letting him overdraw," said Edina.

"Where's his account now? Still in Cambridge, or up here, or where?" Julia asked. "Is it still open?"

"Goodness, we never thought of that. I've no idea. It used to be in Duntroon, with a pay-in and pay-out account in some bank at Cambridge, like I had at Oxford."

"Well, let's ring up Duntroon now, and see if it's still there."

This was done, by Edina. Mr. MacIntyre, the agent, protesting that it was against the regulations, nevertheless vouchsafed the information—"just for you privately, Miss Monro, since I know ye all so well"—that Mr. Colin had closed his account some nine months ago; the balance had been transferred to the Banque Regié Turque in Casablanca.

"There you are!" said Julia triumphantly. "Where a man's bank-account is, there shall his body be also, at least occasionally. We're getting warmer."

"Can there really be a branch of the Banque Regié Turque in Casablanca?" Mrs. Hathaway asked. "It seems most extraordinary. I thought that was purely a Turkish thing."

"Well, Mr. MacIntyre would never pay sixpence into a non-existent bank," said Edina—"There must be. Look!" she exclaimed suddenly—"Nine months ago. But that's just when he stopped writing!"

"Who, Colin?" Julia asked.

"Yes—at least we've never heard since then. He didn't write all that often before, but there's never been such a long gap as this."

"Well, this may be where Paddy Lynch will come in," said Julia—"one banker will sometimes talk to another banker. I'd certainly better look in at Casablanca. But Edina, why don't you write to him there, care of the Banque Regié Turque? It seems the firmest address you've had."

"Well, we could," said Edina dubiously—"but he never answers. If you're going out I should hardly have thought it worth while."

"Oh, very well. In that case, Edina, I think I'll start getting onto the shipping lines: some of them must have offices in Glasgow."

"It's frightfully expensive before the cheap time begins," said Edina.

"Ah, and they're shut when it does. No, on we go; I'll try

to remember to put the charges to expense account," said Julia, with another of those slow pleasing grins. "I'll have them all A. D. & C."

The shipping lines were not very fruitful. Most of the big liners no longer call at Gibraltar when outward bound for Australia or the Far East, and the few that do were booked out till mid-March with sun-seeking Britons. Julie established this fact in a way that amused Edina and Mrs. Hathaway. The bookings were mostly made in London, the shipping clerks told her; they couldn't really say in Glasgow—with languid firmness Julia told them to ring up London, and call her back "collect". "Oh, reverse the charge, if you don't know what 'collect' means," she intoned slowly. "This is urgent—I'm the Press. Do please get on with it." They got on with it, and reported these negative results. Julia, scribbling pounds shillings and pence on the telephone pad, said—"Well, that's useless."

"Why not try a cargo-boat?" said Mrs. Hathaway. "I believe they go to all sorts of small places, and if you want to get the 'feel', as you say, of a banana-boat, or whatever Colin's is, that should be just the thing."

"A good idea," Julia agreed.

"Do you get sea-sick?" Edina put in. "Cargo-boats can be pretty small—I had some chums who went to Greece on one, and it was tiny."

"No—never sea-sick. Yes, a cargo-boat is undoubtedly the thing, but I expect I could fix that more easily in London. In fact, Edina, I think I'd better flash off again tomorrow and get onto it; poor Aunt Ellen, she's in a dismal frenzy herself, and I'm sure driving you frantic—quite apart from your firm howling for you. Do you mind if I ring up Renfrew for a passage? Oh, what a pity—it is so nice up here. I do love Glentoran."

Chapter 2

"WELL, this is the London Docks, lady," said the taxi-man to Julia a week later, pulling up at a huge gateway beyond which black-looking buildings loomed through a grey downpour of rain. "Know which shed you want?"

"Number Nine," said Julia, consulting a paper which the shipping company had given her.

"Ought to be a policeman," said the taxi-driver.

"Hoot," said Julia.

When the driver hooted a policeman appeared from a sort of sentry-box by the gates, and asked what Julia wanted.

"The *Vidago*."

"May I see your ticket, please?" He inspected it, and looked curiously at Julia through the cab window; then directed the driver.

"Go along as far as you can, straight, and then turn right. You'll see her lying." The taxi passed through the big gates, and proceeded slowly over cobbles gleaming in the rain; the buildings formed a sort of canyon, its floor nearly as wet as a river-bed; short broad spaces led off it on one side, piled with crates and wine-barrels; more wine-barrels cluttered the canyon-floor itself—Julia had never seen so many wine-barrels in her life. At length they reached a transverse road; the taxi turned right, and in a few seconds came to the water, where nearly a hundred yards away a ship lay moored alongside the berth.

"That'll be her," said the driver.

Julia stared at the boat with the curiosity which everyone feels about a ship they are to travel on. She was prepared for it to be small, for she knew the *Vidago* to be only thirteen hundred tons, but she was startled by its extreme dirtiness. All the paintwork that should have been white was smeared

23

with black grime, or stained and mottled with rust; it looked very unappetising.

The driver got out, turning up his collar, and began to unstrap her suitcases.

"Oh, leave those," said Julia. "I don't want them put down in this mess." The quayside was quite as filthy as the ship, and wetter. "I'll go and find a steward or someone—wait, please." And she walked off towards the boat along the strip of cement between the water and the open-fronted shed from which goods were embarked, a big resonant place as dirty as everything else, full of crates of goods and, she noted, tractors —innumerable tractors. Her progress was presently blocked by a crane, from whose control cabin, forty feet above her head, a monkey-faced man in blue jeans peered out at her curiously; to circumvent this obstacle she took to the shed, where four or five men were languidly mounting crates on outsize luggage-barrows; re-emerging onto the quay she found herself at the *Vidago's* gangway. This was almost surrealist, she thought; it consisted of a sort of ladder of black slimy wooden steps, with dirty ropes for hand-rails, mounting to the deck of the *Vidago* at an angle of some thirty-five degrees. Julia surveyed it with distaste, and instead of attempting the disagreeable ascent, stood still and shouted.

A porthole close above her was pushed open, and a huge red face poked through it. "Who d'ye want?" it enquired.

"Someone to bring my luggage aboard," said Julia.

"Och, I don't know that there's anyone here—they're mostly ashore," said the red face.

"But we're sailing at four. I'm the passenger," said Julia.

"We're only sailing tomorrow, no the nicht," the face pronounced; it then withdrew, closing the porthole.

"Oh, *God!*" said Julia, crossly and loudly. She stood for a moment, undecided what to do next. To spend the next twenty-four hours in these surroundings was a dismal prospect; on the other hand her taxi was going to cost a fortune, with all that luggage—it seemed absurd to pay it twice over. (Mrs. Hathaway was quite right about Julia's sensible views as to what it was worth spending money on.) She determined to get most of her stuff on board at once, somehow, and walked back towards the taxi; passing as before through the cargo-shed she looked round for a barrow, found one, and wheeled it out along the quay—as she passed below the crane she was once more hailed from above, this time by the monkey-faced man in the cabin atop of it.

"Want help with your baggage, Miss?"

"Yes, please," Julia called up; on reaching the taxi she and the driver began to pile her suitcases onto the barrow. They had just finished this task and she was paying off the cab when two individuals came up simultaneously—one the crane-driver, the other a tall man with a curly brown beard, in a very shabby nautical uniform and a peaked cap.

"Can I help?" the newcomer asked.

"Oh, I think this kind person is going to take my stuff aboard the *Vidago* for me—there seems to be no one else to do it," said Julia coldly. She was feeling extremely cross.

"I'm the mate of the *Vidago*," said the bearded man. "I'll send the boy along—this chap can't go aboard. But we're not sailing till tomorrow, you know."

"I know nothing of the sort," said Julia, more coldly still. "Your passenger manager or whatever he calls himself told me yesterday at six o'clock to be here at three sharp, to sail at four, and I have no contrary instructions."

"Ah yes, but there's been a hold-up," said the bearded man. "Very sorry." He spoke with a very cultivated accent, which contrasted sharply with his shabby appearance.

"I'm sorry too, but I can't help that," said Julia—"I and my luggage are coming aboard *now*, according to schedule. Carry on—take it to the gangway," she said to the crane-driver.

A grin appeared in the depths of the mate's beard.

25

"Oh, very well," he said.

"If your 'boy' can drag this up your ladder and put it in my cabin, he had better," said Julia, walking off after the crane-driver and the barrow; the mate, his grin expanding in his beard, followed.

Her cabin, when she reached it, after negotiating the precipitous gangway and following the mate along decks as black and filthy as the rest of the ship, proved a rather agreeable surprise. It was quite a sizable little room, containing besides a substantial bunk with drawers below it, a hanging-cupboard, a desk-cum-chest of drawers, a fitted basin, and a big padded sofa built against the bulkhead.

"Fine," said Julia, looking around her. "But my luggage won't all go in here. Stop," she said firmly to the boy, who was beginning to pile her cases onto the sofa—"only bring in what I tell you. Yes, the typewriter, and those two small ones; that's all for here." She turned to the officer, who loomed, still grinning slightly, in the passageway outside, and asked— "Where does the rest go? You would hardly have a baggage-room, with only one passenger?"

"No, afraid not."

"Well, will you have it put somewhere—*dry*," said Julia calmly.

"Is the pilot's cabin unlocked?" the first officer asked the boy. "Yessir."

"All right—put it in there."

The pilot's cabin was next door to Julia's, similarly furnished and equally large; she supervised the stowing of the rest of her luggage in it, remarking, "Very handy," to the mate.

"You all right now?" he asked, still looking amused.

"No. I must have the keys to lock both these cabins. You can't leave cabins unlocked in port," said Julia. "And then I want to telephone, as there's this delay. Is the ship connected up by telephone?"

"No—not a liner, you know," said the mate. "But you could ring up from the agents' office on the quay."

"Where is that?"

"I'll show you,"—and the keys having been produced by the boy, he led her down the gang-ladder again and along the shed to a small door with a roughly-painted label outside which read "Forres Line. No Admittance".

"Thanks," said Julia briefly; the bearded man, still grinning slightly, raised his hand to his cap and walked off.

The office was a grubby little hole in which a red-haired individual sat at a desk, telephoning; another, wearing a felt hat and a stained raincoat, stood by the window, which was smothered in cobwebs, holding up long yellowish sheets of paper to catch the last light of the winter's afternoon, and occasionally calling out figures to the one at the telephone, who repeated them down it; a third was tinkering with a very small electric fire, on which he succeeded in balancing a kettle just as Julia walked in. They all looked up, and the man at the telephone, saying, "Hold on," asked if she wanted anything?

"To telephone, when the line is free; to the head office," Julia replied.

The man with the kettle, who was very old, removed a pile of ledgers and a couple of beer-bottles from a chair, of which he dusted the seat with his sleeve before offering it to her; she sat down and waited. Presently the list came to an end, and the man at the desk asked her who she wanted at head office.

"The passenger manager."

The passenger manager was 'not available'.

"Find out when he will be, please, and tell him to ring back. Miss Probyn to speak to him.—Can I wait here?" she asked.

"Oh, surely. Have one of mine," said the man at the window, as she pulled out her cigarette case. He looked at her subdued elegance curiously. "You're not for the *Vidago*?"

"Yes."

Julia enjoyed her wait in the Forres Line's quayside office, in spite of her irritation over the delay in sailing. The old man brewed very strong tea on the electric fire, laid on its side, and they gave her a cup, thick with the glutinous over-sweetened condensed milk beloved of the merchant navy—she found time to wonder how the manufacturers contrived to introduce its peculiar and revolting flavour into this product, with which she was to become painfully familiar in the next few days. In spite of her toughness and temper Julia could be quite a good mixer when she chose, and it always interested her to know how operations were carried on in jobs and trades unfamiliar to her; she soon beguiled the three men in that grubby little room sufficiently to learn not only the reason for the *Vidago's* delayed sailing, but a good deal about dockside labour as well.

"The rain, you see," said the red-haired man at the desk. "It came on heavy about eleven, and you can't load in rain."

"Oh, why not?"

"Soaks the holds; rots or rusts the cargo, and anyhow this docks' shift's short-handed today."

"Oh, why is that?" asked Julia, sipping the old man's brew, which reminded her of a mixture of senna and stewed prunes.

"The fight in Belfast," said the man at the desk.

"Really? How come?" enquired Julia.

What she learned fascinated her. One of the dockers named Murphy had for brother a prize-fighter, who was appearing that night in a big fight in Belfast; so Murphy and his closest pals had chartered a private plane to fly to Northern Ireland to see the show, and large numbers of their comrades had gone off by special train to Liverpool, to cross by boat for the same purpose. This, more than the rain, had held up the loading of the *Vidago*. Julia hugged herself. The poor underpaid dockers, always striking for a living wage! Whoever heard of the so-called idle rich hiring private planes and trains nowadays? These views however she kept to herself.

At length the telephone rang; the passenger manager, at last 'available', was on the line.

"Oh, Mr. Scales," said Julia, taking up the instrument— "Miss Probyn here—yes, down at the docks. Why didn't you let me know that the boat isn't sailing till tomorrow?"

Mr. Scales was evasive. Really, he was extremely sorry, but he hadn't known in time to let her know.

"But the rain came on, and the men stopped work, at eleven —that meant there wasn't a hope of getting her out on tonight's tide," said Julia inexorably; she had picked up a lot of information over her tea. "I only left home at two. Surely there would have been time?—in three hours?"

Mr. Scales could almost be heard to wriggle down the telephone. He hadn't heard quite at eleven o'clock; he really was very sorry it had occurred.

"Well, I call it a very poor show," said Julia. "Don't you instruct your dockside staff to keep you informed when this sort of thing happens, so that you can warn your passengers?"

"That'll mean a raspberry for me," muttered the red-haired man, grinning cheerfully, however.

Mr. Scales meanwhile was asking what Miss Probyn meant to do? Could he do anything to help her?

"I expect so. Have you a car?"

Yes, Mr. Scales had a car.

"Then you could come and fetch me, couldn't you, and take me back to the West End?"

"You're not thinking of sleeping on board, then?"

"Yes, certainly I am—my flat is shut, and I don't see any point in paying for a room at an hotel because of this muddle," said Julia firmly. "But I can spend the evening with friends. No, no hurry—so long as I start about six. Right—thank you." She rang off.

"It won't really mean trouble for you, will it?" she

asked the red-haired man. "What time *did* you tell the office?"

" 'Bout twelve—and they know damn well up there that if the stevedores go off before twelve they never come back till after the dinner-hour, not if the sun was blazing."

"Scales is new," said the man in the raincoat. "He doesn't know the works yet."

"Have you any idea what time we shall get off tomorrow?" Julia asked him.

"Not much before ten p.m., I'd say." He turned to consult a dog-eared tide-table which hung on the wall by the window, near which he had remained standing all the time. "No, about ten she should be moving down into the Pool. But they'll want you on board by nine."

"Oh, *what* a bore!" said Julia. "I did want to go down the river by daylight. Oh, well—and now can I have another call, please?"

She tried to ring up Mrs. Hathaway, but that lady was out and would be out all the evening. Julia cast about in her mind who to try next: she had said goodbye to everybody, her flat was shut and her maid gone off to relations in the country; she felt as if her life in London had already, for the time being, come to an end. At last she bethought her of someone to whom she hadn't said goodbye, nor even announced her departure, out of a cowardly desire to avoid what she privately phrased 'bother', when she was in a rush of packing and arrangements. For after a hurried routing round among cargo-lines she had come on the *Vidago*, sailing for Tangier in under a week and carrying one passenger; she had seized on this chance, but the ensuing days had been a frenzied scurry of what she called 'lining-up' the papers for which she wrote, securing her currency allocation, getting the appropriate visas on her passport and all the rest. The person to whom her thoughts now turned was a young man in the Treasury, who in a rather indeterminate way was an admirer—that is to say she had refused him once, he had sulked for some months, and latterly had begun to hang round her again. He was very nice; it was even possible that some day she might decide to marry him—meanwhile she had rather a bad conscience about having kept him in the dark regarding her trip, and he would, if free, certainly be delighted to take her out to dinner and a movie. So she asked for another call. (She made no offer to pay—this was all the Forres Line's fault, anyhow.)

"Is that the Treasury? Mr. Consett, please . . . Geoffrey? Oh, good . . . Dinner tonight? Yes, I'd love to; in fact I was going to suggest it. What time, and where? . . . Oh, could you make it a bit earlier? Sevenish for drinks? . . . No, not at the flat—it's shut . . . Because I'm going away . . . Well, to Morocco actually—I'll tell you all about it at supper . . . No, don't bother to pick me up . . . Because I'm at the London Docks!" (Here Julia tried unsuccessfully to stifle a giggle.) "No, I'm being brought in to S.W.1.—someone's doing penance! . . . Oh, Geoffrey, don't be sour—I can't explain it all now, and I won't try! Where shall we dine? . . . The Oviedo? Right—but I shan't dress . . . Well then come to my club at seven, for drinks. Goodbye." She rang off.

Both Julia's telephone conversations had brought grins of pleasure to the faces of the other three occupants of the little office—a young lady, going on that little tub the *Vidago*, first ticking off the Head Office and then giving backchat to someone in the Treasury! When she got up and shook hands with them all, with thanks for their tea and their hospitality, each one wrung her hand warmly. "It's been a pleasure. Come in any time," said the old man.

"Oh, I daresay you'll see more of me tomorrow," said Julia airily. "Goodbye, and thank you again."

She went back to her cabin, unpacked and put on a dark frock, with an eye to the gang-ladder, and did her face; on her way up she had yelled for 'the boy', and told him to send Mr. Scales to her cabin when he should arrive. But before that she had another encounter. Emerging to scout about for her escort she almost ran into a small elderly man with grey hair, a smooth grey face, and several gold bands on his sleeves.

"Is it Miss Probyn?" he asked.

"Yes."

"Ah, good evening. I'm sorry we're not starting on time," said this person. "I hope it's not putting you about too much."

"Well, I thought the office might have told me about it," said Julia, who believed in rubbing it in to companies or corporations.

"Won't you come and have a drink?" said the grey-haired man, opening a teak door in the corridor a few yards from her own.

"I'd love to, if someone will tell Mr. Scales where to find me," said Julia, passing through the door. The large, comfortably furnished room in which she found herself told her that she was in the Captain's cabin; it had several of the built-in sofas, a big desk, some arm-chairs, and a cupboard in the wall with a shelf below holding a wooden rack of glasses.

"Scales will find you here all right," said the Captain slowly, moving over to the cupboard—he spoke even more deliberately than Julia herself. "What will you drink?—gin or whisky?"

"Whisky, please."

"Do you like soda?" he asked, holding up a tumbler to the light and squinting at it; as he spoke he opened the lower part of the cupboard, pulled out a spotless cloth, and began to polish the glass.

"Yes, please."

The Captain pushed a bell, meanwhile unlocking the upper cupboard and taking out a bottle of Black-and-White; when the boy tapped on the door he said, "Tell Andrews to bring some soda."

"He's ashore, Sir."

"Is Mr. Harris on board?"

"Yessir—I think so, Sir."

"Then tell him I want some soda, please."

"Yessir."

There was something about the slow formality of Captain Blyth's manner of speaking to his ship's company which was to impress Julia throughout the trip; it began to impress her that first evening when Mr. Harris, who was the chief steward, appeared and said apologetically that Andrews must have gone off with the keys, and he could only find one bottle of soda, which he had borrowed off Mr. Reeder. All Captain Blyth said was—"Thank you. Get some."

"In port, things slow down a bit. The men all like to get ashore, and of course drinks aren't served till we get outside territorial waters," he said, bringing the whisky and soda over to where Julia sat on one of the sofas, and setting them on a table fixed to the bulkhead at her side. "Now, tell me how you like this."

The time passed pleasantly—Julia's lingering vexation gradually melted away under the Captain's slow, cheerful chat. He had a flat, quiet manner and spoke in a gentle, flat voice. He himself liked gin, he said, proceeding to drink it; the agents in the ports mostly liked whisky, and you wouldn't believe how much they would drink; moreover they liked to sit up all night, whereas he, himself, hated staying up late, unless he had to be on the bridge, which was a different thing. He expressed a courteous hope that Julia would be comfortable, and mentioned various people in Tangier who always came out on his ship—"come time after time, the Watsons do. He's a nice man, Mr. Watson—and she's nice, too."

Mr. Scales proved to be a very young man, to Julia's surprise; when she was arranging her passage he had contrived on the telephone to sound almost paternal. When the boy announced him Captain Blyth said, "Oh, I must give you your pass," in his soft voice, and sat down at his desk and unlocked a drawer—everything in his cabin seemed always to be being unlocked and locked again.

"Pass? whatever for?" asked Julia curiously.

"Can't get into the docks at night without. There. Hope you enjoy yourself." He came out with her along the deck to the gangway. "Sorry everything's in a bit of a mess—clean up when we get to sea," he said. "Don't slip, now—that's awkward, that gangway is."

It took Mr. Scales and his small car, caught up in the evening jam of westbound traffic from the City, rather a long time to transport Julia to the discreet club, mostly peopled by women twice her age, for which Mrs. Hathaway had put her up; Mr. Consett was waiting for her, the porter said. Unhurried, Julia went in and found him sitting in the big chintzy drawing-room, reading *Antiquity*.

"I'm sorry I'm late—the traffic in the City was awful, and my penitent didn't drive very well," she said.

"I've not been here long. Who is your penitent, and why?" asked Mr. Consett, locking *Antiquity* away in a black brief-case with the royal cypher on it.

"A *very* incompetent young man—will you have whisky or a Martini?—A Martini and a tomato-juice, please," said Julia to the severe elderly waitress, "and we're not dining here."

"Goodness, Julia, what an ant-heap this place is!" Mr. Consett said in a lowered tone as the waitress moved away, glancing round at the other occupants of the room.

"Well, yes. But the drinks are reasonably good."

" 'A very incompetent young man' you were saying," Mr. Consett prompted her.

"Yes, in the shipping office." She related Mr. Scales's crime. Mr. Consett gazed at her indignantly.

"In fact, you were going to slide off without so much as letting me know! What a *Schweinhund* you are, Julia."

"What is a *Schweinhund*?" asked Julia, sipping her tomato-juice—her languages did not extend to German.

"A mixture of a cur and a swine," said Mr. Consett measuredly. "No, really, Julia—you are *monstrous*."

34

"I was in such a rush," she said, turning the dove's rather than the cow's eyes onto him. "I hadn't a moment to see anyone, Geoffrey; truly I hadn't. Fixing my newspapers, and the visas, and getting extra Travellers' Cheques, and finding a boat to go on—you can't think what an absolute *scrum* it's been."

"Why Morocco, anyhow?" the young man asked. He was very tall; pallid, with thick fair hair, a square intellectual face, and pale blue eyes, he usually looked as severely detached from this world as a youthful St. John the Evangelist in an early Flemish predella.

Julia explained the nature of her quest; Geoffrey Consett immediately became extremely un-detached.

"What is this Colin? A boy-friend? Otherwise, why do you go hooshing off to find him in this completely wild-cat way? I never heard such rubbish."

"Oh, Geoffrey, don't be a clot! People aren't usually boy-friends in at all a *heavy* way if they go off for three years at a time, and never write. But in fact I've hardly seen anything of Colin since he was at Eton."

"Eton? What surname?"

"Monro, you silly. He's Aunt Ellen's son. And I'm only going because Uncle John has gone and died, and Aunt Ellen is in such a fuss, and poor wretched Edina—who makes twice *your* salary, I may say—has got to stay and run Glentoran till someone can find Colin and make him come back and look after his own infernal estate. Not but what it's a most darling place," said Julia.

"Colin Monro—yes, I remember him; he was in Merry-weather's," said Geoffrey, temporarily disregarding all but the Etonian aspect of Julia's remarks. "A pig-headed creature."

"Oh, was he? Well, he's a poor correspondent."

Mr. Consett, during the second round of drinks and over dinner at the Oviedo, continued to cross-examine Julia about Colin and her trip. At one point he asked how the orange-selling venture had been financed. Julia had no idea, but unguardedly let out the fact that nine months earlier the balance of Colin's account at Duntroon had been transferred to the Banque Regié Turque at Casablanca. Mr. Consett pounced on this piece of information like a peregrine on a pigeon.

"Transferred it to Casablanca? How big was the balance?"

"I haven't the smallest clue," said Julia. "Why?"

"Because it's illegal, for a sum of any size. My dear Julia, surely *you* know about currency restrictions?"

"Well, yes, for travelling. I never thought of that," said Julia candidly. "But old Mr. MacIntyre at the Bank of Scotland in Duntroon would never do anything illegal, from what Edina says."

"I must look into this," said Mr. Consett, with more animation than he had yet shown—"the Bank of England will know. Nine months ago, you say?"

"Oh, Geoffrey, *please* don't go making trouble! Edina and Aunt Ellen have quite enough bothers on their plate as it is, without you stirring up the Bank of England with your beastly bureaucratic spoon."

"My dear Julia, do be your age! What all these papers employ you for I can't think," said Geoffrey. He often tried, rather helplessly, to impose his superior knowledge on his love by way of subduing her—a futile process always, and particularly unsuccessful in Julia's case. "If what has been done is within the regulations it can't make trouble," he pursued; "and I agree that the Bank of Scotland are about the last people in the world to slip up. But if the sum was of any size there would have to be special permission for the transfer, and to obtain that reasons would have to be given. I think I might be able to find out what those reasons were. It certainly wouldn't be given for hawking oranges!"

"I wish you wouldn't use words like 'obtain'," said Julia petulantly.

"Oh, darling, what a clown you are! Don't you see that I may be able to help you in this lunatic search-party of yours?" the young man said, reaching for her hand across the table.

Many hands, and often, are held in the Oviedo—Julia was not in the least embarrassed, and suffered poor Mr. Consett to clasp, and even to kiss, her long fingers with their glistening pale pink-tips. Satisfied for the moment—and the waiter arriving with a fresh dish—the young man returned to the subject of her journey, in a more tranquil spirit.

"Where are you sailing to, on your cargo cockleshell?" he asked.

"Tangier—it seems to be the only place boats stop at, going that way. And it's quite a good jumping-off place for all the rest, I gather."

"An excellent one; and a most darling place in itself—like Glentoran," he said, smiling his rather unexpectedly warm smile. "They're doing some very interesting bits of excavation there, too."

"What sort? Neolithic?" Julia knew very little about archaeology, but her prolonged acquaintance with Geoffrey Consett had resulted in her having to hear a good deal about it, and she had picked up some of the words.

"No, no—Roman, and some possible Phoenician too; old La Besse has been working on a fascinating site which is undoubtedly Roman on the top storey, so to speak, but shows signs of Phoenician stuff below that. The amusing thing is that it seems to have been a factory."

"A factory? Goodness, what on earth of?"

"Wine, oil, and they think salt fish—there are pits that suggest fish-pickling more than anything else." He suddenly became enthusiastic. "You ought to see all that, Julia—I envy you going off there now. Look out for old La Besse."

"Who's he?"

"It's not a he, it's a she. An immensely old Belgian lady with a beard! And she sticks at it—she's out on that site day

37

after day, with her rag-time team of Berber labourers, for six or seven hours at a time."

"When were you there?" Julia asked—"I never heard about all this."

"Oh, last winter," said Mr. Consett, trying unsuccessfully not to look too conscious. Last winter had been during the period when he was sulking after being refused by Julia. "She's tremendous fun," he went on rather hastily—"and all that stretch of coast is simply stuffed with Phoenician graves, too."

"What are they like?" Julia enquired, less out of any particular interest in Phoenician graves than from a good-natured desire to co-operate in covering up the embarrassment about last winter.

"Dug out of the rock, I believe, I never saw much of them —I hadn't time. They're mostly rifled; the Berbers go at them like mad."

"What on earth for?"

"Oh, the jewellery. Exquisite golden things turn up sometimes."

"How enchanting!" said Julia; her eyes shone, kindled by the thought of jewellery in any form. "I'd love to see those."

"I'll give you a letter of introduction to Mme La Besse," said the young man—"I'll air-mail it to Tangier. Where shall you be staying, by the way?"

"The Villa Espagnola—moderate, but Cook's say the food and beds are all right."

Mr. Consett jotted the address down.

"There are other things you must do in Tangier if you are going to be there, Colin or no Colin," he said, rather sententiously. "For one, you must go up to the Kasbah, the old Moorish city, on a Friday to see the Mendoub go to the Mosque for his devotions. He has a lovely cavalry guard, all over tassels."

"Who's the Mendoub?"

"The Sultan's representative in the International Zone—a sort of Viceroy, on the smallest possible scale. The Kasbah's lovely, anyhow; the Terence Monteiths have a house there which is quite delicious—look out for them too."

"The Monteiths have a place next door to Glentoran," said Julia—"but I don't suppose I shall meet them."

"Oh, you will—everyone usually meets everyone in Tangier. And don't on any account miss old Lady Tracy—she's lived there for a hundred years, and knows everything; in fact she's quite likely to be able to throw some light on Colin."

"Not an old lady of a hundred, surely," said Julia sceptically.

"You don't know Lady Tracy," said Geoffrey Consett with finality.

Chapter 3

THE *Vidago* got off more or less on time the following night. Julia stayed down at the docks till the ship sailed; it occurred to her that there might be the makings of an article for *Ebb and Flow* in dockside life, so she put on a dirty old featherweight silk mackintosh, such as can only be bought in Italy, visited her new friends in the office and chatted with the crane-driver and the stevedores in the shed; she learned all the details of the fight, anxiously listened to over the wireless by everyone she met, though Murphy's army of backers had not returned—"Oh, they won't show up now till Monday," said the red-haired man in the office. She had various drinks; the first was with the crane-driver, who had taken a fancy to her, at lunch-time; with delightful hesitation he asked if she ever fancied a glass of port?—and when she said she did, led her out to a small cheerful pub, where the fight was also being discussed eagerly. Her lunch she ate on board in the small saloon, along with Captain Blyth and the officer with the beard, who proved to be the Mr. Reeder whose soda the chief steward had 'borrowed' for her the night before; this meal, as it was to do throughout the voyage, took place at twelve-thirty—Julia was late, and when apologising to the Captain explained that she had been having drinks with the crane-driver. She noticed that the mate eyed her rather curiously on hearing this.

"At 'The Prospect of Whitby' I suppose," said the Captain.

"Oh, no—is that near here?"

"Not far off. You ought to see it, if you don't know it."

It rather surprised Julia that the Captain of the *Vidago* should be so accessible before sailing; liners' captains, in her experience, kept themselves *incommunicado* except when on the high seas. But she had still a lot to learn about the ways of cargo-boats: both the hours of meals on board, and the general uncertainty which governs their movements. She was late again for supper, a form of high tea, not having realised that it would be at five-thirty; to repay much hospitality in the little office she had gone over at about five p.m., taking with her a bottle of Bourbon, a farewell offering from an American officer who had fallen under her spell—Julia hated rye whisky, but thought it might go down well in the office, which it did; therefore she was late. But it was over a Scotch with the Captain at nine that she had her real shock. He mentioned casually that they would be putting in at 'Casa'. (He pronounced it 'Cahssa'.)

"Where's that?"

"Casablanca."

"Goodness, are we going to Casablanca?"

Julia had booked to Tangier, understanding that that was the *Vidago's* first port of call; she listened with impatience to Captain Blyth's slowly-pronounced explanation of some failure to deliver part of the cargo for 'Tangiers', as he called it, and how instead they had loaded up with tractors and saloon cars for 'Cahssa'. If they were putting in at Casablanca she might be able to see Paddy Lynch, and cause him to make enquiries about Colin through the Banque Regié Turque; but then, if Geoffrey's probings at the Bank of England yielded any fruitful results, she ought to know what they were before accosting Paddy.

"How long shall we have at Casablanca?" she asked, practically cutting into the Captain's softly-spoken sentences.

"About twelve hours—maybe twenty-four. You never know to an hour or so."

Julia got up, moving a good deal faster than she normally moved.

"Where can I get to a telephone?" she asked. "Do excuse me, but if we're going to Casablanca I ought to get hold of someone at once. The office will be shut of course—damn!"

41

There was a telephone kiosk by the other dock gates, nearer the ship, the Captain told her. Julia remembered those gates, that was the exit which she and the crane-driver had used on their way to the pub.

"Well, if you will forgive me, I'll fly and telephone," she said.

"You'll be back by nine-thirty, won't you?" the Captain said. "I oughtn't to let you off the ship now, it's ten past nine."

"Oh, yes, I'll be back in loads of time. How sweet of you. That perishing Mr. Scales might have told me about going to Casa of course—what a blot the man is," said Julia, hurriedly downing her whisky; she heard the Captain's slow chuckle as she hastened out.

She was out of luck. When she had pattered through the rain to the red kiosk, a desolate little monument to who knows what ardent or despairing last-moment conversations, and put in her three pennies, there was 'No Reply' from Geoffrey's flat. Julia said "Damn" again, pressed Button B, and tried the Garrick—the Club porter, after a prolonged interval, informed her that Mr. Consett was not in the Club. She stood for a moment or two in the cold stuffy little wood-and-glass box, smelling of stale tobacco-smoke, casting about in her mind as to where else she could try, but no brilliant idea occurred to her. Julia had a strongly-held theory, upon which she often acted with success, that in any crisis there is always something clever to do if one can only calm down and think what it is—she therefore calmed down and thought hard, in that telephone box by the London Dock gates; but nothing occurred to her except a strong desire to go and ask kind fatherly Captain Blyth what on earth she could do to get a message ashore at that time of night? Julia did not then know that the *Vidago's* captain was commonly known as "Cheery Blyth", or to his ship's company simply as "Cheery"; but in her moment of need she felt the want of his cheerful kindness, and after splashing back over the wet cobbles and scrambling

42

and slipping up the greasy gangway, she boldly tapped on his door.

"Gracious, you *are* wet," he said, as she entered on his "Come in." "Get your call all right?"

"No. In fact I'm in rather a jam. I suppose there's no earthly means of getting a letter ashore, now?"

"Take off that wet mac thing—I'll dry it in my bathroom," said the Captain; he took it from her and disappeared through an inner door. Returning—"You'd better have some whisky," he said levelly; "don't want to start off with a cold."

"But *can* I get a letter ashore?" Julia asked, as he poured her out a stiff glass.

"O' course—the pilot will take it when we drop him, down the river; easiest thing in the world," said Cheery Blyth, cheerfully.

"Oh, splendid. What time will that be?"

"Some time after midnight. Now you'd better put in your own soda, and get it right."

Blessing the kindly little man, warmed and comforted, Julia sat contentedly in his cabin till a fair rather sleek-haired young man entered to announce that the *Vidago* was about to get under way. Captain Blyth ignored this information till he had effected a rather formal introduction—"Miss Probyn, this is our second officer, Mr. Freeman; Freeman, this is our passenger, Miss Probyn." After which he went leisurely into his inner cabin and emerged in an oilskin and a cap heavy with gold braid, Julia's mackintosh over his arm.

"Oh, thank you. But who do I give my letter to?" Julia asked.

"Put it on my desk—I'll leave my door open, and see that it goes."

By now Julia felt sure that it would. She went to her cabin and scribbled a note to Geoffrey, telling him that they would be calling at Casablanca, and that he should therefore hurry up his enquiries at the Bank of England, and airmail the results to her. Then the idea struck her—where should he write *to*? Poste Restante? A considerable experience of the difficulty attending the extraction of letters from Postes Restantes in France and the Iberian Peninsula had made Julia cautious; she decided that Geoffrey's letter had better be sent care of Paddy Lynch—she must just risk the Lynches being away. She would have written to Paddy too, but she hadn't enough stamps left for airmail, and the Captain and apparently everyone else was either on the bridge or for'ard ringing bells and shouting, as the *Vidago* nosed and edged her way through incredibly narrow locks and channels, gently bumping, sometimes, against the stone sides, on her way to the open river. Tying a scarf round her head Julia went on deck and watched this process for a while. Deck hands ran to and fro, slinging hempen fenders over the side when a bump seemed imminent; arc-lights fizzed above dark water, dirty with refuse of all kinds; figures in oilskins moved about on the wet cement which in this strange world represented land, shouting directions— once one of them bellowed for 'the keys', and some keys tied to a piece of wood were flung down to him. That small circumstance intrigued Julia very much; but it was wet and cold, and on the whole rather monotonous—she went back to her snug little cabin, turned in, and slept.

Julia thoroughly enjoyed her voyage on the *Vidago*. Crossing the Bay of Biscay in January is not normally regarded as a pleasure-trip, but the weather was not excessively bad, and the little vessel rode well, lightly surmounting huge seas that would have dealt shuddering blows to a big liner. Indeed in every way, Julia felt, a small cargo-boat had immense advantages over the leviathans on which she had hitherto done her ocean travel. Personal relations, if slight, were genuine as far as they went; one met the officers at all meals anyhow, and chatted as human beings do over their food—what was wholly and mercifully absent was the forced and bogus heartiness obtaining on large passenger-boats, with their ghastly organ-

44

ised deck-games and evening gaieties. She spent much of her time in her cabin—since except the gloomy little dining-saloon there was nowhere else to sit—or in the pilot's cabin next door, which she used as a study-cum-luggage room, tapping away at an article on 'Dockside Diversions' for *Ebb and Flow*. Now and again, for air, she went on deck; she asked Captain Blyth if he minded slacks on board—such already was her feeling for the little Skipper—when he said "No, very sensible," she wore those, with a duffle-coat and fleece-lined rubber zip-boots to the knee superimposed for her outings. Julia had swithered about taking those boots on a journey into sunshine, it seemed so silly; but she had decided to 'for the Bay'—in fact they were to stand her in good stead on many journeys in Morocco.

The first time that Mr. Reeder, the mate, encountered her on deck thus equipped, he looked her up and down and said —"Jolly good boots. Where did you get the duffle-coat?"

"Buntings, in High Street, Kensington," said Julia—"they go in for war surplus."

She asked him about the shipping that dotted the horizon in all directions—the eastern approaches to the Bay seemed almost as full of traffic as Piccadilly—and had pointed out to her tankers, long, low, and ugly; tramps of various sorts, apparently all familiar to Mr. Reeder: "That's a John Doe Line," he would say of some spot on the skyline; "They're small coal-boats." Near the French coast, off Ushant, lively little fishing craft bobbed about on the grey-blue waters, causing Julia to opine that it must be frightfully difficult to avoid them at night, especially in fog.

"Not any more—radar's made all that easy," he said.

"Oh, have *you* got radar?"

"Naturally," he said, rather huffily.

"I wish I could see it," said Julia.

"You must ask the Old Man about that," said Mr. Reeder, repressively. "I've no objection to passengers on the bridge, in fact I like the company, but it can't be done unless he says so."

Of course Julia asked Captain Blyth at the very next meal, which was one of those rather indigestible spam-and-salad, cake-and-scone collations at the distasteful hour of five-thirty p.m., if she could go up on the bridge some time to watch the radar functioning.

"Yes. Better come up tomorrow night, when we shall be off Finisterre—then you'll see the land on it as well as the ships."

They slogged down across the Bay, that evening and that night; next morning Julia awoke to see a rather thin watery sunlight seeping in at her cabin window. She scrambled hastily out of her bunk—a drawer, half-pulled out below it, she had learned to use as a ladder—and ran across to the window to look out. Yes, sun it was, albeit rather faint as yet; in London one had forgotten that such a thing as sunshine existed. And the sea was blue too—faintly blue; anyhow not that cold steely grey. She felt extraordinarily exhilarated as she climbed back into bed just as Andrews, the steward, tapped on the door with her morning tea; he came in wearing his usual rig-out of shirt-sleeves, no collar, a puce pull-over, and a dark stubbly chin. "It looks a nice morning, Miss," he said—Andrews was evidently slightly exhilarated too.

So was everyone else. A sort of joy pervaded the ship at the sight of the sun; it took the very practical form of doing some washing. A positive efflorescence of washing broke out on both decks, and at the midday meal there were prolonged arguments between Mr. Struthers, the lanky Chief Engineer, Mr. Freeman, the fair-haired second officer, and Reeder as to the best way of washing woollens—*Lux* or *Tide*, and how hot the water should be. The Captain contributed a story of a very nice young fella who had been given a cardigan knitted by his mother, which he had boiled in soda—everyone laughed politely. Julia decided to do some washing herself: by plaintively asking Mr. Reeder where and how she could hang her

46

things, as she had no clothes-pegs, she caused him to run a line for her across the boat deck under the bridge—"When your stuff's ready I'll hang it for you without pegs," he said briefly.

"Ready in half-an-hour," said Julia equally briefly; and half-an-hour later she watched with amusement the big bearded mate attaching her nylon effects to the line. He did this by a most ingenious method: inserting the point of the marlin-spike on his clasp-knife into the cord, he unlayed it enough to slip one corner of a garment through, and did the same to a second corner; the cord, springing back into place, held the sweater or petticoat as in a vice, far more strongly than any clothes-peg.

"That's grand," said Julia admiringly, watching a selection of her wardrobe flapping and fluttering, completely secure, in the brisk breeze. "How clever. Thank you so very much."

"Ah," said Mr. Freeman, pausing on his way up to the bridge to take his four-hour trick to observe these proceedings, "but that will leave nicks on the shoulders of jerseys. Now my wife, she always reeves an old stocking through the sleeves of her jerseys, and pins that to the line at the middle and ends—so the jersey itself doesn't get nicked, see?"

"That sounds very clever," said Julia politely—"but I haven't any old stockings with me, and I'm sure this will be perfect." Reeder, however, for whose benefit the last remark was intended, had stalked indignantly away.

"*Oh*, what fun," Julia thought, retiring to the pilot's cabin to type out more items concerning "Dockside Diversions" before Andrews went round the boat ringing a hand-bell to announce lunch—again she compared these direct simplicities with the atmosphere on large liners, to the latter's disfavour.

That night she had her usual whisky with the Captain about nine-thirty. Andrews always brought cocoa and biscuits to all cabins at eight-fifteen; Julia had amended this, in her case, to having her thermos filled with her own *Nescafé*, which blanketed the insupportable flavour of the condensed milk better than

47

cocoa—and being in a thermos, she could take it when she liked, which was when she was finally installed in her bunk. (She was much struck by the lack of such amenities, apparently willingly endured by the merchant navy.) At ten-thirty that evening—"Well, let's go up," said Captain Blyth, "if you really want to see the radar carrying on." And up they went.

A radar screen is more like a small television set than anything else. In the darkened chart-room behind the bridge proper—where a seaman stood at the wheel, and Mr. Reeder, his beard muffled in a scarf, strode up and down looking both business-like and sulky—there was no light except that from a shaded lamp, falling on the chart spread out on the big table against the bulkhead. The Captain went first to this, and studied the pencil line drawn on it to indicate the ship's course; he went out in front, glanced at the bearings on the illuminated compass in front of the helmsman, and then spoke to Reeder. "Have we picked up Torinan yet?"

Reeder moved rapidly over and stuck his wrist watch into the faint light of the binnacle.

"Three minutes ago, Sir."

"H'm." He went across to the port side of the bridge, remarking—"Like to come and see?" to Julia over his shoulder.

Julia went with him. Several steady lights, small and yellow, pricked the darkness, but after a few seconds a much more powerful one, infinitely far away, winked, flashed, paused—and then winked and flashed again.

"That's Torinan. One always gets it a bit before Finisterre."

"How do you know which light it is?" Julia asked.

"By the number of flashes, and the intervals between. I'll show you"—and leading her back into the chart-room he reached down from a shelf a grey paper-backed volume, rather thumbed and dog-eared from much use, entitled, Julia saw —"Admiralty List of Lights, Vol. IV." He licked a tobacco-stained finger and turned the pages. "There's Torinan."

Julia bent over the chart-table and read, muttering the

words aloud—"Toriñana. 1470. Octagonal tower on white square building, 29 ft. high. I.W. Character and period G.P. Occ. (3) Miles seen in clear weather, 20. Light 5·5 seconds, eclipse 1 second, light 1 second, eclipse 1 second, light 5·5 seconds, eclipse 1 second."

"There you are, you see," said Captain Blyth. "Check the flashes with a second-hand, and you know at once. Now we'll see if Spain is showing yet."

With him Julia peered at the dark glassy screen, on which small luminous objects showed here and there; he explained to her the meaning of the concentric rings of green light surrounding the central point which was the ship, and how each ring stood, at the present adjustment, for ten miles.

"Then that ship," said Julia, indicating a white object like a small maggot, "will be about five—no, four miles away."

"That's right. Four or three-and-a-half. Of course if you get really close you can magnify it." He twiddled a knob, the green rings seemed to shift, the maggot was ever so slightly enlarged—"Now that's set at five miles," said Captain Blyth.

"Yes—oh, obviously now it's three-and-a-half—no, three."

"Well, we're both moving, you see."

Julia was entranced by this magical gadget. "Can you make the range larger too, so one can see further away?" she asked.

"Yes. We'll pick up Spain." He twiddled the knob again, and suddenly the whole screen went dark.

"Silly thing," said Captain Blyth mildly. "We'll have to get Sparks." He pressed a bell on the chart-table, and lit a cigarette, quite unperturbed. To the man who presently appeared, looking rather sleepy and dishevelled, he said— "Fetch Sparks."

A moment or so later the wireless officer, also looking sleepy and dishevelled, appeared. "Sparks, this damn thing's conked out," said the Captain equably. "Fix it."

Julia was familiar with Sparks, the wireless officer, a curly-headed boy from the Midlands; she sometimes went and sat

49

with him in his cabin, next door to the pilot's and full of curious instruments, to listen to whichever English news service he could best pick up at the moment, through the singing tappings in Morse which never seemed to stop for an instant. Sparks, whose real name was Watson, was a happy youth, utterly devoted to his job; he would sit by the hour, headphones clipped round his curly brown skull, listening-in to the inter-ship messages which fill the ocean air with etheric chit-chat. Now however his cheerful face wore a rather sulky expression as he fiddled with the radar, removing and replacing valves—it was getting on for eleven-thirty, and Sparks had been fast asleep. However when he had finished he said, "All right now, Sir, I think," very respectfully.

"Thanks," said Captain Blyth. Once again he twiddled a knob; the illumined maggots seemed to increase, and right up at the edge of the screen appeared some faint curved lines of light, more like the petals of a chrysanthemum, Julia thought, than anything else. The Captain pointed at them with his thumb.

"That's Spain—Finisterre. It'll show up better when we get nearer."

"Can I stay and see?"

" 'Course, if you like. But I think I'll go to bed." He went out again to the bridge, looked at the binnacle, peered over the port side at the flashes from Toriñana Lighthouse; returned to the chart-room, laid the protractors on the chart, ruled a line and made an X in pencil, below which he wrote the time—23.23. Then he called, "I'm going below, Reeder," and vanished down the companion-ladder.

A moment or so later Reeder ceased his pacing of the bridge and came into the chart-room, where Julia was still peering, fascinated, at the radar screen.

"Oh—you're still here."

"Yes, the Captain said I could stay—I want to see the land come clearer on this. Oh, could you explain one thing?"

"I expect so—what is it?"

"All this fuzz of little white dots round the ship herself, just like the Milky Way."

Reeder laughed shortly.

"That's what we call the clutter—it's the ship's own disturbance in the water."

"Oh—oh, how funny."

"Why funny?"

"Because all the other things it shows, like ships and land, are solid—this is only bubbles in the water, like you see over the side. And talking of that, did you notice that there's phosphorescence in the water tonight?—not a lot, just an odd spark, but it's there all right."

"Yes. The beginning of southern waters. Lovely," said Mr. Reeder. He glanced rather keenly at her. "You're fairly observant."

"Not really, a bit—madly vague, in fact. Thanks"—as he gave her a cigarette, and lit one for himself. "Do you like southern waters?" she asked then—Mr. Reeder seemed in a more unbending mood than his usual abrupt aloofness, tonight.

"Yes, adore them—sub-southern, that is; I loathe the tropics. That's why I stick to this run—Spanish ports, Moroccan ports!"

When he spoke of sticking to the *Vidago's* run Julia recalled how Captain Blyth had said of him, over one of their nightly drinks, that Reeder was 'one of the most efficient officers in the merchant navy. He could have had his master's ticket any time these last eight years, but he won't go up for it. Can't understand the fella.' With this in mind—

"Why do you like the Spanish and Moroccan ports so much?" she asked.

"The sun—and the girls! Anything with black hair drives me wild!" said Reeder frankly. "Can't abide blondes—funny, isn't it?"

Julia laughed. But suddenly an idea struck her. "Do you

get to know about other ships in all these ports?—yachts and things like that?'

"Don't know what you mean by 'things'—one hears about some of the yachts, of course. Why? Do you want a yacht?"

"No, but I'm looking for one."

"What's her name?"

"The lunatic part is that I don't even know that," said Julia, more slowly than usual.

"Then I don't see how you are going to find her, unless you know the owner's name. What sort of yacht is she?—steam or sail?"

"Some sail and some engine, I think—I've no idea how big, either. It's all quite mad, but I absolutely must find her. I do know one of the owner's names, but not whether it's registered under that."

"*She's* registered," Reeder corrected. He seemed to hesitate for a moment, and then said—"Why have you got to find her? None of my business, of course."

Julia now plumped for telling this abrupt, rather cranky, man the reason for her quest—after all she needed any help she could get, and the Captain's unsolicited testimonial caused her to regard Reeder as a trustworthy person. In her near-drawling tones she related the whole story: Uncle John's death, and the consequent crisis at Glentoran; Aunt Ellen's distress, Edina's frustration at being stuck in Argyll, and her anxiety to get back to her rich job—finally, Colin's alleged orange-selling, and his failure to write for the last nine months. Reeder listened in silence; at the end he spoke.

"Of course they aren't selling oranges at all—you realise that?"

"No, I don't. I don't realise anything. What would they be doing, if not that?"

"Smuggling, of course."

"*Smuggling!*" said Julia in astonishment, raising her delicate eyebrows. "Smuggling *what*, for goodness sake?"

"Almost certainly currency out of Tangier; watches and cameras, probably, out of Gibraltar. Watches and cameras are duty-free there; they cost about a third of what they do elsewhere. Or American cigarettes."

While Julia stood silent in front of the radar machine, digesting this quite new idea, a seaman in shirt-sleeves came into the chart-room, bearing a dirty high-sided wooden tray with a pot of tea, some chipped cups, and a jug of the horrible condensed milk—Reeder poured out a cup, which he told the seaman to take out to the helmsman; then he offered Julia one.

"Oh, no, thanks, I think tea is quite too revolting, with this unutterable milk—how you all bear it I can't imagine! But do have a go yourself; I have my thermos of *Nescafé* down below."

Reeder laughed, and poured himself a cup of the dreadful brew. Drinking it, rather to Julia's surprise he reverted to the subject of Edina. "She must be quite a considerable girl, to be earning such a huge screw. How old did you say she is?"

"I didn't say. But in fact she's twenty-five."

"Formidable," said Reeder. "And now she's running the farm?"

"Well, they have three farms in hand, actually; she's running those, and the saw-mill and lime-mill—and of course she has to supervise the other eight farms, see to gates and fences and so on; and then the hill sheep, naturally. They simply can't afford a factor, with taxation what it is. Who can?"

"Sheep, eh? What sort? Black-faced on the hill, I suppose?"

"Yes, and some cross lambs on the low ground."

"Do you winter those away?"

"No, it's not worth it. Why, do you know about farming in the Highlands?"

"Not there, but I was brought up on a place in North-umberland." Julia was momentarily struck by his use of the word 'place' rather than 'farm'. "Good heavens!" Mr. Reeder pursued—'What a job for a girl! I should say being a mate is a picnic to it."

"I couldn't agree more. I think life on this ship is one long picnic—if you leave out the food," said Julia.

Reeder laughed again, heartily this time.

"Well, I wish you all luck in your search," he said. "Anyhow you'll be making it in some of the most delightful places in the world. Tangier, is it, that you're making your base? Know it?"

"No—I've never set foot in North Africa. Rather a thrill, really. But any hints and tips will be gratefully received," said Julia, with a hint of her beguiling grin. She felt sure that if Mr. Reeder vouchsafed any information or suggestions about Tangier they would be on quite different lines to Geoffrey's. She was not wrong. He stared rather hard at her, for a moment or two, in the faint reflected glow from the light over the chart-table; then—

"Well, I will give you one," he said at last. "I don't suppose it would normally be given to young ladies, but then I know nothing about young ladies!"

"Well, what is it?" Julia asked with a sort of tranquil impatience. "Don't bother over-much about young ladyhood, because I'm congenitally hard-boiled."

"That was rather my impression, in spite of your appearance," Reeder said, grinning a little through his beard. "Well go sometimes when you're in Tangier to Purcell's Bar—it's a good place, one of the nicest there is."

"Good drinks?"

"Yes, first class: no wood-alcohol to put your eyes out. And Purcell is a most delightful type—*sabe todo*."

"Oh, he does, does he? Might he know Colin?"

Mr. Reeder displayed panic, unexpectedly.

"Oh, for God's sake don't go walking in to Purcell's Bar and asking about smugglers!" he said hastily. "That would put the lid on. No—but when you've salted him, just drifting in and

54

having a gin-and-something for a bit, you might throw a fly over him about your smuggling cousin. He might know or he might not; my bet is that he *would* know, but whether he tells you or not is anybody's guess."

"My guess is that he might—people do tell one things," said Julia. "But I'll go very slowly, I promise you. Thanks."

At that point Mr. Freeman came stumping up the ladder and walked into the chart-room—he checked at the sight of Julia.

"Oh, hullo," he said—"I didn't expect to find you here."

"Studying radar," said Julia. She turned again to the screen. Up in the top left-hand corner the chrysanthemum-petals were now quite clear and strong, and spread much further down towards the ship. "Oh, look, Mr. Reeder—Spain's showing up beautifully now."

Reeder however did not look; instead he went out onto the bridge, glanced at the binnacle, at his wrist-watch, and then came back and did things on the chart with the protractors, as Captain Blyth, had done making a pencil X and writing '23.59 hours' below it.

"There you are," he said to Freeman. "Over to you now. Wish you joy of your trick"—and he strode out; his heavy steps could be heard clattering down the ladder.

"I think I shall say Goodnight too," said Julia and betook herself to her cabin. In bed, sipping her coffee and smoking a last cigarette, she meditated on what Reeder had told her. It was quite a new idea that Colin might be smuggling—and would probably make him harder to trace, she thought; he might even be using a false name. But then—if so, why in the world should the Bank of England allow him to transfer his account to Casablanca? Smuggling currency was about the last thing that the Bank would either smile upon or promote. All very queer—and still thinking how queer it was, and what fun to be trying to unravel so odd a mystery, she fell asleep.

Casablanca, where the *Vidago* eventually tied up at about

nine one morning, gives a rather false first impression of North Africa. What one sees—what Julia saw—as the ship moves along the coast to slip in behind the long long mole which protects the harbour is first the hideous factory zone to the north of the city, and then a conglomeration of high, feature-less, cream-coloured modern blocks, near-sky-scrapers, which constitute the town itself. This is very disillusioning. It might be a lesser New York; lesser, and less ugly than the fantastic Manhattan skyline, but not in the least anyone's idea of Africa, or any part of the Old World. From the deck Julia observed it all—as they approached the dockside she noticed that the local workers, at least, looked very different to Mr. Murphy's friends at the London Docks: not only had they very dark skins, some indeed being obvious negroes, but many of them wore long-skirted garments, and on their heads small brightly-coloured skullcaps, knitted or crocheted in patterns resembling Fair-Isle, and very dirty.

"Good gracious me, what an extraordinary place," she muttered to herself. "Not at all what I expected."

Chapter 4

THE Arab dockers, in their curious garb, were considerably quicker off the mark than their *confrères* in London. The hatch-covers had been got off while the *Vidago* was idling along inside the mole, awaiting the signal to berth, and in no time at all crane-drivers in fancy dress were slinging tractors, endless tractors, out of one end of the ship and small saloon cars, mostly painted a pale green, out of the other; the moment these last touched solid ground swarms of Moors ran them off the rope nets which held the wheels, manhandled them across the wide quayside, and parked them in neat rows between the warehouse sheds. It was a pleasant lively sight, in the bright southern sunlight, and Julia stood watching it with satisfaction —this might make a nice tail-piece to "Dockside Diversions", she thought, if *Ebb and Flow* had the guts to print anything which in the least reflected on English labour.

Almost the moment they tied up a very obvious Englishman in a trilby hat had come aboard, and disappeared into the Captain's cabin; he presently re-emerged, accompanied by Captain Blyth, who brought him up to Julia and made one of his little formal introductions:

"Miss Probyn, this is our agent, Mr. Bond; Mr. Bond, this is our passenger, Miss Probyn. Mr. Bond has a letter for you, Miss Probyn"—and the agent, after shaking hands, gave Julia a letter addressed in Geoffrey Consett's familiar hand, simply to 'Miss Julia Probyn, M.S. *Vidago*, Casablanca'. To her surprise it bore no stamp or post mark.

"Oh, thank you. How did this come, Mr. Bond?"

"It was sent down by hand to the office—from one of the Banks, I believe."

Julia bore it away to her cabin and read it. Like Casablanca, the letter was not at all what she expected. In the first place it

57

was typewritten. Mr. Consett began by explaining that to make sure of its reaching her he had sent it with a covering one to Mr. Lynch at the Banque Anglo-Morocaine, telling him that she was on the *Vidago*—"then he can contact the agents and get it to you at once." "Sensible creature," Julia commented approvingly. But for the rest of the letter she had no approval at all—she read it, frowning, with mounting vexation.

"I made enquiries in the quarter I spoke of," Mr. Consett wrote, "but I think you had better leave that line of enquiry alone. As you know, banks are not allowed to divulge any particulars about their clients' accounts to third parties—it is like the seal of the confessional; and though the Bank of England is practically a Government department since it was nationalised, that rule holds for it too. I regret now very much that I made the suggestion at all—it was foolish of me. My only excuse is that at the time I was thinking of something else." The letter ended very formally—

"Yours ever
Geoffrey Consett."

"Dictated," said Julia angrily. "All official rubbish!" She picked up the envelope from the sofa beside her, intending to crumple it up and throw it into the wastepaper-basket which she had forced Andrews to extract for her from the Chief Steward—she felt a need to crumple and throw something—when she noticed that there was another sheet in the envelope; this was written in Geoffrey's hand.

"Oh, darling, you know what I was thinking of that last evening—*you!* I do wish you hadn't gone away; London really *is* a desert without your beautiful blank foolish face in it. And anyhow, even if you do find your second or third cousin, or whatever he is, I doubt if he will come home quite as soon as you or his family would wish—Edina may have to sacrifice her magnificent salary, so much larger than mine, for a bit longer! But whatever you do don't start your Irish bank-clerk chum snooping round—I do implore you to leave the whole thing alone, from the banking angle."

"One for me, one for the file!" said Julia contemptuously. Poor Geoffrey—he was so frightful when he went all official. "Divulge!" she muttered disgustedly, looking at the type-written letter again. Then she re-read the P.S. Taken together, the two letters made her smell a rat. If Geoffrey didn't like Reeder's friend in the bar at Tangier, *sabe todo*, he knew a good deal more than he was willing to say, even to her. Now quite intelligent young women like Julia often develop a peculiar and really irrational remorselessness towards young men who are their self-professed slaves, but with whom they are not yet in love; she was unreasonably vexed with Mr. Consett for his official caution and propriety. She sat in her snug little cabin, that she had become so fond of, smoking and thinking. Geoffrey was of course a complete clot to imagine that she wouldn't try to make Paddy Lynch find out all he could; *he* wasn't the Bank of England, and nor was she—her job was to find Colin. But the whole business about the B. of E. was most peculiar. Whatever Colin's present occupation was it probably wasn't smuggling—Reeder must have been wrong about that—since it had official sanction; indeed someone at the Bank must know a good deal about it if they could put Geoffrey in a position to hint to her, in the privacy of his P.S., that Colin probably wouldn't come home at once. What could it be?

Anyhow, she decided, glancing at her watch, she had better take some steps about contacting Paddy, even if she did in the end decide to use a certain discretion in tackling him; and also find out from the Captain how long they would have in "Casa".

At that point there was a tap on her door, and Andrews, as he frequently did, entered without waiting for any "Come in".

"Car's come for you, Miss," he said.

"What car?"

"Couldn't say, I'm sure. I was just told to tell you that the car's waiting for you on the dockside."

59

"Thank you, Andrews. Say I'll be there in five minutes."

She stepped out on deck for a moment, to make up her mind about the temperature. It was not yet ten, and there was a light breeze off the sea, but it was already getting gently warm; by midday, in a city, it would probably be hot. She exchanged her woolly for a blouse, her brown shoes for green sandals, matching her broad-brimmed felt hat—that most useful of travelling companions, which had crossed the Bay rolled up into a green cone among her stockings; throwing her pale tweed overcoat across her arm, she went on deck in search of Captain Blyth.

She found him still in conversation with the agent, leaning on the rail watching the cars and tractors being unloaded.

"Oh, Captain dear, someone's sent a car for me. That probably means hospitality—so how long have we got here?"

"Well, we shan't be sailing till tomorrow, anyhow."

"Oh, grand—a night ashore! What fun."

"That's what the crew always think at Cahssa," said the Captain. "And they come aboard again at three in the morning as green as grass, and plucked clean as chickens!—and all they say is that they had *fun*." He spoke in his usual gentle accents of this aspect of human folly in his crew.

Mr. Harris, the Chief Steward, whom Julia had hardly seen since her first evening on board, when he pinched the bottle of Mr. Reeder's soda for her, now came bustling up rather pompously, holding out a note to the Captain.

"This has come for Miss Probyn, Sir," he said.

"Well, give it to her, then," said Captain Blyth flatly—Harris, looking foolishly formal, handed the envelope to Julia.

"Oh, will you excuse me?"

The note was from Mr. Lynch. He would be busy at the bank till one, but was sending his car and chauffeur to show her the sights of Casablanca during the morning, and to bring her to his house for lunch. "Ali speaks tolerable French. The

60

Librairie Farrère is the best place for picture post-cards. It will be uncommonly nice to see you again."

Julia said to the Captain—

"I'm going ashore for lunch. I'll be back before tomorrow morning, anyhow."

"O.K. Don't get shot up!" replied Captain Blyth tranquilly.

"Which is Mr. Lynch's car?" Julia asked Harris. There were two cars near the foot of the gangway, a small black Ford and a beige one considerably larger than the sea-green saloons which were continually being swung up out of the bowels of the ship.

"Oh, the black one's mine," said the agent, hearing her question. So Julia ran down the gangway and got into the beige car, the chauffeur politely holding the door open for her.

Ali was a neat little Arab with a flattened hook nose, a small Chaplin moustache, and dark brown eyes full of a rather sceptical intelligence, indeed his whole expression conveyed a not unfriendly scepticism; he wore a trim chauffeur's jacket over baggy dark-blue trousers, and a red fez. Julia told him to go to the Librairie Farrère. This was a huge bookshop in the business quarter among the tall blocks of buildings which made the streets look like canyons of golden sandstone. Here she turned over masses of picture post-cards, mostly displaying palm-trees, camels, and views of Marrakesh, none of which seemed very appropriate for despatch from this African version of New York; however she bought a few, and then realised that she had no Moroccan currency—whatever that might be. It proved to be a special African type of franc, and the grey-haired woman who served her had no hesitation in changing a £1 note—however she only got 800-odd francs for it.

"Not a thousand?" asked Julia, in her excellent French.

"Ah no, Mademoiselle—not in the Maroc. A thousand is the *French* rate."

Back in the car, Julia learned with astonished amusement in what Ali's idea of the sights of Casablanca consisted. He drove her briefly through the Mella, the Jewish quarter, which was too tumble-down and dirty even to be picturesque, with low one-storey houses and many street markets; but thereafter they proceeded to visit the hospitals of the city, which stood more on the outskirts, in large airy tree-shaded avenues. He took her to nine in all, ending up with the Animal Dispensary! "Hospital for Arab Men," Ali would say complacently, pulling up before high iron gates and indicating a series of modern buildings in spacious grounds full of flowering shrubs and trees; or "Hospital for Arab Children". There were hospitals for Europeans too, of course, but the little chauffeur made the longest pause of all outside "Hospital for Arab Women". He pointed out to Julia the Moorish trained nurses, unveiled and in European dress, but not in uniform, passing in and out through the gates, their up-to-date tartan-covered bags of medical appliances strapped to the carriers of their bicycles, explaining how they went into Arab homes, giving piqûres, applying dressings, administering medicines and treatment. "Do much good," said Ali, with such conviction that Julia was considerably impressed; she sat in the car for some time watching these lively hatless girls, their modern dress and hair-do contrasting so strangely with their dark-skinned un-European faces, chatting at the big gates to numerous Moorish women, presumably their patients—the latter veiled to the eyes and smothered in voluminous white draperies which, as Edith Wharton said long ago, caused them to resemble nothing so much as animated bundles of washing.

After the Animal Dispensary, however, she struck. Among the post-cards she had bought was one of Marshal Lyautey unveiling a memorial plaque to Charles de Foucauld, and she wanted to see it; she had what she herself would have called 'rather a thing' for that strange being, the cavalry officer turned White Father, whose missionary efforts had been so wholly unavailing, his political effect on the pacification of North Africa so great. She showed Ali the picture and bade him take her there. The Foucauld monument stands in a particularly busy avenue; Ali approached it from the wrong side and pulled up level with it, but across the road.

"Wait," said Julia; she hopped out, threaded her way through the traffic and stood quietly for a few moments in front of the memorial, behind its small hedge of bushes. It seemed to bring her monkish hero—so unlike all the pseudo-romantic business of the novelists who write up the Foreign Legion—strangely near. Julia was seldom impulsive, except when moved by temper, but now she did an odd thing: she knelt down on the dusty gravel and said a prayer for the repose of the soul of the saintly eccentric. Ali eyed her curiously when she returned to the car.

Casablanca in recent years has become a zoned city, carefully controlled by the Municipal Council. Factories may only be erected on the northern side—and only factories; impossible to get a permit to build a house there. Out to the south on gently rising ground lies the residential zone, spreading all the time—hotels, some blocks of flats, but mostly villas, of all shapes and sizes, in pretty gardens full of flowering shrubs; in that climate everything grows so fast that this modern quarter has not in the least the unfinished aspect of a new garden suburb in England—shrubs rise from the ground practically with the speed of the Hindu magician's mangrove-tree, while creepers with exotic blossoms smother the walls almost before the plaster is dry. Here no shops may be built; an impassioned petition from the residents was necessary even to get a permit for a petrol-station to be opened for local use.

Out to this pleasant district Ali proceeded to drive Julia, along avenues of older, larger, more sedate houses; she gazed about her with a lively interest, veiled by her customary vacant expression. Paddy Lynch's house was a medium-sized villa in the new quarter, covered in flowering roses, climbing geraniums, and some creeper with dark-green leaves and flowers precisely the colour of tangerine-peel; Paddy himself, lanky, black-haired, with lake-grey eyes set in an Irish smudge of dark eyelashes, was standing waiting for her at the top of a flight of concrete steps—as the car pulled up he ran down to greet her.

"Julia! How splendid! No need to ask how you are—you're radiant!"

"Dear Paddy," said Julia, giving him a cool kiss. "This is so nice."

"Nita's away, such a shame; she'd have loved to see you."

"Why?"

"Oh, a baby—and though a Frenchman produces such splendid pasteurised milk for us all, she thought she'd rather have it in England, and see if she can nurse it herself. But come in."

"Good idea, nursing," said Julia, as her host led her into a large sun-filled room; at the further end, through an archway, was another room with a table set for lunch.

Over drinks—"What on earth are you doing in Morocco?" Mr. Lynch asked.

"Sunshine—and articles for my medium papers."

"Why aren't you staying here? I gather you're going on to Tangier. You ought really to stop and do Marrakesh and Rabat and all that; you could stay with me and I'd drive you over for a week-end."

"I'd love to do that later on; I'm all booked at Tangier now, hotel and everything. Tell me, Paddy, how are things here now?" Julia asked, with a mental eye on her articles.

"Oh, very quiet—there hasn't been an assassination for at least ten days."

Julia laughed.

"Well, that's quiet for Casa," said Mr. Lynch, laughing too. "By the way, what time do you sail?"

"Only tomorrow morning."

"Why not come and stay here tonight, then?"

"Oh, no, Paddy dear, thank you so much—unpack and re-pack, so exhausting. But I'll lounge in your nice garden this afternoon, if I may, and have supper with you if I'm asked."

"Of course you're asked. Only it will be a bit late because I have to go to a cocktail party this evening. I know—why don't you come too?"

Julia made a small face.

"I feel rather like Sir Anthony Eden about cocktail parties. Will it be diplomatic or amusing?"

"Well, the Binghams are nice people—he's in the Banque Régie Turque."

Julia managed to repress a start—when she spoke it was with a real drawl.

"Oh very well—anything to oblige. But I shall have to go back to the boat and change," she said, with a glance at her coat and skirt.

"Need you? You look perfect." She nodded vigorously. "Very well; Ali can take you down about six, and bring you back to pick me up. What did Ali show you, by the way? *Splendeurs et misères de Casablanca?* That's the classic round."

"No; he showed me nothing but hospitals," said Julia, and related her morning. Mr. Lynch laughed, but this curious form of sight-seeing aroused his interest.

"That's a rather significant tribute to the French," he said. "Hospitals and after-care are one of their real achievements in Morocco. It's like drawing teeth, of course, to make the Arabs go to a hospital or a clinic the first time; but once they've been nothing will keep them away. Ali's wife nearly died with her last baby but two, and I simply bunged her into the *Hôpital pour Femmes Arabes* by main force—now he won't hear of her having a child at home. It's a most frightful pity, this muck-up about the Sultan, because the French are doing such a superb job here. Ah, here's Mahomet and the lunch."

Another Arab, in the baggy blue cotton breeches to which Julia was beginning to get accustomed, topped by an impeccable white jacket and a fez, stood bowing in the archway leading to the dining-room; as they sat down Julia observed that though in all other respects so neat, the servant's jaw and chin were covered with several days' stubbly black growth. After he had left the room, Mr. Lynch, forking in mouthfuls of a delicious risotto, pursued his theme.

"Did you notice Mahomet's beard?"

"Well, yes."

"That's all part of the trouble. He used to keep shaved, clean as a whistle; especially on Fridays, when he went to the Mosque. Today's Friday—and just look at him."

"I did," said Julia candidly. "But what has Mahomet's not shaving got to do with the new Sultan?"

"Everything!" said Paddy Lynch explosively. "At the Mosque they pray for the Sultan as their Imam, sort of High Priest, ye-know—but the French have outed the one they recognise and believe in, and put in someone else. 'Tis as though you were to ask Cat'lics to pray for the intentions of a new Pope, put in by the Russians, with the true Holy Father exiled some other place!" In his excitement Mr. Lynch relapsed surprisingly into his native idiom.

"Then why did the French do it?"

"Oh, the ould fella was just hopeless!—wouldn't sign any decrees, even those for reforms that the people themselves wanted; he was holding everything up. The French could hardly help themselves—'twas a regular *impasse*. But the cure is worse than the disease—now a lot of the Moors have stopped wanting even reforms, if they come from the French. Nationalism and traditionalism, fighting now on the same side, and the next minute fighting one another! But you can't touch a Moslem's faith—and that's what the Administration has done, God help them." He sighed, gustily.

Mr. Lynch's words about the Moslem's faith reminded Julia

66

of the curious look Ali had given her after she had prayed at the Foucauld memorial, and she told her host about the small episode.

"Did you do that? Oh, good. No, Ali won't have thought it in the least odd; on the contrary, it will have impressed him a lot. They think Christians fearfully irreligious—and to see one praying at the shrine of a Christian marabout will have bucked him up no end."

After lunch a telephone call came for Mr. Lynch, who hurried away; Julia sat on the verandah among stone troughs full of pink geraniums, revelling in the hot sun, or browsed among her host's books—she also gave some thought to what use she could best make of a cocktail party in the house of someone belonging to the Banque Regié Turque. It was stupid of her not to have found out how high up Mr. Bingham was, but she had been so interested in Ali and Mahomet, and the whole Moroccan set-up, that she hadn't. Oh well, time enough on the way. She was now glad that when Paddy asked her what she was doing in Morocco she had not told him, flat out, that she was looking for Colin Monro—it had been on the tip of her tongue to say so. But she might do better with a total stranger, over lots of drinks, especially if he was a foreigner. Mr. Bingham was obviously English or Irish—then why in the Banque Regié Turque?—but he would inevitably invite all his colleagues to his party.

He had done so, as Julia ascertained after a hurried dash down to the *Vidago*, where in the pilot's cabin she routed out a rather spectacular black and gold cocktail-dress, very décolletée, and black French sandals with straps threaded with gold. She looked out a hat, but decided against it—she knew that her hair, in certain circles, was one of her strong suits, however much Edina might rail against its length, and she might want her strongest suit tonight. When they called at the villa to pick up Mr. Lynch she knew that she had done right: his glance as he looked at her was one of those

67

involuntary tributes that are far more telling than any words. However, he used words too.

"Goodness, Julia, you will smash them! Have you any idea how beautiful you can make yourself when you try?"

She blew him a kiss.

"A pretty fair idea, dear Paddy—thanking you!"

"So I should suppose. A strengthener before the effort?"

"Oh dear no—I want to keep my head, in a strange town."

On the way down—"What exactly *is* Mr. Bingham in the Banque Regié Turque? Do tell me," Julia said.

"Oh, very senior. I think you'll like him, and his wife is a charmer."

"Why is he in a Turkish Bank?"

"Oh, that's a long story. Buxtons were invited, practically, to come here, and refused—I can't imagine why. It was very mistaken. So the Banque Regié Turque stepped in, and a very good thing they have made of it; they very wisely took on Bingham to handle the English side of things."

"I see. And who are his colleagues? Turks?"

"Oh, French and all sorts. There's a very amusing Armenian —you must meet him."

"What's his name?"

"Panoukian."

As they spun down a long boulevard Julia said, very casually—

"Have you run into my cousin Colin Monro out here?"

"Monro? No, I don't think so. What does he do?"

"Nothing very much, so far as I know. He sails a bit about all these ports, I think—oranges, or something."

"Oh, one of these amateur smugglers," said Mr. Lynch, rather contemptuously. Julia was struck by his jumping instantly to the same conclusion as Reeder. "They're such a bore, always getting into prison or some row, and wanting to be bailed out. They're a perfect pest to the Consulate."

Julia held her tongue, and decided to concentrate on Mr.

Panoukian for the moment. Obviously Paddy knew nothing —anyway, Colin's account wasn't in his bank.

The Binghams' was a very large house on one of those earlier and staider avenues between the city proper and the flowery new garden suburb—as they walked up the flagged entranceway a muffled roar of voices greeted them. Julia paused in the warm darkness, and sniffed—"Paddy, what is this heavenly smell?"

"Lemon-blossom," replied Mr. Lynch; he stepped onto a flower-bed to pluck a spray from a tree. "There, you can tuck that in behind your sunburst," he said—"Is it diamonds or Woolworths?"

In the house the party was huge, and already in full blast; Julia studied the company with interest. The women's clothes were very smart, but their hats, oddly, not nearly so good, and their hair and faces either over-done, or not really done at all. Registering such things was a sort of Pavlov reflex with her, but when Paddy introduced their host she concentrated on him. Mr. Bingham was an enormous man, at least six foot three, with iron-grey hair and a huge pale moon of a face, in which a pair of lively grey eyes shone—he flourished a tumbler of whisky-and-soda, rather to Julia's surprise.

"Honoured, Miss Probyn. A great pleasure. What will you drink?"

"Oh, I'd like to follow your example," said Julia, in her slowest tones. "I'll come with you," she said as he moved off towards the buffet.

"Now that's a sensible girl! Would you ever get it, if you didn't come with me? And aren't you wise to choose whisky. Scotch or J.J., by the way?"

"Oh J.J., please," said Julia. She had already decided that her host was an Irish Bingham, and probably in a fairly receptive state, early as it was in the evening; it would be a sound move to opt for Irish whisky, which in fact she loathed. While he was fetching her drink she made a second rapid

69

decision as to her preliminary approach, and when he returned with her glass acted on it at once.

"Mr. Bingham, where is the money here? Who makes it, and from what?"

He stared at her.

"Good God! Whatever makes *you* ask a thing like that?"

"Oh, didn't Paddy tell you I'm a journalist? And where the money is is rather a primary question about a place, don't you think? I shan't quote you, naturally, but that's the first thing I need to know."

"Of course you're quite right," Mr. Bingham said; as he spoke he moved through an archway, holding up a looped curtain for Julia to pass, and took up a position by a bookcase in the next room. "Well, phosphates apart—you know Morocco produces twenty per cent of the world's output of phosphates—the big *quick* money is mostly made in this town," he began.

"From?"

"Real estate: land values in this place keep soaring like in Shanghai in old days, or in some American boom town; and petrol-stations, and the smart shops, and a bit of night-life."

"Is any made outside Casa?"

"Oh, yes; Agadir is developing very fast too—and the citrous fruit industry is becoming quite a big thing. And besides dried peas, they're starting canned peas too, and tinned fish; the French are very go-ahead about all that, and it gives a lot of employment, and brings money into the country."

"Anything else?" Julia asked.

"Well, no one really knows yet what's going to happen about the oil industry."

"Oil! You mean petroleum? Do they get *that* here?"

"Oh, yes—there's that big cracker-plant at Petit-Jean. But I fancy," Mr. Bingham said, leaning towards Julia confidentially, "that the petrol yield may not come up to expectation. Faults in the limestone bedding, they say—don't really under-

70

stand all that myself. But I gather Morocco is never likely to become a second Kuwait."

"That's all most useful," said Julia. "I can't thank you enough, Mr. Bingham."

"Don't you want to write any of it down?" her host asked, looking at Julia with a sort of two-edged interest.

"Oh dear, no. It stays," said Julia, tapping her big white forehead. Mr. Bingham laughed.

"That's the lot, is it? No small handy side-lines?"

"Well, there is one little side-line—no, two."

"Oh, what are they? Readers like side-lines," said Julia professionally.

"Well, it's a funny thing, but there's getting to be quite a trade in Moorish stuff—you know, antiques, leather goods and brass and so on. All that used only to be on sale in Fez or Marrakesh, but quite recently the merchants up there have started sending their sons or nephews down to the coast, to Port Lyautey and Rabat and this place, and even to Mogador and Agadir to open up shops—and you'd be surprised what they're making out of it. A lot of the sons could buy father out now, after only two or three years."

"Fascinating," said Julia. "I must look up these sons! And what's the second side-line?"

Mr. Bingham again looked confidential, and leaned further towards Julia along the top of the bookcase.

"Well, they're doing quite a bit—curious thing—in some of these rare metals."

"What, uranium?"

Mr. Bingham looked slightly embarrassed. "Well, not pitch-blende"—he hemmed a little. "Don't get that here, but they find a lot of queer things, some of the ones with numbers and fancy names—elements, don't you call them?"

"Oh, like titanium and molybdenum?"

"What a girl you are! Yes, they do mine molybdenum, and antimony and cobalt as well. Cobalt of course is enormously valuable; it's worth about a guinea a pound. The French concessionaries are mining that in a biggish way. Wait—I'll bring you the other half."

In Mr. Bingham's absence Julia *résumé*-d what she had heard and stowed it away neatly in her mind. There wasn't much in phosphates and chick peas, even canned ones, for an article, and Casablanca night life had been done to death, but there could be a story in the curio-sellers' rich sons, and possibly in these metals. A guinea per pound was a nice sort of price to write up. When Mr. Bingham returned with their glasses— "Do go on about the cobalt and molybdenum," she said.

"Cheers!" said her host, drinking to her. "I like intelligent girls! I hear they're finding newer stuff than cobalt too," he added.

"Who are? The French?"

"The French have the regular concessions, of course, but— well, don't quote me," he said again, "but it was the Germans who began on these new things."

"What, before the War?"

"No, no, just a year or two ago—the East Germans, they say. But other people have started in now as well, on the Q.T., I gather, and without bothering about concessions too much—though everyone connected with it seems to keep their mouths fairly tightly shut."

"Could I use that at all? I mean, if no one will talk, how do I get a story?" Julia asked.

"Ah, that's up to you," said her host, rather belatedly looking discreet. "I've said too much already, I daresay. But I've given you the tip—a nod's as good as a wink, as we say in the Twenty-Six Counties! And I should think you could make a mule talk, if you gave your mind to it!"

"Oh, how sweet you are! And you have helped me so much. But I'm sure I ought not to monopolise you any longer," said Julia— "You've been so liberal. Push me off onto someone else now."

"Who'd you like to meet? The Prefect and the City Fathers?"

"Well, really, I'd rather talk to your partners. Haven't you any Turks about? I think it's so frightfully odd and amusing, finding the Banque Regié Turque here," Julia said, with Mr. Panoukian well in mind.

"Oh, there are good reasons for that. But if you insist on Banque Regié Turque bankers—Hey!" Mr. Bingham called, above the roar of voices. "Panoukian! Come over here."

A short slender man with a greenish white face, dressed in a tightly waisted suit, with a carnation in the buttonhole, and sharply pointed shoes, obeyed his summons.

"Panoukian, let me introduce you to Miss Probyn, a friend of Paddy Lynch's. She's a journalist, and she wants to know about Morocco, but she only wants to learn it from bankers!" said Mr. Bingham expansively—he then moved away.

Julia deployed her rather varied arts on Mr. Panoukian, who was clearly highly intelligent; his queer topaz-coloured eyes looked at her with the expressionless steady glare of one of the great cats, a lion or a panther; but he shot out information and sympathetic wit in faultless English, and on a higher level than Mr. Bingham's. They got on very well—so well that at last Julia decided to plunge. Leaning a little towards him on that same confidential bookcase, she said—

"Mr. Panoukian, I believe you could help me. Would you?"

"My dear lady, if I can, the thing is done," he said, with an exceedingly sweet smile.

"Oh, thank you. Indeed I *do* hope you can, for we are in such trouble," said Julia, turning the eyes of a distressed dove onto the Armenian. "Look—I feel as if I can trust you; may I be perfectly frank?"

"It is almost always wiser to be perfectly frank, especially if one wants help," said Mr. Panoukian. "In theory the English understand this, and *nous autres* do not—in fact I often find the reverse to be the case."

73

Julia laughed a little, but promptly returned to her role of distressed damsel.

"I'm looking for someone—a distant cousin, whom I haven't seen for years. He hasn't written home now for months and months, and his poor mother is distracted; she needs him, too, because the man who used to look after their very large property has just died, and there is no one to see to things. So I have come out to try to find him."

"The journalism is a blind, then?"

"Oh, no—it finances me. *You* must know all about our currency restrictions in England."

"Yes. How fortunate for the unhappy mother that you are a journalist!" Mr. Panoukian said—was it with a hint of mockery? On that assumption—

"Oh, please don't be unkind!" said Julia.

"I am not. Who could be unkind to you? But please tell me one thing—with this perfect frankness which we agree is so useful: why do you imagine that *I* can help you to trace your missing cousin?"

"Because he has an account with you; here, in Casablanca."

Was it her imagination or did a sort of veil, an almost imperceptible blankness come over those yellow eyes when she said that?

"Indeed! And may I know his name?"

"Of course—how could you help me, otherwise? His name is Colin Monro," said Julia.

This time there was no doubt about it. Mr. Panoukian's topaz eyes seemed visibly to lose all expression before her own; it was as if a blind shutter of refusal were drawn down over that whole curious visage. She did not have to wait for his words to know that she had failed, that this was a dead end; she hardly listened when he said slowly—

"Monro? I must look that up. Where are you staying?"

Mr. Panoukian was not a mule, he was one of the greater cats—and she could not make him talk. But *why* not? she asked

74

herself, as they drove back to a late supper. To her surprise Mr. Lynch drove her himself; the chauffeur had disappeared.

"Where's Ali?" she asked.

"I sent him home—I always do if I'm going to be at all late!"

"But why?"

"So he won't get stoned," said Paddy casually. "He lives in the new Medina, the modern Moorish quarter, and everyone knows he works for a foreigner; if he comes back late the thugs stone him."

"Paddy, it's not *true*! In a modern town, today?"

"Oh, yes, it's happened three or four times. If I *have* to keep him late for some official do I send him home in a taxi."

Over coffee after supper, in the rather chilly drawing-room —the electric power had failed for some reason, as it constantly did, Julia learned—she confided to her good friend Paddy the real reason for her coming to Morocco, and asked if he would do anything he could to trace Colin. (Whatever Geoffrey might say, she had got to find him.)

"His account's with the Banque Regié Turque, is it? Is that what you were making eyes at Panoukian about?"

"Yes," said Julia, unruffled. "I made all the eyes I've got, but it was no use."

"No, I shouldn't expect it to be. You'd have done better with old Bingham—you really have enslaved him! What did Tony say?"

"Tony?"

"Tony Panoukian."

"Said he'd look up the account. But I saw—I mean I'm practically certain—that he *did* know about Colin, and wasn't going to tell—his whole face sort of shut up, went dead-pan, at the name."

"Have you any idea what young Monro really is up to?"

"No, not a clue. *You* said smuggling, and so did the mate on my boat—but I can't believe it's really that, because . . ." here Julia paused, wondering how much to say. Recalling

75

Mr. Panoukian's dictum about perfect frankness, she decided to plunge. . . .

"Because what?" Mr. Lynch asked, while she hesitated.

"Well, I told a chum in the Treasury about Colin's account having been transferred here, and he volunteered to find out the reason for permission being given from the Bank of England."

"A rather *young* man, I deduce," said Paddy Lynch.

"Yes. Well, I got a most totally clottish officialese letter from him this morning, the one he sent via you—*typed*, would you believe it?—telling me to leave it all alone from the banking angle. From which I deduce," said Julia, fitting another of Mr. Lynch's cigarettes into a small delicate silver-and-ebony holder, "that not only does the B. of E. know all about his job, and bless it, but that it is something peculiarly hush. Otherwise why the panic? Geoffrey's letter was panic-stricken."

"In the typed officialese?"

"Oh, no—the panic was in an MS. P.S.," said Julia, grinning a little, while a faint and becoming blush stole over her apricot-tinted cheeks.

"H'm. I think I see."

"And your horrible Panoukian person shutting up like a *clam* at the very sound of Colin's name confirms that, wouldn't you say? If it was all open and in the clear he'd have said, 'Oh, yes, of course—I'll send you his address tomorrow,' don't you think?"

"Um. Yes. I daresay you're onto something. Have you got the letter from your Treasury pal on you?"

"No, I left it on board, locked up. He said I was on no account to start you snooping," added Julia, with a giggle.

"That won't worry me," said Mr. Lynch. "I'm an Irish citizen; I've no commitments to the Old Lady of Threadneedle Street, certainly none to override those to the *young* lady, Julia my dear! I'll snoop for all I'm worth. Give me your Tangier address, by the way—and the telephone number."

"I'll have to post you that; I don't know it."

"Then remember to airmail it. Surface mail from Tangier takes an eternity."

"All surface mail takes an eternity since airmail began—I think they put the letters on ox-wagons," said Julia—and Mr. Lynch laughed.

He drove her down to the docks himself. Having been fetched and carried by Ali, Julia had not troubled to register exactly where her ship lay, and they had to cruise about under the arc-lights for some time till she spotted the small neat shape of the *Vidago*.

"Golly, what a comic little tub!" said Mr. Lynch. "I must say I think you're pretty devoted, Julia, to have crossed the Bay in winter on that! Who is the devotion to, the missing man? Is he worth it?"

"I've no idea. We were both pretty immature when I saw him last. No," said Julia reflectively—"I think the devotion is to a place rather than to any person. I've been happier at Glentoran than anywhere else on earth, I simply adore it— and it can't carry on without Colin to run it. So I'm going to find him."

Chapter 5

TANGIER from the sea presents a far more agreeable aspect than Casablanca. A line of ochre-coloured cliffs stretches away towards Cape Spartel on the right, in the centre the mass of white, indubitably Moorish houses of the Kasbah climbs steeply up a hill; to the left the modern town slopes, also agreeably white and clean, down to the bay and harbour, and beyond to the east rises the Djebel el Mousa, Hercules' African pillar—so much more pillar-like than its European opposite number, Gibraltar, which from Tangier is barely discernible in the distance, vaguely resembling a lion crouching very low indeed.

Julia stood on deck with Mr. Reeder, admiring this pleasant scene spread out in the sparkling sunshine, while he pointed out the various features of it to her. "I envy you a bit, staying here," he said. "Charming place. How long *shall* you be here?"

"I've no notion. It depends on how soon I find my cousin."

"Ah. Yes. Well, I wish you luck in your quest. Don't forget Purcell, he may be able to help you—but go slowly."

"I will."

"I do hope you succeed, if only for your other cousin's sake —Edina, did you say? Pretty name; curious, too."

"It's a family name."

"She must be a tremendous girl, to be able to run a place like that, and yet earn such a huge screw on her own as well," said Mr. Reeder thoughtfully. "Worth knowing. What is she like?"

"Her hair is jet black," said Julia with malice.

"Oh God! She's not tall, by any chance?"

"Very tall—and as slim as a willow."

"Help!" said Mr. Reeder. "I should be sunk if I met her."

"I expect so—she sinks a lot of people," said Julia.

78

After fond farewells to Captain Blyth and the rest of the ship's officers Julia went ashore. Andrews, typically, loaded up "the boy" with so many of her possessions at once that her typewriter nearly fell off the gangway into the water; she shouted a cold, slow reproof at him from the quay, which caused him to bring the rest of her luggage down himself. (She saw Captain Blyth's tranquil grin at this episode as he stood at the rail below the bridge.) More tractors and more saloon cars were being slung ashore, also a piece of deck-cargo which had amused Julia throughout the voyage: several wooden cases of lighter-fuel, which might not be stowed below, and had remained lashed on the main deck. Evidently the cigarette-lighters of Tangier could now be filled.

The Villa Espagnola to which a taxi bore her was really a small hotel, situated at the top of the town at the far end of the big Boulevard, the main shopping street, where this peters out into a residential quarter of large houses in gardens, where most of the Legations are situated; as she unpacked, the great fronds of palm-trees on a level with her window tossed their heads like restless horses in the sea-breeze close outside, and the scent of roses came up from the garden below—by craning her neck a little she could just see the white mass of the Kasbah, a pile of gleaming rectangular blocks, each block a house, poised precariously on the steep slope of its hill. All pretty good as a change from London in January, Julia thought—in her calm fashion she exulted a little.

But she was never one to waste time, and as Purcell's Bar was obviously going to be a slow process, she made a call there her first job. The Spanish proprietor looked a little startled when she asked the way to it, but gave her directions—down through the Medina and the Socco Chico, the Small Market, and then a street on the right, close above the harbour.

Julia had the sensible habit of always buying a plan of any new town the moment she arrived in it; her hotel however had none, so she set off without. Everyone in Tangier speaks

79

Spanish, so she had no difficulty in asking her way to the Socco Chico, revelling as she went at the sight of teams of donkeys laden with unrecognisable merchandise blocking the road for Chrysler cars, or more of those women smothered in white draperies, and men in dark-brown woollen djellabas, straight from neck to ankle, and topped with wide straw hats looped up and trimmed with cords and tassels of wool. Heavenly fun, she thought; delicious entertainment of the eye—no wonder Colin and Reeder liked this part of the world.

But when she tried to go through the Medina to the Socco Chico the heavenly fun became a little too much of a good thing. The old Moorish city of Tangier is a network of steep cobbled alleys, so narrow that the passage of a single donkey sends the thronging pedestrians scrambling into the open-fronted shops for safety; even without a donkey's passing it was hard to push one's way through the swarms of people—Moors and Jews, men and women—and the smells were unwonted and strong; moreover there were so many twists and turnings that she soon felt in danger of being hopelessly lost. She beat a retreat uphill, and managed to find her way back into the big open market lying immediately above, the Gran Socco; here she took a taxi, which circumnavigated the impossibly steep angle and narrowness of the Moorish shopping quarter, and drew up in a quiet, narrow, modern street, where a small and discreet notice said "Purcell's Bar".

She found this to be quite a small place, a narrow room with a bar along one side leading through into a larger one, both with small glass-topped tables and modern leather-covered chairs—it was all as quiet as the street and as discreet as the notice, rather to her surprise; she had expected something more exotic or more rough-and-tumble. It was early in the evening; she took a seat in the narrow room opposite the bar, ordered a drink, and then sat demurely sipping it while she took stock of her surroundings. The man who served her wore an ordinary dark suit, but his face was far from ordinary:

negro blood was obvious in the wide mouth and broad mask, but his hair was brown and straight, his skin merely of a European sallowness, his eyes grey. When he brought Julia her drink he spoke perfect English, but having done so he busied himself quietly among his bottles, not making conversation after the manner of his kind. This struck her; and indeed there was about the whole man a quiet dignity, combined with a look of strong intelligence, which was impressive. Could this, she wondered, be Purcell himself? If merely a barman he was an unusual one.

Her question was answered by the entrance of a little Moor in fez, baggy blue trousers, and scarlet jacket, who carried a basket full of bottles and spoke in Arabic to the grey-eyed man; he was promptly set to washing and polishing glasses, and from the demeanour of them both it was obvious that the half-negro was the boss. Julia studied him with fresh interest. He certainly had the look of a person who might know everything, and would keep his mouth shut on what he knew, she thought, recalling Reeder's words. A few minutes later she received fresh confirmation of his identity. The muslin-veiled door onto the street opened again to admit a small rather seedy man, who somehow had the word 'spiv' written large all over him; he leaned over the bar and greeted the man behind it with the words, "Look here, Purthell, old man"—then he caught sight of Julia and lowered his voice, so that the rest of his communication was lost to her. Julia was pleased—this was the sort of type she had expected to find in Purcell's Bar. But he was not made very welcome—Purcell listened coldly and shook his head more than once. The newcomer had a very slight cast in one eye; presently he cocked the other at Julia, clearly asking who she was?—Purcell shook his head again, repressively, and said something which drove the small cross-eyed representative of the underworld out of the bar. (Julia felt an instantaneous conviction that this miserable little creature belonged to Tangier's underworld, whatever that might

81

amount to, and that Purcell, like King David's wife, despised him in his heart.)

She was sufficiently interested by what she had already seen to sit on, in hopes of more—she asked for another drink, and when Purcell brought it observed that it had been a beautiful day—he agreed, with almost royal politeness, and expressed a hope that she was enjoying Tangier. Julia said that she was. But just then the door opened again and five or six men came in: of various ages, they were all speaking English and wore English-tailored suits; two or three had the quality for which we use the blunt word 'pansy' written as large on them as 'spiv' had been written on the seedy little man. They were manifestly *habitués*—they perched on stools along the bar and asked for "the usual, please, Purcell". One in particular struck Julia rather pleasantly—he was very tall, with flaming red hair and no look of a pansy at all about him; he wore a dark blue blazer above white flannel trousers, and removed a pair of sunglasses after he had settled on his stool. She listened for some time to the conversation of this bunch—all residents, she gathered, since they were discussing their gardens: the bashing of their tulips by a recent storm, and why daffodils would grow so superbly in Tetuan, only fifty miles away, and yet "absolutely *not*, my dear" in Tangier. She hoped for a mention of the Monteiths, for from the glances discreetly cast at her she realised that to form an acquaintance would be easy—but none came. Oh, well, these people might come in useful some time—you never knew. She was satisfied with her evening when she left, with a word of thanks to Purcell.

Next day she embarked at once on what the police call "routine enquiries". She went first to the British Consulate-General, a medium-sized but stately yellow-washed house standing among palm-trees in a commanding position, with open spaces all round it. Most of the other seven Powers who operate the International Zone at Tangier call their missions Legations; the English, with a typical arrogant modesty, describe theirs as a Consulate-General, though the Consul-General enjoys the local rank of Minister. This distinction is rather chic and slightly annoys the more flamboyant colleagues of the British representative; they would hate to be mere Consuls-General themselves, but realise that in Tangier it is really grander *not* to be a Minister—in self-defence they ostentatiously address him as "Your Excellency" or "M. le Ministre".

A very tall Moor, splendid in a dark-blue robe down to his feet, met her at the gate-house which commands the entrance, and led her through a flowery garden to offices behind the house proper, where she had an interview with a very young and most courteous vice-consul.

"Colin Monro? No, I'm pretty certain that he hasn't made his number here, but I'll check in a moment, if you like. What was he doing?"

Julia, still under the influence of Mr. Panoukian's remarks about the value of frankness, said—

"Well, I think they were probably smuggling, though they called it selling oranges."

"Oh, did they? Out here they usually pretend to be fishermen, if they bother with a disguise at all. If you will wait one moment, I'll check." He vanished through a door.

"No," the vice-consul said, when he returned—"He didn't get imprisoned and ask us to bail him out. I'm so sorry I can't help. How long are you staying?"

"Till I find him," said Julia.

"Ah. Yes. Have you put your name in the book? Oh, but you should do that"—and he led her out through a spacious hall where a couple of Moors clad in tunics, fezzes and baggy breeches of brilliant scarlet, were polishing the marble floor. "Here," the young man said—and Julia inscribed her name and "Villa Espagnola" in a large album.

Having drawn a blank at the Consulate-General, she tackled the harbour-master, who was supposed to be found in an office down near the quay. This was a far less courtly proceeding and took much longer; however at last, using a great deal of Spanish and many blandishments Julia achieved access to an official of sorts. Here, though she felt more hamstrung than ever by her ignorance of the name of Colin's boat, she got a bit further. Yes, the harbour-master's chief clerk told her, there was an English yacht, with several Señores on board, hanging about Tangier; he too consulted files, after which he informed Julia that the boat was called "The Frivolity". No, she was not in the harbour now; he thought they had gone to Gibraltar. The Ingleses bathed in the sea a great deal, he volunteered, diving off the boat itself; imagine such a thing! This encouraged Julia, for Colin was a strong and impassioned swimmer. Had the Señor seen them, she asked. Oh, yes, many times. Were any tall and dark? Indeed yes—one extremely tall, and very dark. And did the Señor know their names?

But here the clerk was less helpful: Julia could not be sure whether he was being evasive or really did not know. One, he said, with some confidence, was certainly a lord—but that was as far as he would go. He indicated politely that the office was now about to close for the luncheon-hour—this, Julia guessed from past experience in Spain, would certainly last till four p.m. at least, so with grateful thanks she took her leave and withdrew to Purcell's Bar, most conveniently close by, for a drink and meditation.

As before she was the only patron, except for the red-haired man who had impressed her favourably the evening before, who sat in the furthest corner of the inner room, drinking beer and reading a book. In this agreeable solitude Julia decided to seek some information from Purcell, and when he brought her drink she asked him how one got to Gibraltar?

"By the Ferry—it goes every day."

"Can one go in the morning and come back the same night?"

No, that one could not do; the ferry went about midday, and only returned the next morning.

"How lunatic," said Julia. "Why? Why not come back the same night? It can't take very long to steam across there."

Purcell's strange face with the negro bones and the intelligent European eyes took on a most peculiar expression—combined, it seemed to Julia, in equal parts of vivid comprehension, some secret amusement, and reprobation.

"It just is so," was all he said, however.

"Oh, well—how tiresome. And could you tell me where one can stay in Gibraltar?—a cheap hotel?"

Purcell's peculiar expression was if anything accentuated as he said—"There is really only one possible hotel in Gibraltar —the Rock; and it is not cheap."

"How much a night, do you know? This is very kind of you," said Julia, "but one has to be careful these days, on a travel allowance."

"Wagons-Lits Cooks could tell you exactly, but I believe about fifty shillings a night."

"Fifty shillings a *night*! Merciful God!" Julia exploded— "How appalling." Purcell gave a tiny laugh. "The proprietor of the Rock Hotel is a first cousin of the ferry-owner, I presume," she said—at which Purcell laughed out loud, causing the red-haired man in the inner room to look up in surprise. Laughter was rare with Purcell, Julia surmised.

However, these huge prices—the ferry cost about a pound each way too, she gathered—decided her against going to Gibraltar on what might prove to be a wild-goose chase: after all she had no certainty that the tall dark young man on the *Frivolity* was really Colin, though she knew that he numbered more than one youthful peer among his intimates. Instead she went in the afternoon to Cook's, checked on the exorbitant prices, and then forced a very ill-mannered and recalcitrant clerk to ring up the harbour-master at Gibraltar to find out if the *Frivolity* was there. At Gibraltar, on the other end of the line, all was ease. Julia spoke herself with someone who talked English, and learned that the yacht she wanted had sailed

85

that very morning for Malaga—however she was expected back in about ten days' time, and was then thought to be proceeding to Tangier.

Fair enough, Julia said to herself, as she walked out of the Wagons-Lits office and strolled up a sunny street towards the Place de France; best wait till they come back, staying inexpensively at the Espagnola, and meanwhile work up Geoffrey's local contacts, using his letters of introduction to Lady Tracy and Mme La Besse. And see the local sights, and continue to put salt on Purcell's tail by repeated visits to his very nice bar, till it became possible to consult him. In Tangier in hot sunshine in January, this seemed a very agreeable programme; and after taking a black coffee at a small table on the pavement outside the Café de France, on the Place, she went back to her small hotel in high good humour and typed out "Dockside Diversions"; she was just in time to airmail it from the English Post Office in a street below the Consulate-General, where the stamps sold are ordinary English ones with the word TANGIER printed in heavy black across the face. It was then, as always, crowded with a mob of all nationalities, who wished to profit by the cheap postal rates—sixpence for an airmail letter to the British Isles, for example.

This feature, and the whole business of England having its own post-office in the absurd international set-up that Tangier is, delighted Julia. In common with most of her generation, the post-war, neo-New Young, she had a thoroughly considered respect and admiration for her country; Julia's contemporaries would never be found passing resolutions not to fight for King and Country. And even in the short time that she had been in Tangier, in conversation with the inmates of her little Spanish hotel Julia had learned something which amused and pleased her even more than the existence of the English Post Office—namely the astonishing impression created by the visit of the Royal children to Gibraltar. The Spanish press had been uttering all sorts of menaces about what would happen if the

Queen herself dared to set foot on what, in defiance of treaties, they deemed to be the soil of Spain; her Majesty however not only stepped ashore herself, but for good measure sent those royal midgets, Prince Charles and Princess Anne, up the Rock to see the monkeys. The foreign element in Tangier could not get over this example of *le flegme britannique*; they found it quite overpowering.

"These little children!—to take such a risk!"

This had never struck Julia while at home—monkeys are monkeys, and all children love them. But the effect on foreign opinion of this expedition she found very gratifying.

Next morning she set out to call on Lady Tracy, taking Geoffrey's letter of introduction—to which, in the rather old-fashioned elegance of manners which he affected, he had clipped his visiting card, with "To introduce Miss Julia Probyn" written across the top. The address was some unpronounceable Arabic street name; Julia caused the *patron* of her little pub to read it out to her taxi-driver, who could not, it seemed, read himself; on hearing it he said, in Spanish, that the Señorita must prepare herself to walk. Julia had prepared herself for almost anything, but the approach to Lady Tracy's house succeeded in startling her. The Kasbah at Tangier rises right up to the very lip of that line of cliffs of ochreous earth which overhangs the approach to the Straits; but beyond it, westwards, other houses have been planted on this vertiginous ridge, between the yellow cliff fall to the sea and the steep approach from the landward side—and in such a house Lady Tracy lived. After grinding up a yellowish muddy street between small whitewashed houses which turned blank walls to the roadway, the taxi paused practically in mid-air, reversed several times, and came to rest facing back towards Tangier proper—the taxi-man then indicated to Julia that she must now proceed on foot down a concreted path, punctuated here and there by flights of steps, and that the pink *casa* at the end was the house which she sought. Julia picked her way down this slope, which was inundated now and again by douches of dirty water thrown from the houses overhanging it, where washing flapped in the breeze off the ocean; an iron gate in a small garden gave access to Lady Tracy's front door.

This was opened by a Moor who bowed, took the letter which she held out, and ushered her into a hall or room built in the Moorish style, with narrow arches on slender pillars supporting a high ceiling, and rugs spread about on a floor brightly patterned in small tiles—through curtained archways she caught glimpses of other rooms. From the windows, also arched and with tiny pillars, the view was superb—out across the blue sea of the Straits to that ultra-couchant lion Gibraltar on one side; to the cliffy outline of Cape Trafalgar on the other. Turning back to the room Julia, seeking an impression of its owner, noted that the furniture was partly Moorish, with a few good English pieces; everywhere a clutter of photographs, some of famous people, stood about on small tables along with curios and brass trays; water-colours, some good, more less good, shared the wall space with the typically Moslem decoration of pieces of brilliant embroidery and some very fine old rugs. There were several modern French books lying about, and a good deal of dust was present; the whole room, Julia thought, spoke of a vigorous personality—too vigorous to fuss about coherence in its surroundings, let alone dust.

The Moorish manservant had borne off Mr. Consett's letter to his mistress; after rather a long pause he reappeared, holding back the curtains of one of the arched openings to admit a very old lady indeed, dressed with as much inconsequence as the furnishings of her room in a welter of cardigans, scarves and shawls—she held Geoffrey's letter in one hand, the other she extended to Julia.

"My dear Miss Probyn, how very kind of you to come and visit me! And how good of my young friend Geoffrey to send you."

Julia lost her heart to Lady Tracy at once. By the time she

left, nearly two hours later, she was completely subjugated. Here for once, for a wonder, was a purely golden character: full of intelligence in spite of her great age, and yet almost bursting with benignity; at no point, in spite of her free and lively comments on all manner of events and people, did she display the smallest contempt for those stupider than herself— who must, Julia reckoned, comprise at least ninety-five per cent of her acquaintance. Simplicity, and a sort of divine modesty, characterised all her utterances, shrewd as they were. And Lady Tracy's character, Julia soon came to feel, explained the heterogeneous appearance of her room, and especially the bad water-colours; these had clearly been kept out of an affection strong enough to override the chilly fads of mere taste. One in particular, close above the chair in which the old lady evidently always sat—judging from the litter of sewing, newspapers, half-cut books and knitting on the table beside it —constantly caught Julia's eye; faded and spotted with damp, it was nevertheless executed with the utmost spirit, and repre- sented an exotic-looking boat under full sail, off a coast of savage mountains dotted whitely here and there with temples, villas, and mosques. At last she asked who had painted it?

"That? Oh Jane Digby; Lady Ellenborough, you know. Positively *heading*, you see my dear child, for the wilder shores of love. Don't they look wild?"

Julia, entranced by this, rapidly decided that no time need be wasted in "salting" Lady Tracy; she would cultivate her for all she was worth, for her own pleasure in such a rare being, but in the meantime she sought her advice immediately.

"Lady Tracy, Geoffrey sent me to you not only *pour me procurer un plaisir*—which he has done," she added smiling— "but because he thought you might conceivably be able to help me. May I pour out to you?"

"Oh, yes, dear child, pour away—I am an absolute reservoir of outpourings, though I can't imagine why."

"I can," said Julia; "I can already. Well, this is it"—and she unfolded her mission. At the end—"How *does* one set about finding a person on a yacht in Tangier?" she asked.

"Oh, in various ways. What are they doing? Smuggling? So many try to do that. Are you sure they are really smuggling?"

"No," said Julia, "I'm not sure of anything—it's all utterly vague. Smuggling is just a general suspicion which several people, like you, have thrown out. But I went up to the Consulate-General yesterday, and they certainly haven't been imprisoned; at least they didn't seem to know my cousin's name there."

"Well, that's something. You don't think your cousin and his friends are just young *rentiers* living out here on yachts to avoid paying English income-tax? There is so much of that in *le grand bidet*," said Lady Tracy, calmly.

"*Le grand bidet!* What on earth is that?" Julia asked, still more entranced by this phrase.

"Oh, yes, that's what they call this end of the Mediterranean; its shape on the map, if you come to think of it, is rather like a biddy."

Julia laughed.

"What a pleasing name! Well anyhow, I don't think Colin can be tax-dodging; he's anything but a *rentier*, in fact I shouldn't think his income has ever been large enough to pay tax on at all. Don't people get up to two hundred and fifty pounds free?"

"I daresay, my dear—we don't have to bother much about that out here, thank goodness. Colin!" said Lady Tracy abruptly. "Colin what?"

"Colin Monro. His father was a cousin of my mother's, and I call *his* mother Aunt Ellen, and think of her as an aunt. They have a most heavenly place in Argyll—I really do love it," said Julia, in an unwonted burst of confidence. "And he's needed there now because the old uncle who used to cope—another cousin of my mother's—has gone and died."

"Ah yes—we all die in time," said Lady Tracy tranquilly.

"My turn is really overdue." She turned to the table beside her chair and rang a small brass handbell which stood on it, saying—"I think we might have a glass of sherry to assist us in studying this problem."

A young and very beautiful Moorish girl, swathed in veils, answered the bell; she slid in through one of the archways, stepped noiselessly across the floor and stood behind Lady Tracy's chair; there she bent over her mistress, stroking her shoulder with the gesture of a loving child, and bending down asked her in Arabic what she wanted? Julia could not understand the words, but the sense of them was clear—even more clear was the complete devotion of the handmaiden to her mistress; there was a sort of Biblical beauty about the whole thing, small and unimportant as it was, such as Julia had never seen in the modern world. She was still under the spell of this when the sherry was brought, poured out, and handed to her by that beautiful creature, who looked as she imagined Ruth or Jephthah's daughter to look, or some other gentle Old Testament heroine.

"Colin Monro," Lady Tracy mused, sipping her sherry. "No, I don't remember the name. I will think, and perhaps ask. I don't always ask, one sometimes hears more without."

"You don't know the owners of the *Frivolity*?" Julia asked. "I got a faint idea that he might be on her, but it's only a guess. She's in and out of here, I know."

"Oh, I believe they are all much older, and mostly very rich; hardly your cousin's galère, I should have thought. But I have never met them, and I can't recall their names. One is a peer, I think. My dear child, what a task this is for you!"

"Yes it is—and I really have got to succeed. But any sort of detection is rather fun, don't you think?"

"Oh, yes—the greatest possible fun. It will be so kind if you will let me detect with you, as far as I can from this chair."

"Oh, *please* do," said Julia, with fervour. "Dredge up the

sediment from your reservoir—I'm sure you will come on some dead cat that will furnish a clue."

Lady Tracy laughed; really a high, old, but infectious chuckle. Then she became practical all of a sudden.

"How are you going to live? This may take some time, and a hundred pounds goes nowhere in this place."

Julia mentioned her invaluable papers.

"Oh, that is splendid. How clever you must be! I take *Ebb and Flow*—it's somewhere on that chair, I think." Julia found it for her, on the seat of a splendid Chippendale armchair, of which one broken leg was propped up by a beautiful little Moroccan coffer of crimson velvet, studded with silver nails. "Ah yes—thank you. A good paper. But can they *remit* to you here?" the old lady asked astutely.

No, it was only the extra allowance, Julia admitted.

"Well, that is better than nothing, of course; much better. But I was thinking—let us get Feridah to give us some more sherry," Lady Tracy said, tinkling the brass handbell; once again the beautiful girl glided in, stroked her aged mistress, and re-filled their glasses. Julia felt as if she were in some quite fresh version of the Arabian Nights, sitting in this Anglo-Moorish house—was it old or a modern imitation, she wondered?—perched above the ocean's rim somewhere between the Pillars of Hercules and the Garden of the Hesperides, with this marvellous old lady.

"Do you have only Moroccan servants?" she was moved to ask.

"Yes. They suit me better. 'Abdeslem who let you in is my steward, and butler, and general factotum, a wonderful person; and then little Feridah is what in the old days in England used to be called one's body-servant—which she is: she dresses me and all that. And I have a notable cook called Fatima— you must come and taste her food sometime. And there are all sorts of hangers-on who pretend to weed the garden and feed the chickens, and of course chiefly take a percentage of my peas and eggs." She gave her chuckle. "It is all much more peaceful and happy though than what most of one's friends go through. But let us get back to you, my dear child."

"Oh, well, if we must," said Julia. "I think your household is much more amusing than me."

Lady Tracy patted Julia's hand.

"We must be practical," she said. "I was thinking that if you took some job here, you would be making money to live on, in the first place. Would you take a job?"

"Oh Lord, yes, if I could get one. What had you in mind?"

"Can you type?" Lady Tracy asked.

"Yes rather—I have my typewriter with me."

"Shorthand?"

"No," said Julia without distaste—"not shorthand."

"Ah well—I daresay that wouldn't matter. You could memorise the gist of letters, and take notes and so on—and if you are a writer, I feel sure you could make up very good letters yourself."

"Do *you* want a secretary?" Julia asked, hopefully.

"Oh, no, dear child; I have only a very small correspondence —nearly all my friends are dead. But tell me—what languages do you speak and write?"

"Really well, French and Spanish—Italian only moderate."

"Excellent. Let me hear you speak a little French and Spanish."

Julia, rather embarrassed, nevertheless pulled herself together and first asked her hostess in Spanish about the age of her house, and then in French what brought her originally to Tangier? Lady Tracy laughed, clapped her hands, and without answering either question said in English—

"That will do, perfectly. How unusual in an English girl to speak such good Spanish—and it is so essential here. Now listen, my dear Miss Probyn. I can see that you are tolerant of old people, and for the post I have in mind that is important. I have an old friend, very able but very crochety and very vague; she works extremely hard and has a large correspondence, mostly in French, and she is badly in need of a secretary. I may as well tell you at once that none of them stay with her very long," said Lady Tracy, with a fine little smile; "but you have no thought of staying for ever, and a person of your upbringing is more likely to be patient and gentle than those little girls who do do shorthand, but seem to have so few other interests."

"Perhaps—yes, probably," said Julia. "What does your difficult friend work *at*, Lady Tracy?"

"Well, my dear, I believe it is archaeology," said Lady Tracy, looking rather amused.

"Goodness, can it be Madame La Besse?"

"Yes. Do you know her, then?"

"No, but Geoffrey told me about her; in fact he gave me a letter to her, too."

"Ah yes—I remember that he was very much interested in all that; he spent a lot of time with poor Clémentine out at her excavations. Well, so much the better; she was very fond of him, so you will have a golden entrée—though no entrée, golden or not, generally lasts very long with her, poor thing," said Lady Tracy philosophically. "Well, I will write to her too, and recommend you. Are you interested in archaeology?"

"No, not a bit," said Julia frankly—"but that won't prevent me from typing her letters to learned societies in perfectly good French, unless it's *too* technical; and even then I can make her spell out words like mesolithic."

Lady Tracy laughed again.

"My dear child, I see that you will be *perfect* for this. Now I will write her a note, and you shall take it to her with her beloved M. Consett's letter tomorrow. I am sure she will engage you, and I shall tell her that she must pay you a *large* fee. Then you can live more or less free; and what is more important, you will have a cover, as I think they call it, for your presence here."

"Do I need cover?" Julia asked, rather startled both by the idea and the word itself, in the mouth of Lady Tracy of all people. "Can't I just be here, like any other tourist?"

"I think cover is *always* a good thing," said the surprising old lady. "But it is especially useful when one is making enquiries. You have been making them already—at the Legation, from the harbour-master—for a missing young man in a mystery yacht, whose name you don't even know. Don't you suppose that all the relevant circles in this tiny place will already be discussing this fascinating fact?"

"No, it would never have occurred to me," said Julia.

"Oh, well, you may be sure they are. And a beautiful young lady is conducting the search!—*immensely* sensational," said Lady Tracy, what practically amounted to a grin appearing on her wise old face; this made Julia laugh.

"What are the 'relevant circles' as you call them?" the girl asked.

"Oh, Interpol, if they are smuggling—and the Zone Police and all sorts of other interests," said Lady Tracy airily. Then 'Abdeslem came in, bowing, with some enquiry; Lady Tracy told him to wait while she wrote a note to Mme La Besse, and Julia took it and went away, considerably cheered.

It will be noticed that she had not been *quite* frank with her new acquaintance; she had said nothing about the curious business of the Bank of England. It seemed to the girl more prudent not to do this, to begin with at any rate, especially as Lady Tracy was a friend of Geoffrey's; she remembered Paddy Lynch's comment on Geoffrey's youth in that connection. So she left that part out. She rejoined her taxi, poised at the crumbling edge of the cliff, and went skimming back to her hotel, wondering what Interpol was, and what "interests" could possibly feel concern in her affairs. She could have no idea what that particular piece of loyalty to Mr. Consett was going to cost.

95

Chapter 6

JULIA did not take Lady Tracy's and Geoffrey Consett's letters to Mme La Besse next day, as she had intended. In the morning, writing an account of her trip to Mrs. Hathaway, a glance at the date showed her that it was Friday, and she decided to take Geoffrey's advice and go up to see the Mendoub pay his weekly visit to the mosque. On the advice of the *patron* of the villa she did not attempt to find her way up through the Kasbah; the mosque stands at the very top of the old citadel, and it is a toilsome ascent to it on foot up steep cobbled alleys and flights of steps—moreover, said the Señor Huerta, she would certainly lose her way. So she took a taxi, which after climbing through the high-lying modern quarter to the south passed through the citadel wall and twiddled its way by narrow streets to decant her at the upper end of an irregularly-shaped *place*, sloping slightly downhill; near the lower end of this was the mosque. But, said the taxi-man, who had conducted a brisk conversation with Julia in Spanish the whole way, let the Señorita first go to the *miradoro* close by, and look out over the ocean—the Mendoub was always late, and she was early.

Julia took his advice and went out onto a small terrace, whose parapet wall overhung the cliff itself; below her the sea, blue as heaven under the hot sun, murmured gently about the yellow cliff-foot. The coast of Spain was a deeper blue, as willow-gentian is deeper than forget-me-nots—but what interested Julia more than the soft shapes of Gibraltar and Trafalgar was that she succeeded in descrying, away to her left and also perched on the cliff's edge, a pink-washed house which was certainly Lady Tracy's—her house was a *miradoro* in itself.

Turning back into the *place*, she looked about her. The

square slanted downhill in two directions, so that the buildings on her left lay below those on her right; they mostly presented blank whitewashed walls pierced by a single door, over each of which, incongruously, a blue-and-white enamel plaque carried a number. At the lower end a heterogeneous crowd was already gathered; Julia strolled down towards it over the hot stones, looking for a point of vantage from which to watch the proceedings, and if possible somewhere to sit. Both these requirements, she observed, were met by a short flight of steps leading up to a building with iron-barred windows; climbing the steps she perched on the parapet at the top. Almost immediately, however, an official in a green uniform followed by an Arab carrying a kitchen chair came over, planted the chair on the top step, and bowing politely urged Julia in French to sit on it. The official seemed too grand to tip, so Julia gave a coin to the Arab; then she lit a cigarette and settled down to see the fun.

There was plenty to look at. Immediately in front of her on the lower side of the *place*, which at this end extended still further down the slope in a sort of rectangular bulge, the Mendoub's guard was already drawn up, a line of Moorish horsemen on beautiful little barbs; the men had various weapons stuck and slung about their wild dress, and carried long staves with fanions a-top; the little horses were as betasselled as Geoffrey had led her to expect—tassels depended from saddles, from bridles, and wherever a tassel could be hung, all in bright colours in which red predominated. The guard was smaller than she had expected; only fifteen in all, but it was by no means the only part of the show. There were also two rows of elderly men dressed in robes of spotless cream, with hoods or cowls thrown back to reveal maroon skullcaps bound round with narrow snowy turbans; they stood on either side of the paved road which bisected the cobbles of the *place* from top to bottom, talking among themselves— beyond them a gaggle of populace and children, all strangely garbed, shouted and ran about, constantly harried and called to order by several policemen, and the official in green who had brought her the chair.

All this was amusing enough at first, but presently it began to pall. Half-an-hour passed, three-quarters of an hour, and still no Mendoub. Several Americans, shepherded by two rather officious Arab guides, arrived, and also took up their stance on the steps, crowding these uncomfortably; they had cameras which they held to their eyes as they photographed the Mendoub's guard, but they were restrained by the official in green from photographing the old men in white burnouses. They grumbled about that, and about the unpunctuality of the planes which were carrying them about Morocco and Spain; it was very hot; Julia began to get bored. And then something very peculiar happened.

Out onto the flat roof of one of the Moorish houses which bounded the bulge at the lower end of the square came two men, carrying canvas chairs which they proceeded to set up in the small shade cast by two bay-trees growing in tubs. They then disappeared, to re-appear after a moment, each carrying a large cocktail-glass. The houses below the bulge were so much lower than the northern side of the *place* that their roofs were practically on a level with Julia, and she could see clearly all that took place; for a moment or two she watched the two men idly, envying them the deckchairs in which they presently sat down, the shade of the bay-trees, and above all their cocktails. Then suddenly she sat up very straight, as both rose and came and stood by the low parapet, looking down onto the crowd below. One was the red-haired man whom she had twice seen in Purcell's Bar, wearing as usual his white flannel trousers and dark blue blazer. But the other? The other was much younger, very tall and very dark; and Julia, incredulously, thought that she recognised Colin Monro. She stared and stared, through the glittering blinding sunshine; the range was about seventy yards, and moreover Colin had been four years younger when she last saw him, and this was a grown man. But the loose easy walk, the slouch—so like Edina's slouch—were exactly as she remembered the charming youth at Glentoran; and what she could discern of the face at that distance was Colin's face.

She sprang up from her kitchen chair, and started to go down the steps, disturbing the Americans, who protested loudly—not without reason. For at that very moment a vast cream-coloured motor-car nearly as long as a bus appeared at the upper end of the *place*, and moved slowly down it; the Arab guard sprang to attention, the two rows of old men hurriedly pulled the hoods of their white robes over their heads and stood in reverent attitudes; the police chivvied the crowding children away and awed them into silence, and then stood at the salute as the Mendoub, the local representative of the Sultan, who is Allah's representative on earth as far as Morocco is concerned, drove up to pay his devotions to Allah on high. Helpless, fuming, hemmed in by the eager transatlantic tourists, and in spite of herself awed by the moment, Julia stood, one eye on the two men on the roof, while she watched the proceedings. There was little enough to see—several elderly men in long robes emerged from the car, were surrounded and masked by the police, and shuffled off up a cobbled alley to the mosque. By the time they disappeared the two men on the roof opposite had also vanished, taking their chairs with them.

The moment that it was possible do so Julia ran down the steps and tried to push her way through the crowd of women and children in order to find the entrance to the house on whose roof she thought she had seen Colin; but it was some moments before she could reach her objective, and when she did she was completely frustrated. Only one house had a door giving onto the lower, bulging corner of the square, and that was away to one side; she knocked at it, and after a long pause a veiled Arab woman with cross-eyes opened to her. The inner court revealed by the open door was dirty and filthy to a degree which really precluded that house being lived in by the red-haired man, with his immaculate trousers; nor could Julia exchange a word with the woman, who looked equally blank at the sound of English, Spanish, or French. Julia gave it up. Some distance away an archway led through into a cobbled alley, which was in fact the entrance from the Kasbah; Julia tried this. Here there was a plethora of doors —closed doors in blank walls; not only on both sides of the main alley, but in a sort of court leading off it—she counted at least eight. But in the confused rabbit-warren which an old Moorish city usually is it was impossible to determine which of the eight was the door of the house she wanted. She tried one, haphazard—it opened on another filthy little courtyard, on another Arab woman, though this time not cross-eyed; but she too understood nothing but Arabic. Poor Julia began to feel desperate. It was frightful to think of Colin perhaps being within a few yards of her, and not to be able to reach him. She went out again into the *place*, noted the position of the house with the bay-trees as well as she could, and returned to the alley. One house in the court leading off it seemed to correspond best to that position—moreover the door was of clean-grained wood, not covered with peeling paint, and the knocker was tidily blacked; Julia used this to knock loudly.

The door was opened almost immediately; through it, past the smartly-dressed Moor in a braided jacket who stood in the opening, she caught a glimpse of a neat courtyard with whitewashed walls and geraniums growing in big earthenware jars. This was much more the style, Julia thought, and it was quite hopefully that she addressed the elegant man-servant.

It is always a question in Morocco, and in Tangier especially, whether servants will respond best to Spanish or to French —on this occasion Julia opted for French.

"Monsieur is at home?" she asked.

"I will enquire, Mademoiselle," the Moor replied politely;

he spoke excellent French. "Might I have Mademoiselle's card?"

Now visiting cards are one of the many things that have practically disappeared from England since the Second World War, when they could only be bought, with permits, by diplomats and officials—Julia, brought up without such things, had none. She said so, but gave her name; the servant bowed elegantly as he repeated it carefully—evidently a well-trained man, she thought. And then a still stranger thing happened. It struck her that she might as well ask for Colin at once and she said, quietly—"*En effet*, the person whom I desire to see is Monsieur Monro. I believe he is staying here."

When she said that, this well-trained Moorish man-servant, with no diminution of the elegance of his manners, and without uttering a single word, very quietly shut the door in her face.

For a moment or two Julia stood in that shadowed but nevertheless hot little court, utterly taken aback. One very seldom has a door shut in one's face by a servant unless one is a beggar, or in some other obvious way unsuitable for polite society—which Julia knew she was not. She had a moment of fury, an impulse to hammer savagely with that black-painted knocker on the tidy well-grained door. But she pulled herself together, and did neither. Slowly she turned away—and then turned back to see if there was one of those blue-and-white plaques with numbers over the door. There was not. And there was no street-name at the entrance to the little court; when she turned the corner and stood where she could see up the alley into the *place*, there was none there either. But at the angle where the court and the alley met she nearly bumped into a small lurking figure, European, with a hang-dog look—she recognised the seedy little man who had come into Purcell's Bar the first time she went there, by the cast in his eye. He glanced at her curiously before he scuttled off, silently, on rubber-soled feet, and was lost to sight among the gradually dissolving crowd in the square.

This tiny encounter rather upset Julia, coming on top of what had gone before. Had he *seen* that door shut in her face? The thought was disagreeable; somehow the whole thing was eminently disagreeable. She walked out into the square, suddenly extremely aware of heat, hunger, and fatigue—and how on earth was she to get back to the Espagnola? She really *couldn't* walk it. However this problem solved itself, rapidly. The Americans with whom she had shared those steps had gone, but one of their Arab guides, whom she recognised, promptly accosted her; he conjured up a taxi out of space and escorted her to the Place Pasteur, all the address she would vouchsafe. There, in English, he demanded an exorbitant tip —Julia said *"Par exemple!"* and gave him a very modest one; whereat he smirked, bowed, and took himself off.

The Espagnola being under Spanish management really preferred its patrons to lunch about half-past two, so Julia did not have to worry about being late; this was as well, for she felt a little unnerved. Seeing Colin, if it was Colin, was startling enough—and she felt pretty sure that it must have been him, or why had the mere mention of his name caused that door to be shut? She was troubled. The whole thing was so extraordinary, and seeing the seedy little man from the underworld there, at that precise moment, was somehow the last, most disconcerting touch. *How* was she to get hold of Colin?

Julia, finishing her tortilla and refusing cheese—after all she was not as hungry as she thought, she found—fell back on her usual principle of there being always some sensible thing to do: in this case, she decided after reflection, the sensible thing was to take a nap. She did so, and awoke refreshed and mentally restored; she had tea sent to her room, made a leisurely toilet, and set off in good time for Purcell's Bar; if she went early enough she would be sure to find him alone and—well, one never knew.

Purcell was alone when she went in, sure enough; he greeted

her with a minute degree of extra friendliness, a sort of delicate accent on the gradual progress in their acquaintanceship which really charmed Julia—it occurred to her that she knew no one, in any walk of life, who would have done this better, if indeed as well. Purcell observed that it was a hot day, and while he shook her cocktail for her, neat and small behind his bar, asked if she would like a piece of ice in it? Julia said she would, and when he brought her drink with the clear cube swimming in the liquid he also brought the bottle of Gordon's, and slipped in an extra dash, observing that in his view a washy cocktail was a horrible thing. These agreeable attentions cheered Julia up considerably, and restored her nerve; nevertheless, she resisted the gin-born impulse to ask Purcell some questions, and instead did a sort of mental summing-up. If she had really seen Colin up in the Kasbah today he couldn't be on the *Frivolity*, so *that* was out; and if it wasn't him that she had seen, why the closed door at the sound of his name? Damn!—why hadn't she longer sight?

Purcell broke in on these reflections with a friendly query from behind the bar—had she, he asked, been up today to see the Mendoub? This struck Julia as being a sort of pointer for further action. Yes, she had gone, she said; very interesting and very picturesque. Then she drawled out a question— "Who is that tall man with red hair whom I've seen in here once or twice? You know—he always wears white flannel trousers and a blue blazer."

Purcell hesitated for a moment before replying—did his fascinating Anglo-negro face bear for a moment something of the same withdrawn expression that she had seen on Mr. Panoukian's face down in Casablanca? She couldn't be sure, but there certainly was a perceptible hesitation before he replied.

"I know the person you mean," the bar proprietor said, "but I don't know his name."

"Oh, you must!" Julia protested. "He came in with all

that bunch of pansies!" she added unguardedly—"They're locals."

Purcell gave a little laugh.

"Still I do not know his name. I do not know the names of everyone who comes here—not yours, for example! In any case this particular gentleman left Tangier early this afternoon; he came in to get supplies of whisky and gin before going off to the interior."

"Was there another man with him?"

Purcell eyed her a little curiously, she thought, when she asked that, but all he said was—

"No, he came alone, except for his chauffeur; they brought the car and took the cases away in it."

Julia reflected again for a moment.

"He has a house here, hasn't he?" she then asked.

"Ah, that I could not say. He may be staying at the Minzah—many people stay there. I only see him at intervals."

Julia was about to press her questions when that veiled door opened and let in several people, among them those she had seen on her first visit; she paid and went home.

Next day she took her letters of introduction round to Mme La Besse; she telephoned in advance, and was asked to come early, as the lady had to go out for the day. That suited Julia; this quest was evidently going to be a long job, and the sooner she started earning the better. Mme La Besse lived in a rather indeterminate little house standing in a small muddled garden, down a cul-de-sac high up in the modern quarter to the west of the town; from the main road at the entry to the cul-de-sac there was a splendid view, out over half Tangier lying far below, white among the green of trees, with the misty blue of the mountains of the Rif in the distance; but from the house itself, low and muffled in its rather ugly small trees, nothing of this was to be seen. Mme La Besse was a short stout woman with thick untidy grey hair, and dressed in ugly shapeless clothes; her beard, of which Geoffrey had spoken, was very much in evidence, stiff greyish bristles all over her chin. But she had a pair of very bright lively pale-blue eyes and a thoroughly cheerful expression; this was accentuated after she had read Geoffrey's letter.

"Ah, this dear Con*sett*—he is so charming. I like him enormously. He says you are his friend—his fiancée, perhaps?"

"Decidedly *no*—but I too like him," said Julia. "He is very fond of you, and greatly wished me to know you," she added courteously.

"*Le cher garçon!* and such an ardent archaeologist. And you?"

"I am afraid not—I am completely ignorant of all that."

"Ah well, never mind. Did he speak to you of my beard?" the old lady asked unexpectedly.

"Actually he did," Julia said, embarrassed but candid. Mme La Besse laughed, delightedly; she seemed to think her beard the best joke in the world. When she laughed her whole stout flabby body shook like a jelly, and her rather ugly face became creased with mirth—Julia decided that her new employer was rather likeable.

For employer and employed they at once became. Mme La Besse asked if she could drive a car? The car proved to be a Chrysler, a make which Julia had in fact only driven on her dash to Glentoran a couple of weeks earlier; she had beguiled the long run from Renfrew to Argyll by driving much of the way herself—this entitled her, she felt, to undertaking to drive the La Besse machine, and she hardily agreed to do so. She for her part bargained for a four-day week, in order to have time to write her articles—she had already started one on Casablanca, and how money was made in Morocco. Mme La Besse did not appear to be much impressed by journalism; indeed she gave the impression of not being easily impressed at all—"*Tiens! Les petites feuilles*" was her only comment. But she agreed to engage Julia to work four days a week, for a very fairly handsome sum in francs, which as Lady Tracy had foreseen would enable the girl to live practically free at her Spanish pension; and she also made no fuss about Julia's stipulation for an occasional week off if she wanted it.

The job was a curious affair. It comprised paying the bills (some of them months old), dealing with the Spanish servants, doing the shopping for the household, and buying the flowers —Mme La Besse had a passion for flowers, and liked to have her untidy little house full of them all the time. This was a thing Julia enjoyed; it involved constant trips down to the Gran Socco, the big open-air market, where vegetables, fruit and cheeses were to be bought, and where majestic Berber women, in those huge be-tasselled straw hats, sold flowers of every kind—roses, carnations, freesias, heaths and myrtles; most charming of all one of them, in particular, delighted in concocting bright formal Victorian posies, with garden flowers and wild flowers all mixed together—Julia loved these, and always had one in her room in the hotel, but Mme La Besse preferred grander displays. No accounts were kept that Julia could see; she was given money to go shopping, and brought back the change, but her employer waved aside her neat sheets of reckonings. Nor was there a great deal of correspondence, though now and again she had to type out a few pages of reports on "*l'excavation*". It became clear to Julia that what Mme La Besse wanted was less a secretary than a mother's help, to deal with the practical affairs of life, leaving her free for more congenial occupations. Geoffrey was right, though— she was great fun.

Before the first week was out Julia to her great satisfaction was called on to drive the old lady down to "*l'excavation*"; she had not yet been outside the city at all, and was delighted at the chance of seeing something of the countryside. The site lay in the International Zone—in which the city of Tangier is embedded like the stone in a peach—on the coast, down beyond the airport; Julia sent the Chrysler humming along a superb road, first through suburbs, then across open country through fields either ploughed, or blue with wild Spanish iris standing two feet high, and past streams along whose banks paper-white narcissus bloomed in huge milky clumps. When they turned out towards the ocean the splendid road degenerated, till it ended as no more than a yellow sandy track; cultivation ceased, and a fragrant healthy countryside, full of wild scillas, took its place. Set among the heaths and cistuses Julia presently saw an oblong of low stone walls, of a curious tone between deep cream and pale sand, sloping gently down towards the real sand of the shore, along which the green Atlantic breakers rose and poised, to tumble and fall in a thundering confusion of foam; the noise they made was splendid on that wild sweet-smelling shore, in the strong hot sunshine.

They parked the car near a small roughly-built shed, surrounded by a little courtyard full of the spouts and bases of amphorae, tiles, and archaeological bits and pieces of all sorts; in the shed itself, Mme La Besse explained, the more valuable objects were housed, padlocked. However they did not then enter it; the old enthusiast could not wait to show the newcomer the site itself. In fact it was charming, and laid out with the utmost ingenuity. At the upper end were three large underground cisterns, still holding water—two had vaulted cemented roofs, as the Romans built them, but the third was roofed with over-sailing courses of dry stone, unmortared; this, Mme La Besse stated, was the Phoenician style for such things. Julia asked how the water reached the cisterns, and was shown some sections of stone-cut drain-pipes through which it had been led, from springs a considerable distance away, up on the higher ground inland. In the next enclosure below the cisterns—each activity, in this ancient factory, had had a compartment to itself, on most modern lines—were shallow mortared tanks for treading the grapes to make wine; Julia had once been up the Douro to see the port vintage, and noticed with amusement that these Roman or Phoenician structures were exactly like the *legares* in which, today, bare-legged Portuguese men in flowered cotton pants tread the grapes to make port, the only difference being that in Portugal in the twentieth century the raw wine is led off through pipes, whereas here a small open channel, beautifully cemented, had led it away to an adjoining tank several feet deep. "That must hold at least eight thousand gallons," Julia said, comparing it in her mind to farm tanks installed by the Monros up at Glentoran.

"*Nine* thousand," said Mme La Besse proudly—"Consett said at least nine thousand."

Two Berber labourers in straw hats were busily engaged in shovelling sand out of the bottom of this receptacle and throwing it up over the side; Mme La Besse shouted greetings to them in Arabic, and they shouted back, happy and friendly. The sand kept on blowing in, Mme La Besse explained; that must have been bad for the Phoenician wine, make it salty, Julia observed, which made the old lady laugh and shake.

Next they inspected what Mme La Besse declared to be the *huilerie*, the oil-mill, where olives were crushed before their oil was pressed out; Julia was rather unconvinced by this, since there was little to be seen but a large block of stone surrounded by a shallow circular trench or gutter, mortared as usual. However the fish-pits, which they visited next, were extremely convincing. A range of deep tanks, each some ten feet long by six feet broad, and seven or eight deep, ran round three sides of another enclosure, all lined with beautifully fine close mortar; for fish, whether swimming alive, pickling in brine, or steeping in oil they looked just the thing, indeed it was hard to think of a purpose unconnected with fish to which such structures could be put. Julia—perfectly ignorant of Roman, let alone Phoenician remains—regarded everything she was shown with a fresh and slightly sceptical eye; she listened, also a little sceptically, to the old archaeologist's eager attributions.

The little temple in the middle of the whole lay-out, with its small elegant pillars, she was prepared to accept, and could even pay a happy tribute to a civilisation which insisted on the equivalent of a chapel built into the heart of its factories. But she felt less sure about three long enclosures lying towards the lower, seaward end of the rectangle of buildings, which Mme La Besse declared to have been warehouses for the finished products before they were shipped away—one for wine, one for oil, and one for the pickled fish.

"But how do you *know* that that is what they were for?" Julia asked in her usual slow tones, gazing at her employer from behind her immense dark sun-glasses.

"For what else should they be? And if you had seen the number of shards of broken amphorae that we cleared out of them, you would have thought the same! Oil and wine were certainly transported in amphorae; how they sent the fish we don't know—possibly in rush baskets lined with the leaves of palmettes."

"What are palmettes?" Julia asked.

"Oh, this plant from which the Moors make the *crin végétal* with which they stuff their mattresses—this countryside is full of it, you will see them when we have lunch," said Mme La Besse, rather irritably. She hustled Julia down to look at the baths at the lower end; these too were perfectly convincing. Julia had seen the like in England, when dragged by Geoffrey to observe Roman remains. Hot baths, cold baths, stone steps leading down into both; the tile-vaulted chambers of the hypocaust, where fires were kindled below the sudarium, the sweating-room, immediately above; neat herring-bone tiling floored most of these rooms, and here and there a fragment of gay frescoes, orange and white, still clung to the walls.

Julia surveyed all this with approval; if the place had really been a factory, these dispositions for the workers' comfort were admirable. "Fine; pit-head baths," she said—and then had to translate and explain to Mme La Besse about the English arrangements for coal-miners to wash before they went home from their work. But in spite of her lingering scepticism she was charmed by the idea of such a factory, functioning more than two thousand years ago. Standing there, fingering the curious pock-markings in the beautiful rough golden stone of the wall, for a little while she let her imagination run—an unusual thing with her, picturing those long-ago labourers toiling in the fish-pits or carrying laden amphorae down to the triremes or quinqueremes anchored at the mouth of the small river which ran out just below the site into a bay sheltered by a projecting headland, sweating under the strong sun, as she was sweating merely from walking about. Here, where fragrant scents from the healthy uplands filled the warm air, and the surf thundered on the sands below, there was no suggestion of dark Satanic mills; if one had to be a factory-hand, better to have been a Phoenician one, she thought. And vast earthenware jars full of flowery aromatic wine like that which she drank nightly—free of charge, since it was *vinho de mesa*—at the Espagnola was an amusing counterpart to the tractors and saloon cars which she had watched being decanted from the *Vidago* onto this very coast—amusing, and somehow nicer, as honest wine is nicer than any piece of machinery.

These meditations were only possible because the foreman who directed the labourers had come up to ask some directions of Mme La Besse, but they were soon interrupted; he went away, and the eager old lady led the way down to where most of the actual digging was taking place, in front of the seaward wall of the site. Here five or six more Berbers, in headgear which varied from ragged turbans to torn straw hats, were clearing away the soil to lay bare curious stone slabs, some of them grooved, and several small stone boxes or tanks sunk in the ground, with one sloping side, which reminded Julia of nothing so much as the fitted wash-tubs in the laundry at Glentoran; the men greeted Mme La Besse with gleeful pleasure, and she chatted to them, with a word for each—

clearly she was a general favourite. The excavated soil, to Julia's astonishment, was wheeled away in barrows to be riddled at some hundred yards' distance before being tipped onto the foreshore—no hope therefore, as even her ignorance recognised, of being able to know with any exactitude where any particular object, revealed in the wire sieve, had come from. Had Geoffrey seen this extraordinary proceeding, she wondered?—however, she said nothing.

Mme La Besse was worried about those small stone tanks or boxes, and asked Julia if she had any idea what they could have been used for? Julia mentioned the laundry wash-tubs—"If you dug along behind them you might find a spout or something that led the water into them," she said; she had already been shown parts of the underground system of stone channels through which water had been brought by gravity from the cisterns at its upper end down to every part of the site, and had admired its ingenuity. Mme La Besse was delighted with the laundry idea; she whipped a mason's trowel out of her belt and began to dig herself, and called up a Berber to help. Julia looked on, wishing that she had a trowel or spade with which to dig too, while Mme La Besse, on her knees, continued to speculate aloud as to whether this could have been a laundry or wash-house.

"I know!" Julia exclaimed suddenly.

"What do you know?" asked the old lady, squatting back on her heels and wiping her perspiring face with an earthy hand.

"Won't this have been the place where they gutted the fish? Right down here near the shore, you see, and keep the pickling chamber clean. London fishmongers always clean fish in sort of sinks, with running water—you can see them in the backs of the shops."

Mme La Besse was even more delighted with this second suggestion; she stood up to pat Julia on the shoulder, and said that she was *une fille très intelligente*, then shouted to the foreman to come over and discuss this new idea. Presently she abandoned the foreman, and led Julia off again—"You must see *all*," she said, "and then we will have lunch."

There was not much more to see. Out on the open space, as yet undug, between the lowest wall and the sea lay several large blocks of that pock-marked limestone, placed there till either their use or their original positions could be established; one or two had large phalluses carved in relief on the sides, definitely proving, Mme La Besse thought, that they were Phoenician in origin. Julia, her hair spectacular in the sun, and in her huge dark glasses looking like a peculiarly vacant film-star, said in her slow tones—

"Couldn't they be Mithraic, and Roman?"

The old woman cocked her head sharply at the young one.

"I thought you were so ignorant!" she said.

"Oh, well, everyone knows about Mithras now, since that place in the City was being dug up," said Julia blithely.

"*Tiens!* Yes, well, it is possible that these are Mithraic—but I think not."

They lunched near the shed, sitting on the last fringe of the heathy slope where it fell away to the shore, and Mme La Besse showed Julia some low bushy dumps of palm-leaves which she said were the palmettes from which *crin végétal* was made. Julia was hungry, though the lunch was not very good; she made a mental note that if she was going to come to the site often she would organise the picnic food herself. However, there was a bottle of the good red Moroccan wine which helped down the rather dry sandwiches and the lump of hard Moroccan cheese.

"What impression does the site make on you?" Mme La Besse asked.

"Fascinating! And so much has been done; I suppose to begin with—well, what was there to see?"

"Nothing!—except for a few fallen pillars among the cistuses."

"Extraordinary," said Julia. "What fun you must have had."

The old lady was pleased with these rather moderate tributes, and developed her theories while she masticated the withered sandwiches. The archaeological sites in England to which Geoffrey Consett had sometimes borne Julia in his little car had all been completely excavated, determined, and written up—she had not realised the part that speculation and intelligent interpretation has to play in archaeology. Now she did, and in her casual way she sympathised with her employer's problems; she was really rather moved when the old lady said—

"You like it out here? You will come often? I see that you have intuition, good ideas; you could be a great help to me in the excavation. This notion of cleaning the fish outside the walls—it is formidable!"

Julia asked nothing better than to spend as much time as possible out in this delicious place, thunderously musical with surf along the shore, sweet with wild scents—she said as much, and Mme La Besse patted her hand.

But while they lunched something else held her attention. When Mme La Besse had left the site to eat the Berber labourers also knocked off work; they went out onto the dry white sand of the upper shore and there knelt down with their faces towards Gibraltar—which also happened to be towards Mecca, more or less—and recited their midday prayers, bowing their foreheads to the ground, before they started to eat. Julia remembered what Paddy Lynch had said about a Moslem's faith, and how irreligious they considered Christians —well, there you were. If she were a Catholic she might have said the Angelus, and so might Mme La Besse. *Was* she a Catholic? Julia felt too lazy to ask—she drank another glass of wine and then, poking her head into the shade of a palmette plant, while her body relaxed in the sun, she fell into a doze.

Chapter 7

JULIA waited rather impatiently during the next few days for the promised letter from Paddy Lynch, which was to report the results of his "snooping" about Colin; she was busy with her work, she wrote away at her Casablanca article, but she had quite sufficient time to wonder why he didn't write, and to ponder uncomfortably over the episode up in the Kasbah. When at last Paddy's letter did come it was profoundly unsatisfactory.

"No go," he wrote. "I'm frightfully sorry—I did all I could. Johnny Bingham knows nothing, I'm sure of that—so it wouldn't have been any good your using those eyes of yours on him! Tony Panoukian certainly *does* know something, I can see, but he is keeping utterly mum about it. I was very much surprised, really. Your cousin must be on some tremendously hush job, because Tony will usually tell me anything I want to know. They've got his account all right—I got that, quick like the fox, from a clerk before I tackled the high-ups."

Julia thought Mr. Lynch's letter over carefully, sitting in her room at the Espagnola. She was thoroughly intrigued by this whole series of dead ends—a dead end at the Bank of England, two dead ends in Casablanca, that closed door (than which no end could be deader) in the Kasbah. What *could* be going on? She had said up at Glentoran, she remembered a little ruefully, that detection would be a frolic—but it wasn't really much of a frolic to be thwarted at every turn, and find out *nothing*, delicious as it was to be in Tangier in the sun among flowers, and much as she was enjoying her days out at "*l'excavation*", searching for thresholds and floor-levels, digging herself with the trowel she had bought at Kent's Emporium, and writing up reports for the old lady.

Time was marching on, and she was getting nowhere. She remembered that Lady Tracy had also expressed a fondness for detection—from her chair; and that afternoon she chartered a taxi by the hour (Spanish-speakers can do this in Tangier) and went up to the house on the cliff.

Lady Tracy was out on the roof—which was flat and festooned with lines of washing—sitting in a deckchair and screaming jests over the low parapet at the Moorish occupants of some rather hovel-like little houses down on the slopes below. The cliffs here were, so to speak, in two tiers: first an upper cliff, then a talus of scree overgrown with grass, now full of grazing goats and those small houses dotted about; then a second vertical fall to the blue water, crashing ceaselessly against the yellow line of rocks.

"They are so *nice*," Lady Tracy said, when Julia had greeted her and been kissed, waving a gnarled old hand over the parapet. "From here I can watch every detail of their lives: the washing, the cooking—do you see that little stove out in the garden?—milking the goats, and the hunt for eggs. I *must* remember to tell Nilüfer that her brown hen has a nest in that big clump of thistle—do you see it, under the rock? The fact is, I know almost more about them than they know themselves, from this eyrie."

This was another pleasing facet of Lady Tracy's character, and Julia liked to think of her sitting on her roof-top, watching Moorish domestic life and enjoying long-range conversations with her friends a hundred feet below. However she was glad when presently the old lady asked—"Well, and how is your search going?"

"It isn't going at all. I wanted to ask you if your detection had produced any results, because mine hasn't."

"Oh, I am sorry. And I am afraid I have been rather useless too. I have a nephew who goes about a lot, and often seems to know things, but unfortunately he is away just now—such a bore."

"Yes," said Julia, flatly. "It is, rather. You see I haven't the faintest idea what to do next. When do you expect your nephew to get back?"

"Dear child, I have no idea. One never knows, with him. He's a botanist, and goes flitting off after some flower or other like a butterfly! He knows just where to look for the rarities —which I don't suppose real butterflies care about," said Lady Tracy, looking vague. "I expect they just want honey, don't you?"

"I suppose so," said Julia, rather dully. She suddenly felt depressed; she had hoped a good deal from Lady Tracy's help, and now none seemed to be forthcoming.

The old lady saw her depression. She leaned over and patted Julia's hand.

"My dear child, I am *sorry* not to have helped you. I will try to bestir myself somehow, even before Hugh comes back —and in the meantime, do remember what St. Paul said about possessing one's soul in patience. *Was* it St. Paul?"

"I can't remember."

"Tell me," said Lady Tracy, with a sudden switch of subject —"How are you getting on with Mme Le Besse?"

"Oh, the dig is heaven," said Julia more cheerfully, "and she's great fun."

Lady Tracy said that the Belgian was delighted with Julia and her help. "She says that you have intuitions!" she said with a gleam of amusement.

"Oh, yes, I'm bursting with intuitions," Julia replied gaily. "And she's nothing like as tatty as you led me to expect—not so far at least."

"Ah, wait!" said Lady Tracy.

Julia decided to follow one of her intuitions that very evening. Since Lady Tracy had learned nothing—again Julia had failed to put the old lady in possession of *all* the facts, but she overlooked that point—the time had clearly come to ask Purcell flat out about Colin. It was too early for the bar to be open when she got back to the Espagnola, so she filled in the time by writing a much overdue letter to Edina; that is to say, knowing her Aunt Ellen she wrote two letters: a short boring one saying that she hadn't found Colin yet but hoped to soon, and how lovely Tangier was, and she had taken a job as secretary to support herself—and another for Edina's private eye.

"Colin is evidently up to something quite extraordinary," she wrote, "though so far I can't find out what, and nor can Paddy"—and she gave a lively version of her encounter with Mr. Panoukian. "I think he was probably *smuggling*, to begin with," the letter went on; "the mate on the boat, a most odd bearded type called Reeder, suggested it at once—and everyone I've seen puts that up as an hypothesis, Consulate-General and all. *No one* sells oranges seriously, Mrs. H. was quite right about the smell of *that* rat; and out here they don't even call it orange-selling, they usually dress up as fishermen—that nonsense was just for home consumption." Then she pursued the theme of Mr. Reeder.

"He's really quite an enigma. Madly efficient, the Captain told me; he could be at the top of his profession by now—but he sticks on in this subordinate job because he loves this run—so he says. And I couldn't place him at all. He looks *terrible*, in a ghastly old uniform and with that beard, and he is crusty and curt to a degree; but he talks like a complete gent—really rather an ultra-gent, if you follow me—and he knows all about sheep, and wintering away and first-cross lambs. It seems he was brought up in Northumberland, where they have to do much what one does in Argyll about sheep." And she added as a P.S., in an access of leisurely mischief—

"He says anything with black hair drives him wild."

As she walked down to post this missive in the English post office on her way to Purcell's Bar, through the calm bright evening air, and the golden light which conferred a certain beauty on even the dullest villas, Julia's depression suddenly left her. She was beginning to feel at home in Tangier, as if she "belonged"; and she liked the place more than ever—she was no longer afraid of losing her way in the old city, and after buying one of these delicious posies from her enormous flower-woman in the Gran Socco, who greeted her with cries of pleasure, she cut down through the swarming alleys to the Socco Chico, with its thronged cafés and strolling crowd of idlers, and made her way to the quiet little street where Purcell's notice so discreetly beckoned.

She was still too early—the muslin-veiled door was locked. Julia tapped on the glass with the stem of her bouquet; in a moment it opened, and the little Moor peered out. When he saw who it was he drew the door wide to let her in, with a bow and a greeting in what he conceived to be French—Julia felt still more at home. "Monsieur Purcell?" she asked, seeing no sign of him, as she sat down at her usual table; the Moor scurried away, and in a moment Purcell himself was there behind the bar, small, neat, calm and courteous, with a smile of welcome.

"Sorry if I'm too early, Mr. Purcell, but I wanted to talk to you," the young woman said. "Yes, a Martini, please."

"That will be a pleasure," said Purcell, pouring things into a mixer. "What pretty flowers!"

"Aren't they? There's a heavenly old Berber woman up in the Gran Socco who always makes them—a giantess!"

"I know her," said Purcell, bringing Julia's drink round the end of the bar and setting it down on the table. "She is a witch with flowers."

"Yes, she is. Look, Mr. Purcell, sit for two minutes, till people come—I hate shrieking through space!"

Purcell sat.

"You won't drink yourself? You never do, I think?"

"No, I never do. I will have a cup of coffee, though." He called in a low voice, and ordered coffee from the little Moor.

"Mr. Purcell," said Julia, "did you ever know a young man

called Colin Monro, who was in and out of here for two or three years on a yacht with some other young Englishmen?"

"Yes, naturally I knew him. He was often here; they hung about for some time, as you say."

"What were they doing?"

"Oh, smuggling, of course. I am sure you know that already"—with a fine glance.

"Well, I guessed it."

"Yes, that was it. But after a time I imagine they made the place too hot to hold them; probably the Zone police got busy, or Interpol—they combine, you know—anyhow those young men seem to have cleared out altogether. I haven't seen anything of them for the last year—well, say ten or eleven months."

The last four words clicked in Julia's head like a bolt into its slot. Ten or eleven months—ten fitting in exactly with the transfer of Colin's account from Duntroon to Casablanca. But another thing struck her about Purcell's words. There was a lot of information, but all made somehow indefinite: "I imagine", "probably", "they seem". In her turn she studied Purcell curiously, with a long slow look, in silence.

"May I ask, if it is not indiscreet, why you are interested in Mr. Monro?" the man asked.

"Of course. He's my cousin, and we've had no news of him now for ages. I hoped you might know something. Do you know the name of the yacht, for instance?"

"No, I have no idea. Those sort of people do not talk much about themselves."

His face still puzzled her. *Sabe todo*, Reeder had said—and might be reluctant to say what he knew. She determined to fire all her batteries, now at last.

"Look, Mr. Purcell dear," she said with the eyes of a mourning dove—"you've simply *got* to help me about this! I'm desperate. I must find him."

"Why are you desperate? Why must you find him?"

"I must find him because he's wanted at home, badly. Listen—please listen." She poured out the story of Glentoran; Purcell did listen, in silence. "Anyhow his mother is frantic —he's her only son," Julia ended. "Surely you see?"

"Why do you not consult your friend Lady Tracy?" Purcell asked.

At this instance of Purcell's all-knowingness Julia laughed; she couldn't help it. She had a very pretty laugh, deep and gurgling, and slow, like her speech, as if she were chewing and tasting her amusement—it made Purcell smile.

"Why is that funny?" he asked, with genuine curiosity.

"Oh, a private joke. Anyhow, I did ask Lady Tracy, and, she promised to help, and she hasn't been able to. Her nephew, who it seems *sabe todo*,"—Julia grinned again, privately, at the phrase—"and might have been able to find out, has gone jaunting off after wild flowers, so he's no use."

Purcell's face, so mobile and expressive, once more seemed to Julia to register some impression which she could not fathom at the mention of the nephew and the wild flowers, but he said nothing.

"So there's no one to help me but you—don't for goodness sake suggest that I try Mme La Besse! I know there's no reason why you should help me; but I am really in trouble, and I ask you to."

He looked at her for some moments in silence when she said that; there was an expression, almost of compassion, on his queer face.

"It is *really* urgent, serious, that you get in touch with him?" he asked at last.

"Yes."

Still he studied her, as if trying to come to a decision.

"*Yes*," Julia said again, nodding her head.

He smiled.

"You are very persuasive, and I assume that you have some good reason for thinking that I can help you; I am curious about this, but I shall not ask what it is. I will do what I can, if you for your part will promise not to say *to anyone* that it is I who have told you what I now tell you."

"I promise that," said Julia quietly, though she was tremendously excited. Was she really going to learn something at last?

"Good. Well, if I were you I should go up to Fez—you have not been to Fez yet, have you?" Julia shook her head. "While you are there, simply *en touriste*, go to the shop of a very well-known dealer in curios called Bathyadis: any of the guides will take you to him. He may be able to tell you something—but speak to him alone, out of earshot of other people. If he cannot, or will not, tell you himself, he may at least put you in touch with a compatriot of yours, a Mr. St John."

Julia was all ears—this was quite unexpected. But another of those clicks took place in her head, and after thanking Purcell she said, quite lightheartedly and casually—

"Is Bathyadis one of the ones whose sons have started shops in Casablanca and Agadir and places?"

The effect on Purcell of this innocent question was electric—he started in his seat, for a moment he looked almost angry—or was it almost frightened?

"How do you know that?" he asked sharply.

"What, that they've started curio-shops down on the coast—the sons of the dealers in Fez and Marrakesh, I mean? Oh, someone was telling me about it in Casa, when I was asking who made money, how, out here."

"Who was this person, may I know?" He spoke with a curious urgency.

"A rather dumb bank-manager, to be exact," said Julia. "At a cocktail party. Why? Is it important? I just thought it was fun that the sons and nephews had got so rich in two or three years that they could buy Papa out, now," she said, tranquillisingly.

Purcell appeared to be tranquillised; his expression relaxed.

"No, it is not important," he said. "And it is, as you say, an amusing development." He paused for a moment. "But it is a very recent one, which few people, even those living out here, know about—so naturally I was surprised that you, so newly arrived, had heard of it."

"Yes, of course," said Julia smoothly; but to herself—"Covering-up" she said.

"You have many contacts in Casa?" Purcell asked, now with all his usual blandness.

"Oh, no—just one friend, in a bank. His wife and I were at school together," said Julia. "My boat put in there for twenty-four hours, so I looked them up. Horrible place, Casa, don't you think? I like this so much better."

"Ah, who would not?" said Purcell. "Tangier is unique."

At that moment the door opened to admit the young men whom Julia had now come to call "the bunch". At the first shadow on the muslin veiling, even before the tiny click of the latch, quick and silent as a cat Purcell was on his feet; before the door opened he was the other side of the table; and when the bunch entered, giggling and calling to one another, he was bending across assiduously and saying, for all to hear—"You are *sure* you will not have another, Mademoiselle?"

"Quite sure, thank you," said Julia, rising and taking a note from her purse. In fact the pansies could not have arrived more opportunely: she had got a line out of Purcell, and to continue to sit exchanging elegant cover-talk with him about the uniqueness of Tangier and the horribleness of Casablanca was the last thing she wanted. She had plenty to think about, and wanted time for that.

But thought, though amusing and exciting—*why* the fuss about the curio-dealing sons in the Atlantic ports?—it seemed quite inexplicable—did not take her very far. What was obvious was that she must go to Fez as soon as possible, and follow up this clue, faint and mysterious as it was. Next day she told Mme La Besse as she drove her out to the site, spinning along the blue-grey tarmac between the blue fields of irises, that she wanted to take a week's leave at once. The old lady was rather cross.

"What, already? But you have only just begun! Does my work bore you so soon?"

"No, *aucunément*—I adore the work," said Julia, heartily and truly. "But I must go now. I told you I might have to, dear Madame, as you will remember."

Mme La Besse grunted. "And where 'must' you go, now?"

"To Fez."

"Fez? *Tiens.* If you go to Fez you might do something useful to me," said the old Belgian, suddenly mollified and with a return to her usual childish eagerness.

"I should have the utmost pleasure in doing this, if it is within my power," said Julia, turning on some of her more elegant and formal French—she had already learned that this had a subduing effect on Mme La Besse when she became irritable. "Pray tell me, dear Madame, what it is that you desire of me."

Tame as a lamb, ardent as a little girl, Mme La Besse told her.

"I wish that you would go to Volubilis, the ruined Roman city near Fez. I am told that there is there a very good example of a Roman oil-mill, and I should like you to examine this with the greatest care, and write down a description on the spot, so that I may compare it with our little *huilerie* here. Perhaps," said Mme La Besse, peering hopefully sideways at Julia, "you could make a sketch?"

No, Julia could not sketch, and she had no camera; but she promised to take a tape-measure and bring back accurate measurements of the *huilerie*.

"And please observe closely, how it resembles or differs from ours here. Volubilis is said to have been built on the site of a Berber city, the name is derived from a Berber name. The Phoenicians were there also. I have a theory, though as yet I cannot prove it, that it was the Phoenicians who began the cultivation of the olive and oil-production in l'Afrique du Nord, long before the Romans; all information is therefore valuable."

Julia promised to do her best. Then she put a practical question.

"How far is Volubilis from Fez?"

"Oh, a nothing—sixty or seventy kilometres, perhaps."

"Is there a bus?"

"*Chère enfant*, how should I know? But in any case you could not travel in an autobus in le Maroc! You must take a car."

"Um," said Julia, wondering what this would be likely to cost. The trip to Fez would be pretty expensive, anyhow. But just then they arrived at the site, and the moment the Chrysler had been turned and parked near the shed, the old lady, glowing with enthusiasm over this new project, led Julia up to look at that so unconvincing oil-mill again. They stared together at the round block of yellow stone, the circular cemented channel, and at some other squarish blocks about whose use the old lady confessed herself at a loss—Julia for her part had no intuitions on this occasion. They stood speculating for some moments; a chilly wind had sprung up suddenly, and dark clouds were looming over the bronze-coloured mass of the headland which protected the bay on the south-west—Julia shivered.

"I think I'll go and fetch my coat," she said.

"Let us just go up to the wine-press enclosure, and see if Achmet and Abdul have got all the sand out of the big wine-tank," said Mme La Besse. "This wind will blow it in again, and I want to see the bottom."

The wine enclosure was the next above the one where they stood; they went into it and looked down into the deep tank. Abdul and Achmet had cleared out all the sand and were wheeling the last of it away in barrows; the bottom seemed to be covered with dark mud. Mme La Besse drew Julia's attention to some discoloration on the cemented sides, observing that to her it had a purplish look, like the stains of wine——Julia felt that to see this required the eye of faith, but did not say so. The two Berbers had carried away the short ladder they used for getting in and out of the pit; Mme La Besse lamented this, she wanted to climb down and examine the stained cement with the magnifying glass which, like her trowel, she invariably carried stuck in her belt. Julia volunteered to go for the ladder if she could be told the Berber word for it; Mme La Besse could not remember this for the moment, and while they stood undecided, on a sharp gust of wind down came the rain. Julia had only a cardigan—damn, if only she had fetched her coat.

"Here, under the wall—we shall get some shelter there," exclaimed the old lady, as she spoke unbuttoning her rather aged burberry; she drew it off and threw part over Julia's shoulders as they crouched together immediately above the tank under the low wall, which did afford a certain amount of shelter from the wind-driven rain. Julia thought she had never seen such a heavy downpour; the silver rods rebounded from the earth like hail, causing a white mist a foot high to rise above the surface of the ground; the rain hissed among the stones, and drummed—a different note—on the floor of the tank at their feet. Watching all this idly, and still rather cross at having been prevented from fetching her coat in time, the girl presently saw a sight which filled her with something like awe. The rain was so heavy that small runnels of water were soon streaming away downhill on all sides, and in a matter of minutes there was water all over the floor of the ancient wine-vat; the rain, hammering into this, brought it up in foam—and the foam was *red*!

"Look!" Julia almost gasped. "Mme La Besse, look at the tank!"

"Ah! You *see*," the Belgian said, in slow triumph. That was all. The old woman was awestruck too, as well she might be;

in silence, together, they watched a twentieth-century rain-storm stirring up lees of wine nearly two thousand years old.

Julia lost no time about setting off for Fez, though the more she thought about it, the more dubious the adventure seemed. Would Bathyadis tell her anything?—even how to find Mr. St John? On him, at least, she determined to try to secure a second string to her bow; she went up to the pink house on the cliff to consult Lady Tracy.

"Mr. St John? Oh, yes, of course I know him," said the old lady. "He comes down here sometimes, though not as often as one could wish. Such an interesting man—he has lived in Fez for ages, fifteen years at least, and quite *among* the Moors; he has a house in the Medina. My dear child, if you could get him to take you about a little, he is the most perfect cicerone; he knows everything and everybody. Shall I give you a letter to him?"

"Oh, yes, *do*. Do you think he would take me about to please you?"

"My dear child, once you have met I am confident that he will take you about to please *you*—or indeed to please himself," said Lady Tracy, bending her beautiful old eyes on the girl with a sweet aged archness. "I will write at once—" She rang her little brass bell as she spoke. "Feridah shall find my pad for me." Julia could see the pad on the table, poking out from under some knitting and *Life*, but refrained from mentioning the fact; she could never see enough of the lovely Feridah, who slid in, smiled through her veils at the visitor, stroked her mistress, and produced what was required. "When do you go?" Lady Tracy asked, pausing in her careful deliberate writing.

"Tomorrow."

"By car?"

"Oh heavens no—by train."

"My dear, it is an *awful* journey! And do you realise that

126

there is *no* restaurant car? Be sure to take a good picnic-basket and a bottle of wine, so that you don't starve."

Julia had not realised that the Moroccan State Railways seldom provide food for the traveller even on long journeys, and gratefully ordered herself an ample picnic meal on her return to the Espagnola. Señor Huerta had booked a room for her in a small hotel at Fez in the Medina, the old city, when she explained that she could not possibly afford the prices at the Palais Jamai, ravishing as she knew this to be; it was French-run, he said, and she would be all right there.

The storm which had so dramatically afforded proof of the authenticity of the wine-vat out at the site continued to blow and deluge Morocco, and when Julia went down to the station in good time for the three-thirty train to Fez it was only to learn that it had not even arrived—there were floods, the Espagnola porter told her; roads were washed away, and the train was delayed. Julia sat rather gloomily on her suitcases in that curious place, Tangier railway-station, watching the milling crowd of Moors, French *colons*, tourists, and hawkers of cigarettes and sweets who filled it, and used the time to inform herself about the journey from the hotel porter. What about customs, for instance? Oh, there were plenty of *them*, the man said grinning: customs out of the city of Tangier—the officers would come presently, to those benches where people were placing their baggage, as the Señorita saw for herself; customs again into the Spanish Zone; more customs on entering the French Protectorate of Morocco. It is a fact that the town of Tangier and its surroundings have a certain resemblance to one of those nests of wooden boxes beloved of the Chinese: the great French Protectorate, stretching from the Sahara on the East to the Atlantic on the West, and reaching southwards almost into Equatorial Africa, is the vast outer box; the much smaller Spanish Zone is the next; then the minute International Zone with the absurd little city at its heart. Absurd only because this tiny entity is politically unique, an

127

internationally-administered territory of a bare two hundred and twenty-five square miles, containing a population of only a hundred and seventy thousand souls; yet this doll's-house unit has its capital, its diplomatic corps, a judiciary of no less than eight judges, in fact most of the paraphernalia of statehood—it is really much as if Bournemouth had become a state, full as the place is of the delicate and the elderly.

About five the train from Fez came in; half an hour later it moved out again. The Espagnola porter was surprisingly efficient, and while most of the passengers were still screaming harassedly round the customs benches Julia found herself relaxing in a first-class carriage, her suitcases in the racks. Here she was presently joined by an exasperated and sweating individual who slung some rather military-looking baggage up onto the opposite rack, cursed his Arab porter in American French, over-tipped him, and sank back into his seat to light a Chesterfield—with typical courtesy he held out his pack to Julia before he did so.

"Oh, thank you, but I'm smoking," said Julia. "May I later?"

Her travelling-companion, whose age she judged to be about thirty, next began to ask about customs; thanks to the Espagnola porter Julia was able to enlighten him. And was there a restaurant-car? No there wasn't, she told him.

"Gosh! This is a hell country! How will I eat? With this hold-up I won't get to Port Lyautey till around two a.m.," said the American aghast.

Julia made no comment on this; instead she asked him what he was going to Port Lyautey for?

He was stationed there, it seemed, at the American Naval Air Base. Julia had not yet realised the highly important political fact of the huge American air bases in Morocco, but she pricked up her journalist's ears at once (with *The Onlooker* and *Ebb and Flow* well in mind) and set about cultivating the airman. Port Lyautey was sandy, she learned, and pretty upstate; there really wasn't much to it beside the Base; nor was there all that much to the Base—it was dull, apart from the jets. They had a library, but he had read mostly all the books; he amused himself by writing letters. Julia drew him out on the jets, about which he was enthusiastic—wonderful machines! They had given a number to the French for their base at Meknes and sent instructors up to teach the Frogs how to fly them—he had been doing that before he went on leave to take a look at France; he hoped to get sent up again. Meknes was a hick town, though it had a pretty gate—"Kinda arch, y'know; funny, but really pretty"—but when he went there he often drove over to Fez. "Fez is a swell town, so unique. Know it?"

Julia said she was going to Fez.

The airman at once said that he'd try to fix it to get sent up to Meknes right away—anyway he had four or five days leave in hand; he'd gotten fed up with France and came back, so he might come up any time. Where was she staying?

Julia told him the name of her small hotel.

"That's in the old town, isn't it? A small French place? Oh, I'd not stay there if I was you. Little French hotels are awful. Ever stay in one? That's what drove me away, the French hotels. Their notions of *plumbing*!"

Julia laughed and said that she had lived in France, and didn't mind any of it, not even the plumbing. She continued to cultivate her Yankee acquaintance, with her usual regrettable eye to the main chance: if he came up to Fez with his car it might solve the problem of getting out to Volubilis and checking on the Roman *huilerie* for Mme La Besse. He was quite nice really, she decided; rather lonely, rather bored—bored, living in Morocco! Julia constantly kept one eye out of the window, observing the country-side, the houses, the flocks of white tick-birds in the sodden fields, the storks wading majestically across the flooded land, a group of animals she couldn't identify scampering beside a reed-bordered stream—

could they be deer? Were there deer in Morocco? She asked her new acquaintance, who had already informed her that his name was Steve Keller, and that he had "done" two years there.

He didn't know—he knew strangely little about this place where he had lived so long. He had obviously never had any real curiosity whatever about the country or its inhabitants: the Moors were a crafty crowd, he said, but just the same what business had the god-damned French there, sitting on top of them and making money out of them? Julia, startled by this attitude, mentioned the hospitals in Casablanca as one instance of something the French had done *for* Morocco—it was, so far, the only thing she knew of that tremendous work. Oh, well, maybe, Mr. Keller replied; he hadn't seen the hospitals, he didn't know. But he was against imperialism and colonialism, any place.

"Why?" Julia asked. "The French have done at least one good thing, which you've never managed to learn about in all this time—don't tell me the Arabs would organise hospitals on their own; they never have anywhere. What harm have they done to the Moors?"

He couldn't answer her. It was just this vague emotional feeling, supported by incuriosity and ignorance, with no more solid basis than an inherited mass-memory of one instance of a Colonial dispensation gone wrong, gone sour; but issuing in a mass-attitude which presented a blank wall to facts. Julia was startled and rather horrified—she had met several Americans, but all of a much more sophisticated type than the airman: either too well-educated to be at the mercy of these primitive concepts, or too wise to give them expression. She relapsed into silence, a thing which always came easy to her.

Dusk began to fall, ending the resource of looking out of the window; the unheated train grew very cold—Julia was glad she had put on the fleecy zip boots admired by Mr. Reeder. She was hungry, and made up her mind to have supper; clearly she must offer some to her companion and as she lifted down her basket and began to unpack it on the little table under the window she said—

"Won't you have something to eat? I have lots. That is, if you don't mind sharing it with an impenitent imperialist, who is a convinced believer in the colonial system for backward races."

He laughed very nicely.

"You have me there! I am hungry." He fairly beamed as he watched her spread out a long loaf, a packet of butter, slices of raw smoked ham, tomatoes, and a jar of black olives, with a bottle of Moroccan red wine standing up in the midst.

They supped in amity, now talking again; Julia had a little thick travelling glass, Steve Keller fished an aluminium cup out of his baggage, from which they drank. The raw ham troubled his timid ignorance about strange foods. "Nonsense, it's delicious; what absurd ideas you have," said Julia firmly.

"It's *raw*," objected the American.

"Yes, and so are oysters—it's raw and it's *good*. No, you'll get no more bread till you've eaten a slice," the girl said, tucking the loaf back into her basket—and in fact when Mr. Keller had tried the raw ham he admitted that it *was* good.

Just as they were finishing supper the ticket collector came along—after snipping their tickets he informed them both that they must change at Petit-Jean. This was one thing on which the Espagnola porter had failed to enlighten Julia; she thought the train went through to Fez. They would reach Petit-Jean about 9.30 to change trains—oh, abundantly of time; yes, and plenty of porters. And when would they reach Fez? Julia asked. Ah, it was impossible to be precise—at one in the morning, or perhaps at two.

Julia groaned—this was going to be ghastly. Her little hotel was to have sent to meet her train at the normal time, but would they wait till one or even two a.m.? However, she put all that aside till the time came, with her usual calm.

When they reached Petit-Jean, they found that the collector was wrong both about the abundance of time for the change and the supply of porters. Of the latter there were none. Julia and Steve Keller tumbled out in the darkness on to a platform empty of everything but other distracted passengers tumbling out too, while a French voice screamed *"Depart pour Fez en deux minutes!"* The airman gathered up her suitcases, gallantly abandoning his own luggage, and led her, running and stumbling, round to another stationary train, which proved to be the one for Fez; hastening after him, cumbered with her typewriter and food basket, on the further platform she bumped into a small man who swore at her in some guttural language as he recoiled from the painful impact of the basket. "The same to you, with knobs on!" Julia muttered —in the light falling from the high train windows she saw that he had a cast in one eye, and thought she recognised the seedy little man from Purcell's Bar. But there was no time to make sure—Steve was already throwing her cases up the four feet which always separate the doors of French trains, Heaven knows why, from ground level, and hollering to her to hurry. Discomfited, furious, panting, Julia climbed in after them just as the train drew out.

"Oh, thank you *so* much!" she shouted at him through the window—and "See you in Fez, Thursday," the American shouted back.

Chapter 8

FEZ is a strange city. Withdrawn, remote, secretive, it is so compressed, both within itself and by its gloomy encircling hills, that it is one of the most difficult towns in the world to *see*—its most famous monuments, like the Kairouine Mosque, can never be entered by Christians (or any other infidel), and there are no open spaces from which to gaze even on the exterior of these wonderful buildings. The most the visitor can do is to climb to the top of one or other of the Medersas, or sacred colleges, and thence look out over the roofs of the greater wonders, and perambulate the narrow steep streets, catching a glimpse, here of a fountain, there of the carved doorway of a shrine. It is very revealing of the character of the place that the only views it permits of itself as a whole should be of its walls, seen from the slopes of the hills outside—Fez allows no view within those walls.

And yet it is full of magic: the magic of things half-seen in a dream, the magic of the barely visible or the partly remembered, which are the very stuff of dreams. Fez is full of rivers—seven, I believe—but they all run underground; the narrow alleys are full of the mysterious sound of invisible rushing water, but even the rivers may not be looked upon. These subterranean streams serve the useful purpose of sewers and also of rubbish dumps; here and there, under dank and clammy vaulted archways, one comes upon a mortared chute where the sound of the hidden water is extra loud—two women with baskets, or a mule-drawn cart, are to be seen emptying part of what Fez has done with and wishes to be rid of down the chute into the roaring hurrying stream, below and out of sight. Earth has not anything to show, not more fair, but more peculiar.

And the people are as strange and as secretive as the place.

Hawk-like Arab types predominate, striding along in silence on slippered feet, their stern splendid faces closed, inward-looking; the women's great sombre eyes look out from above swathing white veils with none of the languor or gay curiosity of the eyes which look out above veils in Tangier or Marrakesh; even the Berber women, unveiled and with deep blue designs tattooed on brow and chin, seem, in Fez, to lack the bold chattering gaiety which they display elsewhere—sitting inviting the passer-by to inspect their wares in Tetuan, for example. And since the secretive, the mysterious, are apt to be also slightly sinister, or at least intimidating, Fez at first often creates a faintly alarming impression.

So at least it seemed to Julia Probyn—especially when the Oran express, into which she had to make another unexpected change at Meknes, decanted her at the station at half-past one in the morning. The railway of course has been kept well away from the mediaeval city, brooding within its walls; it only touches the new town. There were few passengers besides herself, and these got into cars and drove away; a solitary taxi was parked under the arc-lights on the space outside the station. This Julia hailed. It was free—it had not been sent by her hotel; an aged Arab with a beard, leaning in his djellaba by the station entrance, heard her question, and vouchsafed in curious French that the hotel had sent a car earlier, but that it had gone away. So Julia drove off in the taxi, cold, weary, and in spite of her usual calm a little nervous—what, for instance, would the taxi cost at this unearthly hour? It cost five hundred francs; but after driving along what seemed miles of wall, and through innumerable gateways and archways, looming high and shadowy above her, it did at last deposit her at her hotel, where a lot of hammering and bell-ringing at length produced a sleepy servant who led her to a small but decent room—fifteen minutes after she entered it Julia was in bed and asleep.

Next morning, over the familiar French breakfast of rolls and

butter, with chicory in the coffee, she wrote a note to Mr. St
John enclosing Lady Tracy's letter, and saying that if it was
not "a bore" she would so much like to see him—this the hotel
undertook to send by hand at once. Señor Huerta at the
Espagnola, and Lady Tracy too, had impressed on the girl
that no European woman of *any* age could with propriety walk
alone in the streets of Fez; anxious to lose no time—though the
prices of her small hotel proved, mercifully, to be fairly
moderate—Julia asked the management to lay on a French-
speaking guide for eleven o'clock. When she went downstairs
this individual was already waiting—a tall Arab in flowing
robes, whose excessively handsome face was only slightly dis-
figured by a rather noticeable wart on one side of his high
hawk-like nose. He spoke fair French, but in spite of his hand-
someness—or perhaps because of it; there are women who
instinctively distrust handsome men—Julia took against Abdul
from the moment she set eyes on him, and she was really
rather relieved when in the middle of their colloquy as to
where she should go and what she should see, the hotel porter
announced that a Monsieur Anglais desired to speak with
Mademoiselle, and she found herself face to face with Mr.
St John.

Mr. St John, Julia decided at once, could not possibly be
as old as he looked, or he simply couldn't have walked about
at all. He looked incredibly old. He was very short, not much
over five feet, with bushy snow-white hair and a face so brown,
leathery, and wrinkled that he strongly resembled a lizard—
but a very *nice* lizard; his expression was charming, benevolent
and intelligent, in spite of his disconcerting saurian face, with
the little hooked poking nose, so like the nose of a questing
tortoise. He spoke with extreme deliberateness and a curiously
beautiful enunciation; his words came out like small carved
beads of sound from his tight withered lips. Julia was fascinated
by him, and by his brief way of dealing with Abdul, the
guide.

"Another time," he said in French, waving a small claw-like hand in dismissal. "Today it is *I* who escort Mademoiselle." (The 'moi' in this speech was even more elaborately carved than the other verbal beads.) Abdul, clearly intimidated, gave a deeply respectful Moslem salutation and took himself off.

"Now that we are rid of this *shameless* exploiter and profiteer, what do you want to see?" Mr. St John asked.

"Well, Fez," said Julia. "But don't let me be a bore."

"That were impossible. And if Fez could bore me—which it never has yet—I should console myself by looking at you," the old man said, with a prehistoric twinkle from under his extraordinary dinosaur's eye-lids. "But do you, in the first place, wish to shop?"

"No, not really. You see I haven't much money for shopping —this hellish travel allowance!" said Julia. "But some time, when we've done the main sights, I should like to go to Bathyadis. I hear he has lovely things, and that one can look at them without buying too much."

"Ah, this delightful Bathyadis! A great friend of mine. Who told you of him?" Mr. St John asked, with a keen glance.

"Lady Tracy," Julia lied glibly. She had rather been caught on one foot by Mr. St John turning up so promptly, and with her customary deliberation she decided not to rush matters but to hold her fire and see what happened—she had intended to do a preliminary visit to Bathyadis alone and try out the ground before embarking on the Englishman at all. As it was, she would be passive today. Something might eventuate.

Quite a lot eventuated, as it turned out. Mr. St John, with a stout walking-stick, led Julia on a skilful round of Fez, which he accompanied by a learned and lively commentary: through *souks* full of leather, of copper, of pottery, of silks, of spices— each commodity in its separate street; past fountains with exquisite carved plaster above them, past the doors, equally ornate, of famous and forbidden mosques; under those vaulted echoing tunnels where the rushing noise of underground water filled the air, and women tipped rubbish into the subter-ranean streams. He told her of the seven rivers, and their names.

"Yes, but where do all these Alphs come out?" Julia asked, "if they do come out? They must look pretty ghastly when they emerge, with all this garbage in them; they'd really do better to stick to caverns measureless to man, don't you think?"

Mr. St John laughed, a dry articulated laugh such as a tortoise might give, if tortoises laughed.

"Dear young lady, how practical and factual you are! Do you know, I have never observed them after they emerge—which they certainly do, ultimately."

"Oh, well, I expect you're wise," said Julia carelessly. She was beginning to get tired, young and strong as she was, after yesterday's journey and her short night; moreover Fez is built on two slopes of considerable steepness, so that when perambu-lating the old city half one's time seems to be spent in climbing Mount Everest, or descending something equally abrupt. She was much relieved when at last Mr. St John, turning into a courtyard with a fountain, and shops opening all round it, said—

"Here is Bathyadis's."

The shop was really two, and was not in the least like a European shop. It consisted of a couple of rooms, with most of both their fronts open to their full width on the court, causing Julia to wonder how the place could be shut up at night. One half was given over solely to carpets, the other was full of curios of every sort—silverware, antique jewellery in cases, lamps, brass trays, exquisite embroideries, woven saddle-bags and djellabas, and fine old leather-work; the whole place glowed and gleamed with colour like Aladdin's cave.

Bathyadis, in spite of his Greek-sounding name, was to all appearance a complete Moor, dressed in a long woollen robe with a fez on top—Goodness, that's why they're called fezes, Julia thought to herself, now at last in the city that gives its meaning to the word; he had a splendid presence, a flowing grey beard, and courtly manners. He greeted Mr. St John by name in passable French and with evident pleasure, and invited them to sit down and have mint tea; Mr. St John looked enquiringly at Julia.

"Oh, yes, do let's—I'm longing to take the weight off my feet," the girl said in English. Mr. St John nodded to Bathyadis and introduced him to Julia, who figured in the introduction, she recalled afterwards, as "a friend of mine".

They sat on a sort of bench covered with rich carpets. A youth in Arab garments brought the mint tea in glasses; it was sweet, scalding hot, and very minty—Julia thought it rather nasty, but sipped peacefully while Bathyadis and her escort talked. They spoke in French, and she listened idly, glad to be sitting down; Bathyadis was asking if Monsieur St John wanted to look at the tray again? No, not today, the old gentleman said—nevertheless the dealer had the tray brought out, a lovely antique one in wrought brass, of exquisite workmanship; Mr. St John continued to say No. Meanwhile Julia's eye, roving round the cave-like gloom of the shop, was caught by a little coffer or trunk covered in plum-coloured velvet studded in a graceful pattern with silver-headed nails, for all the world like the one which propped up the broken Chippendale chair in Lady Tracy's house in Tangier; she thought it quite enchanting, and presently she drew Mr. St John's attention to it. "Would that be fearfully expensive?" she asked. "I'd love to have it, if I have to starve for a week!"

"The little trousseau-trunk, do you mean? Oh no, they are not in the least costly—two pounds, or two pounds ten at the most. They have become a drug in the market." He spoke to Bathyadis, and the little object was brought over by the youth who had fetched the tea, and opened for Julia's inspection; inside it was lined with some flowered material, there was a tiny lock and a delicate silver key.

"It's sweet," said Julia. "I will reflect upon it," she told Bathyadis in French, waving the pretty thing away.

"How wise you already are," said Mr. St John approvingly. "One should always tell an Arab that one will reflect upon a purchase; the longer one reflects, the less a given object costs."

"Why do you call them trousseau-trunks? And why are they a drug on the market?" Julia asked.

"For a sad reason, in answer to your second question. For centuries, here, the trousseau of a Moorish bride has always been carried in the wedding procession—on someone's head, usually—enclosed in one of these velvet coffers, varying in size of course according to the wealth and social status of the family; most of these little pieces of luggage are between two and three hundred years old, handed down with love and respect from mother to daughter from generation to generation. But recently," said Mr. St John, emitting a whistling sigh which again reminded Julia of a tortoise of her childhood, "it has become dated, out-moded, arriéré, to use these beautiful things for this purpose; it is considered much more chic, more up-to-date, to send down to Casablanca, or to the New Town here, for some very dreadful modern suitcase in compressed fibre—if possible with an imitation of the skin of the lizard or the crocodile stamped on its surface—in which to carry the bride's trousseau to her new home."

"God, how revolting!" said Julia fervently.

"You are right. The deity may with propriety be invoked to condemn this practice. However, it obtains; and that is why these lovely objects of art—for they are that—can now be bought at bargain prices."

"Well, I'll buy one next time I come. If I wait, shall I perhaps get it for thirty-five shillings?" Julia asked.

"Oh, you are admirable! I daresay you may. I will speak to him about it," Mr. St John said—and did so.

"Mademoiselle, my friend, desires a coffer, which you will sell her at the proper price—not at all the *prix de touristes*, you understand." The immediate result was to cause Bathyadis to have half the contents of the crowded shop pulled aside in order to display to Julia another trunk of the same sort, only in a more crimson shade of velvet, and five times bigger. "*Non, non,*" Julia said, laughing and shaking her head—the old Englishman for some reason grinned broadly at this point.

However Mr. St John, still speaking French, now asked a question of Bathyadis which caused Julia to sit up and listen. How was his son doing in Casablanca?

Oh, marvellously—he was making a fortune. Such a place for money, Casablanca! "But he is here, just for a week—you would like to meet him?"

Mr. St John said he would, and the Arab youth, who had been quietly putting back the displaced objects in front of the vast velvet trunk, was sent to fetch young Mr. Bathyadis. Julia hugged herself in silence—as easy as all that.

The young man when he arrived proved to be much less picturesque than his father, since he wore neat European clothes; but his manners were equally good. He greeted Mr. St John with the utmost warmth, thanking him with all his heart—rather to Julia's surprise this—for having made that wonderful suggestion. "Only a year and a half I am there, and already such gains! It is formidable!" More mint tea was brought to celebrate the occasion; the young man was presented to Julia, who said she would be going to Casablanca later, and would so much like to visit his shop and take her friends there—young Bathyadis whipped out a card and handed it to her; she stowed it away in her purse with great satisfaction. A second article on the Moroccan financial sidelines was practically in the bag, if she could only get onto that business of the rare minerals, somehow or other.

As they left, bowed out by old Bathyadis and his rich son, Julia had a small, unpleasant shock. Leaning against the wall in the open courtyard, in conversation with the Arab youth who had fetched the tea, was—this time quite unmistakably—the seedy little man with the cast in his eye whom Julia thought she had recognised when she bumped into him at Petit-Jean the night before. She walked quickly over, determined to tackle him; but with his beetle-like run he nipped out through the archway leading from the court to the street, and was gone.

"What is it?" Mr. St John asked, as she fell back, baffled, beside him.

"That revolting little man! I really believe he's following me," said Julia indignantly.

"Dear young lady, it should no longer surprise you that men follow you, surely?" said Mr. St John, with calm and slightly mocking benevolence.

"Oh, well—" said Julia; she was by nature all in favour of calm, and gave that up for the moment.

Mr. St John said that they would now visit the museum. The museum is at the top of Fez, or Everest, Bathyadis' shop is at the bottom; they toiled upwards. Julia began to feel extraordinarily tired—so tired that the sight of lush growths of plants on the tops of yellow plastered walls, and the trees that occasionally overhung them, could no longer charm her; she could think only of her back, which ached, of her feet, and the appalling cobble-stones in which her feet trod. But even in this near-coma of exhaustion, one thing drew and held her attention. Now and again, in fact quite often in their exhausting progress uphill they encountered some wonderful old man, swathed from head to foot in impeccable robes of creamy wool, a woollen hood covering his ice-white hair, and revealing his ice-white beard—they were the *cleanest* human beings that Julia had ever beheld, and moreover she observed that the crowds in the thronging alleys made way for them with reverent respect.

"What *is* that old man?" she was at last moved to ask Mr. St John, as they passed yet another of these ultra-clean white-clad figures.

"He is a leading member of one of the religious brotherhoods, which are such a feature of Muslim life here," Mr. St John replied.

"Religious life? For charity and so on, like the Spanish *hermandads*?"

"Originally, yes; and for that reason they are held in great veneration and wield a prodigious influence. But latterly, with the growth of nationalism and the disturbed state of public feeling, a good many of these brotherhoods, or the leaders of them, have begun to bend their organisations to political ends, alas!"—he ended with another of those whistling sighs. Julia was so much interested that she almost forgot her fatigue— this would be splendid for *Ebb and Flow*.

"I suppose they are rather anti the new Sultan, then?" she asked. "I mean, he's like a schismatic Pope, isn't he?"

"You are astonishingly well-informed"—he bent his bright lizard's eyes curiously onto Julia's lovely blank face. "Yes— well—yes and no. The late Pope, as you so amusingly regard him, presented great difficulties to the Administration; but the installation of the schismatic one has presented even greater. And in spite of their strong religious leanings not all the Moulays—for I should explain that these leaders and many others besides, being descendants of the Prophet, are entitled to be called Moulay This-or-That—are 'anti': amusing transatlantic word, but how briefly expressive! Where was I?" Mr. St John asked, suddenly lost in his own parentheses.

"You'd got to where not all the Moulays were anti-something, but you didn't say what—you got held up on the word anti," said Julia, amused.

"Ah—yes—thank you. Well, by no means all of them are 'anti', or against the French Administration, since it has brought such undoubted benefits to Morocco: peace, stability, order, wealth; progress in agriculture, and in the development of natural resources such as oil and minerals— all things unknown here for two thousand years; moreover things which the Arabs and Berbers, delightful and splendid though they may be as individuals, are congenitally incapable of creating for themselves. And these men, wiser and more forward-looking than most of their compatriots, have tried to use their influence, both religious and political, to achieve co-operation with the French régime. Since the régime has installed a schismatic Sultan, or Pope, they have supported him too."

"That sounds very sensible to me; fine, in fact," quoth Julia.

"It *is* fine, it *is* sensible," said Mr. St John. "But what is the lamentable result? Do you read the papers, here? If so you will have seen that the Moulay X was murdered in Casablanca last week."

"No, I hadn't seen it. Good gracious, that must be since I was there! And everyone thought it was getting so quiet."

" 'Everyone' was wrong. This Moulay X was an excellent man, learned, wise and sufficiently statesman-like to realise that the best thing for Morocco, whatever mistakes the French may have made, was a long continuance of the Protectorate; and he threw all his weight into that end of the scale. But that sufficed for him to be branded as a quisling, and all he got for his pains was a bullet."

"Fired by whom?"

"A nationalist—or more probably a common assassin hired by the extreme nationalists—who are neither learned, nor wise, *nor* statesman-like," said Mr. St John, an astonishing bitterness suddenly infusing his clipped delicate accents. "So-called patriots!" he said angrily, tapping sharply with his stick against the corner of a house. "Oh," he said, with a sudden change of tone—"We have passed it. I am sorry."

"Passed what?"

"Marshal Lyautey's house. Would you like to see it?" He looked backwards as he spoke.

"Not if it means going down that hill again," said Julia firmly. "Another day, perhaps." They appeared to have reached the top of Mount Everest at last, and had turned into a fairly level street whose surface was, thank goodness, sand and not cobbles.

143

"Very well—we will go on to the museum—it is quite close by."

"Look, Mr. St John, couldn't we—I—go to the museum some other time? I'd far sooner go on hearing about the French and the Nationalists than look at the finest museum in the world, if there is any place, besides Bathyadis' shop, in the whole of Fez where one can *sit*," said Julia.

He was full of compunction.

"Of course—you are tired, and I am thoughtless! There is a charming garden attached to the museum; we can sit there." And there in a few minutes they did sit, on the kerb of a fountain in the sun, among beds full of bright flowers, with exotic trees growing darkly overhead against the blue African sky.

"That's *lovely*," said Julia, stretching her feet out in front of her luxuriously. "Heaven fountain; heaven garden. Now please, would you tell me what mistakes, exactly, the French have made? You said just now that Moulay What-Not wanted to play in with the French, in spite of their mistakes. I thought from what I saw in Casa that they had done a lot for this country—but of course I don't know anything yet."

"What did you see in Casablanca?" Mr. St John asked—his stress on the full word was a minute rebuke, Julia felt.

"Oh, all those hospitals—" she described her morning with Ali.

"Yes, the French have done that: created wonderful social services in the larger towns. And they are struggling to educate the Moors to a point where they are fit for self-government, and to create a competent indigenous bureaucracy; have you seen the great college that they have built at Rabat, devoted entirely to courses in political administration?"

No, Julia had not yet been to Rabat.

"Well, you will see it. But—" the old gentleman paused, and emitted another of those hissing sighs. "Their mistakes—how difficult they are to analyse! Intellectual mistakes, spiritual

144

mistakes, emotional mistakes—all intangible, but how appallingly potent and dangerous intangibles can be! That is what the modern world so fatally tends to forget, obsessed as it is by material and economic progress. Spiritual values?—idealistic rubbish! But they are the ultimate ones, even in things political." He darted a diamond-bright lizard's eye onto Julia, seated beside him on the fountain's rim, her face turned up lovingly to the sun with closed eyelids, her thick tawny lashes resting on her apricot-coloured cheeks. "This really interests you?" he enquired a little sharply.

"Yes. That's why I asked," said Julia, without opening her eyes. Mr. St John chuckled—cool himself, the coolness of this young woman pleased him. He pulled a small notebook out of his pocket, ruffled the pages, and said—

"Then I will read you a prophecy about the French mistakes in North Africa—made by one of the two men who loved it most, and understood it best. If you care, that is, to listen."

"I'm listening," said Julia, still without opening her eyes; and Mr. St John proceeded to read.

" 'If France fulfils her duty, if she behaves towards her peoples as mother and not exploiter, doing to others what she would wish done to her, she will have an admirable Empire. If she does not, the mass of the population will necessarily remain alien and aloof, without attachment to us, different from us in everything; it will be influenced only by the local aristocracy. This aristocracy, composed of the middle class, the small chiefs, and the marabouts, will study in our schools, but without acquiring there any affection for us; from their schooling, owing to the ease of communications, will arise the idea of a patriotic union between all the lettered, educated, or distinguished people of the Barbary countries, from Fez to Tunis, all with a single aspiration—that of throwing us out.' "

The words rang, somehow, vaguely familiar in Julia's ears, but she could not place them at once.

"Goodness, that's accurate enough as a prophecy," she said. "It's exactly what *is* happening. Who wrote it?"

"It was written in the year 1911, please remark," said Mr. St John.

"Yes, but who by? Oh, I believe I know—was it de Foucauld?"

"You surprise me more and more! Yes, it was. Do you study him?"

"Well, I read that Fremantle book—so good, I thought— and the French life—not so good, wouldn't you say? But it was a long time ago, and I had rather forgotten. Good Heavens!" said Julia reflectively—"he *was* a prophet. But then he would be."

"Please note what he says about the 'ease of communications' at that time," said Mr. St John. "In 1911 there was no airmail, spinning a deplorably rapid web of postal deliveries all over North Africa—still less was there the even more lamentable diffusion of ideas by the wireless. Today every small town in Morocco can, and does, listen to false, vain, and utterly subversive broadcasts in Arabic from Cairo radio."

"Do they do much harm?"

"Infinite! It is largely, mainly, Egypt's fault that the situation here has got so completely out of hand. Egypt!" said Mr. St John, putting a serpent's hiss of contempt into the word. "Weak, effete; futile in armed conflict—look at her ignominious performance in the war with Israel!—and yet this vaulting ambition. *She* will lead the Arab world. The whole Egyptian army is not worth one corps of Moroccan tribesmen! But because she has the technical capacity to disseminate these ideas, she is a disruptive force throughout North Africa."

"Yes, I always gathered that the Gyppos were pretty wet," said Julia, still reflectively. "Some older friends of mine were there during the war, and they took a dim view of them, I must admit. But you still haven't told me what the French mistakes were," she persisted. "Did de Foucauld prophesy them too?"

146

"He indicated what would have to be done to avoid them—and it has not been done. This," said Mr. St John, turning to his little notebook again, "was written in 1915,"—and once more he read.

" 'We French have in Africa two essential duties to perform. The first is the administration and civilisation of North-west Africa—Algeria, Morocco, Tunis, the Sahara are united for the first time in history, and form a single block. Our second duty is evangelisation—and we do, we might as well say, absolutely nothing about it. The White Fathers are fifty-six in all North Africa! . . . Moreover I do not know anyone, colonising farmer, officer, or missionary, who knows the indigenous population sufficiently well.' There you have it—the 'not knowing the people sufficiently well' has all along been one of the major French mistakes," said Mr. St John sadly.

"Could the Moslems have been evangelised? I thought it was next to impossible. Even Fr. de Foucauld never baptised a convert, did he?"

"No—and perhaps evagelisation, in his terms, was impossible. But they could have been loved and understood as he loved and understood them. His influence was incalculable —the influence of the Christian spirit; that, in spite of all the great good that the French have done, has been lacking, and that alone might have prevented what he foresaw so terribly clearly. Hear him again—how wise he was!

" 'My thought is, that if the Moslems of our colonial Empire do not gently, little by little, become converted, a nationalist movement analogous to that in Turkey will arise; an intellectual élite will be formed in the big cities, taught *à la française* without having either French hearts or minds, an élite which will have lost its own Islamic faith, but which will keep the label in order to influence the masses. . . . Nationalist sentiments will be exalted by this élite, which when it finds an opportunity (such as would be provided by difficulties threatening France from without or from within) will use

147

Islam as a lever to rouse the ignorant multitudes, and will try to create an independent African Moslem Empire.' "

"Goodness, what price Isaiah now? That *is* today, to a hair!" said Julia.

"Yes, it is. I give the French two more years here, at the outside."

"No!" Julia was shocked. Little as she yet knew of Morocco at first hand, the idea of the French leaving, or being driven out, and so soon, put coldly like that, appalled her. "Do you really think that, after all they've done?"

"I do indeed." Mr. St John sighed again, loudly, elegiacally. "Alas, alas!"

That was on a Tuesday. Julia would rather have waited longer before going to see Bathyadis again, but Steve Keller had said that he was coming up on Thursday, and if he arrived in time she thought they had better go to Volubilis and check on the *huilerie* for Mme La Besse at once; then she would have another day in which to tackle Mr. St John about Colin— always supposing that she got no satisfaction, or not as much as she needed, from Bathyadis. After which, unless one or the other could put her in the way of finding her cousin at once she would return to Tangier. Of course if either of them told her where to reach him she would throw everything aside and go; but Julia was getting rather dubious about all these clues and contacts which seemed to lead nowhere, and modest as it was, her little French hotel in Fez was a good deal more expensive than the Espagnola—moreover in Fez she wasn't earning.

The following morning, accordingly, she laid on Abdul, the handsome voluble Arab guide whom Mr. St John had so unceremoniously waved aside the day before, and told him to take her to Bathyadis. Abdul like all Arab guides had ideas of his own, and began by leading her to all sorts of irrelevant sights; Julia in her most *cassant* tones told him that M. Saint Jonne had already taken her through the street of the silks and the street of the spices, and would he please take her directly to the *magasin* of M. Bathyadis. All the same she inhaled with intense pleasure the varied, heavy, penetrating odours which filled the air in the *souk* of the spices; she longed to know what all the different-coloured grains and powders, spread out in shallow oval baskets, were, and sniffed their varied aromas as she passed through.

Bathyadis greeted her with a most disarming appearance of warmth, and again sent his youth hastening to fetch mint tea. Julia told Abdul to wait outside, but the guide interpreted this instruction rather liberally, hanging about the opening of the shop while Julia successfully negotiated the purchase of the delicious little velvet trunk, or coffer, which she had seen the previous day for the equivalent of thirty-seven-and-sixpence. She held it on her knees, gloating over it, as she turned to her real business. A friend had told her, she said, that Mr. Bathyadis might be willing to help her with some information— no, not M. Saint Jonne, though no doubt he would say the same, she added, as a piece of corroborative detail—this was another friend in Tangier. She lowered her voice as she saw that Abdul had now come right into the shop and was hovering within earshot—"Remain outside," she told him curtly. Abdul withdrew. The matter was confidential, Julia explained, and then said quite flatly that she had come from England to make contact with a young Englishman called Monro, who happened to be her cousin; she had reason to believe that he had been, or was, in Fez, and in touch with Mr. Bathyadis.

Almost for the first time since she had started her enquiries the mention of Colin's name produced no reaction at all. Bathyadis looked benevolently blank; apparently Monro meant nothing to him. With one of her intuitions, as Mme La Besse called them, Julia drew a bow at a venture. "I believe," she went on, "that he is in company with another Englishman, very tall, with hair as red as fire."

That *did* register, she saw—Bathyadis looked serious, and

suddenly much more alert, too. "My cousin however is very dark with the face pale," she added, watching the old man closely; and she thought that that description registered too —Bathyadis continued to look serious, and did not answer at once. "He has a curious trick with his right thumb," Julia pursued—what *was* the French for double-jointed? Never mind. "When he is nervous he pushes the joint out, as if it was broken, with a small noise, *plutôt désagréable.*"

At that Bathyadis actually laughed.

"I think I know *le jeune Monsieur* you mean," he said carefully, "but could you perhaps indicate to me why you ask *me* about him?—since you know that he is here, and who he is with?"

Julia could have jumped with excitement at the last words. Her arrow had gone right into the gold—it had quite undoubtedly been Colin that she had seen up in the Kasbah with the red-haired man. But she remained calm outwardly, and told Bathyadis in vague sentences of her urgent need to get in touch with the young man immediately. (She did not, this time, say why—another intuition.) Most unfortunately she had just missed him in Tangier, she added casually, as if she would certainly have seen him had she arrived in time; and she had been sent on to him, M. Bathyadis.

The old man listened, and made a sympathetic reply, but Julia got a curious impression that he was puzzled by something; he kept on glancing at the little trunk, which she still held on her knees. At last he said, slowly and doubtfully—

"But if Mademoiselle is interested in the affair, why does she require the *little* coffer?"

Julia was completely taken aback by this. What affair? And what had velvet coffers to do with it anyhow, little or big? She lit a cigarette before replying, to gain time, and thought quickly. Blowing out smoke she said at last, non-committally and airily—"A coffer can always come in useful, can it not?— and for all sorts of purposes? And this"—she touched the object on her lap—"is also beautiful."

"Beautiful, yes—but it is so *small*. Would not the larger one be better?"

"I wonder," said Julia, still trying to gain time, and putting on a vague, meditative air. For one thing she couldn't possibly afford the big trunk, that was flat. "You really think so?" she asked, looking at the old Moor confidingly, enquiringly.

"It is usually the larger ones that they buy, and several at a time, Mademoiselle," he replied positively.

This astonished Julia more than ever. Who were "they"? Presumably Colin and the red-haired man—in French Bathyadis' words were perfectly clear: he had said "Ils"—they, not "on"—one, as in "people buy" or "one buys"; in the context he could only be referring to Colin and his red-haired friend. But why in the world should they be buying velvet trunks, and big ones, in bulk, in Fez? Her mind flew to possible reasons— Colin wanting to make a little money on the side, poor darling, in the new curio-shops down on the coast? Seething with curiosity, quite at sea, but with this idea in her head she observed, still looking vague—

"I suppose they do business with your son in Casablanca— my cousin and his friend, I mean."

When she said that old Bathyadis bent on her the indulgent look that a kind and wise elder bestows on a peculiarly ignorant or idiotic child.

"But *naturellement*, Mademoiselle. This is how the *expédition* is arranged, as Mademoiselle of course realises."

Julia didn't realise—as she herself would have said, she hadn't a clue. Obviously Bathyadis assumed that she understood all about Colin's activities, whatever they were, whereas in fact she knew nothing. For a moment the word *expédition* held her up—Purcell had said that the red-haired man had bought cases of whisky and gin to take on a journey, therefore on an expedition; but why vast velvet trunks to put the booze in? Then she remembered that in French *expédition* can also mean the despatch of goods; the man who sends one's luggage

and furniture from one place to another in France is called
an *expéditeur*—so the velvet trunks might conceivably be used
for the transport of something, somewhere. Probably that
was it. But transport of what and where to? About Morocco? Hardly. Her mind, behind her blank face, raced
wildly. Curios at the ports, dealings with the son in Casablanca, a port; *expédition*—oh, she *must* find out. Putting on
her most vacant expression she risked another arrow at a
venture.

"The export, you wish to say," she asserted, very slowly.
And equally slowly a benignant smile showed itself above M.
Bathyadis' beard, the smile of one who approves at least one
piece of intelligence on the part of the ignorant child. He didn't
even nod—but the smile was enough for Julia. She had got it
—or got something.

Unluckily, at that precise moment she happened to observe
that Abdul had again come into the shop, and had edged his
way up close beside them. In her anxiety, her intense concen-
tration, and her bewilderment, this was the last straw; she
completely lost her temper. "*Ôte-toi de là!*" she fairly shouted
at the guide—"Remain outside, as I have already twice bidden
you!" As Abdul withdrew she saw another smile—small,
shrewd, but still approving—appear in M. Bathyadis'
patriarchal beard.

Temper throws one off balance; Julia felt then like an actor
who has lost his cue. She returned to the charge, but on
another line.

"Is my cousin here just now?"

"Ah, no, Mademoiselle—they were here some days ago, but
they have gone."

"Where?"

Bathyadis waved a vague hand.

"To the South, as usual, I imagine." Again he spoke as if
Julia would know what was meant. This was all inconceivably
tantalising: Bathyadis, with his wholly mistaken assumption

that she knew all about Colin—though why he should have made that assumption she couldn't for the moment work out —was clearly perfectly willing to talk to her, willing as no one else had yet been, if only she could manage to ask the right questions. She had had extraordinary luck so far, but she must go very warily, and continue to feel her way.

"Ah, yes," she said, nodding her head wisely. Once more she took out her cigarette-case, and this time offered it to the dealer, not realising that devout Moslems (unlike the Berber labourers at the dig) do not smoke; he declined majestically. She lit one herself.

"How soon do you expect them back?" she asked. This seemed a safe question, and it was really more important to contact Colin than to find out what he was expediting abroad in Moroccan trousseau-trunks.

"Probably after the usual interval," the old man replied.

God, what *was* the usual interval? How maddening. She blew out smoke, and then chanced her arm again.

"In a month, perhaps?"

"Ah, no, *voyons*, Mademoiselle—it is usually six weeks at least, more often two months, before they return."

"*Tiens*," said Julia non-committally. *That* was no good. "Two months is a long time," she said reflectively. "Since my business is so urgent, I think perhaps I had better follow my cousin, and see him."

"Ah, *non*, Mademoiselle—that is impossible!" The old man was evidently shocked at this idea. "They work in horrible places" (*viles endroits* was the expression Bathyadis used) "where a young lady like yourself could not possibly go. How could you stay in those *cantines*?—a young lady alone? And it is a desolate country, terrible!"

Poor Julia groaned inwardly. Where were these "*viles endroits*"? And what on earth, in a Moroccan context, were "cantines"? In England one never *stayed* in canteens—they were places where factory-hands or soldiers ate.

153

"Then I must have his address, that is all," she said, with a firmness she was far from feeling.

At this Bathyadis recoiled in absolute horror.

"But no, Mademoiselle—no, no, no! To begin with they are naturally constantly moving from one place to another; and as Mademoiselle must very well know, above all one must never *write* anything—least of all the names. A name on a letter, in a *bureau de poste*!—this could be fatal. Mademoiselle does not reflect," the old man said, gently reproving, with a return of his kind benignant manner.

Julia, who had been reflecting till her brain almost cracked, smiled wryly—only no smile ever came out awry on her beautiful mouth, and her eyes remained doves' eyes even when she was frowning above them with worry, as now. Bathyadis smiled benevolently at her, returning a smile which to him merely seemed ravishing.

"Then what do I do?" she asked helplessly.

"Wait till they return, and repose upon the Merciful Goodness of God," said the old man, with a splendid calm confidence.

Those words and the way in which he spoke them did in fact give Julia, suddenly, a strange sense of peace. It might have lasted longer if at that very instant she had not seen, over M. Bathyadis' monumental shoulder, the seedy little cross-eyed man from Purcell's bar peeping into the shop from the entrance. Mastering her exasperation she spoke slowly, and very low.

"Please, after some instants look round, and tell me if you know who this little man is, who regards through the door. He was here yesterday also."

With elephantine deliberation Bathyadis turned slowly, and moved to a show-case behind him, which he opened, taking out a piece of jewellery; he had a fair view of the entrance before the little man with the cast in his eye bobbed hurriedly out of sight.

"Well?" Julia asked.

"It is a Jew—a German I think by nationality. Mademoiselle says he was here yesterday?"

"Yes—when I went out he was talking with your boy."

"Ah, *méfiez-vous de cet homme-là*! I do not like the little I know of him. Where has Mademoiselle seen him before?"

"Several times in Tangier, and I also thought I saw him at Petit-Jean on the way up—probably it was him, since he is here now."

"Then greatly beware of him. If he is what I think, German, he will be of our enemies," said Bathyadis. He looked troubled. "It is bad, this, very bad, if someone already follows Mademoiselle. They will have been alerted."

Dared she ask who "they" and "our enemies" were, Julia wondered, without giving away how far she was from being what Bathyadis so fortunately imagined her to be? While she pondered this question, looking appropriately serious, a number of American tourists suddenly surged into the little shop, escorted by a replica of Abdul, except for the wart on the nose. That, for the moment, was *that*. She said goodbye, gave Abdul the little coffer to carry—which he instantly passed on to an urchin the moment they reached the street—and returned to her hotel. On the way Lady Tracy's remark about the value of having cover popped up into her mind. Well, perhaps *Yes*.

Chapter 9

JULIA sat eating rolls and drinking coffee in her room next morning, wondering what she should do if Steve Keller didn't come. He was only a stray pick-up in the train, anyhow; but she didn't much care to go out with the inquisitive Abdul again, who anyhow cost a lot, and what else was there to do, except get hold of Mr. St John and see if he would tell her what all the mystery was about? She had lain awake half the night, trying to piece together the various items of fact that the old Moor had let fall, and to make some sense out of them—now, by daylight, she ticked them off on her fingers. Whatever Colin was doing, he was doing it with the red-haired man, who either had that house, or stayed in it, in the Kasbah at Tangier—that was one fixed piece of information. Second, they went at intervals to *viles endroits* in 'the South', remaining from six weeks to two months at a time—but not in one spot, they moved about, and stayed in *cantines*. Probably St John could tell her what *cantines* were, and very likely would, if she asked him without letting on why she wanted to know. (Julia was acquiring a very reasonable distrust of anybody's willingness to tell her anything that they knew to relate to Colin Monro.) Third—she drank some more coffee and buttered another roll; very few things ever interfered with Julia's appetite—they dealt with Bathyadis' son in Casablanca for the *expédition*, or export. But export of *what*? Not of the velvet trunks—munching her roll, Julia now totally rejected this hypothesis. There could not be so much mystery about straight sales of antique Moroccan bridal coffers; moreover the Bank of England would surely never facilitate the financing of such a simple and modest enterprise. Then what was the real enterprise? And why the bigger coffers? Presumably to contain as much as possible of something, but once again, of *what*, in Heaven's name?

Well, she had her three facts, Julia thought with a certain satisfaction as she continued to eat her breakfast; sometime or other they might fall into place and make sense. This really *was* detection!—trying to make the pieces of the puzzle fit. At least the 'export' part of it explained Purcell's getting into such a fuss when she had spoken of the curio-dealers' sons in the ports—yes, oh yes! How much, she wondered, did Purcell really know? *Todo?* Quite a lot, if not all, evidently. But one thing still bothered her: why had old Bathyadis so readily assumed that she knew what Colin's activities, still a complete mystery to her, were? She ran over their conversation in her mind, and decided that the first key point had been her reference to the red-haired man—after she had mentioned him the Moor had spoken freely; he was obviously the important person in this queer business. And—oh yes, she might have thought of that before—very likely, almost certainly, the fact that Mr. St John had brought her to the shop had pre-disposed the antique-merchant to think she knew about the whole affair, since, according to Purcell, St John himself was also a source of information. And, of course, she had at once tried to buy a trunk. But who were "they"?—Germans, Bathyadis thought; and "enemies". Who *had* talked to her in Morocco about Germans? She still could not remember. And—was it in Tangier or Casablanca? Bother!—why need she have forgotten this?

Her cogitations were interrupted at this point by a rather raggle-taggle Arab servant, who entered to say that a Monsieur demanded Mademoiselle below. Julia said "I descend", and then did not do so; she paused to reflect while she put on some lip-stick. If it was St John again, what should she ask him? About *cantines*, certainly; but should she risk also asking, flat out, the name of Colin's red-haired companion? That was a thing she needed to know, letters or no letters. It was still so early that the idea of the Monsieur being the airman had never entered her head, but when she at last went downstairs it was

Steve Keller who came towards her, in uniform this time, a cheerful grin on his nice plain face.

"Well, here I am! How are you making out?"

"Beautifully, thank you. But where on earth have you come from, at this hour?"

"Meknes. Got there last night, and drove over this morning. Now what do we do? Will I show you Fez?"

"Not unless you have a helicopter and a parachute," said Julia. "Those hills have half killed me already." Then as he looked rather dashed she said quickly—

"There's one place I do very much want to see, if it isn't too far."

"Nowhere's too far! Where is it?"

"Volubilis."

"That's easy—fine. I have the car right here. Don't you want a coat, though?"

Yes, Julia wanted a coat, and thicker shoes too—she went up to put them on, and with the *huilerie* in mind stuffed a notebook, pencils, and a centimetre-tape into the pockets of her short loose leather jacket. This was of a warm reddish-orange shade, and set off the peculiar tawny tones of her hair and complexion wonderfully—Steve stared in open admiration when she reappeared.

"You look wonderful!"

"Ought we to take some food along?" Julia asked, ignoring this tribute.

"No need to—we'll be back in time for lunch, latish. Let's go."

In the entrance to the hotel they nearly ran into the minute figure of Mr. St John; he greeted Julia gaily. "Good morning! Good morning! Do you feel strong enough for another round of Fez?"

Bunched together in the small entry-way, Julia effected introductions. "Mr. St John, this is Mr. Keller, of the American Air Force."

158

"American *Naval* Air Force," the airman corrected her. Julia swam over this obstruction—"And this is Mr. St. John, who lives in Fez, and knows everything." The two men shook hands, Keller looking slightly damped by the interruption.

"Mr. Keller has just driven over from Meknes," Julia proceeded equably; "we thought of going to Volubilis. I want to look at the Roman oil-mill there."

"Admirable! I did not know that you went in for archaeology. There are several *quite* good examples—" the old gentleman went into details.

Even Steve Keller saw that there was nothing for it but to invite Mr. St John to accompany them, which he did with a good enough grace to win Julia's admiration; for obviously this was not in the least the sort of outing he had intended. Mr. St John was delighted, and they set off, Julia sitting in front gazing about her; a certain packing of Moroccan agriculture would fill out a general article for *The Onlooker*.

She was immediately impressed, in fact, by the excellence of the cultivation. The pruning of the olive-trees was in itself a work of art—their flattened tops were cut so regularly that on level ground a ruler a kilometre long could have been run the length of the rows and hardly shown an inch of variation; new plantings were to be seen everywhere, the white bindings of the fresh grafts standing out sharply in the sun. Under the trees in the almond-orchards Moors were hoeing rows of vegetables, beneath the curious dull greyish pink of African almond-blossom; out in the open fields dwarf peas, barely a foot high and already in flower, spread for miles—the chick-peas now used for canning, Julia imagined—or could you not can chick-peas? She must ask sometime.

Presently they left the main highway to Meknes and Rabat and began to climb up into hilly country; here, though the olives and almonds still persisted, there was less tillage, and flocks of sheep grazed on the open slopes. Up in the hills they passed Berber farms, groups of rough buildings surrounded by high irregular fences of dried camel-thorn, a curious mauve-brown in colour, or the far more spectacular hedges of agaves, brandishing their huge curved saw-toothed leaves like giant pale-blue swords; these lines of great silvery-blue plants, so menacing in form, so startling in colour against the drab tones of the countryside, enchanted Julia. They dropped into another valley, where small oil-derricks stood up incongruously here and there—yes, they yielded a little oil, Mr. St John told her, when she leaned back to ask; it went down to Petit-Pean in tankers. They climbed up onto an outlying spur of the Djebel Zerehoune, and dropped on a long slant into the valley to west of it; here, facing the sun, sheltered from the north and east, the olive-trees grew thickly, and of enormous size—Mr. St John leaned forward to tell Julia that from pre-Roman times this had always been a famous centre for olive-growing; even before the Phoenicians came Volubilis, lying in the valley below, had been a wealthy Berber settlement, and the Romans had developed the oil industry to such a pitch that in and around the city not less than thirty oil-mills were still to be seen.

"Gracious," said Julia, aghast. "One will do for me." Keller laughed.

Volubilis is an exquisite place. The French have carried out the excavation and preservation of the ruins with the same thoughtful skill and competent thoroughness that they invariably display on the spot in Morocco, when the local administration has a free hand. A pleasant building houses a small museum, where the principal treasures are on view; neat paths through pretty plantings of shrubs and flowers lead up to the remains themselves, with unobtrusive sign-posts to indicate the way to the various points of interest. One of these, which the small party came on almost at once, said *Huilerie*, and there they went forthwith; a guide sought to accompany them—Mr. St John brushed him off as easily as he had brushed off the horrid Abdul on Julia's first morning in Fez.

Julia found the *huilerie* rather bothering, since it in no way resembled the one at Mme La Besse's site. There was no circular block of stone with a cemented channel round it: instead they saw a huge flat slab of what Julia took to be granite, with a number of narrow shallow runnels carefully chased out in the stone, leading down into two great oblong tanks, also floored and lined with dressed stone. Julia made measurements and wrote them down, Mr. St John the while explaining that the two tanks were for two different types of oil: the best from the first pressing, the less good from the second. Steve Keller lit a Chesterfield and looked bored—Julia was relieved when she had done her duty, and they were free to wander about the charming ruins of a remote but exquisitely civilised past. Storks, newly returned from the South, were turning over the remains of last year's nests on the top of the triumphal arch and some high columns topped by ornate capitals, with clattering beaks, enquiring claws, and a general expression of disgust—storks have a capacity for looking disgusted almost equal to that of camels. A small mauve wild-flower bloomed everywhere among fallen marble; the sun shone down, African and hot, on the gay mosaic flooring of rooms nearly two thousand years old, still depicting in brilliant colours the scenes from classical antiquity ordered by interior decorators twenty centuries before Elsie de Wolfe and Sybil Colefaxe began.

It was the private houses which above all entranced Julia. Mr. St John knew his stuff quite as well at Volubilis as he did in Fez, and led her and the still bored American up beyond the triumphal arch and the Forum into the residential quarter of the city, where Roman citizens had lived, presumably loved, and above all undoubtedly bathed. In many of these houses they came on small round baths, six feet or more across and about the depth of a modern bath, cemented within, their raised rims decorated with designs in mosaic: one of these bore a pattern of goldfish. Julia was instantly reminded of

Linda's bath, with the swimming goldfish in its glass sides, in *The Pursuit of Love*, and was ravished; she drew Mr. St John's attention to this resemblance, and he gave his dry prehistoric chuckle—they had to explain the joke to the airman, who had not read Nancy Mitford, and was less amused.

Walking back towards the entrance the sky was suddenly rent by a high mechanical whine, a piercing and threatening note—it seemed to come from the east, and Julia looked up, but nothing was to be seen there but a trail of white vapour leading across the blue; the American, laughing, took her elbow and turned her towards the west just in time to see a plane vanishing behind the hills, while the noise continued to fill the empty sky.

"That's one of ours," he said. "Great, aren't they?"

Julia thought them appalling, and somehow the more so, standing among the lovely relics of an age which had never been tormented by jet propulsion or atom bombs; but Mr St John promptly entered on a conversation with Steve Keller about the jets, the air-base at Port Lyautey, the instruction being given to the French air-force at Meknes, and concerning the other great American bases further South, near Casablanca. In this the American showed up well—he was intelligent, keen, and knew the technical side of his subject thoroughly; but presently he got on to the political aspect, and again gave utterance to some vague anti-colonial sentiments. "The poor toads of Moors, why should they live in shanty-towns and work for a silly wage, when the French are living in grand apartments or smart villas?"

"Why, indeed?" Mr. St John asked, with deceptive mildness. "Who brings the Moors to the towns?"

"Why, they just come, I guess."

"Exactly. You don't suggest that the French Administration brings them? They come of their own free will, and constitute a great problem—the eternal problem of the lure of city lights, and the possibility of making money more quickly than by the long monotonous processes of agriculture. What do you suggest that the French should do about it?"

"Well, they could put them in decent houses," the young man said, looking rather surprised.

"Could they? Could they? At a rent they could pay? And would this *check* the flow to the big towns? Would not more come, and still more? What was the result of building the new Medina for the Moorish workers in Casablanca?"

"I don't know."

"No, I supposed not. And have you seen the new *bidonvilles améliorées*, the improved shanty-towns which the French have arranged on empty spaces outside Casablanca with piped water and drains laid, ready for the Moors to use if they persist in coming and putting up their horrible petrol-tin shacks?"

No, the airman hadn't seen them.

"Again, I supposed not. It would seem that you have not seen very *much* of what the French have done here. However, these new sites represent an honest attempt at a solution of an almost insoluble problem. Criticism, to be of value or even admissible, should be based on facts, do you not think?" said Mr. St John primly.

Julia stole a glance at Steve to see how he took this. As she feared, the rebuke was too elegantly wrapped up really to register; Steve just felt vaguely that he was being 'ribbed', and said rather sulkily—"Oh well, one can't help the way one feels. I just feel an*ti*-colonial."

"Regardless of the facts before your eyes?"

"Facts don't alter feelings," the American said stubbornly. "Anyway, I just tell all the Moors I come across that they'd be better off without the French, in my opinion."

"You count your feelings as an opinion, then?" said Mr. St John, with dry exasperation.

Julia felt it was time to intervene. Poor Steve was utterly hopeless, in his crass ignorance and his refusal to look facts in the face, but trying to teach less lettered Americans about the

Old World was obviously about as much use as setting out to empty the Atlantic with a teaspoon—and anyhow they were in his car. She glanced at her watch.

"Is there anything else to see near here?" she asked. "Mr. Keller, how far are we from Meknes? Didn't you say there was a pretty gate there?"

Keller said there was. Mr. St John, however, quick to take a hint, proclaimed that Moulay Idriss, the holy city of Morocco, was only a few kilometres away—should they not rather see that? As they got into Steve's roadster again Julia noticed another car waiting on the sandy space outside the museum; an Arab driver lounged over the wheel, and Abdul, her inquisitive guide of the day before, leant against the wing —the wart on his handsome nose made him unmistakable. He glanced at her and her two companions with some interest, and spoke to the driver.

"Look, there's Abdul," she said to Mr. St John.

"Where? Oh yes. He's a pestilential fellow," the old Englishman said. He seemed rather upset.

The road to Moulay Idriss wound round the contours of the Djebel Zerehoune among those enormous olive-trees, bordered by more hedges of the savage agaves; silver-green above, silver-blue below—what a landscape, Julia thought, while Mr. St John was telling them from the back seat that Moulay Idriss was one of the most purely Islamic cities in existence, since owing to its great holiness neither Europeans nor Jews were allowed to settle there. From the road they had a view of the twin bosses of hill, covered with the white flat-topped cubes of Moorish houses, with a green-tiled mosque away to the left.

One cannot take a car at all far into Moulay Idriss, because the streets are mere alleys, and anyhow far too steep, steeper even than those of Fez; but the party took a rather brief walk through the exquisite little holy city. Now and again they emerged onto terraced paths almost as narrow as goat-tracks, which wound round outside the town, and afforded views of the hilly slopes around them and the valley below, a shimmering sea of olive-groves shaken in the breeze—Mr. St John reiterated that the olives were bigger and thicker to the acre here than anywhere else in the world. Moors as usual constantly offered their services as guides, and were as constantly waved aside by the Englishman with courteous skill; but as the party was descending towards the car again one caught him by the arm and said in French—"Come, see Berber oil-mill!"

"Oh yes, do let us see that," said Julia. "It might be interesting."

To Julia, at least, it was. The Moor led them through a dark descending passage to an underground chamber where by the light of an oil lamp a blindfold mule walked round and round in a circle, rotating a large stone wheel set on edge in a hollow mortared channel full of black olives which were in process of being crushed to pulp; two or three men with long-handled shovels kept nipping skilfully in behind the mule and throwing the black strong-smelling oily mush back into the path of the wheel—Steve opined that this was 'a kinda one-horse way' of doing things.

"One-mule way, surely," said Mr. St John. Julia however had espied a second chamber opening out of the first and went into it. Here the pulp, enclosed in flat round bags or nets of coarse rope, was being pressed under a complicated arrangement of a stone slab and a long wooden beam, wound down by a handle on a vast screw of polished wood; the clear oil oozed and dripped in bright beads from between the rough fibres into another mortared channel surrounding a circular stone block, on which the bags of pulp were set. This block and the channel surrounding it were in fact exact replicas of the block and channel at Mme La Besse's excavation. Julia exclaimed "Goody!" at the sight.

"What have you found?" Mr. St John asked, tapping his way after her with his stick over the uneven earthen floor.

"Only something that will thrill my employer," the girl answered casually.

When they got back to Fez, late and rather hungry, Mr. St John tactfully insisted on leaving the young people to lunch alone; but before they parted Julia made a point of asking him if they could have "another go at Fez" the next day, as she might be leaving the day after—he at once promised to call for her in the morning. Steve was rather plaintive over lunch—"I saw we had to take your dwarf Methuselah along, and he knows a lot; but he's not quite the girl to go to Venice with, is he?" Julia laughed, and after lunch allowed the American to drive her round the wonderful road along the slopes surrounding the city which the French call the *Route du Tour de Fez*; from it one sees from a score of different angles all that Fez permits to be seen: its walls and its heaped flat roof-tops, with a few rather bulky minarets looming over them. The day had turned gloomy and threatening, the mountains were the colour of ink, and below these dark shapes the city seemed to crouch, pallid and hostile—Julia thought it more sinister than ever. Steve extorted from her her address in Tangier, and a promise to let him know if she should come to Port Lyautey.

She did another brisk tour of *medersas* and *souks* with Mr. St John next morning, including the Moorish house once lived in by Marshal Lyautey; but the tiny old gentleman seemed a little abstracted, the flow of his carved pronouncements less ready than usual, while his whistling sighs occurred constantly. Another thing struck Julia that morning: in the crowded alleys they constantly came on knots of people which were really congealed, standing so close that it was impossible to filter through them as one can usually filter through a Moorish crowd; edging round was the only way. And in the centre of each knot was an Arab with a newspaper, reading aloud to the grave concentrated faces round him.

"Why are they all so keen on the press today?" Julia asked at last.

"The murder," said Mr. St John soberly.

"Not *more* murders! Who is it this time? Another Moulay?"

"No—a French doctor in Casablanca, a man greatly beloved; his practice was largely among the Moors, to whom he devoted himself. He was shot from behind as he was leaving his clinic in the New Medina."

"How horrible! But why, if he did so much good?"

"Aah!—that is the insane part of it. If a prominent Moor is assassinated, a prominent Frenchman will be assassinated too, to redress the balance; and then another Moor, and another Frenchman—it is as endless as an Albanian feud or a Corsican vendetta." He sighed again. "In this case there is particular concern and bitterness among the Moors, because just as Moroccan elements killed the Moulay for being on too good terms with the French, it is suspected that French elements murdered the doctor for being on too good terms with the Arabs."

"You don't mean it!"

"I do, unhappily."

"But that is simply *hopeless*," said Julia. "That understanding, I mean, that de Foucauld wrote of becomes impossible if it's just the people, on both sides, who *do* understand who get murdered. They can never get together if they go on like that."

"No, they can never get together," the old man said in a tone of unutterable sadness.

Julia mused. "It ought to be prevented," she said presently. "It's ridiculous. If it's the prominent people who get killed, they must be known—couldn't they have guards or police or something, to go about with?"

"That is what the French doctors in Casablanca whose work takes them into the Medina thought," Mr. St John replied with acerbity; "they asked the Municipality to provide them with guards, since their hours at the clinics are known, and they were therefore sitting targets for the thugs."

"And didn't they get them?"

167

"They were offered them, at a price—which they were to pay themselves."

"Good God! The French and their *ça coute*," said Julia, with real anger in her voice. "How much, for heaven's sake?"

"In English money it would have come to about twenty pounds a month. That is a good deal for a man who does more than half his work for love. Some of the wealthier ones agreed to pay it; this doctor refused, as a matter of principle."

" 'And he's just as dead as though he'd been wrong,' " Julia quoted bitterly. "Do you know, Mr. St John, to me that sort of meanness really *smells*."

"The people in Casablanca agree with you. It is not in the papers yet, but I hear that the Préfet was hissed by the crowd yesterday when he attended the funeral—by Moors as well as Europeans."

"Serve him right."

"Not altogether. He is a good man, sympathetic to the indigenous population, broad-minded; but he is tied by regulations, and above all by matters like the vote for colonial expenses at home. The people who really '*puent*', to use your so expressive word, are the French politicians—ignorant, self-seeking, eternally manœuvring for position for their miserable parties, regardless of France's real interests, let alone those of her dependent peoples. Blame them."

"Oh, I do! I've been blaming them for years—ever since I was at school, in fact. France has been the sick woman of Europe for over a century, hasn't she?—and a spoilt invalid at that."

Mr. St John laughed.

"My dear young lady, you have a formidable gift of expression! One which, if I may say so, your appearance would seem to belie," he said.

"No one can help their appearance," said Julia, who knew quite well that she looked the dumbest of blondes, but didn't particularly mind. At the moment she was glad that her so unmatching views on the French had cheered the little old gentleman up, and was delighted by his obvious pleasure when she asked if they couldn't go and sit in the museum garden again.

"Ah, you liked it? So do I—a charming spot. Yes, let us go there."

But Mr. St John was very far from showing pleasure when, once more seated on the kerb of the fountain, Julia asked him how she could get hold of Colin Monro at once. He started, dropped his stick, upon which he had been resting his gnarled old hands, picked it up again, and asked quite petulantly—

"Good gracious, what in the world do *you* know about young Monro? And what on earth do you want him for?"

"I want him to come home. But unless I find him, I can't tell him that he's got to."

Mr. St John looked like a very cross tortoise indeed.

"And why should you imagine that he is here?"

Julia, however half-baked she might in Edina's opinion be as a journalist, had at least learned in that profession that to display such facts as she was already in possession of frequently led to the disclosure of yet other facts—and she employed this technique now.

"Oh, I know he isn't here at this moment," she drawled, casually—"he went down to the South just a few days ago, with that red-headed type he goes round with, and a fresh consignment of those pretty velvet trunks, but I want to contact him *quickly*."

This pronouncement created a considerable effect. Mr. St John dropped his stick again, and assumed the appearance of a quite furious tortoise; when he was able to speak—Julia picked up the stick this time—he was almost stuttering with vexation and bewilderment.

"Who—who are you? And how do you come to know all this?"

"I'm Colin's cousin—his mother sent me out here to find

him. And as for knowing things, of course one has one's contacts," said Julia, rather grandly, but again with careful casualness.

Mr. St John looked so worried and upset that her heart rather smote her for a moment; but after all she had come all this way for one single purpose, and being thwarted so often had aroused her obstinacy; she must not allow pity, even for this rather darling old man, to deflect her. His next question surprised her, though.

"But Lady Tracy—*she* wrote to me about you." He looked immensely puzzled. "Does she know of this—this quest of yours?"

"But of course. She promised to help me, only then her nephew—the botanist one, I expect you know him—went hooshing away, so she couldn't do much. He seems to be her special link with the outside world."

"Ah!" Mr. St John became a reflective tortoise—Julia got a curious impression of a hitch, that she had lost a point somehow, or given something away; but the old gentleman was still upset, sufficiently so to make a remark which he failed to finish: "Ah, then she cannot know—" He checked himself abruptly.

Julia was dying to ask what Lady Tracy could not know, but checked herself too; she must not let her tongue run away with her, or give anything more away—if indeed she had done so; it was only an impression, and a vague one at that. She remained silent, waiting for Mr. St John to speak again, and meanwhile gazed up at the strange shapes of the trees in the museum garden, silhouetted against the brilliant Moroccan sky.

It was some time before her companion did speak again. When he did, he went off on a fresh tack. "*Why* do you want young Monro to come home?"

Gloomily, like an actor speaking a boring part for the hundredth time, Julia went through the reasons: the estate,

Uncle John's death, Edina's rich money-making career. Colin had *got* to come home.

"Well, he can't," said Mr. St John very curtly. "For the present he is obliged to stay here. I am sorry to disappoint you, but really you had better give up this search of yours. Moreover, I think I should warn you that it is not very prudent to go round asking for this young man by name."

"Oh, because of those infernal Germans?" Julia felt that it would be as well to learn a little more about "our enemies" if she could, while the poor old gentleman was available, and in this slightly dislocated state. The result was pretty good—Mr. St John gazed at her in absolute stupefaction.

"H—h—*how* do you know that?" he stuttered angrily. "Of course!"—again he checked himself. "I believe you are being un-candid with me—you are not what you pretend to be, a friend of my old friend, just an English girl!" he said bitterly.

"Oh, yes, Mr. St John, I am precisely that. Only I happen to know a little more than you expected," said Julia hardily. "Do tell me more about these Germans, won't you?"

"No, I will *not*," said Mr. St John, quite furiously banging the butt of his stick on the stone pavement which surrounded the fountain. "I will tell you *nothing*! How, I cannot conceive, but you know far too much already."

Julia deployed her eyes at their most dove-like on the angry old man, and laid her long pink-tipped hand caressingly on his sleeve.

"Oh Mr. St John, dear, don't be so upset, and horrid to me," she said. "You've been so kind, but now you're really being a pest."

"So are you!" he exploded, actually throwing her hand off his arm.

"I daresay. I expect I often am. But you've been so sweet, and I'm so grateful. Look, won't you at least tell me this— which is it imprudent for, me or Colin, if I go about asking for him?"

"Both!" said Mr. St John. "Imprudent for you, possibly mortally dangerous for him."

A little silence fell after that. Dislocated or not, Mr. St John had remained totally uninformative about the Germans, the enemies, except to confirm their inimical existence. Germans, Germans—*who* had talked to her, in Morocco, about Germans, Julia wondered, trailing the fingers of the hand Mr. St John had so summarily rejected in the cool water of the pool behind her. Twice she had tried to remember, and couldn't; now, with the unaccountability of memory, suddenly it flashed back into her mind—Mr. Bingham, rather lit up at his own cocktail-party in Casablanca, had mentioned as one of two side-lines in Morocco the exploitation of rare minerals, started since the War, by the East Germans! And he had said that everyone kept their mouths pretty tightly shut about it, too. LAWKS! —Could it be some rare mineral that Colin and the red-haired chum were expediting, or exporting, in the velvet trunks? Out of pure curiosity, combined with this new obstinacy born of frustration, Julia once more employed shock tactics on the unhappy Mr. St John.

"I'd hate to do anything to jeopardise Colin, naturally," she said gently—"But they are shipping out some odd mineral, aren't they?"

For a moment she thought the old man was going to have a stroke. He became purple in the face, and looked as if he were going to choke.

"Monstrous!" he exploded. "This is absolutely monstrous! You must be a spy!"

"I'm *not*—I do assure you I'm not," Julia said pleadingly. "I only want to get hold of Colin."

"Well, *I* shall not help you—indeed I shall warn Lady Tracy about you! If you did succeed in contacting your cousin—if he *is* your cousin—he could not possibly go home now; no miserable estate, property, inheritance, is of comparable importance to the work he is engaged on! Oh, you shock me!" The poor old man paused, looked wildly round, and as once before asked helplessly—

"Where was I?"

"You'd said Colin couldn't come home, however urgent it was," Julia said, now really alarmed by his state. "But look, Mr. St John, I think you'd better go home. Let me go and find a taxi."

"There are no taxis here. No, I will go to the Consulate, which is just opposite—if you will accompany me so far?"

Julia, rather penitent, took his arm and accompanied him to the gateway with the superb baroque plaster effigy of the Lion and the Unicorn stuck on the wall outside it; she rang a bell, a Moorish servant appeared, and led her old escort in through a pretty courtyard. But before Mr. St John disappeared he turned back to her and spoke again, with menacing finality.

"Go home. Give this up. Don't try to find him; make some other arrangement for his wretched inheritance."

"I can't give it up, and I won't," said Julia. "Oh, but I am so sorry."

"Never mind that—you have been warned," said Mr. St John, as the door of the Consulate closed behind him.

Julia was rather shaken by the painful termination of this interview. She liked Mr. St John, he had been, as she had told him, very kind to her, and now she had left him upset almost to the point of illness by her questions and assertions—upset moreover to such a degree as to have left her alone and unescorted in the street, in Fez. She made her way back to her small hotel without adventure, wondering on the way why anyone so old, and so easily made to lose his temper and inadvertently let things out, should be allowed to be in on anything so secret and so important as Colin's activities appeared to be—indeed as Mr. St John himself declared them to be. For really he had, if only by his rage, let out quite a lot. He had confirmed Bathyadis' implication that the Germans were the enemy—presumably the East Germans, in view of Mr. Bingham's remarks; and his violent reaction to her suggestion that a rare mineral of some sort was the object of the operation was tantamount to a confirmation of that idea, too. One did not turn purple and go completely to pieces about something that *wasn't* true. All rather exciting; and *fun*, really, Julia thought as she sat down to a thoroughly French lunch, nibbling the carved radishes among the *hors d'œuvres* with appetite, and shovelling in the sliced tomatoes, the hard-boiled eggs in mayonnaise, and the inevitable sardines.

One thing however bothered her—she had completely forgotten to ask Mr. St John about *cantines* before she embarked on the vexed subject of Colin. What a clot she was!—now he would tell her nothing, indeed he would probably never speak to her again. After she had consumed some veal followed by salad—the veal, she learned from the waiter, flown in from France—she asked to see the proprietor, who came to her in the little salon while she drank her coffee, and asked politely if he could be useful to her in anything?

Only to satisfy her curiosity, Julia said—she was in fact *journaliste*, and everything about Morocco was of great interest for her. The manager bowed, pleased and impressed; for some reason *hôteliers*, unlike the rest of mankind, have a passion for journalists. To what, he asked, was the curiosity of Mademoiselle directed? To something in Fez?

No, Julia said, not in Fez. She desired to know more about the *cantines* in the South of Morocco.

As it turned out, she could not have applied to a better person than the *patron*. The *cantines*, he told her, were the official hotels or rest-houses in small towns strung out along the bus-routes; a network of motor-buses now covered much of the Protectorate, and for the convenience of travellers there were, at the end of each day's stage, these *cantines* where they could spend the night, with bedrooms—yes, sometimes even with showers—a bar and a restaurant. Arab-style, of course—

all on one floor, rooms opening on a corridor on one side, usually on the garden on the other. He used to run one at Beni-Issar before he came to this hotel in Fez—ah, that was a fine *cantine*, the garden full of roses! Many were directed by ex-members of the Foreign Legion—he himself was *ancien légionnaire*; oddly enough, said the *patron*, expanding on what was clearly a favourite theme, many of these managers were Germans, who had joined the Legion between the two wars —after completing their term of service they married Arab or Berber wives, and abandoning the Fatherland settled down in Morocco as *cantiniers*.

Julia was greatly pleased by this unexpected bonus, as it were, to her enquiries, which were usually so difficult, if not fruitless; she asked the *hôtelier*, as indifferently as she could, whether these expatriate Germans kept up any links with their homeland? Oh indeed yes; once a German, a German to all eternity, the Frenchman replied rather acidly; the door and the heart always open to never-mind-who of their compatriots! But did many Germans come to Morocco, Julia enquired. Yes, quite a few, especially in the last year or two. Tourists? Yes—and others besides.

Julia was rather nervous of risking any very direct questions about these others, even from the unsuspecting *patron*—she tried a more oblique angle. What sort of travellers went to the South, she wanted to know.

Oh, *colons* going to and from their farms, after shopping or business in Casablanca or Agadir; many Moors—with the advent of the autobus the Moors had become great travellers; then there were the members of the Administration of Indigenous Affairs, who frequented the bars, though they usually had official cars; and finally of course the personnel of the mines.

Julia pricked up her ears again, meanwhile carefully looking as stupid as possible.

"Mines? What mines?"

"For the chrome, principally, naturally. Does Mademoiselle, as a journalist, realise—" and out came a piece about Morocco producing so much of the valuable useful chrome. *That* was a place to see: the gaunt dressing-plants, the great refuse-heaps, the water-pumps, all in a perpetual haze of dust—*un paysage Dantesque*, said the landlord, with a surprising flight of imagination. Julia said that sounded fascinating, and she must try to get down to see it all, if she could arrange an escort. And was anything else mined besides chrome? Oh, yes—the cobalt, the molybdenum, strategic minerals of all sorts, so rich was the Protectorate; and new discoveries were being made all the time, as science advanced and the prospectors explored further and further. What a future lay there, for the whole country, if only the *sacrés nationalistes* would cease to make agitations, and recognise the benefits which France was bringing, and if those animals of Communists would desist from stirring up trouble!

The idea of communism in Morocco was new to Julia, and she allowed herself to be deflected into enquiring about that. Mostly in the big cities, she supposed? *Mais non!*—there probably also, but they were everywhere, even down in that desolate country of the mines: talking to these poor ignorant creatures of Berbers, creating discontent, denouncing la France, who had done all, but *all*, for the country—he had seen this going on with his own eyes. Many of them were Spaniards who had fled after the Civil War and now sought only to undermine the well-being of other happier people by playing on nationalist feeling, and exciting the envy of those who, for the first time in their lives earning a regular, a decent wage, instead of being at the mercy of droughts and bad harvests, yet saw that their employers were richer than themselves—most naturally. "For developing mines, for machinery, for paying wages, *capital* is required, Mademoiselle; and what capital can the Berber offer? His she-camel and his ass!" Julia laughed, and asked if the Communists were more dangerous, injurious, than the broadcasts from Cairo, remembering Mr. St John's remarks. The landlord fairly exploded.

"But Mademoiselle, it is one and the same thing! Moscow courts the Arab world today, and fosters, if not finances, Moslem nationalism for her own ends; she desires a pan-Arab North Africa, a single unit from Egypt to Morocco, communist-dominated. Ah, their eyes will be opened, *ces pauvres bougres*, if this ever comes to pass!"

Communism, Julia reflected, was one thing that de Foucauld had not foreseen. But though all this would come in very nicely for an article she had her own fish to fry; and presently she reverted to the matter of the mines. Where were they?

South of the Atlas—but a new area, whose development had only started a year or so ago, lay further south still near Tindouf, practically *en pleine Sahara*; this was enormously rich, and as it was situated inland from the Spanish territory of the Rio do Ouro, the construction of a railway to bring the products out onto the French coast was in contemplation. And how, Julia asked, were the products from the older mines, south of the Sahara, taken to the coast? (This was a question in the answer to which she felt the deepest interest.) Was there a railway? Ah no, all went by *camion*; the value of the exports, especially of the cobalt, made even the vast expense involved by lorry transport worth while, especially to such powerful interests as the *concessionaires* who were behind the affair.

Hum, Julia thought—lorry-loads of velvet trunks, perhaps? But the word *concessionaire* caught her attention, and she asked about that. Oh, quite evidently for the exploitation and still more the export of strategic minerals a concession from the Government was necessary; nothing was possible without it. Legally, that is to say; of course one heard rumours of underhand doings. The landlord shrugged his shoulders.

Underhand doings by whom? the girl asked.

Oh, but naturally by these detestable Germans!

"But do they not have concessions?" Julia enquired, now

easily recalling what Mr. Bingham had said about the East Germans having actually started the drive for the rarer minerals.

"Some do, some do not," the landlord answered. "I, I have my friends down there, my sources of information; and you may believe me when I say to you that there is plenty of dirty work going on, illicit exploiting and exporting, to avoid paying the heavy fees for concessions and export licences."

"But how do they manage it?" Julia asked, genuinely interested—cobalt-running was still quite a new idea. Was this what lay behind the tip-off that Mr. Bingham professed to have given her, when he said that a nod was as good as a wink?

"Oh, these types have their methods—disguises, false passports; heavy bribes, naturally, to right and left; and the commodity itself concealed in something else, so that it appears other than what it is," said the landlord breezily. "And they stick at nothing, *ces messieurs-là*—if anyone becomes too curious he is liable to have a nasty accident. For my part, I am glad that I am no longer in the South, things have become so unpleasant down there. Imagine to yourself that an official was killed, not so long ago, in the bar of my own *cantine*!"

"Good heavens! How?"

"With a home-made bomb. Several were injured, but they made sure of the man they wanted, who had been too pertinacious in his enquiries, and knew too much."

"But weren't they caught?—the ones who threw it, I mean?"

The *patron* gave another shrug.

"Mademoiselle, whenever a bomb is thrown in Morocco it is thrown by a nationalist terrorist, or by a counter-terrorist! —so at least it can always be said, and will always be believed. This affords a wonderful camouflage to murder for quite other motives, such as commercial or international rivalry."

"How beastly," said Julia slowly. She was thinking of Mr. St John's words—"possibly mortally dangerous"—if she persisted in enquiring for Colin. Perhaps this particular piece of detection wasn't going to be quite so much fun, after all.

Chapter 10

IN Julia's favourite books on detection, much time was always spent in reflecting on evidence, checking it over, and summing it up to assess its importance—most detectives, whether professional or amateur, wrote down lists of suspects or telling facts in parallel columns for the help of the active-minded reader. Her two conversations that day had given her so much to chew over that a sheet of paper and a pencil would have been a great help, but she decided against this—who knew but that Abdul or the squinting man might not get into her room, somehow? Seated in that same room, after her very revealing talk with the *patron*, she did the best she could in her head.

What had she got? She counted it out, slowly.

From Mr. St John's intemperate exclamations she now knew pretty positively that it was the Germans who were Bathyadis' "enemies", and from the same indiscreet source she had quite sufficient confirmation of the fact that what Colin and the red-haired man were doing was to ship some mineral out of Morocco. It must be very rare and very important, in veiw of the poor old gentleman's insistence that Colin must stay where he was, inheritance or no inheritance—and Julia paused for a long time to consider this aspect of the matter. If it would really be impossible, or even wrong, for Colin to come home, was there any point in going on with her search?—especially if it might possibly involve him in danger? The landlord's account of the metal racket certainly sounded as if that could be true, and Julia placed rather more reliance on his statements than on Mr. St John's angry ejaculations. On the other hand it seemed very silly to have come so far and learned so much, and then give up now, without at least seeing Colin. If she could manage to see him she could anyhow tell him the situation at Glentoran, and then let him decide for himself; he was twenty-three, after all, and quite old enough to make up his own mind where his duty lay.

Moreover—though Julia didn't argue this out very clearly with herself—by a succession of strokes of extraordinary luck such as Mr. Bingham's indiscretions and Bathyadis' mistake about her, she had found out quite a lot, and she wanted very badly to go on until she had unravelled the whole mystery. That would be one in the eye for Geoffrey—and for the Bank of England too! No, she would go on, for a bit anyhow, and as carefully as possible. Very well—and she returned to her assessment of facts. From Bathyadis she knew that whatever was exported went in the velvet trunks: this was confirmed directly by Mr. St John, and indirectly by the landlord, who had said that the mineral-smugglers sent their commodity out "concealed in something else, so that it appears other than what it is". He was talking of the Germans, but what better concealment for a precious mineral than to put it in velvet trunks and—*yes*! send these down to antique-dealers at the ports, who could easily, somehow, ship it out. It must be that or "thatabouts", Julia thought, smiling as the old nursery expression at Glentoran rose of itself in her mind. That of course was where young Bathyadis came in, and there flashed back into her recollection how he had expressed such surprising gratitude to Mr. St John for suggesting that he should start up in business in Casablanca. Aha!—the old boy had been responsible for organising that; no doubt it was because with his immense local knowledge he could arrange such things that he was "in on" the business, in spite of his age and his indiscreet tongue.

But now, what was the next step towards finding Colin? He was in the South, with the red-haired man, staying in *cantines* and moving about: that was all she knew—except that the landlord had said that metal-runners, if illicit, used false passports and disguise. She didn't of course know for certain that Colin's activities *were* illicit, but if they were completely above-board, why the mystery everywhere, and the velvet trunks, which were a sort of commercial equivalent of false beards? No, for the moment she would assume that their business was *not* above-board. Therefore it was pretty useless to attempt to follow them and find them herself; that would involve a lot of arranging, since she spoke no Arabic, and would cost a great deal—besides, she suddenly realised, she didn't know in which of the two areas they were operating, the one south of the Atlas, or the new one *en pleine Sahara*, near Mindouf?—Dindouf?—no, Tindouf, that was the name—of which the landlord had spoken.

Very well—following them was out, for the moment any-how. And if they were not coming back to Fez for six weeks or two months it was senseless to wait there for them. Julia paused at that point for some time, sitting staring in front of her, looking perfectly blank. She was wondering if it would be any good going to see Bathyadis again, with some other guide than the nosey Abdul, and trying to arrange with him to let her know when they did return by telegram or telephone, using some code expression like—oh, "Carrots received" or "House on fire". She grinned a little at these ideas, but finally decided against that too. Very likely the old Moor would be unwilling to do either, with his panic about names in *bureaux de postes*; he would probably refer her to Mr. St John, which would be quite hopeless. No—really the best thing would be to return to Tangier at once and try to make Purcell tell her some more, using some of her newly-acquired knowledge to "bounce" him. What Purcell stood for in the whole business was another thing to find out, but that he was pretty accurately informed was certain—he had been right about Bathyadis, right about Mr. St John, and he certainly knew about the antique-dealers at the ports, because he had been so startled when she mentioned them. And sooner or later Colin and friend were pretty certain to come back to that house in the Kasbah.

Right—back to Tangier. In her lethargic-seeming fashion Julia was quite a fast worker, and she now went leisurely downstairs and informed the landlord that she had decided to leave the following day. The landlord expressed regret; so did Julia—there was still so much to see in Fez. She had decided upstairs to make a false excuse, and now smoothly said that she thought she ought to go down to Casablanca to investigate the matter of the doctor's murder. (She already knew that the train from Fez went direct to Casablanca, but by changing at Petit-Jean she could get back to Tangier.) While they were talking "Madame" appeared; the landlord had married a Frenchwoman, not a Moor, and Julia asked her politely how she liked being in Fez, and whether she preferred it to life at the *cantine*? Oh, but infinitely! Beni-Issar was so *triste*, so isolated—for shopping, for instance, nothing was obtainable nearer than Mogador, or at the best Marrakesh where the shops were *plutôts indigènes*; nothing in the way of clothes in the least up-to-date, and the price of having one's hair set in the Mamounia Hotal! Julia smiled her slow smile, and sympathised —Madame was in fact a surprisingly trim and chic little person. The couple invited her to take an *apéritif* with them, and they sat in the small hall; Madame pursued the subject of the discomforts of life in "the South". Ah, if only these travelling vendors of clothes had been going about when they were there!

Julia made an enquiring sound.

Yes, just in the last few months travelling salesmen had started making journeys round the southern regions in *camion-nettes*, the landlord said; mostly clothes for men, of course, but he had heard that they had a tolerable selection of garments for women too; stockings, blouses, even *petites robes*. This was clearly a subject of the highest interest to both husband and wife; they pursued it alternately, in strophe and anti-strophe.

Such a boon for the personnel at the mines, who could at least see what they were purchasing when they bought a new shirt instead of getting it by mail-order from Casablanca, said Monsieur. Yes, and equally for the ladies, when they required new stockings, Madame chimed in—and these Austrians and Swiss brought really good *marques*, her friends informed her, like "Nylons Guy".

Oh, it was not the French who conducted this new enterprise, Julia asked, interested—Mr. Bingham had omitted this particular side-line, but it would all fit in nicely to yet another article.

No, no—Austrians and Swiss. Really they were public benefactors, Madame was saying fervently, when the hall door opened and Steve Keller walked in.

"I have the week-end off, so I came to look you up," he said, when Julia had introduced him to the landlord and his wife, who promptly retired to the bureau.

"*Is* it the week-end?" Julia asked vaguely—so much seemed to be happening in Fez that she had almost lost count of time.

"Well, day before yesterday was Thursday, when we went to Volubilis, so I make today Saturday," said the airman, grinning.

"So it is."

"How's Methuselah?"

"Not very well, I'm afraid," said Julia, guiltily—it occurred to her that she ought before this to have rung up the Consulate to ask if the poor old creature was all right. Should she, or would that introduce more complications? He might have already denounced her to the Consul as a spy, in his frame of mind when they parted—feeling even guiltier she decided to let it alone.

Mr. Keller took the news of Mr. St John's indisposition very cheerfully.

"Then he won't want to come on any more trips," he said.

"Fine. What are you doing tomorrow? Care to come for another drive?"

"But I'm going back to Tangier tomorrow," said Julia, thoughtlessly—and then looked quickly round. No, the *patron* was not in sight. "Or rather to Casablanca," she said, more loudly, in case he had been within earshot all the same.

Steve looked puzzled, and also rather dashed.

"Let's get this straight—" he began, rather crossly.

"No—don't let's; at least, not here," said Julia, almost hurriedly for her—"and don't shout. Come outside."

In the sunny street—"I wasn't shouting," the American said rather sulkily. "What's the mix-up, anyway. Where *are* you going?"

Julia felt foolish. Frankness, at least up to a point, seemed the best course.

"I am really going back to Tangier," she said; "but the people here had expected me to stay longer, and they've been so nice—so as an excuse I said I was going to Casa to write up the murder."

"What murder? Oh, that doctor. But what d'you mean write up? Are you a writer?"

"Well, I'm a journalist."

He stared at her.

"You don't look like one! Well—maybe a bit like Virginia Cowles—she's pretty chic," he said, still staring. "But don't you have to go down and cover this murder?"

"Oh, no—I write for weeklies, so I can send what I like."

"Then why do you have to leave tomorrow? Why not come for a drive with me, and go Monday?"

Julia hesitated for a moment, but only for a moment.

"No, I must go," she said. "I have a job in Tangier, and if I get back tomorrow I can start work again on Monday. My employer wasn't very willing to let me come up here at all."

"What kind of a job? You are full of surprises, aren't you? —I thought you were just a rich tourist."

"No English tourists are rich nowadays," said Julia. "We get exactly a hundred pounds, which isn't quite three hundred dollars, to spend abroad in a whole year; so if we want to stay abroad we have to earn abroad—that's all."

"Three hundred dollars a *year*! That's just silly," said the American.

"Silly is the word," Julia replied.

Mr. Keller appeared to reflect.

"Say, are you an early riser?" he asked at length.

"If I have to be. Why?"

"How would it be if I drove you down to Tangier to-morrow, if you absolutely have to go? If we started early I could get back to Meknes the same night. What do you say?"

Julia said Yes. It would save the fare, she would see more of the country, and it would completely fox the little man with the cast in his eye, unless *nos ennemis* sprang him a car. Steve said, "And you fix one of those raw-food picnics of yours, can you?" in tones of great satisfaction.

Julia did not start worrying about Steve, obvious as his pleasure at spending another day with her already was. It was common form for young men to keep on turning up, once she had met them, and to want to take her for drives, or to the theatre, or sailing in uncomfortably small boats. As for the early start, her train would have left at seven a.m. anyhow. She whispered a reminder to him that their destination was supposed to be Casablanca, and then ordered her breakfast and a picnic lunch for two, and went off to dine with him.

And the next morning, sharp at eight o'clock, they set off, with the picnic-basket in the back of the car; the sun struck silver through the olive-groves as they spun through Morocco, down towards the coast and Tangier.

That same Sunday morning, Mrs. Monro, Edina and Mrs. Hathaway were sitting at breakfast in the gloomy dining-room at Glentoran. Olimpia was rather a failure at porridge and even at poached eggs, which she was wont to serve on a bed of fried onion-rings, to the horror of Mrs. Monro and Forbes; but she made a wonderful hispanicised version of kedgeree which Edina and the guest were enjoying; Mrs. Monro, who disliked its strong spicy flavourings, had boiled herself an egg in a little electric boiler. Presently a strong smell of burning bread filled the room, and Edina leapt up and ran to the side-table.

"Damn that machine! Why on earth can't it throw the things out?" she exclaimed, removing two charred and blackened pieces of toast from the shining gadget. She peered at it, and then turned indignantly.

"Mother! Forbes really is unutterable! He'd turned it to *six*. Two is the outside. I can't think why you put up with him," the girl added, adjusting the knob and cutting two more slices of bread—"he really is the *world's* fool."

"No washing-up," Mrs. Hathaway murmured.

"True enough—but Mother might try to make him do what little work he does properly. I can't run the place *and* the house," said Edina impatiently.

Her mother wisely said nothing. The fact was, as Mrs. Hathaway had already observed the previous evening, that Edina was getting thoroughly restive at her enforced stay in Scotland, and the older woman understood now why Mrs. Monro had sent her that muddled and inconclusive appeal to "come up and talk things over", which had brought her to Glentoran the day before. Characteristically, however, Ellen Monro had so far shown no disposition to talk on any but the most trivial subjects, and was presently driven off by a neighbour to attend the Presbyterian church at Duntroon. Presbyterian services held no appeal for either Mrs. Hathaway or Edina, and since the nearest Episcopalian one took place over forty miles away they abandoned all idea of Sabbath observance, and settled down over the fire.

"When did you last hear from Julia?" Edina asked, kicking

a labrador out of the way in order to put on more logs from the vast wood-basket.

"Just this week."

Julia had in fact written to Mrs. Hathaway within a day or so of writing to Edina, and to much the same effect, except that she had omitted the account of Mr. Reeder, and had suggested that if Mrs. Hathaway "happened" to be in touch with Geoffrey Consett, she might "exert a tiny spot of superior-age pressure, and see if that wretched young man can't be made to spill the odd bean". Mrs. Hathaway, who knew Geoffrey quite well, had promptly asked him round for a drink: the conversation which ensued had left her puzzled and rather ill at ease. Mr. Consett, when she questioned him about Colin, had given a life-like representation of a worm on a pin; but he presently stressed what he had written to Julia at Casablanca, only in even stronger terms—that whatever Julia or anyone else did, or said, or wished, it was quite impossible for young Monro to leave his employment for the moment.

"Oh, he is *employed*, is he?" Mrs. Hathaway had asked, promptly and quietly seizing on that ill-chosen and unfortunate phrase. "Who by? The Bank of England, or the Government?"

Mr. Consett's representation of a writhing worm had become more life-like than ever at that question. He stammered, hedged, contradicted himself, and had finally begged Mrs. Hathaway not to press him on a subject on which he was not free to speak. "In fact I really know no more than I have told you, that he can't leave this work, whatever it is. I was not told what it was."

"Official work, anyhow," Mrs. Hathaway responded smoothly.

"I felt that I ought to warn Julia not to go on poking about," Mr. Consett had said then, rather unhappily—"but she has never answered my letter. Do you know where she is, and what she is up to?"

"She's working at archaeology with an old lady in Tangier," Mrs. Hathaway had replied.

"Oh, with Mme La Besse! Good—that will amuse her, and keep her out of mischief." Mr. Consett had seemed considerably relieved at this news, displaying what Mrs. Hathaway felt to be undue optimism, in Julia's case. But she had merely listened sympathetically to his praises of Julia, promised discretion on the subject of Colin, and sent the young man away comforted.

All this was in her mind now as she sat in the ugly pleasant drawing-room at Glentoran, and answered Edina's question. "Has she written to you?" she asked the girl in her turn.

"Yes—I got this last week," said Edina; she pulled the operative portion of Julia's double letter out of the pocket of her porridge-coloured tweed jacket and handed it across the hearth. Mrs. Hathaway read it, and handed it back.

"She doesn't seem to be getting on very fast, does she?" Edina observed.

"Not very—though I wonder whether anyone else would have got on any faster, supposing there was anyone else available," said Mrs. Hathaway thoughtfully. "It seems a complicated business."

"Did she tell you about the hush job too?"

"Oh, yes—and how frightfully frustrated she felt."

"I wonder what on earth it can be. Intelligence or something do you suppose?" Edina speculated. "You'd hardly think they'd take on an ex-smuggler for that!" she said, with a small grin.

"Oh, I don't know. Poachers made such wonderful Commandos," said Mrs. Hathaway blandly.

Edina grinned again—then her face clouded; she put out a long slender leg and stirred the logs on the fire with her foot, restlessly.

"Look, Mrs. H., I expect it is all very difficult for Julia, but it's a month now since she went—and I can't stay up here for ever," the girl said; as she spoke she clicked her right thumb out of joint, making a small, soft, sickening sound. Mrs. Hathaway recognised this family trick as a bad sign, in Edina as in her brother.

"I know you can't, Edina," she said. "Tell me this—how much longer *can* you stay, without jeopardising this special work that was waiting till you get back?"

Edina looked gratefully at her mother's friend. Who but Mrs. Hathaway would have remembered that there was a particular job waiting on her return?

"Another month, at the very outside," she said.

"Then I should advertise for a temporary factor at once—unless you know of someone. If you can pick up a suitable person within the next fortnight you could show him the ropes and get him into the saddle before you go back to London."

Edina gave a startled glance at the older woman.

"Good Lord! Why do you say that?"

"Well, you must go back in a month, and what guarantee can we have that Julia will find Colin, let alone haul him home off this secret mission of his, in four weeks? Surely the estate can stand six months of a junior factor's salary?—especially in view of what you earn yourself."

"Well, yes—I suppose it might," said Edina thoughtfully. Suddenly she glanced rather suspiciously at Mrs. Hathaway.

"Why do you suggest that?—not that I'm saying it isn't a good idea. Do you know something I don't know about this?"

"No," Mrs. Hathaway said smoothly, remembering Mr. Consett's agonised face, and lying in the grand manner. "I'm simply going on the facts we have. Colin is doing a job so 'hush', as you all call it, that even Julia's friend Mr. Lynch, on the spot, can't find out what it is; we assume that it must be something more or less official, because the transfer of his account to Morocco was allowed. But if—or when—Julia does find him, is it likely that he can or will throw up such a job to come home at a moment's notice? I should hardly have thought so."

"No—I getcher," said Edina vulgarly. "I dare say not." She reflected, no longer looking suspicious, and stopped clicking her thumb-joint in and out, to Mrs. Hathaway's great relief—the older woman loathed this particular inherited trait. "There was that boy who was at Cirencester with Colin, what's this his name was?—who went to the Mackenzies to understudy their old factor and train on, but he chucked it after a time."

"Was he no good?"

"Oh, I wouldn't say that. Burns, the factor, was an appalling old toad in his own right, and I expect put it across poor Struthers—*that* was the name, Jimmy Struthers—good and proper, because one day he was to step into his shoes. I don't really know how much use he was."

"Can you get hold of him?"

"I'll write to Maisie Mackenzie. I think they rather liked him, and I'm sure she'll know his address. I'll ask her to ask Roddy how much good he was, and what they thought of his work, Burns apart. Mrs. H. dear, what a boon you are!"

"Failing him, you might try for Julia's officer with the beard," remarked Mrs. Hathaway lightly. "He sounds very knowledgeable."

"Yes, he does, doesn't he? We might have a stab at him if Jimmy's no go," said Edina in the same tone, getting up and going over to sit at her mother's confused writing-table. There she swivelled round in her chair towards the guest.

"There's one other letter I think we might write," she said —"I mean to Colin himself, care of that bank in Casablanca. You remember we didn't before, when Julia was here, because she was going out and we all thought she would find him quite quickly. But don't you think we might, now?"

"They don't sound very helpful," said Mrs. Hathaway.

"No—very much the contrary! But surely, however tatty

they are about *giving* information about a client, a bank can hardly hold up letters to him, can they?"

"I simply don't know. No, I suppose not. Anyhow I think it is quite worth trying, Edina."

"Good so. Right, I'll get going—if you will excuse me? I'd like to get them done before lunch—the Macdonalds are coming."

"With Ronan? Then Olimpia is sure to give us quite superlative food," said Mrs. Hathaway contentedly.

"Oh Lord, yes—*ne plus ultra*! God, where *has* Mother put the writing-paper?"

While Mrs. Hathaway, the Monros and the Macdonalds were eating Olimpia's exquisite food at luncheon at Glentoran, the rain as usual beating and streaming on the window-panes, which rattled in frequent savage gusts of wind, Julia and Mr. Keller were sitting in blazing sunshine on a heathy slope above a Moroccan highway, also eating their lunch— Julia, in an unwonted fit of mercifulness, had ordered cold veal this time instead of raw ham, and there were tomatoes and hard-boiled eggs; a bottle of local red wine was propped among the rust-stemmed, dark green leaves, so neat and small, of a pistachio-bush. Tiny blue scillas starred the reddish earth, and a minute mauve daisy; here and there a cistus, hardily, had opened an odd bloom—the air was warm and fragrant. Steve was a good driver, fast but safe; they were already in the Spanish Zone. And when they resumed their drive he deposited her at the Espagnola soon after two-thirty.

"Come in and have another lunch," she invited him.

"*Now?*" the American exclaimed, glancing at his watch.

"Yes. This is a Spanish place—they'll hardly have begun."

So Steve went in, and Julia watched with amusement his efforts to control his expression of dismay over the abundant oil and garlic of the Espagnola food. He wanted to take her to a movie, but Julia refused saying that she must unpack and deal with her mail, so as to be ready to start work next morning.

"It still seems silly, you having to work," the American said, looking hard at her.

"Oh, no, it's fun. Thank you *so* much for bringing me—it was a lovely drive."

"Thanks nothing!—you know I loved it." He wrung her hand rather hard. "I'll be seeing you again—I know where you are, now. Maybe you'll come up to Meknes some time, to look at that gate."

Chapter 11

AFTER the American had driven off Julia did read her letters and unpack, and rang up Mme La Besse to say that she had returned and would be round in the morning. But her real reason for wishing to get rid of Steve was that she wanted to get to the bar early to see Purcell. If he proved to know a good deal more than he had told her, which she thought quite likely, it was important to twiddle it out of him. Watching palm-trees outside her window tossing their heads in Tangier's sea-wind, she gave a good deal of thought as to the best means of doing this. Try the familiar technique of displaying some of her newly-won information, which had worked so painfully well with Mr. St John? Perhaps—though Purcell was rather a different proposition. Anyhow she promised herself a little fun with the all-knowing Purcell, since she had learned so unexpectedly much.

So, gay and feeling rather "on her day", she walked down across the Gran Socco, where the great plane-trees behind the wall of the Mendoubia gardens stood up golden in the evening light, through the crowded alleys of the Medina, and down the Socco Chico. It was nice to be back in Tangier; even her short absence had increased her sense of being at home there.

At Purcell's Bar this happy mood received a check. Julia had expected the door to be locked, for it was still very early; but when the little Moor opened it he announced that Mr. Purcell was not in, and he did not know when he would return. At this perfectly normal statement Julia had a moment, suddenly, of quite irrational panic. Her dismay revealed to her, rather to her own surprise, how much she had come to rely on that strange personality and how confidently she had been looking forward to this meeting with him. She turned slowly away, realising for the first time how isolated she was in this quest of hers. Lady Tracy up on her cliff-top was full of sympathy and good-will, but had not done anything, and she had fatally alienated poor old Mr. St John. Except for Purcell there was in fact *no one* to help her; if he was going to close his door—like that horrible door in the Kasbah—she might as well give up and go home, as Mr. St John had advised. And at that very moment, as she was about to turn back into the Socco Chico, Purcell's voice said—"Oh, good evening. Were you coming in? I am so sorry I was out—won't you come back?"

No sight could have been more welcome to Julia just then than that odd, half-negro face, no words more welcome than this greeting.

"Yes, I was—and I will," she said, turning and walking beside him. "Mahomet said you were out—but of course I am early."

Purcell let them in with his latchkey and passed straight round behind the bar, hanging up his hat as he went—from there, with his usual courteous formality, he asked her what she would take?

"A Martini, please." But she did not sit down at her usual table in the narrow portion immediately opposite the bar; she walked on in to the inner room and sat in a corner— Purcell brought her drink there.

"Is it permitted to ask how you got on in Fez?" he asked.

"Yes—and it's permitted to sit, too."

He sat at the next table.

"I got on rather well, really," said Julia very cheerfully. Purcell cocked one of those surprising grey eyes of his at her tone.

"You saw Bathyadis?"

"Yes indeed. I bought one of those velvet trunks of his," said Julia, her own eyes on his face.

He gave her a keen glance.

194

"Ah." He paused; Julia guessed that he was wondering if she meant more than what she said. "Why did you do that?" he asked at length.

"I'll give you three guesses!" said Julia, laughing—this was the fun she had promised herself. He looked at her, something like concern coming slowly into his face, but he said nothing. "You won't guess?" she went on. "Shall I guess for you? Because it was so pretty?—right. Because Mr. St John helped me to get it cheap?—right again." Purcell looked relieved. "Because I thought it might be useful to take something out of Morocco in, without its being recognised for what it was?" Julia pursued. "What is your answer to that one, Mr. Purcell?"

The man got up and came over to her.

"It would appear that you have not wasted your time in Fez," he said.

"No, I haven't. I'm only teasing—I am really infinitely grateful to you for sending me there."

"Thank you. I should however very much like to hear more."

Yes, and how I found it out, wouldn't you? Julia thought to herself. Aloud she said—"Oh, I have quite a bit to tell you. But I should rather like to begin by asking some questions myself."

He looked faintly amused.

"Ladies first!—though I am not very fond of telling."

Julia hesitated for a moment. There were so many things to ask Purcell that she hardly knew where to begin. She plumped for the display-of-knowledge technique.

"Why did you stall when I asked you about the man with the red hair? Why didn't you tell me that my cousin is working with him?"

Purcell gave a start.

"Did Mr. St John tell you this?" he asked sharply.

"Oh, no, poor old thing—at least only indirectly. Bathyadis did."

He stared at her.

"I think you must be a witch," he said slowly. "That is the last thing I should have expected Bathyadis to tell you."

"No, I'm not a witch. Merely lucky, and a little putting two-and-two together. For one thing, Bathyadis' son from Casablanca happened to be in Fez, and I met him, too," Julia pursued.

Purcell started again at this rather equivocal statement—for a moment or so he said nothing, and Julia watched the effect of her insinuation sinking in, contentedly. At last—

"I should very much like to know exactly how much you do know," the half-caste said.

"I'm sure you would. And I should love to tell you, if you will promise to tell me the rest," Julia riposted.

Purcell laughed.

"I think I must ask first a question myself," he said.

"Fire away."

"Have you seen your cousin?"

"Now look, Mr. Purcell, be your age!" Julia expostulated, slowly. "How *could* I have seen him? You know when they left here, with all that gin, as well as I do, and you know how long it takes them to load up the big trunks in Fez—and to fix the rest," said Julia, guessing glibly. "Do you want me to believe that you *don't* know how long they usually spend grubbing out their mineral down in the South? I couldn't have caught up with them without a plane, possibly."

His eyes never left her face during this speech—and Julia watched him too. Surprise; something like consternation; but also, unmistakably, a hint of amusement.

"You are alarming," he said at length. "But since you know so much, what more can you want to hear from me?"

"Lots. I want to know *where* I can most quickly get hold of them, and see my cousin. For instance, do they go to Casablanca themselves to arrange about exporting the stuff, or do they leave that to young Bathyadis?"

"This too," Purcell murmured, half to himself. "Would you be willing to tell me from whom you have learned all this? It is quite important to me to know."

"Yes, gladly—when you have told me precisely where and how to contact Colin. It is no use my going off into the blue, trying to locate him at all those German-run *cantines*; I should need a car, which I can't afford, *and* an interpreter—which I can't afford either," said Julia. "So please give me a time and a place. I'm sure you can."

Purcell again stared at her, she noticed, when she spoke of the *cantines* run by Germans.

"I wish I knew your sources of information," he said. "In one week!"

"I'll spill every single bean, once you have told me where I can meet him," Julia replied.

Purcell was silent then for quite a long time. At last with characteristic percipience he said—

"I am sure that at this point I ought to tell you to give up this attempt to find your cousin, and that it will be useless even if you succeed—but I am equally certain that it would be quite fruitless to do this."

"Totally," Julia agreed. She began to feel quite hopeful —though she still did not know where Purcell stood, his last words sounded as if he meant to tell her something.

"Therefore," Purcell pursued, "I suggest that in about a fortnight's time you go to Marrakesh, and—"

A tiny crash, quite close by, made them both look round. The little man with the cast in his eye had entered unnoticed; in stealing round the corner to the inner room and creeping in under a table he had dislodged an ash-tray. Julia fairly exploded with rage.

"Will you *please* tell that loathsome little wretch to clear out! I won't have him hanging round me all the time!"

Purcell had risen, like the unhappy man; he took him by the shoulder and led him out, ignoring his protests "Purthell,

I wanted to thee you!" After shutting the door on him Purcell locked it, and knocked on the bar-top; the Moor appeared looking frightened; Purcell berated him in Arabic—Julia couldn't understand a word, but it was evident that Mahomet was getting a terrific tongue-ing; he cringed and clasped his hands in entreaty before his master returned to Julia's table.

"Mahomet must have let him in by the back entrance," he said, sitting down again. "We should have heard the door. But now will you please tell me what you mean by this man's hanging round you?"

"He follows me everywhere," said Julia, still indignant. "He was at Petit-Jean when I changed trains, going up, and then he was after me in Fez—I saw him twice."

"Where, may I know? At your hotel?"

"No, I never saw him at the hotel. But he was at Bathyadis's both times that I went there."

Purcell looked grave.

"Have you seen him anywhere else?"

"Yes, up in the Kasbah here, when I went to look for Colin in that red-haired type's house. You still haven't told me why you fibbed and pretended that he was staying at the Minzah," said Julia coolly—"but let that pass. Anyhow he was hanging about up there too. Who is he? And why does he follow me?"

"I may point out that you did not tell me about this visit to the Kasbah," Purcell said. "I *see*. You saw them on the roof, of course, when you went up to watch the Mendoub's procession. It is so unwise to sit out there, but Mr. Tor—" he bit the word off.

"He will do it, will he?" said Julia, trying hard to think of names which began with Tor—there hardly seemed to be any.

Purcell ignored this question.

"And Moshe was up there? Where?"

198

"Hanging about in the alley. I didn't get in, of course—otherwise I shouldn't still be in Morocco! But who is this creature, and why does he follow me?"

"He is a miserable little Jew, who earns a living as best he can—usually by rather unsavoury activities."

"So I should suppose," said Julia scornfully.

"Jews have a hard time in Morocco," said Purcell with detachment. "They are not over-popular with the Moslems, especially the new nationalist element; they would like to go to Palestine, but Palestine is already overcrowded, and only a few get permits. I believe there is in Morocco a waiting-list of 250,000 or more would-be emigrants—so be merciful in your judgements."

Julia liked him more than ever for saying that, but she pursued her enquiry.

"But why does he follow *me*?"

"He was probably not following you when you went to that house in the Kasbah; most likely he was just watching it. But having seen you there, no doubt he reported the fact, and was detailed to follow you."

"But—" Julia's head was full of questions, jostling one another to be asked first—and there was the business of Marrakesh to be followed up, too. The winning question popped out.

"How could he have known that I was going to Fez?"

"How did you buy your ticket?"

"The hotel porter got it for me."

"There you are. Hotel porters, too, get a nice little *douceur* for supplying such information."

"Yes, but Mr. Purcell, who for? *Who* wants to have me watched and pays that creature for doing it?"

Purcell's face took on one of its gleaming expressions of amused intelligence; Julia was watching him with happy expectancy when a violent hammering on the door began. The half-caste sprang up, glancing at his watch.

"I left it locked," he murmured; "but of course it is time. Can you come in tomorrow at eleven?"

"No, I can't. I must go to my job."

"In the evening then, early. Five o'clock?"

The hammering was renewed, with redoubled violence, while Julia wondered whether, if she had to go out to "*l'excavation*", she could possibly be back by five. She decided that she would, come hell and high water.

"Yes, five tomorrow. I'll pay then." As Purcell opened the door and the bunch, protesting loudly in high voices, surged in, she went out.

It was raining next morning. Julia was glad of the weather, as it meant that there could be no question of going out to the excavation—Mme La Besse was like a cat about the wet. Tangier in rain has a strange, dis-orientated aspect. The colour-washed flats and houses, so brilliant in sunshine, look stained and shabby, the tossing fronds of the palms fling showers of heavy drops into the air; the usually lively little donkeys patter dolefully along on the wet tarmac with drooping ears, their backs darkened with moisture; as for the Arab women, their sodden white draperies cling dismally round them, making them resemble, now, bundles of washing still dripping from the tub—a most unhappy sight. But dampness accentuates scents and odours, and since residential Tangier is full of flowering gardens, in rain its air is unbelievably fragrant; Julia snuffed it up happily through the open window of her taxi.

She was touched by the pleasure with which the Belgian greeted her. They sat down to con over Julia's measurements and descriptions of the *huilerie* at Volubilis; and when she produced a neatly-typed description of the Berber oil-mill in Moulay Idriss, Mme La Besse's pleasure and excitement knew no bounds.

"But this is wonderful! Evidently, our *huilerie* is of this type. Probably the Berbers still use a Phoenician kind of mill; or possibly the Phoenicians adapted a mill already used by the Berbers." She instantly dictated a long and enthusiastic letter to a fellow archaeologist in Tunis—after typing this Julia drove off to post it and to shop in the Gran Socco, where all the Berber women looked pinched, drops falling from the brims of their vast straw hats. She told Mme La Besse firmly that she could not stay late, and sharp at five she was tapping lightly on the door of Purcell's Bar. To her surprise a new Moor opened it, and ushered her in.

"Have you fired Mahomet?" the girl asked Purcell as she sat down; she meant it jokingly, but he answered in all seriousness.

"Certainly. I cannot employ someone who takes money from others."

"Do you think the Jew paid Mahomet to let him in, then?" Julia asked in surprise.

"I *know* he did. Mahomet was bribed."

This episode sent Julia's thoughts back to her unanswered question of the previous evening, when the bunch had come hammering on the door. She did very much want to know who was having her followed, and why—but it was more important to get Purcell to amplify his hint about Marrakesh, which had been interrupted by the entry of the Jew, and she went for that first.

"Horrid little creature," she said. "But now tell me about going to Marrakesh—in about a fortnight, you said?"

"Yes, about that. I think you might learn a little more— much as you seem to know!—and even see your cousin, possibly. Marrakesh is an *entrepôt* for many wares," said Purcell, looking crafty and amused.

"Oh, *how* good of you! *See* him!" Julia exclaimed, delighted.

"Do not thank me too soon. It is a very speculative venture; I should not suggest it to most people. But you seem to have the knack of success."

"Goody," said Julia. "Well, that will suit me perfectly—I

want to see Marrakesh anyhow, and I can get driven there from Casa."

"Excuse me, but driven by whom?"

"An Irishman—that friend of mine I told you about. How do I proceed?—who's the local St John? Not that he was much good," said Julia reflectively. "He really did very little but tell me to call it all off."

Purcell laughed.

"Poor Mr. St John. I can imagine him in your hands! Well, in Marrakesh you will really do best by frequenting the Café de France, on the Djema el F'na, the great square—you should eat all your meals there; the food is delicious."

"Expensive?"

"I am afraid so. But it is the place where most Europeans, except the tourists, eat."

"I see."

"And sometimes go up onto the roof to drink coffee; there is a wonderful view of the Atlas mountains, but also it commands the whole square. Have you a pair of field-glasses?"

"No. Oh, dear, and they cost the earth!"

"Possibly I might be able to get you a pair fairly reasonably," said Purcell.

"Ah, yes—from Gibraltar, where everything is so cheap, I suppose. What do I want them for?"

"To study the crowds on the Djema el F'na—unless you have exceptionally long sight."

"No, mine is very short. Oh, what a worry! Well, never mind—do get them," she said resignedly. If she could only find Colin through a pair of field-glasses, field-glasses she would have. "How much shall I have to pay?"

"I think I might get you a really good pair, second-hand, for about twenty-five pounds."

"Right—how kind you are! Will you go ahead and do that? Unless Lady Tracy has a pair, just the sort of thing she would have. I'll let you know tomorrow, shall I?"

"By all means."

"Well, when I have them, what do I do? Spot my cousin from the roof of this Café place, and then plunge down and find him?"

"Exactly that; unless you meet him in the bar."

"It sounds rather complicated," said Julia dubiously. "Suppose he's walked on by the time I get down? How many flights up is this roof?"

Purcell laughed outright.

"You are so practical! I am not sure—four or five flights, I think. But there is always the chance that he would not have moved on, but would be standing in the same circle watching dancers, or a juggler, or a snake-charmer."

"Fun!" said Julia. "Right, I've got that. But suppose I don't spot him? Is there a local Bathyadis?"

"More or less, yes. At least there is a house in a garden, where curios are sold, and tea is served *à la marocaine*; there is a tall blonde woman there, Swiss or Swedish, I don't know which—anyhow she is called Mademoiselle Hortense."

"No surname?"

"If she has one I don't know it. Hortense is enough."

"Is her shop stuffed with velvet trunks?"

Purcell smiled.

"I imagine not. But go there and look at her things, and drink mint tea, and talk, to begin with."

"How often? As often as I came to you before I asked about Colin? Anyhow, mint is cheaper than gin," said Julia.

Purcell's face crinkled with amusement.

"How long shall you be in Marrakesh?" he asked.

"Only a few days—a long week-end, I should think, unless I stay on alone."

"Then you cannot take too much time. Go and drink tea at once, the first day, and arrange to return next morning to look at some piece again. Then get Hortense alone, and ask if she can help you to find your cousin."

"H'm. Do I ask for Colin by name?"

Purcell reflected.

"No, I think not—it is always better not to use names. Describe him; you could mention that thumb of his." Julia started a little at Purcell's mention of Colin's thumb—*sabe todo* with a vengeance. He smiled one of his fine smiles. "You might perhaps even say that he is an admirer, a follower, of Mademoiselle Astrid."

"Goodness! Does she exist?"

"Very much so!" His smile was finer still.

Oh Lord, Julia thought, was there girl trouble too, to add to the other complications? What a worry!

"Beautiful?" she asked, slowly, but with a certain anxiety.

"No—but very rich!" Purcell replied; at this point his smile had to be seen to be believed, so full was it of some secret enjoyment. Julia watched him, puzzled—as he so evidently meant her to be; there was some catch which was entertaining him. But he certainly meant something and she thanked him again, and asked for Hortense's address. This he gave in a curious form. No street, no number—but starting from the small garden outside the Post Office in Marrakesh, a series of second, third, or fourth left or right-hand turns, and then a garden wall with a medlar-tree leaning over it, and the upper part of the house visible above. Julia pulled out her diary and wrote these details down.

"I am not sure that that is wise," Purcell said.

"I haven't written down the starting-point, I can remember that," said Julia—at which the man gave a sanctioning nod.

"I suppose your Irish friend will escort you about Marrakesh?" he asked.

"While he's there, yes; if I have to stay on can I walk about alone?"

"Oh, yes—certainly by day. Marrakesh is not Fez. But if you visit the souks take a guide, or you will lose your way."

Remembering Abdul—"I'm not all that keen on Arab guides," Julia said.

"Why not?"

She told him how troublesome her wart-nosed escort had been when he took her to Bathyadis' shop—"and when we went to Volubilis, there he was waiting by another car, wart and all. Perhaps I'm getting suspicious, and it was just a coincidence, but somehow I didn't altogether like it."

"I do not like it either. And this reminds me, what have you done with the velvet coffer that you said you bought?"

"It's at my hotel, of course."

"Did you bring it by train?"

"No, I came back by car, with a friend."

"You went by car to Volubilis, I suppose. In the same car?"

"Yes."

"Then the number will be known." He looked concerned. "Is it open?"

"What, the car?"

"No, no, the coffer."

"No."

"Well, *leave* it open—with the lid up," Purcell said, urgently. "No—better not to have it with you at all. It has been there twenty-four hours already; I ought to have seen to this last night, but that wretched Moshe!"—He broke off, and glanced at his watch. "You cannot bring it here tonight, there isn't time—the place will be full. Can you take it to Lady Tracy's?"

"Well I could, as I'm going there. But if it's unwise for me, what about her?"

"Lady Tracy is different," Purcell said brusquely. "Nothing can happen to her."

"Why not?"

"The Moors love her too much. Please take it to her this evening."

"All right," said Julia, slightly puzzled by all this. "In

fact I'd better go now"—and after paying for two evenings' drinks she took her departure.

"Take a taxi off the rank when you take the coffer," Purcell said at the door—"Do not let that porter telephone for one."

"Oh, very well."

The girl duly picked up a taxi on the *place* at the top of the boulevard on her way home, as before booking it by the hour; when she ran in to collect the little coffer she took the precaution of wrapping it in her old duffle-coat, and so swathed carried it out under the curious gaze of the Espagnola porter. "Drive to the Mountain," she told the taxi-man; only when they were out of earshot did she give the address of the pink-washed house on the cliff.

As the taxi wound up onto the high ground west of the Kasbah the girl felt a certain nervousness, a thing rather foreign to her nature. Suppose Mr. St John had really carried out his threat of writing to Lady Tracy about her, what sort of reception might she expect? It was true that the old lady had not, so far, done anything at all concrete to help her, but Julia recognised suddenly what it would mean to her to lose the affection and friendship of this golden character—as earlier in the afternoon she had realised how lost she would be without that other strange character, Purcell. Nervously then, on the cliff's edge, in the dark, she bade the chauffeur wait, and shouldered the duffle-coat bundle down the cement path to the door of the pink house.

'Abdeslem opened to her, and insisted on relieving her of her burden, which he carried through into the arched hall where the old lady sat in her corner, beside her cluttered table and the broken and equally cluttered Chippendale chair—at her first words, as she rose in greeting, Julia's fears vanished.

"Oh, my dear child, how *delightful* to see you!" A warm embrace. "Sit down and tell me *everything*. 'Abdeslem, have some sherry brought. But what is that?" She indicated the oblong shape wrapped in the duffle-coat.

"Darling Lady Tracy, how good to see you. That isn't a *present*, I'm afraid," said Julia firmly—"it's something I bought in Fez, that I thought perhaps you would house for me; my room is so tiny," she said untruthfully. As she spoke she unwrapped the little coffer.

"Oh, charming! Just like mine, but more beautiful. Of course I will keep it for you. Where did you get it?"

"At Bathyadis'," said Julia, watching Lady Tracy's face. No reaction whatever. "Mr. St John helped me to get it cheap," she pursued, still watching her hostess; and this time there was a slight change in the old lady's expression—a wise, careful look appeared.

"Poor Mr. St John! Oh, yes—what did you make of him?"

"Oh, he's tremendously learned, and explained all about Morocco, and these Moulays, and quoted de Foucauld," said Julia with rather studied vacuity. "He was tremendously kind."

Lady Tracy bent an acute glance on her.

"Did you get on well?"

Now why does she ask that? Julia thought. Instead of replying she in her turn asked—

"Lady Tracy, have you heard from him since I was there?"

"My dear child, *yes*—I have. A mysterious note which someone from the Consulate brought down today. He warns me against you, and thinks you are a spy!" The old lady gave a happy chuckle.

"Is he all right?" Julia asked rather anxiously—"I mean not ill or anything? Did he write from the Consulate, or from his own house?"

There was something peculiarly sweet and benignant about the glance which the very old woman bent on the very young one at that string of questions.

"My dear Miss Probyn, I should love you and trust you if

twenty people told me that you were a spy! Yes, he wrote from his own home, and he did not speak of being ill, though he was clearly disturbed in mind. Why did you suspect illness?"

"Oh, I thought he was going to have a stroke!" said Julia, much relieved. "He asked me to take him to the Consulate, and I did, but he was terribly upset. I *am* glad he's all right." She paused. "Did he say *why* he thought I was a spy? I'm not really, you know."

"No, he explained nothing. The note was infinitely confused. Perhaps he really *is* getting a little old," said Lady Tracy, detachedly.

Julia, drinking sherry, wondered if she should attempt to explain fully what had so upset Mr. St John. But she decided against this, and instead merely said that some enquiries she made about Colin seemed to have disturbed Mr. St John, and that he got quite cross and told her to go home!—"which I really *can't* do."

Lady Tracy seemed satisfied by this, and said of course not—whereupon Julia asked her friend if she could possibly lend her a pair of field-glasses?

Lady Tracy was desolated—her nephew had asked if he could borrow them for his latest botanical trip. Julia began to hate this unknown nephew: always away when he was most wanted, and now carrying off the field-glasses as well, thereby setting her, Julia, back by some twenty-five pounds. Lady Tracy presently said that she hoped the weather would improve by the time Mme La Besse's experts arrived, so that they could get to work on the Phoenician graves. This was all news to Julia, and she enquired about it.

"Oh, yes, my dear child, someone immensely famous, from Cambridge; he wants to open some new graves. She thinks there are some that haven't been rifled on that headland close to the site, so he is coming out to excavate."

"When?"

"In about a fortnight, I fancy. Didn't she tell you?"

"Not a thing." Inwardly Julia was rather dismayed. If the expert came while she was in Marrakesh she would miss the grave-digging, a thing she really wanted to see; and Mme La Besse would make a frightful fuss about her going away again. However there was nothing to be done about it—and presently she rose and kissed Lady Tracy in farewell.

"Goodbye, my dear child. I expect you will find your cousin soon," the old lady called as she went out. Julia was tempted to turn back and go into this rather enigmatic statement, but didn't. Mr. St John must have said something about Colin in his note, but it was no good pressing things. Come to that, she had been rather selective herself in her statements to her aged friend.

Chapter 12

JULIA wrote to Paddy Lynch that same evening after supper by airmail, asking if she would be welcome for a visit in about a fortnight's time, and if he would be able to take her to Marrakesh—"which is really the object of the operation. I believe I may be onto something, but I won't write, tell you when I see you. Will Nita be back?" She further said that she would be glad of two or three days in Casa as well, if it suited, and added a P.S.—

"*Don't* repeat *don't* ring me up—write your answer, please."

The answer when it came was completely satisfactory: she was always welcome, even though Nita was still at home, and Mr. Lynch had arranged to take from Friday to Wednesday off for the trip to Marrakesh. "As for this fancy business about the telephone, don't let Bruce Lockhart go to your head."

Meanwhile Julia promptly tackled Mme La Besse on the subject of the expert who was coming to dig the Phoenician graves. His name, Professor Carnforth, was one which would have kindled Mr. Consett; to careless Julia it meant nothing, but she was glad to learn that he was arriving exactly a week hence, so that she would be able to see something of his operations, anyhow, before she went down to Marrakesh—a subject on which she continued to preserve a discreet silence to her employer. She did not omit to flit down to the Bar the very day after she had seen Lady Tracy, to ask Purcell to get her second-hand Zeiss glasses; that individual displayed his usual rapid competence, and only three days later handed Julia a parcel and a bill for £23.11.9.

"If you prefer to pay that with a sterling cheque, you can," he said.

"Really? Oh, splendid. Of course Gib. isn't really abroad,

is it?" said Julia, causing the proprietor to laugh. "Are they good? Did you look at them?"

"Naturally, or I should not have accepted them. The field is not particularly large, but the magnification is very high indeed, which is what you want for your purpose. Practise using them as much as you can before you go; there is an art in using Zeiss glasses. Stand above the Gran Socco and learn to sweep them over the crowds, slowly, so that you can see every face in each group clearly."

Julia took her sterling cheque down the next evening, and reported having successfully picked out her Berber flower-woman in the market—"and *not* at her stall; she was walking about talking to her chums."

"Continue," was all Purcell said.

Julia did continue—but not only in the market. She took the field-glasses out to the site with her next day, and walked up onto the high headland to the south of it, where the Phoenician graves soon to be excavated by Professor Carn-forth were alleged to be. The headland was a strange place, with vast bronze-coloured blocks of hard smoothish stone, mostly sharply rectangular, and often standing upright, giving the impression of Cyclopean doorways—the spaces between them might have been the entrances to passages or even to graves, Julia supposed. Blown sand filled the interstices between the huge rocks, making walking difficult, but at last she reached the top of the long whalebacked ridge, and could look down on the further side.

To her surprise she found herself looking into a quite different world. Instead of the dark heathy slopes and low hills behind her, the country in front was green and almost flat; a shining lagoon bordered with reeds ran into it, separated from the ocean by a sand-bar on which the Atlantic breakers tumbled and thundered. Julia sat down, unslung her new acquisition from round her neck, and focussing the glasses studied this fresh landscape. The flat ground immediately below her was marshy; flocks of small white egrets were pecking and feeding on it, storks strode slowly and majestically about—it was fascinating how the powerful glasses brought these creatures right up to her eyes. Ranging further, she saw that at the far end of the sand-bar, a narrow channel appeared to lead in from the ocean to the lagoon—and in a moment, as she swung her glasses inland, she saw that this must in fact be the case, for tucked in close under the landward end of the ridge on which she sat was, of all things, a small white yacht. *How* amusing—what a queer place for a yacht to be! Fiddling unskilfully with the lenses, Julia managed to get a close-up of the little vessel. She was manned, not laid up for the winter, for washing flapped from her rigging, and a couple of Arabs in very miscellaneous clothing were padding barefoot about her deck, apparently cooking on some form of stove or brazier for'ard. Out of the most idle curiosity Julia tried to see her name—the gilt letters were there, but it required a lot more of her inexpert twiddling before she got them into focus where she could read, or nearly read them— *Finetta*, it looked like. Funny—Finetta was the name of one of the Monteith girls; the prettiest, with whom Colin had carried on one of those childish innocent boy-and-girl affairs that last summer when she had been up at Glentoran. How silly she was—she had never done anything about the Monteiths, and contrary to Geoffrey's prediction she hadn't met them.

Still a little curious about the yacht's name, Julia rang up their house in the Kasbah that night when she got home—only to learn that the family had gone off some weeks earlier to South Africa for several months. But her curiosity about the yacht with the familiar and unusual name was still not satisfied, and on her next free day—four days a week was her stipulated contract with Mme La Besse—she strolled round to the Consulate-General and once more saw the young and courteous vice-consul.

Had they a Lloyd's Register? Julia enquired.

"I think so, Miss Probyn. But can I help at all?" the polite young man asked.

"Well, perhaps—I just wondered who the owner of a yacht called the *Finetta* is."

At the name "Finetta" a faint disturbance became evident on the rather ingenuous face of the polite young man.

"The *Finetta*—oh, well, yes, she was here at one time."

"Where is she now?" Julia asked innocently.

"I've no idea."

Whose name had she been registered in, Julia wanted to know.

"Well, she has changed hands since then—she was sold getting on for a year ago." He continued to look uncomfortable.

"Was there some trouble about her?" Julia asked—the young man's disquiet was so manifest that "trouble" of some sort stood out a foot.

"Actually yes—there was."

"What, smuggling or something?"

But the vice-consul would not be drawn any further. If Miss Probyn wanted the owner's name she could probably get it, he said, from Lloyd's representative in Tangier, whose name and address he furnished her with. Julia thanked him, and apologised so charmingly for bothering him that he relented to the point of saying—

"The owner's name was certainly not Monro. Wasn't it a Mr. Monro that you were asking about before?"

"Yes. Anyhow I'll see this Lloyd's functionary—thank you so much." And on she went to the Lloyd's agent.

This individual glanced at her rather curiously when she asked in whose name the *Finetta* had been registered up to a year ago, but turned up some files.

"Mr. John Grove," he read out. Julia got the impression, she couldn't have said why, that the man had known the name all along, and that looking in the files was just a piece

213

of what the theatre calls 'business'. "Do you know him?" he asked, she thought slightly suspiciously.

"No—I never heard that name. I expect there's some mistake. And whose name is she registered under now?"

"Mr. Charles Smith," the man said without troubling to refer to the files again.

"Thank you. I am so sorry to have bothered you. For some reason I thought she might have belonged to one of the Monteiths."

"Good Lord no!" the man exclaimed, taken by surprise— "What an idea! Mr. Monteith! He never had anything to do with *that* outfit!" He paused. "Do you know Mr. Monteith?"

"Well, they're neighbours of ours in Scotland, and one of the daughters is called Finetta—that gave me the idea," said Julia, with her usual serene vagueness.

"I assure you all the same that there is no connection whatever," the Lloyd's man said, very repressively.

"And Mr. Smith?" Julia asked.

"Oh, he's a man who is fond of sailing, and comes out here, so I understand, for his health from time to time."

"Is he here now?"

"Ah, that I couldn't say. The yacht isn't in the harbour at the moment, anyhow, so he may have gone off cruising somewhere."

The devil he may, Julia thought to herself, and not so far off either—but she thanked the Lloyd's man, and wandered back to the Espagnola. She didn't for a moment believe that Mr. Smith was actually on the *Finetta* now—crews, whether Arab or British, don't normally hang out their washing and do their cooking on deck while the owner is aboard. Probably the whole thing wasn't in the least important—it was just a bit funny. She must ask Purcell some time about Mr. Grove —he would be sure to know all the dirt. Or Lady Tracy.

In fact it was Lady Tracy whom she asked about the *Finetta* at that point. She had nothing particular to do for the rest of the afternoon, and decided to go up to the pink house and find out if the old lady had any hints and tips to offer about Marrakesh.

Lady Tracy greeted her with her usual affection, and said that she had some news for Julia—"Though negative, I am afraid. The *Frivolity* is in, and I've learned *all* their names—and none is Monro. But one is a Duke!"

"Oh, lovely!" said Julia. "The harbour-master said one was a lord—all the same to him no doubt." Nothing but yachts today, she thought, and being now certain that Colin was in the interior she couldn't have cared less about the crew, or passengers or whatever they were on the *Frivolity*.

"I wanted to ask you about another yacht, Lady T. darling," the girl said then. "What was all the scandal about the *Finetta*? Do tell me—I'm sure you know."

"Oh, my dear, that was a *horrible* business! There were three or four young men on her, I believe quite nice creatures, just smuggling away perfectly innocently—cameras and things from Gibraltar, and American cigarettes, and perhaps a little currency from here—just what everyone else does," said Lady Tracy serenely. "But suddenly one of them started carrying *drugs*!—quite unbeknown to the others, I gather; *they* said so, and no one gave a moment's credit to anything *he* said," said the old lady, something approaching harshness appearing most unexpectedly in her voice.

"And what happened?"

"Oh, the Zone Police and Interpol caught him, and he was sent to prison in the end."

"And the others?"

"They disappeared. I heard they were all quite furious with this wretched creature, and it seems they really weren't involved—I know my nephew thought they were not—though I believe Interpol still has its eye open for them. Such a *hideous* brush to be tarred with!" said Lady Tracy indignantly.

"Goodness *yes*. And the yacht?—the *Finetta*?"

"Oh, I've no idea what happened to her. I suppose some-one bought her, or perhaps the others went off in her. Hugh would have known," said Lady Tracy, vaguely.

Julia guessed Hugh to be the tiresome botanical nephew but didn't trouble to confirm the fact. Useless creature!

"How long ago was all this?" she asked.

"Now let me think. It was some time last spring—would it have been April or May? Wait"—the old lady rang the brass handbell. "Feridah will know," she said.

"What, about the drug-running?" Julia was genuinely startled.

Lady Tracy chuckled.

"No, no!—though quite a number of the richer Moors do use hashish and things, of course. No, but she will remember when Nilüfer's goat—you remember, the pretty woman who lives down on the slope—had three kids. It all happened at the same time."

Julia was entranced by this rather unusual method of establishing facts about drug-smugglers. She watched with her usual pleasure the graceful movements of the Arab maid as she glided in and hung affectionately over her aged mistress. A prolonged nattering in Arabic ensued.

"It was April the 13th," Lady Tracy pronounced triumph-antly, while the lovely Feridah and her veils slid out again. "'Abdeslem brought the third kid up here, and we reared it on a bottle. And that very same evening Hugh came in and told me about this horrible Mr. Glade."

"Grove?" Julia murmured.

"Oh, yes, it *was* Grove. So alike, glades and groves—all pure Milton," said the old lady. In fact since Lady Tracy had mentioned the previous April or May, sums had begun to do themselves, almost unbidden, in Julia's head: last April was just nine months from this January, when up at Glentoran she had been shown Colin's last letter, in which he said that one of his chums had left the boat! There might be nothing in it, of course—just one of those coincidences; but it was worth remembering. However for the moment she put that aside and turned to her more immediate preoccupation, which was Marrakesh.

"Lady Tracy, can you keep a secret for about five days? Because if so I want to ask you something."

"Dear child, I once kept a quite *lurid* secret for forty years! —by which time of course it had lost most of its luridness. What is it?"

"Well, I don't want Mme La Besse to know too soon, and be upset just with this Cambridge V.I.P. coming," said Julia slowly, "but I'm going to Marrakesh in about ten days."

"Poor Mme La Besse! Yes, she will be terribly fussed. However I suppose it is something to do with your cousin, or you wouldn't leave her just then." Julia nodded. "In that case you must go," the old lady pursued. "Do you think there is really a chance of your seeing him down there?"

"A faint chance. But I have to try."

"Of course. I do hope you succeed."

"Anyhow I shall see Marrakesh," said Julia.

"Oh, yes—such an exquisite place. You are going with friends I hope? Do they know it well?"

"I've no idea. They're not madly learned. Is there anything I especially ought not to miss?—that's what I wanted to ask you."

"Oh, indeed, yes. The Saadian Tombs are unbelievably lovely; you must see them—though even the *least* cultured people would probably take you there."

Julia scribbled in a little book.

"And then you must see the Apartment of the Favourite in the Palace that Marshal Lyautey used as his headquarters. He put Edith Wharton in it!" said Lady Tracy, with antique glee.

"*No!*"

"Yes, he did!—*absit omen*, we all said—when she went to stay with him. The Palace itself is nineteenth-century and really nothing except for its vastness—and showing how gay and elegant even quite late buildings can be in Morocco; but the apartment is fascinating, when you think of that *ultra*-American woman living in such surroundings. Wait—I'll get you her book." The old lady struggled to her feet, and with Julia's arm perambulated her bookcases till she found the volume, and handed it to her young guest.

"She saw so *much*—Lyautey thought a good deal of her, and she was on the spot so early, before the interior was really opened up at all. It wasn't a *good* book," Lady Tracy mused, "although she was such a good writer—Africa muddled her; it often seems to muddle Americans."

"*And* how!" Julia said, thinking of Steve.

"Ah, you find that? But there are things in it about Morocco that you will find nowhere else. Bring it back—she wrote what they call 'a sentiment' in it for me!"

"I will," said Julia.

With Professor Carnforth's advent imminent, Mme La Besse kept her young secretary on the run practically non-stop, and Julia's conscience about taking leave at this juncture smote her to the extent of causing her to offer to work six days instead of four in the ensuing week, and to work late on all of them—too late for it to be of any use going to the bar to ask Purcell about the *Finetta*, since the place would be full. Indeed she was so busy, and by nightfall so tired, that for the moment she more or less passed the *Finetta* up. Certainly it was an odd affair, and the yacht's unusual name suggested a link with Colin, while the dates undoubtedly fitted in with his last letter—but it was all too indefinite to bother about.

Julia chose the moment for telling her old employer that she wanted to take another fortnight's leave with some care —in fact a few minutes after she had fetched the eminent man in the Chrysler from the airport, and deposited him in

Mme La Besse's ugly little house. By mentioning the subject hastily, over drinks, and in a stranger's presence, she hoped to avoid a scene, but she was wrong. Mme La Bessse emitted a screech which caused the Professor to jump and drop his cocktail, breaking the glass.

"*Now* you will leave me? Now, NOW? Just when I need you most? Oh, *c'est une saleté!*"

"I'm not going till Monday; that gives us all this week," said Julia mildly. "I am so terribly sorry, but I can't help it —I must go."

"What is a *week*? And why 'must' you go?"

"Because I have to." Professor Carnforth watched with interest how the slow, calm firmness of this pretty young woman—who looked so silly but who drove so uncommonly well—gradually mastered the rage and dismay of the so much older one, by whom (for some reason) she appeared to be employed. Still suffering from suppressed indignation, Mme La Besse at last accepted the inevitable, and even sealed the reconciliation with a bearded kiss. And next day they all drove out to the site and began the examination of the headland.

One of Mme La Besse's great merits was knowing when she was beaten. Of course she was dying to show Professor Carnforth the factory site, in detail and at length; but when he said firmly that though he hoped to see that later, graves he had come for and with graves he would begin, she shook with chuckles and gave way. She also suggested that he and Julia should proceed ahead to the summit of the headland, while Achmet and Abdullah could haul her up after them.

As the advance party toiled upwards through the clogging white sand between those strange bronze-toned rocks—

"You are interested in archaeology?" the Professor asked Julia.

"Oh God, no! I don't know the first thing about it."

The Professor had been a surprise to Julia. In her usual

total ignorance of matters academic she had expected someone very old and untidy, with moths flying out of his clothes and probably a long beard—whereas Carnforth was relatively young, clean-shaven, rather good-looking, and neat in his dress to the point of nattiness. He had a nice voice and a pleasant laugh, which emerged at this frank statement.

"Then why—?"

"Oh, the travel allowance. I'm out here about something else, and I have to earn my keep. But I'm a *good* secretary—when I'm there!" said Julia blithely. "I can't be there all the time—I warned poor old Mme La Besse of that. And in fact I hate missing this grave-robbing—I'm dying to see all that gold jewellery! *Do* find some!"

"I'll do my best," said Carnforth, laughing his pleasant laugh again. By now they had reached a point in the ascent where the wind-borne sand ceased, and was replaced by stony reddish earth set with stunted shrubby plants; here the rocks were further apart, and the Professor paused before a low mound rising from the soil.

"This could be a grave," he said. "Where are those Arab creatures with the spades?"

The creatures were far below, pulling up Mme La Besse; so the Professor marked his mound with a minute cairn of small chips of rocks, and proceeded upwards—they found several more promising spots, which he similarly marked. On the top they sat down for a breather, rejoicing in the sun and the keen salty Atlantic air; Julia took her field-glasses out of their holder and established the fact that the *Finetta* was still lying in the lagoon, and her Arab crew still cooking on deck. When the old Belgian and her escort arrived digging began.

The next few days saw feverish activity on the headland. Carnforth insisted firmly that at least six of the Berbers from the site should come up every day as soon as he arrived, to dig under his directions, bringing their midday meal with them to avoid loss of time—thus he was able to work on more than one mound at once. There are several peculiar features about Phoenician graves, in Morocco anyhow. One is that ninety per cent of them have already been opened and rifled —this was the case with the first three or four which the Professor tackled. Another is the troublesome circumstance that once you have started opening a grave you must go on till you have finished—either by establishing that it is empty, or by removing the contents; otherwise the ingenious Berbers from the surrounding villages will swarm up at night, complete your operations, and carry off anything of value. The only way to avoid this is to mount guard over an unfinished excavation during the hours of darkness.

The first grave of all was a beauty and fascinated Julia; it was entered through an elegant little doorway with stone columns and lintel, from which a short flight of steps led down into a chamber walled and roofed with beautifully cut slabs of stone. As the Berbers' spades removed the last of the soil which masked the entrance Carnforth gestured them aside, and did the final clearing himself carefully, with some help from Julia and her trowel. When the doorway was clear it could be seen that earth had fallen down the steps and into the interior; this Carnforth allowed the Berbers to remove under his supervision—he was considerably impressed by the fact that they had brought up rush baskets in which to carry it out.

"*Ah, ils ne sont pas mal débrouillards, ces types-là,*" Mme La Besse commented acidly—"It is not the first time that they uncover a grave!"

Within, by the light of the Professor's torch, they saw along the sides of the tomb narrow stone-cut niches in which the coffins of dead Phoenicians had once been reverently placed, now empty. It was all rather touching, Julia thought—these non-Christian people caring so deeply about an appropriate and beautiful resting-place for their dead.

But however elegant, however touching this particular

tomb was, it was now empty. The Professor made notes and measurements—twelve foot long, six foot wide, seven foot from the floor to the peak of the gabled stone ceiling—but that was all it held for him, and he went on to others of his little cairn-marked spots. Julia, though excited by the first tomb, in her bird-witted way soon lost interest, and during the succeeding days pottered idly about the ridge which formed the headland, watching storks and herons in the marshy land below through her glasses, watching the culinary operations of the *Finetta's* crew on her rather dirty deck. But in the course of her casual wanderings she came on several more of those unmistakable stone-lintelled entrances to empty tombs; with her cigarette-lighter she examined them—empty, vacant, but perfectly cleaned out. She reported these to Carnforth, and he went with her to look at them—yes, well, there you were, he said; the place was stiff with them, but all rifled and from his point of view useless.

On the evening before she left for Casablanca Julia went down to the bar, hoping for a last word with Purcell, but early as it was the place was not empty; a tall man in tinted glasses sat on one of the high bar stools, reading *Le Mensonge de Tanger*. Julia, annoyed, barely glanced at this intruder as she turned towards her table; the tall man however had lowered his paper and got quickly down off his stool crying— "My dear Julia! What in the world are *you* doing here?"— and kissed her warmly.

"Gracious, Angus, I never recognised you in those ghastly glasses," Julia said, returning the Duke of Ross-shire's kiss with temperate affection. "And why are you here? Oh, I know—you're on the *Frivolity*. All the same, what *are* you in fact doing?"

"My dear Julia, what we all have to do—trying to *live*, in spite of the Chancellor of the Exchequer! Look—what will you drink? Oh, what fun this is!"

"*Scotch* with you, dear Angus, I think," said Julia—"but

not on one of those pylons. This is my table." She sat at it, and the Duke brought his drink over. Purcell observed this encounter with considerable interest.

"Well, tell me"—Julia said, when his Grace had raised his glass to her with the regrettable expression "Cheers!" "Go on."

"My dear Julia, I simply can't afford to buy bread and cheese, let alone drink, if I stay more than two months of the year in the U.K.! I have it all worked out; I spend three weeks in London with Mollie in the season; *three* daughters, dear child!—and what their schools cost! Then three weeks in August at Inverglass for the grouse, when I entertain a few of my friends, and a fortnight for the stalking—in *total* and most blessed solitude—at Gartavaigh. And that's the lot."

"It's rather horrid," Julia mused. "Is old Mackenzie still buttling and running everything at the Castle?"

"Oh, yes, bless his faithful heart; and he's marvellous with the tourists—did you know that we're open now six days a week in the summer? That's what supports Mollie and educates the girls."

"Where on earth do the tourists eat?" Julia asked, remembering the cooking at Inverglass's only hotel, a small one.

"Cafeteria in one of the wings!—and a huge car park for the charas out where the old rose-garden used to be. All that pays hand-over-fist," said the Duke cheerfully.

"Well, I expect it's all right, and you have to; but I still think it's rather beastly," said Julia. "What *would* your mother have said? However, let that pass. Why do you live on a yacht? Do you smuggle?"

"Good Heavens no!" Angus Ross-shire stared at her in horror. "What an idea! We live on a yacht, dear girl, because the sea is now the only untaxed and untaxable form of 'normal residence'. Neither the avaricious French nor the contemptuous Spaniards nor the affable Portuguese nor the venal Africans can mulct you of income-tax if you only haunt their shores. So that is where, and how, I live. And mostly in agreeable climates." He paused, with a gusty sigh. "Sometimes I have a great nostalgia for my own *disagreeable* climate," he said. "But however—tell me about *you*. What are you doing out here?"

"Odd pieces for my papers. That gives me an extra allowance, of course; and as well I'm working for an archaeologist, as secretary."

"Good God! What like?"

"A beard."

"My *dear* Julia! Since when have you taken to beards? Tell me all about him."

"It isn't a him, it's a her," said Julia with a giggle. "And about seventy."

"Good Heavens! Oh, well, we must try to brighten your life, which does sound very drab, poor Julia, and so unlike you. No boy-friend anywhere about?"

"No, worse luck."

"Extraordinary! I thought Tangier was full of men—they must all have cataract," said the Duke meditatively. "Well, come to supper on board tomorrow. I'll fetch you in our gig."

"Angus, I can't. Oh *bother*!—what fun that would have been."

"Why can't you?"

"I'm going to Casablanca tomorrow."

"But Julia, so are *we*—next week. Wait and come with us; cruise down and save the fare! You see how my mind runs on money."

"Oh, Angus dear, what a shame! How I wish I could."

"Well once again, why not? We shall be there in a week. What is the hurry?"

Julia hesitated—not over her decision, but as to what to say.

"Everything is fixed up," she said at length. "And I'm going on to Marrakesh."

224

"Dear Julia, this is all *quite* absurd—we are going to Marrakesh too! You really must come along and make a party of it. My co-tax dodgers are very nice harmless creatures; and one of them, though of my sex, is of the same age as your Bearded Lady—so he can act as chaperone, surely? Purcell, please be most kind and bring Miss Probyn another whisky—it may assist her thoughts."

Julia laughed rather helplessly at Angus's nonsense, but held to her point—everything was arranged, and she couldn't change it now. The Duke looked rather hard at her.

"Julia, you have something up your sleeve, I fancy. I wonder what it is? Does your aged employer go with you to Marrakesh?"

"Angus, don't pester me! You know perfectly well that if I could come with you, I would. But I can't and that's that."

"No boy-friend, and yet she has her secrets! Very well, we will respect them. *Parlez-moi d'autre chose.* How is the very beautiful Edina? She really is such an exquisite creature."

Behind Julia's back the bar door had opened, letting in a puff of cool air; whoever it was that entered sat down at the table by the door, also behind her—she paid no attention.

"She's up at Glentoran," she said, in answer to the question.

"Ah, yes. Such a lovely place, in spite of the ghastly house. Didn't old John Monro, the uncle, die the other day?"

"Yes."

"Then who's running it? Not poor old Ellen M.?"

"No, Edina's doing it—and *hating* it."

"Why hating it? Oh, yes, she had a *riche* amusing job in London, hadn't she? But where is young Colin? It's his pidgin now, surely."

"My dear Angus, if only we knew! He was last heard of on a yacht somewhere out here—only he *was* smuggling. But we can't trace him." Julia was rather pleased with this answer of hers, which she brought out quite pat—but it caused Angus Ross-shire to look thoughtful.

"You don't mean to say he was one of that crowd on the *Finetta*?" he asked. "Not that anyone but Grove was really involved, I gather, but it was a horrid business."

Julia was startled. "Why do you ask that?" she demanded. As she spoke she glanced across to where Purcell stood behind the bar, and saw his face. It told her, as plainly as any words, that he had heard what her companion said, and that Colin *had* been on the yacht that was now lying in the lagoon behind the headland.

"My dear girl, naturally the whole of *le grand bidet* was ringing with the story, and I thought I remembered the name Monro—but of course I never connected it with Colin. They tried to pull *us* in for it at one point—poor Interpol, they try so hard!—but the Zone Police soon cleared that up." The Duke gave Julia a shrewd amused look.

"You wouldn't be out here *looking* for Master Colin, by any chance, and doing archaeology with your circus sideshow as a supporting bye-line?" he asked.

Julia could not refrain from glancing at Purcell. He had heard again—a veiled discreet delight showed in his face. Bother Angus—he was too intelligent by far.

"You'll be cutting yourself soon if you aren't careful," she said coldly—and to her surprise heard a stifled laugh. It was not Angus, who was merely grinning at her smugly; and it was not Purcell, smooth and correct, carrying a drink to the table behind her, though still carefully enjoying himself, evidently. Her companion now leaned across to her, and spoke in a lowered voice.

"Don't look now, but there's a rather sinister type sitting just behind you who seems to be taking a deep interest in us."

"Was it he who laughed?" Julia asked, in the same tone.

"Yes, damn his impertinence."

"Then I shall look." Slowly and deliberately she turned fully round. At the table behind her sat Reeder.

Julia did rather well, Angus Ross-shire thought. She got up very slowly, and held out her hand.

"Good evening, Mr. Reeder. How nice to see you again. Won't you come and join us, properly?" And as he rose, a little shamefacedly, she made the introductions—"Mr. Reeder, the Duke of Ross-shire. Mr. Reeder was First Officer on the boat I came out on, and was very kind to me," she said equably.

In fact Mr. Reeder also did quite well. He shook hands with the Duke, sat calmly down, and said to Julia very nicely—

"I do apologise for laughing just now. I couldn't help over-hearing, but I oughtn't to have laughed."

Julia swam over that.

"I daresay I was talking rather loud. Tell me, what are you doing here? Is the *Vidago* in?"

"Not she. Poor old *Vidago*—Freeman piled her up, going in to Seville to collect sherry."

"No! Is she done for?"

"Well, we hope not—but it will be quite a while before she's on the run again, so I'm taking a bit of leave."

"Was anyone hurt? Is the Captain all right?" Julia asked, with an eagerness which rather surprised Angus Ross-shire.

"Oh, Cherry's as right as eight trivets. But you should have heard him swear!—you know he never does as a rule, but he let Freeman have it superbly."

"I *wish* I'd been there! Precious Captain Blyth!" said Julia, with enthusiasm. She turned to her friend. "The *Vidago's* the most darling boat, I was so happy on her—and Captain Blyth is an angel. So you're hanging about here for a bit?" she asked Reeder.

"Yes. I thought I'd go inland now I have the chance—see Fez, and Marrakesh, and all that; there's never been time before."

"It looks as though we shall all be 'piling up' at Marrakesh,

227

though let's hope not actually wrecked," said the Duke. "You are going, Miss Probyn is going, I and my party are going. I hope we all meet there and have a drink. Where shall you drink in Marrakesh, Julia? The Mamounia?"

"Mercy, no!" said Julia. "The Café de France."

Chapter 13

"NOW what *is* all this nonsense about not being rung up on the telephone?" Mr. Lynch asked, as he steered his car skilfully through Casablanca's traffic on the way from the station.

"It may be nonsense, as you say, Paddy, only I have been being shadowed pretty persistently—even as far as Fez."

"Who on earth by?"

"A seedy little creature who was pretty unsuitable for the job because he had a squint which one simply couldn't mistake."

"And in whose interest is this flatty employed, do you imagine?"

"I don't imagine, and I don't know. I can only guess—and I want you to help me with my guessing. In fact, a car is such a good place to talk in—do you think we could potter about a little instead of going straight home? I've got a lot to tell you."

"God help you, you have got it on your mind," said Mr. Lynch. "O.K.—we'll potter."

Julia had decided on her way down in the train to tell Mr. Lynch everything. He was intelligent, trustworthy, and had lived in Morocco for a considerable time; moreover not being a British subject he would be free from certain inhibitions. Her cogitations about this had been constantly interrupted by what she saw from the train windows—the endless young plantations of eucalyptus inland from Port Lyautey; the curious fact that all the orange-groves, gleaming with fruit in their neat squares, were surrounded by 20-foot hedges of some evergreen thing like a cypress; the large pale-brown winged insects that sprang up in clouds from beside the line in several places as the train passed—could they be locusts? She *must* ask Paddy about all these things—but also, she managed to decide, she must tell him her whole story. And while they sat drawn up by the kerb in the open space near the new Cathedral—that inspired combination of Gothic form with the characteristic Moroccan open-cut plaster-work in the windows, creating quite a new sort of beauty in ecclesiastical building—she did tell him. Julia had no great gift for lucid exposition; she began at the end rather than at the beginning, and continued with many parentheses and flash-backs. But from the moment when she said—"Well, I know what Colin is doing: he is digging out some rare mineral somewhere down in the South and shipping it out in velvet trousseau-trunks which they buy from an old Moor in Fez"—she held Mr. Lynch's attention. There was no more mockery; now and again he asked a question, but on the whole, at the end, he accepted her piecing together of facts from so many different sources, including his friend Mr. Bingham.

"Old ruffian," he said cheerfully. "He told you much more than he ever has me! I knew about the chrome and molybdenum of course, and I'd heard vague talk of some rarer things being prospected for, but I'd no idea the East Germans were doing it. I'd better see what I can find out. There are others who know things besides Bingham."

"Oughtn't we to go and see young Bathyadis?" Julia asked.

"Oh we will, by all means—I'd like a good tray as a baby-present for Nita, anyhow. But we shan't get anything from a Moor."

"I did from his father," Julia pointed out.

"Yes—that's the queerest part of the whole business. *Very* odd, his assuming you were in on it, and an amazing stroke of luck; everything else has flowed from that—though I'm not saying you weren't almighty smart, dear Julia. Whoever'd think it, to look at you? Your face really *is* your fortune!"

"Yes, isn't it?" said Julia tranquilly.

Mr. Lynch continued to meditate.

"I wonder if it would be any good having a go at the *Affaires Indigènes.*"

"Why?"

"They keep tabs on all travellers: everyone has to have a *fiche*, a sort of *permis de circulation* with their name and so on, which is checked and stamped in each Administration Post. Car-drivers are even asked at one post where they are making for, and the French check by telephone to find if they've clocked in where they said."

"Goodness, do they? They ought to be easy to trace, so, Paddy."

"Not if they're using false names and false passports. And one person may dig a thing out, but there are probably whole echelons of men of straw between him and whoever ships it —in this case presumably young Bathyadis." He reflected. "I'll think about it. Anyhow, come on home now and have a drink."

"There he is!" Julia ejaculated, as Mr. Lynch swung the car swiftly round.

"Who is?"

"My shadower—look, the little man in the bad hat, on that seat. Oh, he's going off."

Mr. Lynch pulled the car sharply back onto the wrong side of the road and overhauled Moshe; springing out, he caught the little Jew by the shoulder, and stared relentlessly in his face.

"I shall know you if I see you again," he said in French— "And if I do see you again you will come to call on the police! Why do you pursue Mademoiselle?"

"I do not, I do not! I take the air only."

"Well, take some other air! Go back to Tangier! Where's your notebook?"

Even as the little Jew said piteously—"Monsieur, I have no *carnet*," one hand flew protectively to the breast pocket of his shabby jacket; Paddy's followed it, and drew out a small book.

"*Très-bien!* I keep this. Be off—it is not permitted to pursue

231

young ladies in Casablanca." He returned to the car, tossing the notebook into Julia's lap as they drove off.

They studied it together over their drinks in Paddy's villa. There were various dates: Julia identified the two days when she had called on Bathyadis, with a small "f" in front of them; the number (which she happened to remember) of Steve's car, with the date of her return in it to Tangier, and such a quantity of entries with "P" and a date that Paddy laughed out loud when Julia explained that these must presumably represent her visits to Purcell's Bar.

"No wonder you needed to seek 'gainful employment'—you seem to have lived in that bar!" he said, delightedly. Julia ignored this and went on studying the notebook—in view of what Purcell had said about the Jew's probably having only started following her after he had seen her outside the house in the Kasbah, she was looking for the date when she went up to see the Mendoub. There it was—with "XO1" and "XO2" against it. She showed these to Paddy, with great satisfaction.

"There's a car-number on the next line," he said. "See? Moroccan, by the look of it."

"Goodness, so there is! That might be the car they fetched the gin and whisky in. *Paddy!* Couldn't we trace them with that?"

"Might do. We'll have a fair try, anyhow. Do you want to change?"

In the pretty downstairs bedroom allotted to her Julia found an airmail letter on her dressing-table. "Oh, yes—sorry; that came this morning," said Mr. Lynch, "but with all this Inspector Alleyn stuff I forgot to tell you. Dinner in half-an-hour?"

In spite of unpacking and dressing in a hurry, Julia found time to gobble her letter while she smeared stuff on her face and wiped it off again. It was from Mrs. Hathaway, to whom she had written about her impending stay in Casablanca, and brought news. After describing her visit to Glentoran and her suggestion to Edina about getting in a factor Mrs. Hathaway went on—"And young Struthers *was* free, and is there now; Edina is running him in, and she says he's shaping so well that she hopes to be able to come South next week. She is delighted, of course. And from what your friend Geoffrey said (but don't tell him I told you) it seemed of little use her hanging on indefinitely waiting for Colin."

"Good for you, Mrs. H.!" Julia ejaculated. "But I wonder exactly *what* Geoffrey has been saying." She herself had mentioned confidentially to her old friend that she thought she might be on Colin's track, though it was far from certain that he could or would return even if she found him; but that letter could only have reached Mrs. Hathaway some days after the visit to Glentoran, when she had already suggested getting a factor at once—so Geoffrey certainly had said something.

Mr. Lynch, who had a very sound sense of priorities, called on Casablanca officialdom on his way to the bank next morning; he rang Julia up to say that lunch would have to be pretty late, as he proposed to have "some useful drinks", and would she tell Mahomet? Julia relaxed in the sun on the balcony among the geraniums, still studying Moshe's grubby little notebook. There were various entries of "XO1" and XO2" prior to the day when she had seen Colin on the roof of the house in the Kasbah, but none after; presumably these figures represented him and the red-haired man, and when they left Tangier someone else had followed that line and Moshe been told off, as Purcell had suggested, to tail her. She smiled slowly when she noted that the last entry of all bore yesterday's date, with a small "c" and a car-number, presumably Paddy's. Would the little Jew also have memorised it?

Mr. Lynch came back in high spirits.

"Well, I've got the name of the owner of that car," he said, throwing a slip of paper to Julia—"English all right, though not Monro." Julia took up the slip—on it was written: "M. Charles Smith."

233

Her air of stupefaction as she read was so marked that Paddy got up and came over to her.

"What's the matter?"

"Nothing—only I think it means that Colin must have been on the *Finetta*."

"That drug-yacht? Why on earth do you deduce that?"

She told him why, at some length; when Mahomet appeared in the archway leading to the dining-room he was told—"Five minutes more."

"I didn't bother to tell you all this yesterday, because it was just a possibility," Julia said at the end. "The dates fitted all right, and Angus Ross-shire mentioned that *he* thought Monro was one of the *Finetta* names—but I couldn't be positive. I think this ties it in, though."

"So do I. But what on earth is the yacht doing in that lagoon where you say you saw her?"

"What indeed? That will want some thinking about. But isn't the first thing to find out where Mr. Charles Smith's car is now? Won't your *fiche* experts be able to tell that?"

"They should be. It'll take a little working, but I'm pretty *bien* with one of them, luckily. I'll tackle that the moment after lunch—and after tea, what about a call on Master Bathyadis?"

The visit to Bathyadis produced no fresh information, as Mr. Lynch had foretold, except concerning the situation of his shop, which was just outside the Old Medina, the original Moorish quarter, and therefore quite close to the harbour. Young Bathyadis expressed polite pleasure at seeing Julia, but seemed rather reserved otherwise, though he sold Paddy an exquisite old brass tray rather cheap. There were no velvet trousseau-trunks on view, and Julia refrained from asking to see one.

"We'll just call round at the Bureau to see if they've traced that car," Mr. Lynch said as they drove off. Julia waited in the car—her companion presently returned with another slip of paper.

234

"Garaged, and in *this* town," he said. "I think we'd better check right away." They drove to the garage, where Julia again waited outside.

This time the pause was prolonged. Presently Paddy came out—"Got any money on you?"

"About 20,000 francs."

"I daresay that will do."

She handed over the notes and then waited again. When at last Paddy emerged he drove off very fast.

"*Very* sticky, Monsieur Martin," he said. "The car's there all right—I saw it; a black saloon. But it took most of your good francs, my dear Julia, to elicit what I so badly wanted to know: which is that for his trips to the interior Monsieur Smith leaves his car there and takes a closed *camionnette*."

"Golly! Did you get its number?"

"Yes, I did—that was what cost the money. How *are* you off for cash, by the way?"

"Oh, masses. I earn a salary in francs now, you see."

"I don't see—but here we are. Wait again, will you?"

They were once more outside the Administration Offices —and this time the pause was brief before Mr. Lynch returned.

"Mr. Smith has now metamorphosed himself into a Swiss," he said as he drove away. "Herr Nussbaumer. He travels in men's clothing and ladies' dresses, down in the South. What do you make of that? Can it be the party we want?"

"Oh, *yes*—it sounds exactly right to me. I know all about these Swiss and Austrian travellers: they sell shirts to the personnel at the mines, and frocks and nylons to the wives of the cantiniers."

"And how do you know *that*, my girl? You seem to have plenty up your sleeve."

Julia explained about the hotel *patron* at Fez and his wife, who had been so informative. "It all seems to me to tie in. Couldn't one put coffers, or sacks of ore, on the floor of the camionnette under the suits and dresses? And they'd have a perfect excuse for cruising about near the mines."

"They would that. Yes, so far so good. I wonder how Mr. Smith gets away with two passports, though."

"Two cars, and a false beard on one passport, do you think?"

"Yes—plus a venal *garagiste*."

"But what can this ore *be*," Julia asked, "to be worth so much fuss?"

"Ah, yes—I never told you about that at lunch, you got so het up about Mr. Smith. It *was* the East Germans who found it originally—old Bingham was quite right—helped by a Swiss metallurgist who'd been in the Legion, and stayed on here; they went for it bald-headed because it gave them something unique to trade to the Russians, so's they could keep their end up a bit, see? They have some proper concessions, mostly for chrome and molybdenum, but they get this stuff as well, and ship it out along with the other, secretly."

"But Paddy, what *is* it?"

"Some very queer ore. I had to make the man who told me so tight—hence our late lunch—that I could hardly understand him at the end! But it has some special properties, besides being practically *pure* uranium, with next to no waste products, so it's worth sending out unprocessed, in those trunks of yours." He swung the car smartly into his drive at this point —Julia got out, and after a minute or two he joined her in the sitting-room and poured out drinks. During those few moments alone Julia had been thinking back—recalling Mr. St John's emphasis that what Colin was doing was too important to be left for any inheritance.

"So I suppose our people want it too," she said. "Oh, yes —I'm beginning to see. It will be the East Germans who are tailing Colin and Mr. Smith as rivals, and now me—Bathyadis and poor old Mr. St John really agreed that the Germans were '*nos ennemis*'."

"Could be. Anyhow England would certainly like to be

sure of a supply of this stuff, Astridite or whatever they call it."

Julia sat up. "Say that again," she said quite sharply for her.

"Say what?"

"The name. Did you say *Astri*dite?"

"Yes, that's what I gathered through my acquaintance's hiccoughs. Mean anything to you?"

"Yes, it means a whole lot," said Julia slowly. She was thinking that this practically answered the question she had never cleared up with Purcell, as to where he stood; he had spoken of "Mademoiselle Astrid", and if he knew that name he must be in the whole business up to his neck, surely?

"Did your informant make any fuss about telling you that name?" she asked.

Paddy looked surprised.

"Actually he did. When I repeated it to him, to be sure I'd got it right, he crossed himself and said—'Mother of God, did I say that? I must be drunk.' 'Poor man, you are that,' I said. But why?"

"Just confirmation of another tip I got. Paddy, we couldn't go to Marrakesh a bit sooner, could we?"

"No, my dear. Friday at dawn is the earliest possible! But it seems to me that we haven't done badly so far, in the time."

"No, indeed, Paddy dear. You've been wonderful." She thought. "Where shall we put Moshe's book? I'd rather it didn't lie about."

"Where is it now?"

"In my handbag." She gave it to him.

"Well I hope I don't get leprosy," said Mr. Lynch, putting the unsavoury object in an envelope before tucking it into the inner breast pocket of his jacket. "I'll seal this tomorrow and leave it in the safe."

Julia passed the next two days quite contentedly—she had the use of Paddy's car in the mornings, and caused Ali to take her first to see the *bidonville*, the shanty-town created by the

237

Moors who persisted in pouring into Casablanca in search of higher wages and a gayer life than were obtainable in the *bled*, the agricultural country-side. It was nasty enough: the shacks, crammed together, were constructed of every sort of rubbish—old sacks, straw mats, decayed fabrics of indeterminate origin; those that were really made of hammered-out *bidons*, or petrol-tins, were mansions compared with the rest. And they were minute in size. She commented on this to Ali, who as usual became informative. They were no smaller, he said firmly, than the Moroccan country-man's normal habitation, the *nuala*, a sort of tent of straw or rushes, some eight or nine feet across at the base at a maximum; he would take Mademoiselle to see some of these if she wished. Mademoiselle did wish, and they spun out into the country, where Ali led her along a muddy track to a group of three *nualas*, standing within an untidy straggling hedge of camel-thorn. Ali continued to expound—he would have made a splendid P.R.O., Julia thought. The *nualas* were in fact pre-fabs—a newly-married Moor bought one ready made, erected it on his plot, and lived in it; after a year he bought a second, lived in that, and turned the first into a kitchen or store-house; a year later he bought a third to live in, and turned the original one into a stable for his animals. In four years a *nuala* simply fell to bits, so the Moor of the *bled* bought a new one every year, and continued this extraordinary turn-round of differing uses.

It wasn't, Julia thought, a very high or energetic way of life, this huddling on one spot in fragile impermanent dwellings, less solid and elegant by far than the highly mobile tents of the Bedouin which she had once seen in Syria. Next day she made Ali take her to one of the *bidonvilles améliorées*. There, shacks were going up in quantities; there were the stand-pipes, with an occasional ragged woman drawing water at one; but of any use being made of the facilities for sanitation there was no sign—slops were being emptied, and evacuation taking place, on the open ground.

"*Ah, ils ne se fichent pas mal de tout cela, ces autres,*" said Ali, with the high contempt of the already urbanised man for his rural brethren.

Julia set out for Marrakesh with a considerably higher degree of anticipation than she had felt on her journey to Fez. For one thing, any tips of Purcell's were now proved to be reliable, so that she was more curious to meet "Mademoiselle Hortense" than she had been to see Mr. St John; for another, they had found out so much, quite independently of Purcell, that she really felt herself to be fairly hot on Colin's trail. Mr. Lynch had cajoled his acquaintance in the Casablanca Bureau to produce a note of introduction to his opposite number in Marrakesh, and hoped to be able to arrange for notice to be given them if—and when—Herr Nussbaumer's camionnette turned up in the oasis city—this seemed a more hopeful line than studying crowds through field-glasses from the roof of a restaurant. It was a fine sunny morning, and as they left the city for the open country Julia began to hum a little tune.

"Feeling good?" Mr. Lynch asked.

"Quite good."

"We're just coming to the big Yank air-base," her companion said presently. "It's a vast place; they say the runway is 11,000 feet long."

"*Is* that long?"

"Dear fool, it's immense. The most enormous bombers can use it. Look, the barbed wire's just beginning; on your right."

Julia took a glance at the speedometer and noted the figure of kilometres already run before she turned her attention to the American air-base. There was little to be seen at first behind the high barbed-wire fence but huts and sheds; the runway and main hangars lay out of sight, in the middle, Paddy explained—but presently they came to a well-guarded entrance, beyond which sanded roads led off among tidy bungalows, with creepers on trellises and flowers in bloom, at which Julia looked with interest; were these the sort of quarters lived in by Steve at Port Lyautey? A large notice said "T.V.A.", and she asked Paddy what it meant.

"Temporary Village Accommodation—that's where the officers and their wives live."

The base was certainly large. When at last they left the barbed wire behind Julia looked at the speedometer again— they had done 25 kilometres, or roughly 15 miles. She pointed this out to Paddy.

"Yes, it's immense—and we're coming to another soon on the left, that they run in conjunction with the French, like they do at Meknes. And then there's the one at Port Lyautey. These great Yank air-bases are one of *the* dominating factors in North Africa today, and come to that, in South-West Europe too—though very few people seem to realise it. You might do a piece about them for your paper."

Some distance beyond the bases they came into camel-country. Even close round Casablanca an odd camel may be seen, ploughing yoked to an ass or mule, but here they were everywhere—ploughing in pairs, walking in circles at well-heads winding up the water-buckets, or merely grazing on the stony reddish land like cows: some, like cows, with a calf at foot, delicious little creamy creatures. When they stopped to eat their lunch in the shade of a wood of young pines a commotion presently arose on the far side of the road—a troop of sixty or more of the huge beasts was being driven along a track through the spindly trees, headed and followed by a Moor riding a donkey; they threw up their great saurian heads, snarling and hooting, as they plunged along.

"Oh, good," said Mr. Lynch. "There must be a fair on in Settat. I'd like you to see that."

Settat is for North and Central Morocco in the matter of camels what Ballinasloe is for horses today in Ireland, or the Falkirk Tryst used to be for cattle in Scotland—*the* great mart, where fairs are held frequently, and the animals are driven long distances to be sold. When Julia and Paddy took the road again the resemblance to the outskirts of Ballinasloe on a fair-day became very marked, except for the uncouthness of camels compared with the neatness and grace of Irish horses—in threes or fours, or in bunches of up to a hundred, the earthen track beside the road allocated to four-footed traffic was alive with camels. Mr. Lynch sighed for Ireland; Julia was delighted —something more for *Ebb and Flow*. They pushed slowly through Settat, a rather undistinguished town of white houses, since even the main highway was jammed with the grunting snarling creatures and their brightly-clad buyers and sellers, the latter displaying the same total indifference to the needs of motor traffic as Mr. Lynch's compatriots do; but out in the country beyond the animals were once more confined to the earth track, and the car shot ahead. A range of low mountains rose in front of them: that was the Djebelet, the Small Mountains, her companion informed Julia—"and the French are doing some interesting afforestation work there."

"Oh—why?"

"How pitifully ignorant you are, Julia! Forests bring rain, and also hold the water in the soil instead of letting it pour out over the land below in great scours, smothering what wretched topsoil there is with silt and stones. This country suffers from drought for more than half the year, and from ruinous erosion for the rest of it; the French are spending a fortune trying to correct that—not an enterprise that would occur to an Arab!"

Indeed when they entered the defile by which the road passes through the low range of the Djebelet Julia could see for herself what the French Administration was doing: trenches two or three feet deep following the contours of the hills, with trees planted along their lower edges, thus at the same time securing a supply of water to the roots, and preventing scouring.

In the pass through the hills the camel-track was crammed

close up against the highway; rounding a blind turn Mr. Lynch prudently gave a blast on his horn. This startled the leaders of a troop of laden camels coming round the bend from the opposite direction, and as the car came in sight two or three of them appeared to shy violently, dancing awkwardly at the end of their head-ropes. They were laden with *crin végétal*, the fibre, made from leaves of the palmette, with which Arab mattresses are stuffed; the hairy greenish stuff bulged through the holes of the big rope nets in which it was carried, slung pannier-wise on either side of the hump. Mr. Lynch pulled up: the caravan-men hauled agitatedly at the head-ropes, trying to drag their charges back on to the track, below which a gully ran down to a stream-bed; but one camel got completely out of hand, and plunged so wildly that its load came adrift and fell off onto the road, breaking the net—out from among the hairy mass tumbled a plum-coloured velvet trunk, which also burst open, scattering lumps of stone of a peculiar pinkish orange all over the grey tarmac of the highway.

Julia was out of the car in a flash.

"Paddy! This is *it*!" she cried, and ran towards the mess-up.

"Take care—don't upset them," Mr. Lynch called after her. But Julia never heeded him—here was Astridite itself under her very nose, or she was a Dutchman, and she pounced on two or three of the fallen lumps. That particular camel-man was too busy trying to calm his beast to take any notice, but the Moor in charge of the caravan came over to her gesticulating angrily, obviously demanding his bits of rock back. Mr. Lynch also hastened up.

"Give it back; we don't want any fuss," he said.

"Oh, woe!" But Julia obediently pulled a couple of pieces out of the pocket of her orange suède jacket and gave them to Mr. Lynch, who handed them to the Moor with some pacificatory remarks in Arabic.

"Well, there you have it," said Julia as they drove off.

" 'Confirmation strong,' as the Victorians used to say. *What* a piece of luck!"

"I'm not so sure. I expect *he's* taken our number now. That was rather stupid, Julia."

"Oh *no*, Paddy dear. I had to have a piece—and how could I know he would be so tatty?" She felt in her pocket again and drew out a lump about the size of a cake of bath soap, worn down to little more than an inch in thickness, and examined it. "It's frightfully *heavy*," she said, balancing it in her hand—"like lead. And it's got funny marks on one side, almost like the bark of a tree. Look"—and she held it out.

"Really, Julia, you are a crazy creature!" said Mr. Lynch, laughing in spite of himself, as he took the piece of rock from her hand. "Golly!—it *is* heavy," he said, handing it back. "But do for goodness sake put it away where it can't be seen."

"Handbag," said Julia, opening the article. "I suppose that consignment is on its way down to Master Bathyadis."

"Undoubtedly, I should think."

There are two ways at least of entering Marrakesh by road. The main highway from Casablanca goes straight into the town, showing nothing of the astonishing oasis with its miles and miles of palms, their dark fronds swinging in gentle restlessness against the sky in the perpetual movement of air from the High Atlas beyond; there is however a détour which leads round into this lovely and peculiar place to enter the city from the South—this Mr. Lynch took. Julia gazed entranced as they passed through grove after grove of the strange plumed trees, rising from creamy sand; this, unlike Casablanca, was wholly Africa—and African too were the long low castellated walls, sandy-pink at all times, rose-pink then in the rich sunset light, through which they passed under a gate-tower into the town, and drove through a relatively modern quarter to their hotel.

The Mamounia is not in the least African, in spite of gallant attempts with rugs and furnishings; it is pure cosmopolitan comfort, plus a splendid view and a delightful garden, in which the wise have breakfast. Julia and Mr. Lynch were among the wise next morning, and ate rolls and drank coffee in air heavy with the scent of stocks in full bloom.

"It's rather a bore to come to a place like this, and then spend one's time doing Scotland Yard stuff," said Mr. Lynch, leaning down to pick a carnation, which he put in his buttonhole. "However when you've finished I suppose we'd better hustle off to the Administration and enquire for Mr. Nussbaumer."

"I've been thinking about that. Would he have come through here on his way South from Fez?"

"He needn't, if he was coming direct from Fez and going down to Tagounite or Ouarzazate or Zagora—he could cut through the Atlas by the pass from Azrou to Boua Sidi; the road isn't so good, but the buses use it. But mustn't he have come to Casa to switch from the car to the camionnette?"

"Of course—but *when*? Would he pile all those trousseau-coffers into the saloon? I should have thought they'd be a bit conspicuous. Wouldn't he be more likely to go straight to Casa from Tangier, change machines, go back to Fez, and pick up the trunks, and then on South?"

"I think you're right—yes. In which case there's no means of telling whether he'd have come through here or not."

"Except by asking." Julia leisurely poured herself out another cup of coffee. "I hope your friend's friends play. And then to the blonde Hortense." (Julia had told Mr. Lynch about Hortense.) "I shall feel a frightful fool talking about Mademoiselle Astrid, knowing what we know now."

"I should see her all the same. She might give you a line on when to expect them, or even more exactly where they are."

"Yes—especially if I show her this," said Julia, taking the orange-coloured piece of rock from her handbag and fondling it. "Look—it exactly matches my jacket!"

"Do put that thing away!" said Mr. Lynch, almost irritably. "I wish you hadn't got it."

At the Administration offices a tall courteous official, looking slightly like General de Gaulle, led them, Paddy's card in his hand, into a typical French office; rather untidy, and reeking of Gaulois cigarettes—excusing himself, he read the note brought from Casablanca. He seemed a little surprised, stepped to the door, and asked someone unseen for files; then he turned to the two English people. "If one might ask why—?"

Mr. Lynch was very ready. Mademoiselle was *journaliste*, and concerned herself with all aspects of life in Le Maroc. Julia, taking the hint, whipped out her Press card and did some patter about her interest, and that of her readers, in conditions of living for *women* in the remoter areas—which, she understood, were ameliorated by activities such as M. Nussbaumer's. The Frenchman smiled; partly no doubt at Julia but, Paddy guessed, a little also at her mission—the French are apt to consider that 'the woman's angle' takes care of itself. Some papers were now brought in, which the official —again saying "You permit?"—studied, occasionally consulting his assistant. Then he turned back to the visitors. Yes, M. Nussbaumer was quite well known; for the past year, or nearly, he had been making regular trips, going South about every two months, though he did not always pass through Marrakesh. He had however gone down five or six weeks ago, and should be back any day. If it would assist Mademoiselle, it might be possible to establish from one of the more southern posts when he was likely to return.

This was an unhoped-for boon; Julia, turning eyes of a loving dove onto the handsome officer, said that this would in effect assist her immensely. She would call again—when should she call again?—to learn the result of M. Le Commandant's so kind enquiries.

If Mademoiselle was at the Mamounia, the officer replied, there was no need to derange herself; he would give her a blow of the telephone.

"I prefer to call—I detest the telephone," said Julia. "Towards six?"

"Yes, towards six. By then I should know."

Outside—"Now to the Post Office," Julia said.

"What for?"

"To find Hortense."

"What do you mean? I thought you had her address."

"So I have—but it begins at the Post Office." She got out her diary, and from that small garden outside the yellow building they turned and twisted through the bright sunny streets, following Purcell's directions, till over an ochre-coloured wall leaned a medlar-tree, with a building much taller than most of the houses in Marrakesh rising behind it. "Here we are," said Julia.

This preliminary visit to Mademoiselle Hortense was of course intended to be inconclusive, and was—but it had side-effects. They went through a small door into an untidy but charming garden, and rang a bell at the door of the tall house; Hortense herself let them in and led them upstairs, to floor after floor, a room or two on each, all full of really beautiful and valuable antiques—the best, Paddy muttered to Julia, that he had seen yet in Morocco. But already Julia's heart was not in this visit, nor in the antiques, though she forced herself to praise a lovely eighteenth-century robe, woven in tones of plum-colour and dull gold. On the top floor of all, mint tea was offered them as they sat in comfortable armchairs.

"Funny place. I must say I'm glad to know of it," said Mr. Lynch while they waited for the tea—"Colin or no Colin. They've got superb stuff."

"I hate it!" said Julia unexpectedly.

"Why on earth?"

"I don't know. It makes me feel nervous, for some reason. Do let's get away as soon as we can."

"Must drink the tea," said Mr. Lynch.

Julia got up and went over to a window, restlessly—suddenly she unslung her field-glasses and put them to her eyes. "Paddy, come here," she said, rather low.

He got up and went over to her. The window commanded the street; there stood his car, and behind it a tall Arab, writing something in a book.

"Take the glasses, and tell me if that man has a wart on his nose," Julia commanded.

"Yes—as pronounced as Cromwell's. Why? Know him?"

"It's Abdul, the guide I had at Fez. Look, Paddy, either Moshe did memorise your car-number, and he's checking, or this place is being watched. Anyway he's taken it now," she said, as the Arab stowed away the notebook in his voluminous robes.

"Come back and sit down," said Mr. Lynch—"don't let it get on your nerves." They regained their armchairs just in time, before an Arab brought in the tea, followed by Mademoiselle Hortense. Julia, sticking rather grimly to Purcell's directions, arranged to come the following morning to have another look at the prune-coloured robe.

As they drove away—"Of course, if these people are known to be contacts for Herr Nussbaumer—or Mr. Smith—I expect the house would be watched as a matter of routine," Mr. Lynch said.

"Yes, I daresay—but why a guide from *Fez*? I don't *like* it, Paddy."

Chapter 14

MARRAKESH has none of the withdrawn, enclosed, secretive quality of Fez. The whole city in its wide plain lies open to the sun, within its low peach-pink walls; the exterior, at least, of every building can be seen, nothing is hidden—one would say that Marrakesh has no secrets. Least of all does it attempt to hide its own highly peculiar life—on the contrary, on the Djema el F'na, the great open *place* in the centre of the town, this life is lived in fullest publicity, but in a strangely absorbed fashion. The dense crowds which fill it all day and till late into the night comprise practically every race from Northern and even Central Africa: sitting in circles on the ground round the professional story-tellers, watching every gesture of the narrator, or standing five or six deep round the dancers—white-clad men ranging from grey-beards to young boys—craning their necks to miss no detail of the beautiful foot-work; eager groups crowd about the vendors of cures, herbal or magical, or even modern proprietary brands from Europe; jolly groups sit outside the open kitchen booths, eating happily; veiled women throng the stalls where sweet-meats and strange foods are sold.

It was the self-containedness, the absorption in their own affairs of this vast mass of exotically-clothed people which chiefly impressed Julia when Mr. Lynch led her through the great Square after leaving Mademoiselle Hortense, judging, quite rightly, that the Djema el F'na is enough to afford distraction to anyone, however nervous. When they pressed into a circle to watch the entertainment going on within it no one paid any particular attention; even the man who took round the collecting-bag seemed to do so at the same regular intervals.

"Yes—it's not done for tourists; this is the playground of

Africa," said Mr. Lynch, when she remarked on this. "Now come and have lunch."

The Café de France lies at one end of the Djema el F'na, separated from its crowds by a not very broad street, along which cars pass all the time; that end of the square is closed by a mosque, beyond which a wide passage leads through into the maze of the souks or bazaars; just beyond the café a side-street leaves the main street on the right. The whole front of the café is occupied by a broad verandah filled with small tables and divided in two by a screen of coloured glass; it is raised barely a foot above the level of the street, and since there is no railing, Moors of all ages, from little shoe-shine boys to the sellers of musical instruments, freely step up to pester the European patrons—the sedate Arab habitués who sit for hours drinking coffee they leave severely alone. A door at the end furthest from the glass screen opens into the bar, which is indoors; beyond it flights of stone stairs lead up to the coffee-terrace on the roof.

The bar is rather smoky and murky, and Julia opted for having their drinks and lunch on the verandah, where she could watch the coming and going on the great *place*. The casual African tempo prevailed in the Café: the drinks took a long time to come, so did the lunch; various pedlars, with uncanny persistency, sidled up to the table over and over again, stealthily laying on it something that they desired to sell —Julia laughed, Mr. Lynch repelled them good-humouredly. The food when it did come was quite as good as Purcell had said; in particular there was a rich mutton stew over which one had to sprinkle a brown powder as fine as flour, with an unknown and delicious taste—when Julia asked the waiter what it was he said "Cumin".

"*Oh* what fun!—'tithe of mint and anise and cummin' like in the Bible."

Passing through the bar on their way up to the roof for coffee, Julia was greeted by someone—"Good afternoon,

Miss Probyn"—peering through the gloom, she saw Mr. Reeder.

"Oh, how do you do? I hardly knew you in those clothes!" the girl said. Indeed the *Vidago's* mate was curiously altered by civilian dress; in his rather good tweeds he looked like a country squire. He invited them to have a drink. "No, we've eaten; we're having coffee on the roof; come with us,"—which Reeder did.

There are two things which everyone must do on the roof of the Café de France: look at the view of the High Atlas, and eat Cornes de Gazelles, long slender curved cakes of ground almonds, with their coffee. The High Atlas that day was shrouded, a distant blue line with here and there a cold snowy gleam among high clouds; the party were thus able to concentrate on the Cornes de Gazelles, which are too sweet for most tastes.

"Know Toledo?" Mr. Reeder asked. "At that restaurant in the Square there they give you marzipan cakes just like these, only stumpier."

"Yes, I remember," said Julia. "How funny."

"Not really, you know. Did you notice the metal clappers those dancers use down on the square? Just the same principle as castanets. Spain really is practically Africa; down the southeast coast even the butterflies are the same."

Mr. Lynch was rather impressed by the sailor's display of knowledge, but the mention of the dancers drew Julia to the parapet; leaning on it, she tried to use her field-glasses, but found herself completely baffled. The square was so vast that even when she could pick out faces in a particular circle, when she put down the glasses it was hard to be sure which circle she had been looking at. "Hopeless," she said to Paddy, re-seating herself.

"I travelled down from Petit-Jean to Casa with a friend of yours," Reeder said to Julia—"an American called Keller."

"Steve? Goodness, what's he doing there?"

"Looking for you, I fancy. He said he'd gone to call on you in Tangier and heard you were at Casablanca, so he was going there. I told him you were coming here, and he must have followed on; I saw him in the bar this morning." The smile in Mr. Reeder's beard was rather marked.

"I wonder where he's staying," said Julia.

"Here, same as me," Reeder replied.

In the afternoon Julia demanded to be taken to the Bahia Palace to see the Apartment of the Favourite—Reeder came with them. That curious suite of rooms opening out of one another through archways without doors leads off the vast painted and balconied court which once housed three hundred concubines. No one, as Reeder said, can really take any interest in *three hundred* concubines, but both he and Mr. Lynch were highly entertained by this strange setting for an American novelist. In the centre was a tiny courtyard open to the sky, with a tinkling fountain; rooms brilliant with colour from walls and tiled floors opened off it, in one of which stood a huge four-poster bed upholstered in crimson cut velvet—"She could see the fountain as she lay in bed!" Julia breathed, "What a place. I must say I wish I'd known Marshal Lyautey. and been allowed to stay here."

They idled about in the souks after that, watching various craftsmen at work; Julia bought for Edina one of the crocheted cotton caps which every other man on the *place* wore, and an inlaid cedar-wood travelling-mug for Mrs. Hathaway—then they dropped Reeder on the *place* and went on to the Bureau, where the good-looking French officer had accumulated quite a budget of information about M. Nussbaumer and his assistant.

They had been lately at Tinerhir, near the rocky gorges of the Dadès and the Todra—*un drôle d'endroit* for them, since it was rather wild country, though there were cantines there. But he was expected at Ouarzazate tonight, and if he came straight on he should be in this town sometime tomorrow. In which case, "since Mademoiselle dislikes the telephone so much," he, the Commandant, would send a note to her hotel.

"Paddy, this is wonderful!" Julia exclaimed as they drove away. "What sucks for old St John, telling me to give it all up. *Dear* Colin! It will be lovely to see him."

"Don't talk too loud," said Mr. Lynch, using his native idiom for not provoking Providence.

In the hall of the Mamounia they came on the Duke of Ross-shire, seated alone over a beer; he rose and embraced Julia.

"Well, here some of us are, anyhow! My ancient friend, who would have chaperoned you, has gone sick in Casablanca; the others *said* they were staying to succour him, but I think they really wanted a little night-life. So I came on by myself, by the bus."

"What spirit, Angus. Look, this is Mr. Lynch, who's brought me"—the men shook hands, and Paddy ordered drinks— "Beer is very unwholesome in Morocco at sunset; abandon it and have whisky."

"Mr. Reeder's here too," Julia said, as Angus Ross-shire laughed and agreed to whisky.

"What, your nice eavesdropper?"

"Yes, we're all going to dine together on the Djema— you'd better come too."

"Indeed I will, whatever the Djema may be. I need both company and a guide. But what an exquisite place this is."

As they sat talking Steve Keller entered that brightly-coloured hall, and stood staring round at the various groups scattered about it.

"Here!" said Julia, holding up a languid hand; the young man hastened over, and greeted her with a warmth that was innocently obvious.

"How you do get around!" he said, grinning.

"Well, yes—I'm seeing Morocco. But you must meet my

252

friends. The Duke of Ross-shire—Mr. Keller, of the American Naval Air Force; and Mr. Lynch—Mr. Keller."

At the first of these introductions a curious expression, compounded of astonishment, embarrassment, and a faint hostility, appeared on the ingenuous countenance of the American—Julia saw it.

"Sit down and have a drink, Steve, and talk to the Duke. He was a Pathfinder in the war, though I don't think there were any jets then. Mr. Keller is a jet-fiend, Angus," she said. And in no time at all, Mr. Keller, to his amazement, found himself talking with real pleasure to a man who might be that legendary thing, a Duke, but to whom the air was a familiar place, and who possessed a surprising knowledge of technicalities—Julia, with satisfaction, overheard Angus Ross-shire receiving a warm invitation to come and take a look at the base at Meknes.

"Dear Julia, you *said* no boy-friends," Angus murmured in her ear as they stood waiting on the steps while Paddy brought round the car, "but were you being quite candid? What do you call your so delightful mechanical chum?" Julia giggled—

"They occur, you know, Angus," she said.

They all dined together at the Café de France, where Reeder awaited them; Steve had borrowed a car from an acquaintance at the Casablanca base, and came on by himself. Afterwards they all strolled again on the Djema el F'na. There was a full moon, and the great Koutoubia minaret—to eyes familiar with the minarets of Turkey, slender as knitting-needles, so much more like a tower—stood up almost transparent in the moonlight, in all its immense dignity and beauty. At night, under the naphtha flares, the tempo of pleasure and entertainment on the great square—the "*place folle*", as the French call it—is heightened: the circles round the dancers are more dense, the grey-bearded performers leap more wildly, while the metal clappers, the original castanets, rattle like machine-gun fire; the gestures of the story-tellers are more

253

dramatic, the serpents of the snake-charmers writhe like souls in torment. Public enjoyment for its own sake here achieves an expression unparalleled elsewhere on earth—it is indescribably stimulating. But it is also exhausting, and presently Julia declared for bed.

Going upstairs Julia said—

"Paddy, it seems *too* silly to waste time going to see that Hortense person again."

"Oh, nonsense! Snap out of it, Julia. We've no idea where they'll be staying, or even if they will stay in Marrakesh at all. You can at least ask her if Colin will be going to see her."

"As Colin, or as M. Nussbaumer's assistant?"

"Both, I'd say."

"Honestly, I'd rather go to the Saadian Tombs," said Julia.

In fact on the following morning they did go to these before visiting Hortense, taking Angus Ross-shire with them. The Duke especially was quite ravished by this exquisite flowering of Hispano-Mauresque architecture: the slender marble columns supporting the high shadowy vaulting of the roof of carved cedar-wood, whose gilding and delicate colours glowed richly and dimly in the airy gloom; the lace-like fragility of the incised plaster-work of the walls, combined with dazzling glazed tiles; and on the ground the reason for it all—the tombs themselves, of grooved marble, peaked like a roof and the colour of old ivory, where Ahmed the Golden, his son, his grandson, and various male and female kinsfolk lie at rest. Julia was rather disappointed that one no longer, like Edith Wharton, had to wade through nettles to reach this exquisite place; instead, the Administration has created a neat garden, set with brilliant flowers.

They dropped the Duke off at the Post Office, and then once again took that complicated set of turnings to the tall house with the medlar-tree; but Julia absolutely refused to go in alone.

"You *must* come too—I'll say you're my brother."

Hortense—when Julia, fingering the prune-coloured robe again, began to put her questions—was extremely cagey and suspicious.

"Who sent you to me?"

"That I cannot say."

"But I must know *why* you come—*enfin*, I must have some credentials."

Julia, to Paddy's horror, opened her handbag and took out the orange-coloured lump of Astridite.

"There are my credentials," she said.

The woman positively recoiled.

"Put it away! It is dangerous. You are crazy!" She became angry all of a sudden. "And since you come, yesterday, *des mauvais sujets* hang about the place. I do not like it."

Paddy said firmly—"Do not tell me, Mademoiselle, that this is the *first* time your house has been watched." Hortense shifted her ground.

"They took the number of your car—I saw them."

"Yes, so did we," said Julia coolly. "Abdul is always taking car-numbers."

"Ah, you know this man?"

"Yes, damn him!—and I'd like to know why he's taking them here instead of in Fez."

For some reason this remark caused Mademoiselle Hortense to relent slightly—she even smiled a little.

"I also should like to know this, though I fear I can guess; if he had your car-number in Fez he will have traced you here."

"Oh, no, he won't—not by the number; *that* car has never come nearer to Marrakesh than Port Lyautey."

The blonde woman shrugged her shoulders. "Anyhow you are under suspicion from that quarter—and if I may permit myself the expression, with good reason," she said, with a meaning glance at Julia's handbag.

Julia smiled, slowly.

"Mademoiselle Hortense, I don't want to worry you—I see that it is a bore for you to have us here. Tell me one thing and then we will go, and leave you in peace. Where does M. Nussbaumer eat when he is in Marrakesh?"

"But on the *place*, naturally."

"In the booths, or at the France?"

"It is uncertain. I think the France, as a rule."

"Thank you very much."

"I told you that would be a waste of time," said Julia as they left.

"Why didn't you ask her where they stay?"

"A, she wouldn't have told me, and B, I wonder very much if they do stay here at all. In their place I should be inclined to blind on to Casa, get in after dark, park the camionnette with the avaricious but venal M. Martin, and go and curl up for the night in an outsized coffer chez Bathyadis."

Paddy laughed.

"Perhaps you have something there. Anyhow it's time *we* ate now—the others will be waiting." It had been settled the night before that they should lunch at the Café de France with Reeder, Steve, and the Duke.

"Paddy dear, let's *just* flip round by the Hotel, in case there's a message from your high-powered acquaintance," said Julia urgently; Mr. Lynch obediently drove to the Mamounia.

There was in fact a note at the desk for Mademoiselle Probyn; she went into the hall and sat down to open it. "The Messieurs you seek entered the city half-an-hour ago," it said, and nothing else, except "12.46 *heures*" written under the date. Julia folded it up slowly, put it in her handbag, and went and washed.

"They're here," she said to Paddy as she walked out to the car. "Got in at 12.15."

Paddy glanced at his watch.

"Ten past one. That's early to eat, by Moroccan hours; still, we'd better keep an eye open for them at the France."

"Always allowing for those false beards. Damn, if the red-head wears a wig I'm sunk!"

"We'll take a scout through the bar before we settle down, anyhow," said Paddy.

Reeder, the Duke and Steve were all in the bar when they arrived. Julia accepted a drink, and then stood peering round her in that dark smoky place. It had occurred to her that even with false beards their exceptional height might give the pair she was looking for away, but she realised immediately that it is not easy to judge the height of a man seated on a bar-stool. There were eleven people in the bar besides themselves: three young Moors drinking orange squash, five stumpy elderly Frenchmen, whose little round pots entirely precluded their being the two she sought, two French officers in uniform, and the Commandant.

"No beards," Julia muttered to Paddy. "Let's get out of this smog."

Out on the verandah, though the sun poured in there was a little teasing breeze; they had two tables pushed together right on the inside and close up against the glass screen, where it was relatively warm and sheltered, and sat over another round of drinks while awaiting their lunch. Julia had carefully seated herself with her back to the screen, facing the door leading through to the bar, beside which a small French police officer sat sipping a Pernod—she could thus watch the whole length of the verandah except the smaller portion behind the glass screen. Just as the *hors d'œuvres* were being served two tallish men stepped up from the street and began to cross towards the door—one had a scanty and immature black beard, the other a heavy and rather improbable-looking reddish moustache; both wore bérets which practically concealed their hair, and dark glasses, but this time they were so close that even Julia could not be mistaken.

"There they are!—the two in bérets," she murmured to Paddy. "The one with the beard is Colin." She rose as she spoke, and also began to thread her way between the tables towards them. Just as they reached the door she called "Colin!" softly—which caused the Duke, amused and inquisitive, to get up and follow her. The younger man looked round, paused for a second, and then followed his companion into the bar—Julia continued to make her way slowly in that direction between the large forms of the coffee-drinking Moors.

Suddenly there was a bright flash and a loud explosion—Paddy Lynch could never be sure afterwards whether it took place inside the door or out. What he did see, in that first instant, with horror, was that Julia and the Duke both fell. After that all was confusion—French voices within the bar crying "Les Nationalistes! Les Terroristes!", while excited crowds surged across the street from the *place* to see what was going on; there was broken glass everywhere, from the windows and the shattered screen.

Steve was quicker off the mark than either of the others—he fairly shot down the length of the verandah, knocking over Moors and tables impartially; he had reached Julia's prostrate shape and stood pugnaciously over it just in time to prevent her being trodden on in the panic-stricken stampede out of the bar. Mr. Lynch, following him, saw the two tall men in bérets emerge in the wake of this rush, but at a more reasonable pace; the bearded one paused and looked down distressedly at Julia's fallen body—the Irishman noticed that he jerked his right thumb-joint outwards in a sickening distorted fashion. But his companion with the red moustache turned and beckoned him on—he followed, and they were instantly engulfed in the swarm of Africans which filled the street. It was impossible to follow them, or even to see which way they went.

A van-full of police arrived almost at once, and with the Commandant began an assessment of damage and casualties; a doctor, summoned by telephone, arrived with commendable promptitude. The *agent de police* who had been sitting at the table by the door was dead; so was a waiter, emerging with a tray of coffees at the instant when the bomb exploded. Julia, who was lifted and laid on the bar, was unconscious, blood pouring from a cut in her big white forehead; the Duke, who had been a little behind her, was able to pick himself up, but sat rather dazed in a chair, also streaming with blood from a gash in his head from flying glass. The police began to demand identities—which caused a rapid melting-away of the indigenous crowd. Paddy during this interrogation happened to glance round towards their table; he raced back just in time to seize the wrist of an Arab who had picked up Julia's handbag—the man, he saw, had a wart on his nose. Furious, Lynch wrenched the bag free, and with his other hand took a twisted grip of the folds of the man's robe, yelling at the pitch of his voice to the police—"*Ici!* This is one of them!" Abdul twisted like an eel, but it is impossible to wriggle *out* of a djellaba, with its long sleeves, and Lynch was very strong; a couple of *agents*, delighted to secure at least one prisoner after the outrage, seized Abdul and bore him away. The Irishman's one idea now was to get that infernal piece of rock out of the handbag before the police began looking for papers—turning away, he extracted it and stowed it in an inner pocket and then returned to the bar.

Here the doctor was taking Julia's pulse and lifting her eyelids—he diagnosed shock and concussion, while Lynch showed her passport and *fiche* to the Commandant. At this point a little French pressman appeared and also began taking names, by the simple method of looking over the shoulders of the police while they examined the papers of the casualties. Steve now cut across officialdom.

"Let's get her hospitalised!" he said. "Isn't Casablanca the best place?—she said it was good on hospitals. I have a car right here—I can get her in, fast. This Marrakesh seems a pretty hick town; surely we'd better get her to Casablanca?"

Paddy Lynch was inclined to agree—"But, Mother of God,

there's all her stuff at the hotel!—she won't want that left after her."

"Well, why don't I drive her in, and you collect her things and bring them along, when you've done talking to these police guys? She's sick, and we're wasting time! Give me the *ad*dress, and I'll go."

Both the police and the doctor had by this time got round to the Duke; the doctor put a temporary dressing on the cut in his head—he had already done this for Julia—while the little pressman greedily copied down all the particulars given to the police. Angus, who was coming round gradually, hearing of Steve's plan said—"I could come along, and hold her head steady. Perhaps, Lynch, you would be so good as to collect my gear too and bring it. Oh, yes—and pay my bill." He handed a bundle of notes to Paddy.

So Steve fetched his borrowed car and Julia, still unconscious, was placed along the back seat, her head resting on the Duke's further arm; Mr. Lynch furnished the address of the appropriate hospital, and the American shot off in the best film style.

"What about your things?" Paddy shouted to him at the last moment.

"I'll be back," the airman shouted in reply.

As sometimes happens, the explosion of that bomb on the Djema el F'na really made more noise in England than in Morocco. Londoners are not so prone to listen to the nine-o'clock news as country dwellers, since they are usually having dinner, or at the theatre, or attending a "cocktail *prolongé*", so it was poor Mrs. Monro who first heard of it, sitting at Glentoran over her wretched fire with Jimmy Struthers. She was so upset that she tried to ring up Mrs. Hathaway, but that lady was watching a new French film at the Academy Cinema—"Ask her to ring you back," Struthers prompted, and finally did this himself for his agitated employer.

But next morning a selection of banner headlines announced the episode to every breakfast-table or tray in Britain. "TERRORIST OUTRAGE IN MARRAKESH. TWO BRITISH CASUALTIES" said the sober journals; "SCOTTISH DUKE SERIOUSLY INJURED—GIRL JOURNALIST NOT EXPECTED TO RECOVER" screamed the more scare-minded prints: in either case, their friends soon learned from the smaller type that both the Duke of Ross-shire and Miss Julia Probyn had been blown up in a restaurant in Marrakesh by a bomb, and rushed to hospital in Casablanca, while two other people (fortunately French) had been killed outright; Miss Probyn had serious injuries to her face.

Ringing up Mrs. Hathaway was a habit with others besides poor Ellen Monro—Edina telephoned before 8.30, asking if she might come in at lunch-time, and was told that she could be given lunch; Mr. Consett, more restrainedly putting his call through from the Treasury at 10, was also bidden to luncheon. They found their hostess very much distressed, though still her usual sensible self.

"What was she doing looking for Colin in Marrakesh? Surely that's right inland," Edina said.

Mrs. Hathaway glanced at Mr. Consett.

"I think she thought he might have gone inland," she said smoothly.

"Was she with that Lynch man, do you suppose?" Consett asked.

"Oh, yes—he was taking her to Marrakesh."

"Then he must know something. God, what did I do with his address?"

"I can give it you. But I telegraphed to him this morning to ask for more details."

Edina was turning over the mass of morning papers restlessly, throwing them aside, and jerking her thumb-joint in and out.

"I think I shall go out and see what's happening," she announced suddenly. "After all, she went on our account, and this is pretty rotten for her. One doesn't know what the hospitals are like, or anything."

Mrs. Hathaway looked relieved.

"If you really can get away, that would be splendid," she said. "Geoffrey, can one fly direct to Casablanca?"

Mr. Consett thought B.E.A. to Gibraltar and on would be the best—"Besides, you must have visas for French and Spanish Morocco, and those, as I know to my cost, take ages here, whereas in Tangier you can get them in no time." He added that he had a friend in the Foreign Office who would help to "hurry" the Spanish and International Zone visas.

"All right—I'll go to Tangier. It will take forty-eight hours at least, I suppose, to get all this, and the currency; but I'd better get on to B.E.A. at once. Mrs. H., may I use your telephone?"

"I expect the Consulate-General will help you about telephoning to Casablanca even before you get the visas, as Julia is a British subject," said Mrs. Hathaway.

"Yes, and poor Angus Ross-shire too—he's such a sweet. I'd hate him to be badly hurt."

When the Foreign Office tries it can arrange things rather fast, and it was only three days after her sudden decision when Edina set off by air for Tangier. She rang up Mrs. Hathaway triumphantly just before she left.

"I've got my exes! We've thought up an African lay-out for camel-hair coats for some rather big clients of ours, and they've jumped at it. It may take some time, so I shan't be rushed, and I can go anywhere."

"That's good. But Edina, be sure to telegraph me the moment you've seen her, and let me know, won't you? And about her face."

"*Dear* Mrs. H., of course I will. What did Paddy Lynch say?"

"Only 'Still in hospital injuries less serious than feared firstly,' " said Mrs. Hathaway, laughing rather weakly.

"What a man! *Firstly!*" said Edina with contempt. "Well *I* won't cable you in journalese! God bless—and look after poor Mother."

"Oh, yes—I've promised to go up to her tomorrow, by the way, so telegraph to Glentoran, please."

In fact if Mr. Lynch had delayed his cable to Mrs. Hathaway for another twenty-four hours he would have been able to send a much more reassuring one. Julia's concussion proved to be slight, and her naturally calm, not to say lethargic, nature greatly lessened the effects of the shock; the cut on her forehead, though disfiguring, was not deep enough to require stitches, and was merely strapped up with plaster; on her third day in hospital, when visited by Mr. Lynch she declared herself "as fit as a flea", and demanded to be taken away. "Dr. Gillebeaud says I can go—wait, let's see if we can get him, if you don't believe me. Go and shout for the nurse."

Dr. Gillebeaud when he appeared showed himself to be helplessly under Julia's spell; he pronounced that yes, if Mademoiselle could have reasonable attention, she might leave.

"You can give me reasonable attention, can't you, Paddy darling? Fatimah is *so* good."

"I shall have to push out either Reeder or Keller—they're both staying with me," said poor Mr. Lynch.

"Well, push them out, in God's name! Who's your *old* friend? *Really*, Paddy!"

Keller was pushed out, and Julia returned to her charming ground-floor rooms the same afternoon; Mr. Reeder, whom Paddy rightly judged to be much less flush of foreign cash than the American, remained. The Duke, who had telephoned regularly to the hospital, turned up at the villa almost immediately after Julia's return, to enquire.

"Dear Julia, I would never have believed that anyone could look so lovely with Elastoplast all over their face," he said, kissing her affectionately. "We ought to have you photographed and send a glossy to the advertising Edina; I am sure it would put on sales."

"Well, yes, perhaps. How is your scalp, Angus? Oh, lucky you—only a scalp wound! Though you seem to be doing quite a bit in the bandage line."

"Yes, my sweet; but under it there are *eight* stitches—and oh the horror of having them tweaked out! I am going back to Tangier for *that* martyrdom; my sickly elderly friend is better, but he is insular enough to put all his faith in the English doctor there. So now that you are better, we shall probably sail tomorrow." He turned to Reeder. "What are your plans? If you are returning to Tangier, would you care to pilot us up?"

Reeder looked towards Julia.

"What are you doing, Miss Probyn? Staying here? If you are going back to Tangier I don't think you ought to travel alone."

"Oh, thank you so much, but Steve is going to drive me back to Tangier when I go, the kind creature."

"Then, thank you very much, I should like to come up with you on the yacht," said Reeder to the Duke. "In fact I believe I could take any ship into Tangier harbour blindfold!"

"You'd better come on board with me tonight, then, so that we can sail tomorrow at the hour which the tide, or the moon, or the pilot, or whatever it is dictates," said Angus Ross-shire.

When they had left—

"I don't suppose it will be a ha'porth of use going to see young Bathyadis again, do you?" said Julia.

"No, quite futile. Besides, now that they've gone, I have a bit to tell you. The police are letting it be believed that terrorists threw the bomb, but I think they have a pretty fair idea of what lay behind this particular one."

"Do you mean thrown who *by*, or who *at*?" Julia asked ungrammatically.

"Both. I didn't tell you in the hospital, with all those nurses dodging in and out, but I copped Abdul trying to pinch your bag, and handed him over."

"Goodness, did I leave my bag?"

"Yes, you foolish creature!—and I had to do a nice bit of sleight of hand to get that infernal piece of rock out of it and into my pocket before the police examined your papers. But they grilled Abdul pretty thoroughly, I gather from my friend here, and learned that he was employed by we-know-whom."

"You mean the East Germans?"

"Of course. But Abdul, in a very natural fit of pique—no one *enjoys* being grilled by the French police—seems to have made it abundantly clear to them that others besides his employers were probably exporting strategic minerals without concessions, and that it was the people in this organisation that the Germans were gunning for."

"In fact Colin and the red-haired man?"

"Yes, presumably."

"What did they have to say about that?"

"Not much. The French are always pretty cagey, and out here they've got to be nearly as mute as the Arabs. But unless the British have some top-secret agreement somewhere else, I'm beginning to wonder how much longer the velvet-trunk industry will last."

Julia frowned in thought, as well as she could for the Elastoplast.

"It *must* be official, or why the B. of E.?" she said at last. "But it's all rather funny. Anyhow as far as we are concerned I think the only thing now is to watch the *Finetta*—don't you?"

"Yes—and that house in the Kasbah."

"Of course. Well, the day after tomorrow, Paddy dear, I think I'd better get Steve to drive me back to Tangier."

"Sure you're fit for it? It's about six hours' run, you know."

"Oh, I think so. I do really want to be on the spot, in case they turn up. Maybe Purcell could arrange to have that house in the Kasbah watched for me—I wouldn't put it past him! And I want to go out and see what the Professor has dug up in those graves, if anything."

"You're completely mad, Julia, God help you!" said Mr. Lynch, laughing.

"Well, I should think you'd be glad to be quit of me and my chums, flooding your house out! I hope you realise what an angel you've been."

"I like all your chums—the Duke best perhaps, but Reeder's a grand man, and your poor besotted Yank slave is uncommonly nice too. What'll you do about him?"

"Oh, the soft rub-off that turneth away wrath. I thought the drive would be a good opportunity to get that over with."

"May the Lord have mercy on you for a cold-blooded creature! However, I suppose practice makes perfect."

"That's about it," said Julia equably. "But oh Paddy dear, isn't it *sickening* to have missed even speaking to Colin, when he was within *feet* of us, and we'd been so clever?"

Chapter 15

IN fact the long drive from Casablanca to Tangier, plus the anticipated emotional interlude with poor Steve *en route*, tired Julia more than she had expected. The urgent simplicity and sincerity of the American made the soft rub-off not so easy to administer—Julia, the cool and composed, found herself in tears before she could convince him that she would not marry without love, and that she did not love him "in that way". She was too shaken and exhausted when she arrived at the Espagnola to think of going to Purcell's; all she craved was her bed, where she ordered supper to be served. But to her dismayed surprise she found herself a heroine and a centre of interest; the manager wrung her by the hand, praising God for her preservation; the other occupants of the pension crowded round, full of eager questions—Julia escaped to the manager's office, whence she rang up Mme La Besse.

"Ah *dieu merci* that you are back!—what an escape! I will ring up Lady Tracy at once; she has been in anguish about you—as we all have. But I must tell you that we have found an *intact* grave!—at last! We only began on it today, and the Professor guards it tonight."

"How splendid. Shall I come out tomorrow?"

"But yes, if you are able. *Chère enfant*, how glad I am that you are safe! Now I ring Lady Tracy."

Julia was doing a little hasty unpacking when she was summoned to the telephone again—this time it was Lady Tracy.

"Oh, my dear child, I won't keep you a moment, I'm sure you ought to be in bed, if not in hospital! But I did just want to hear your voice! How merciful that you were not killed, like that poor French policeman, and the Arab waiter—imagine, he was a cousin of 'Abdeslem's."

Julia, rather faintly, made some suitable response, and asked how Lady Tracy was.

"Oh, quite as well as I need to be. And *Hugh* is back—he arrived today; he says the flowers were marvellous further South. When you are up to it you must come and meet him —in fact I think I shall arrange a small sherry-party."

Julia said that would be lovely, and as soon as she could rang off. It amused her that in spite of their genuine pleasure at her safe return, both her elderly friends felt constrained to tell her about their own concerns, of which the grave interested her much more than the advent of Hugh.

In the hall the manager confronted her with a neat little man who implored "but two small minutes" with Mademoiselle, a reporter from the *Mensonge de Tanger*—behind him loomed a tall individual with a slight air of habitual inebriation, who said he represented *World Press*. Julia protested.

"No, *really*, Señor Huerta; I'm too tired. They must go away. I'm sorry, but I won't see *anyone*. Is that understood?" Indignant, she went upstairs.

As she was eating her supper in bed, eagerly fussed over by Natividad, the chambermaid, the porter came up to say that a Señorita below wished to see the Señorita, urgently. Damning all journalists Julia told him that she would see *no one*, and to say that she was away. She made Natividad lock the door for good measure till she had finished her supper; when the maid went out with the tray she slipped in again after a moment with a bunch of flowers, a mixed posy of the sort made by Julia's Berber flower-woman; on the card was written—

"*Très-respectueusement*
J. Purcell."

"Heaven Purcell!" Julia muttered as she closed her eyes.

She woke after thirteen hours of the solid sleep of youth feeling perfectly refreshed, and went round to Mme La Besse in time to drive her out to the site; there she hastened up to see the new grave. It was some distance down the slope of the ridge on the farther side, above the lagoon, and Julia's first glance as she topped the rise was for the *Finetta*. Yes, there she lay—but no washing fluttered from her rigging, the cooking apparatus had disappeared from her deck, and the two Arabs were swabbing her paintwork vigorously. Ah!—Mr. Smith had presumably returned, or at least was expected. She must see Purcell tonight and try to fix something about having the house in the Kasbah watched, she thought, as she descended the slope to where Professor Carnforth, rather bleary-eyed, was directing the Berbers' operations—a sleeping-bag and a thermos lay under a rock. Julia had bethought her to bring her own thermos with fresh coffee and some buttered rolls from the Espagnola; the weary man sat down and consumed these gratefully while Julia peered into the partly excavated chamber. In a wall-niche on the left the end of one coffin was already exposed; it appeared to be covered with Egyptian hieroglyphics, and Julia went out into the sun again to ask about this. The Professor expounded, between mouthfuls of *croissant*: yes, certainly; the Phoenicians constantly used Egyptian coffins, which they purchased ready-made—there was a continual passage of vessels to and fro along the whole coast, and what easier than for a quinquereme, coming in ballast to pick up a cargo of wine, oil, and pickled fish at the factory, to bring down a score or so of coffins from the Nile Delta?

They made good progress that day. Three more coffins were quite literally un-earthed, but by the afternoon the Professor was yawning so pitifully that Julia volunteered to take that night's watch. The grave was just at the stage when it would be most tempting to the local Berbers, and Mme La Besse, who had often slept in partly excavated graves in her time, told the Professor that if the old Spanish foreman stayed with her Miss Probyn would be quite all right—he might not resist Berber bribes alone, but he would certainly guard her faithfully. "He can sleep in that empty grave a few yards away, and she can shout to him in need." So it was settled that Julia should take Mme La Besse home early, get a few hours' sleep, and drive out to relieve the Professor at eleven.

This suited Julia perfectly. After dropping Mme La Besse she parked the Chrysler outside the Espagnola, ran swiftly down the familiar route through the Gran Socco and the Medina, and walked into Purcell's Bar—there, at her old table, sat the Duke, Reeder, and Edina.

"Here she is, herself!" Angus Ross-shire exclaimed, rising. "So you've got her at last, Edina."

Edina had risen too, and rather to Julia's surprise kissed her warmly.

"I was beginning to think you'd been kidnapped as well as bombed," she said—"I couldn't find you anywhere."

"But Edina, whatever next? When did you turn up, and why?"

"When, yesterday morning—usual plane hold-up at Gib. Why, to look after you—the papers practically had you dead, and everyone was mad with worry; all our fault too, of course. But you don't look too bad," Edina said, staring rather anxiously at Julia. "Will it show?"

"Far from looking bad, a photograph of her as an ad: for Elastoplast, we thought," said Angus, who had an affection for his own jokes. "Whisky, Julia? Now you're no longer concussed, alk can do no harm."

"Yes, thank you, Angus. But Edina, why couldn't you find me? I'm at the Espagnola."

"My dear Julia, you're *not*! I've been there over and over again, and either you hadn't come, or you'd gone again. I know my French isn't much good, but that manager's worse! 'She has not come'; 'she has come, but she has gone'; 'she is gone again'—the place is a perfect looney-bin!" said Edina indignantly. Mr. Reeder laughed.

"All very well for you!" Edina said to him, in a tone which rather startled Julia—it was the tart casual note of reproof usually reserved for one's intimates. "And Casablanca was just as bad," she pursued, turning to her cousin again. "I try your chum Lynch—he's at the Bank; by the time I've found out *what* Bank, he's gone to lunch! When I get him after his wretched lunch, he says you've left for the Espagnola! Well I've told you how useful *that* was."

Julia, sipping whisky, laughed rather weakly. A little checking of times made what had happened clear. Edina had first called at the Espagnola just half-an-hour before she and Steve arrived; the second time she, Julia, had refused to see her, thinking that she was a reporter. And today she had been out at the site, when Edina, twice, went again. "Just a second," Julia said when this had finally been elucidated—she left them, went over to the bar, and held out her hand across it to Purcell.

"Thank you for the flowers, very much," she said.

"You are really all right? This will not be too disfiguring?" the half-caste asked, like Edina with an anxious glance at her forehead.

"Usen't women to marry German officers for their duelling scars?" Julia said. "Please don't worry, Mr. Purcell."

"I warned you that it would be speculative, but I never thought anything like this would happen," he said ruefully— then he leant across the bar and lowered his voice. "Did you see him?"

"Not to speak to—the bomb interrupted us! But I have an idea that they'll soon come here—could you keep tabs on that house in the Kasbah for me?"

"Oh, they are back—they arrived yesterday."

"Well, look, now I *must* see him"—Julia was beginning, when Angus Ross-shire's arm was slung round her shoulder.

"Precious Julia, come back and drink. And Mr. Purcell, to whom you naturally want to talk, must for once break all his rules and join us. Purcell, you can't refuse to drink Miss Probyn's health."

Purcell did not refuse. There was no one else in the bar, and he sat with them, saying little but smiling quietly, while Edina expounded to Julia her secondary concern with camel-hair, and hence with camels.

"Oh, for camels you must go to Settat—it's full of them." She explained where Settat was, and Edina said that she should hire a car and drive there from Casablanca—"The sky, thank God, is the limit, where expenses are concerned."

"In that case do go on to Marrakesh—it's so beautiful."

"My *dear* Julia!—and have her blown up too? What a notion!"

"I don't think Edina will be blown up, Angus," said Julia, slanting a glance at Purcell, who gleamed at her in response.

"I remember saying, at this very table, that we should all pile up in Marrakesh, but not, I hoped, be wrecked," said the Duke. "In fact you and I, Julia, damn nearly did pile up there for good."

The cheerful inconsequent talk went on, but Julia noticed presently that Edina and Mr. Reeder returned to what was apparently an unfinished conversation about sheep, marginal land, hill-cattle subsidies, and similar highly technical subjects; while the Duke and Purcell discussed what forms of drink paid best in bars. When other customers, including the bunch, came in Purcell had to leave the party, and Reeder startled Julia by asking them all to dine with him at the Minzah "to celebrate". The Minzah is Tangier's most expensive hotel, and as they walked there through the picturesque crowds and the vivid lamp-lit evening, in twos—Edina and Reeder, Julia and Angus Ross-shire—Julia expressed slight misgivings at this extravagance on the part of the *Vidago's* mate.

"Oh, don't worry about that. I found out about him on the way up. He's one of the Northumberland Reeders; they have a most lovely place in the Cheviots. He took to the sea, I gather, because he can't get on with his father; no wonder,

I met him once, and he's a most cantankerous old party. There's an older brother who'll come into the property, but a remote aunt of Mollie's married one of them, and left all she had to this man—it all came back to me afterwards. He can afford to feed us on caviare, if he wants to! But he's a most splendid fellow—Edina will be lucky indeed if she gets him."

Julia was startled a second time.

"Goodness, do you think there's any question of that?"

"Well watch them. I should say Yes. They haven't done badly in forty-eight hours."

"How did they meet?"

"She was in Purcell's when Reeder and I went in the morning we arrived."

Julia did watch the pair during dinner—at which in fact they were given caviare—and decided that Angus, sharp old thing, was not so far out. She recalled the mate's interest in Edina, and his questions about her, on board the *Vidago*; in particular what he had said when she told him that her cousin was black-haired and slender—"If I meet her, I'm sunk!" It was plain that Mr. Reeder, if not actually sinking, had already taken a heavy list.

It was easy to escape early from the party on the score of fatigue. The Duke drove her to the Espagnola, where she collected her duffle-coat, torch, a thermos of coffee and some food and wine; at the last moment she snatched a pillow off her bed, threw the lot into the Chrysler, and roared off into the Moroccan night.

The Spanish foreman rose stiffly out of the shadows by the shed at the site, and helped to carry her effects up onto the headland. By night it was a strange, out-of-this-world place: the waning moon cast strong shadows from those fantastic rocks onto the white sand, making it hard to recognise the now familiar way up, and on the further slope they had considerable difficulty in finding the right grave—Julia finally stood and shouted "Professor *Carn*forth," till he emerged and led them to the spot. He then went off; the old foreman crept into a neighbouring tomb, and Julia proceeded to arrange her effects in the one just vacated by the Professor. It amused her to wedge her cup and thermos into one of the coffin niches, opening like oven-mouths along the walls; indeed the tomb was altogether the strangest sleeping-place imaginable. The light from her torch, propped on the floor, showed the outlines of the sloping slabs of the roof and the dressed stones of the walls through the pale stucco, clean and fresh in the upper part of the small chamber as when it was put on nearly two thousand years before, while in their dark niches along the sides the Phoenician dead lay quiet all round her. She put her pillow at the head of the Professor's sleeping-bag, still comfortably warm from his tenancy, and then went and sat outside to smoke a last cigarette. It was perfectly still, and not in the least cold; a faint rumble of snoring indicated old Fernando's resting-place, but otherwise, except for the distant roar of the Atlantic on the sand-bar, there was not a sound; below her the lagoon gleamed like dull metal between its dark shores. Hullo, there were lights on the *Finetta*, whose white shape just showed away to her left; the port-holes were not lit up, but small lights moved about her decks, as from torches or lanterns. How tricky the moonlight was!—Julia would have sworn that the yacht was lying closer inshore than yesterday, but in that deceptive illumination it was impossible to be sure. Promising herself to look out often during the night, in case Mr. Smith was up to some funny-business, she turned in, snuggling down in the Professor's flea-bag among corpses nearly two thousand years old.

She had not meant to sleep, but she did. She was awakened by a small noise quite close by; cocking an ear, she decided that it was at the entrance to the tomb. Silently, a little frightened, she groped for her torch, turned it towards the doorway, and switched on The sharp white light revealed a figure in Berber dress, on all fours at the foot of the short flight of steps; but it was an English voice that ejaculated sharply—"Good God! Who's that?" Under the hood the face was that of Colin, now without his Low beard.

"It's Julia," said Julia calmly, lowering the blinding light a little. "Don't you think you might come in and have a talk, Colin, since you *are* here? I've been looking for you for a long time."

"I know you have, and a nice mess-up you've made of things," the young man growled. "Anyhow, what the devil are you doing here at this time of night?"

"Guarding this tomb from marauding Berbers, like you," said Julia, with a giggle.

Perhaps it was the slow gurgling sound of Julia's giggle, an infectious source of amusement from his earliest childhood, that caused Colin to relax his hostile attitude—anyhow he crawled further in, sat down with his back against the wall, and said—"Why guarding?"

"Tomb's half-excavated—probably that coffin behind your head is full of gold jewellery."

Colin grunted.

"Are you all right?" he asked. "I thought you'd still be in hospital."

"Not too bad—poor face a bit the worse for wear."

"Let's see." Julia turned the torch onto her forehead.

"Golly, that's big," the young man said, leaning across and fingering the long line of plaster—the intimacy of the gesture, and the simplicity with which he made it, carried Julia straight back to Glentoran, and the long happy days there, with Colin, always Colin, as her inseparable and dearest companion. "Will it show permanently?" he asked—like everyone else, Julia reflected.

"'Fraid so. But I don't much mind."

"I *hated* having to go off and leave you on the ground like that," he said unexpectedly. "I didn't even know if you were

275

dead or not. But we simply had to get away at once. Who was that Yank who stood guard over you?"

"Oh, a *frightfully* nice creature called Steve Keller—I mean, I never saw him keeping guard, but he was the only Yank about, so it must have been him."

"*How* nice? Nice enough to marry?" Again Colin Monro's words were unexpected, and his eyes were fixed on her face, in the rather dim glow from the torch, now lying on the earthen floor.

"No—I refused him yesterday." As she spoke Julia felt about among the pile of provisions beside the sleeping-bag for the bottle of wine.

"What about a little drink?" she said, holding it out. "I've got eats too, if you'd like some. Frankly, I'm hungry."

"Greedy, you mean!—you always were greedy, Julia. Yes, we might as well have a mouthful—I'm pretty peckish, too. But I mustn't stay long."

Julia produced buttered rolls and slices of her favourite raw ham; the wine they drank from her cup, in turns. It was a happy little meal, eaten in those highly peculiar surroundings; the past came flooding back—other meals they had eaten together, in caves along a Highland shore, or in ruined houses to get out of the wind when out after black-game in January: "Do you remember?" they said to each other. Julia had a curious feeling that Colin was perhaps clinging to the past to avoid the difficulties of the present; but at last he asked— "How has that new salmon-pool on the Toran worked out, that we made just before I came away? Did the logs hold?"

"Oh yes, and the gravel piled up against them splendidly; Uncle John got no end of fish there the last two years." She paused and then said—"You know he's dead?"

"Of course I know—I see the papers," he said, half sulkily.

"Well, *can* you come home, Colin? That's what I've been trying to get near enough to you to ask for the last two months!

Someone's got to run it—you can't let Glentoran just go down the drain, and you know Aunt Ellen simply isn't able."

"Why can't Edina do it?"

"Because she's earning £1,500 a year, and they need that money—she makes your mother an allowance!"

"Fifteen hundred! Good God! What at?"

"Advertising. And her screw's going up to £2000 this summer, with any luck."

Colin whistled at the figure.

"Two thousand a year for *advertising*!" he said. "Edina always was a great apostle of the phoney."

"That's not fair—she isn't," said Julia hotly. "You're just being a jealous beast, Colin, as you often—not always—were. Anyhow, *can* you come home?" she persisted.

Colin began to jerk his thumb in and out.

"I'm simply not sure," he said. "In the ordinary way this job would have gone on for quite a time, but you've managed to stir up so much dust that we may have to chuck it."

"Whatever dust have *I* stirred up?"

"What haven't you, you mean! First diddling old Bathyadis into spilling the beans to you—though I gather that was mostly St John's fault, silly old man; he really is too old for this job now, only he's so damned good with the Arabs. But what was much worse was your goings-on in Casa and Marrakesh. Affaires Indigènes aren't *quite* blind, and when two foreigners start displaying so much interest in the camionnette, they naturally did a bit of checking-up on their own account."

"Did they tie in Monsieur Smith with Herr Nussbaumer from Martin at the garage?" Julia asked, beginning to gurgle again.

"Goodness, *that* was how you found out, was it?" he asked, startled. "But how did you get onto the name of Smith?"

"Seeing the *Finetta* in the lagoon here, when we were digging —so I went in and asked Lloyd's man what name she was registered in."

"You infernal diggers!" he growled. "But I still don't see how you traced the car."

Julia explained about Moshe, and the capture of his note-book—"but it cost 20,000 francs to get the number of the camionnette out of Martin. I hope Affaires Indigènes got it for less."

"You bet they got it for nothing! But Julia, don't you see that your Jew tailer will have tipped off the lot he was working for that you'd got his book? So you can bet they kept an eye on you both in Casablanca and Marrakesh, and knew you'd gone to the Bureau in both places."

"I see that all right, but—so what?"

"So a bomb, silly! Try to mop us up before we could be hauled in and spill what we knew about *them*, as they knew we damn well would, of course, if we got into trouble ourselves."

"But Colin"—Julia was trying, not very successfully, to keep all this straight. "Is what you and 'Smith' are doing legal or illegal?" she asked bluntly.

"Illegal here, of course, but perfectly legal in Paris, because—" he broke off.

"But how—?" Julia was beginning, but he interrupted her.

"Leave all that, would you mind? Forget I said it."

"Oh, very well." She reflected for a moment while she got out a cigarette, and handed her case to Colin, who took one eagerly. "More wine?"—she held out the bottle again. As they drank in turns—

"You don't half do yourself well, Julia!" the young man said, with an impish grin. "Still the same old greedy-gub, luckily for me! But tell me, why are you mixed up in this archaeological racket?"

"My dear Colin, I had to *live* while I was hanging about after you, so tiresomely elusive!—so I took a job as secretary to an archaeologist."

"Oh, the old La Besse. Well I must say she has a *toupet*, to make you come and sleep in her tombs!"

"She didn't—I offered. But come to that, Colin, what are *you* doing, creeping into our tombs in fancy dress?"

"You mind your own business!" he grumbled, with a return to his familiar youthful surliness when in a difficulty. Julia had smoothed this over a hundred times; now she poured him out a cup of coffee, and as he drank—

"I bet I know!" she said gleefully. "You've got masses of velvet trunks full of Astridite hidden in tombs on this slope, all ready to go on board the yacht, and you just happened to hit the wrong tomb. What sucks for you!"

"Julia, I shall slap you in a minute!"

"No, no—don't slap Julia, fresh from the jaws of death! But aren't I right?"

"Damn you, yes, as a matter of fact. I remember I never thought you as stupid as everyone else did, even as a child," he said reflectively—"you always had a way of hopping onto things. Remember the time you spotted the rifle of those deer-poachers, and got Andy Mac to take the contact-breaker out of the distributor of their car, so they couldn't get away?" He laughed and thumped her knee.

"Yes, of course. So you *have* got some stuff here? What a joke!"

"Well, we had to bring the last lot here—we've had to pass up young Bathyadis, with all this fuss. His place is almost certainly being watched." The young man explained how Mr. St John had managed to get word to them down in the South, through trustworthy Arab channels, that Julia was not only on their track, but had also met young Bathyadis; but this information reached them too late to prevent the despatch of a camel-convoy to Casablanca with two-thirds of the fruits of that period of digging.

"Oh, that was the caravan we met in the Djebelet," Julia interrupted blithely. "So handy—a trunk fell off and burst."

"I know it did," the young man said wryly. "You've had the devil's own luck, all along, Julia."

"Well, you silly, it's all your own fault. Why couldn't you at least answer letters, and all those ads? Then no one would have come chasing you."

"In our show we aren't supposed to give our whereabouts away," Colin said, rather pompously.

"And what may 'our show' be? One of these Protean forms of the Secret Service, I suppose, since the Bank of England backs you up."

"Julia, you are a devil! What do you know about the Bank of England?"

"Oh, one has one's contacts," said Julia, airing her favourite tease-phrase. "Never mind, I'll forget that too if you want me to," she added hastily, as he seized her wrist with some violence. "Ow! Don't hurt me, Colin—that's your old nasty trick. Anyhow, how do you get the trunks aboard through all those reed-beds?"

"In the dinghy. There's a good firm track on the east of this ridge that a jeep can come up, and we man-handle the stuff up and into the tombs one night, and get it on board the next."

"And where do you take it when it's on board?"

"Out to sea, where we meet a boat, and trans-ship. But you'd better forget that, too," he said hurriedly.

"Oh, I'll forget anything you like. Who sails the *Finetta* on these jaunts?"

"*Me*. I'm the master now," Colin said, with rather touching pride. "Isn't she a lovely boat, Julia? Very different to the poor old *Thomasina*! Do you remember how you piled her up on Gigha?"

"I *didn't*! You were steering!" said Julia indignantly. "At least, you were holding my arm."

At that, laughing, the young man leant over and held her arm again. "Oh Julia, what fun we've had!"

"Yes, heavenly fun—and please God we'll have more, Colin dear."

At that he edged up the tomb, wriggled in beside her, and sliding an arm round her waist rubbed his cheek against hers, confidingly.

"It's good to see you," he said. "Such a long time away. Julia—" he stopped.

"Yes?"

"Don't you see that one reason why I didn't answer the letters was all that absolute *beastliness* about Grove? I couldn't know how you'd all feel about that. But none of us but him knew a thing about it—I *swear* that."

"Nor did any of us know a thing about it—it never got into the English papers at all."

"Didn't it? How extraordinary. Oh, well, I suppose Torrens must have fixed that."

"So *that's* the name that begins with Tor! Good-oh—another point cleared up," said Julia with satisfaction. "He's your boss, is he?"

"Well, he was starting to work up this show out here just about the time that Grove got copped; we others were pretty fed up with smuggling, with *that* label tied on to us, and didn't know what on earth to do with the boat—I had a third share in her, of course. But he thought it might be handy to have a yacht for this sort of job, with someone who could sail her, and knew the coast, so he bought us out and re-registered her. *How* he got onto me, I really can't think, for we were lying pretty doggo."

"Purcell, I should imagine," said Julia.

He turned to stare at her.

"I believe you're right. I never thought of that." He paused. "But how do *you* know Purcell?"

"Oh, just a regular client. It's the nicest bar in Tangier."

"That isn't why you suggested what you did," he said suspiciously. "Nice bars aren't the same thing as—well, contacts."

"Aren't they? I should have thought they made the very

best kind of contact," said Julia. "Anyhow, I contacted Edina there this evening."

"Edina? What on earth is *she* doing out here?"

"She flew out to see how I was. Some people quite minded my nearly being killed."

"Julia, don't be idiotic! I told you I hated having to leave you there on the floor. What do you think I should have done?"

"Socked Mr. B. Torrens one over the head and told him to go to hell, and then succoured me," said Julia readily.

"Nonsense! Angus Ross-shire was there to succour you. I saw him—and your Yank. You had plenty of succour, and I had a job to finish. So put a sock in it," the young man said firmly.

Julia was pleased; this stout-heartedness was new in Colin, who used to be unduly nervous and sensitive. She was all the more touched when he pulled her to him and kissed her lightly on the cheek. "Oh, darling, there never was anyone like you, for all your monstrousness—and there never will be," he murmured in her ear. Then, in the manner of men, he let her go, reached for the torch, and looked at his watch. "God! It's half-past one! I must go. I wonder where the devil those other tombs can be, with the stuff in."

"I bet I can find them—there are three or four half-right from this, a bit downhill; but don't make a noise, because of Fernando."

"Who the devil is he?"

"The foreman at the site—my watch-dog! He's asleep in a tomb a bit above this."

"Damnation! He's bound to hear my chaps."

"I tell you what—when we've found the place I'll go up and sit outside his cubby-hole, and if he does hear anything I'll tell him it's me, and keep him occupied. Come on."

They crept out—Julia led the way downhill and to the right, where sure enough the light of her torch presently

282

revealed, in three tombs, the rich gleam of velvet studded with silver, stowed in the niches intended for dead Phoenicians. She began to laugh softly.

"What is it?"

"The whole thing. It's so funny. Never mind—cancel laugh! How do you summon your merry men?"

"Whistle," said Colin, putting two fingers to his lips. She snatched his hand away.

"You can't do that, idiot—or not till I've fixed Fernando; but whatever I do he'll hear a whistle. Try my torch—press the button and flash it."

The young man did so, and an answering wink of light presently appeared below them.

"That seems all right—I expect they'll come up. Now you buzz off and muzzle your infernal watch-dog."

"Yes, but how do I see you again? There's masses more to talk about. When do you get back from your cruise?"

"This evening, probably. Where are you staying?"

"The Espagnola."

"Oh, I know. Is Edina there too? I'm not all that keen on seeing her just yet, till I know more where we are."

"No, she's at the Minzah—on expense account!"

"God Almighty, what a girl! Well look, J. dear, I'll come round and see you."

"I'll be at the site all day—I'm a wage-slave! But I can be in after supper. No, I can't—I'm dining with Angus on the yacht tonight. Oh, dear, what can we do?"

"Wait till tomorrow night. I'll leave word with Purcell, one way or the other—how's that?"

"Fine." As she spoke a sound of feet was audible on the slope close below them.

"Here they come! Breeze off!" said Colin hastily.

Julia moved away uphill, and sat down outside Fernando's gîte. A thin veil of cloud was obscuring the moon, but she could just distinguish figures with objects on their shoulders moving down towards the lagoon, and then she heard the splash of oars. Fernando's snores came steadily and undisturbed to her where she sat, and continued to do so while again, and yet again, shadowy figures crept up the slope, and descended it bowed under gleaming burdens. She sat there, happy, quiet —still moved and warmed by the recent presence of Colin, and his evident affection; darling creature, he hadn't changed a bit!—or only for the better. She waited till she saw port and starboard lights run up on the *Finetta's* rigging, and heard the groan of the winch and the rattle of the chain as the anchor came up; then she went back to her tomb, crept into the Professor's flea-bag, and went to sleep. When she woke in the morning the lagoon was empty.

Chapter 16

JULIA slept so well in her tomb—"Like the dead, really," she observed to Professor Carnforth when following her example he came up to her with coffee and rolls—that on hearing that he proposed to open one of the coffins on the spot that afternoon she insisted on returning to the site then, perfectly refreshed after a bath, a couple of hours snoozing, and lunch. By the time she arrived the coffin had been brought down to the shed; Carnforth, ingenious man, had purchased a hammock from one of the ships' chandlers in the port, in which it could be slung down the steep slope between the rocks without injury. It now lay on an improvised table in the little courtyard, and Mme La Besse, Julia and Fernando crowded round, seething with curiosity and pressed from behind by all eight Berbers, who breathed heavily down their necks, as the lid was raised. Carnforth, who was experienced as well as ingenious, had arranged with the archaeological section of the Administration to have two *sergents de ville* of the Zone Police sent out, whom he posted himself at the tomb to mount guard while he was busy with the coffin, lest the well-informed local villagers should attempt a daylight raid. "No one came near you last night?" he had asked Julia when he went up to relieve her. "Not a soul," she told him blandly.

The "funerary furniture", as archaeologists call it, fully came up to Julia's ignorant but eager expectations as the Professor, with infinite care, lifted out object after object and laid them on cotton-wool in a large cardboard dressbox. Two small terra-cotta figurines of deities—one was Ashtaroth, serpent-entwined. A tiny amulet, to ward off evil spirits; a hand-mirror with an exquisite design on the back; a minute delicate cosmetic-box. "Poor love, she used rouge," Julia said, turning it in her hands and noting the faint trace of colour

285

within. At last came the jewellery. Clearly the dust within this coffin was that of a woman, for out came a pair of ear-rings, crescent moons hung on slender chains; a fine gold bracelet, to fit the narrowest of wrists; a couple of rings. Finally, after much blowing into the coffin, and soft sweepings with an old shaving-brush, the Professor lifted out a magnificent necklace.

"Mon Dieu!" exclaimed Mme La Besse. "That was worth the trouble!"

"Do let me try it on," said Julia, opening her flap-jack and propping it against the coffin-lid; she held the jewel round her own throat and peered into the tiny mirror. "Suit me a treat," she said. The Professor laughed.

He decided that all the remaining coffins should be taken back to Tangier that same afternoon, and placed in safety in the Museum. The hammock was called into play again to bring them down, and Julia, accompanied by one of the police sergeants, was kept busy driving the Chrysler in and out with these unwonted passengers, dead Phoenicians, in the back. She tore to and fro at a shameless pace, with dinner on the *Frivolity* in view; besides if possible she wanted a word with Purcell—the rendezvous was to be at the Bar. In the end she had no time to change—clean stockings, fresh sandals, a hurried wash and face-do, and she spun off in a taxi.

Only Purcell was there. "Beaten them to it, thank goodness!" she exclaimed, dropping into a chair.

"You look exhausted," the man said. "I think you should have a whisky."

"Yes, I will. Thank you. But let him get it"—she said, as the new Moor appeared. "I want to speak to you."

Purcell at once came to her table.

"I've seen him!" she said, her face alight.

"Excellent. Where?"

"In a tomb!" she brought out triumphantly. But the gleam in the half-caste's face told its own story. "Oh, you know that too! There's no surprising you," she said, with a *moue*.

"Indeed I am surprised, for how in the world came *you* there, at such an hour?"

"Oh, I was guarding one of our tombs, full of lovely coffins, and he came in by mistake."

"This was rather imprudent, if you will forgive me for saying so—you should surely have been in bed, after your accident."

"No, I slept very well, except while he was there. Oh, such jewellery!—we opened one of the coffins this afternoon."

Purcell ignored the coffins.

"Did you meet the other?"

"Cold-blooded fish Torrens? No, and I don't want to!"

"He is very nice," the half-caste said, smiling.

Julia in her turn ignored this statement.

"Listen, dear Mr. Purcell—tell me something quickly, before the others come. It *was* you who put him onto Colin, after all the stink about Grove, wasn't it?"

"Did your cousin tell you this?" Purcell asked.

"No—I told him! But it's true, isn't it?"

"Yes, it is true."

She looked at him in silence for a moment. Then—

"Well look—now that the whole thing seems to be in process of being broken wide open, can't you indulge me a little, and tell me just *where* you come in?"

He gave one of his rare laughs.

"Since you will quite certainly find it out for yourself if I don't, yes, I will. I have for a considerable time—shall we say acted in concert with?—the British Intelligence people. After all, I am a British subject."

"Really?"

"Yes. I was born in Edinburgh—or rather Leith. And when that most disagreeable character Grove got caught I was sorry for the other three boys, who were perfectly innocent; I guessed most of their capital was in their boat, but the ill-repute round her name made her unusable for ordinary harmless smuggling."

"Was Grove in her from the start?" Julia asked.

"No, he only joined them about two years ago—tools ready to his dirty hand!" Purcell said bitterly. "He bought out one of the others, who was short of cash, and re-registered the yacht in his own name; then he started picking up drugs here or in Ceuta and ran them to Marseilles, where he was spotted somehow—and Interpol and the local Sûreté got to work. He was caught here. But I knew that Major Torrens was starting this new enterprise just then, and was on the look-out for a boat, and someone to sail her who knew the coast; your cousin was far the most competent of the lot, so I recommended him. He's a born sailor."

"How did you know that?" the girl asked.

"I was born in a port, and I have been at sea myself; I heard them talking—and also I made enquiries. That is how it happened, Miss Probyn." He paused, and suddenly laughed again.

"What's funny?" Julia enquired.

"Well, when this was arranged, it was necessary to cause all three of them to disappear rather suddenly. The Major had the other two shipped home, but the Sûreté here, which is headed by an Englishman, are still looking for '*ce jeune brigand Monro*', while in fact he is in the pay of the British Government."

Julia's laughter at this revelation was still resounding through the bar when the door opened to admit the Duke, Edina and Mr. Reeder—it was so loud and hearty that it startled them.

"Goodness, Julia, what is it?" Edina asked.

"Mr. Purcell was telling me a funny story," said Julia, dabbing at her eyes. "Angus, I do apologise for not having changed, but I was terrified of being late."

"What have you been doing to make you late, beautiful and dear Julia?"

"Chauffeuring the dead."

"My dear child, what *can* you mean?" Angus asked.

"Yes, literally. Phoenician corpses. I've brought in six; the dust of ages is in my hair."

"It suits it," said Angus, kissing the top of her head. "Everything suits you—even plaster! But please amplify this extraordinary statement of yours. Why do corpses, even Phoenician ones, require 'carriage-exercise', as my grandmother used to call it?"

Julia's account of the unrifled tomb, the Egyptian coffins, the business of getting them down and the jewellery in the one so far opened kept the party going all through drinks, and during a good part of dinner on the *Frivolity*, to which they chugged across the harbour in a neat fast launch. Angus and his fellow tax-dodgers did themselves quite well, Julia thought, as a smart steward in a white jacket handed round excellent food, and the other dodgers were, as he had said, pleasant harmless people enough; but she could not help recognising in all of them a certain rather pitiful nostalgia for a less comfortable, perhaps, but more *directed* way of life. The one they led was entirely pointless except, in the Duke's case anyhow, to rescue enough money from penal taxation to educate his children and preserve the property on which his family had lived for seven centuries. Beastly war; and beastly social revolution, Julia thought to herself, remembering Murphy and his fellow-dockers and their private plane to Belfast. What values were *they* upholding to compare with the learning, the benevolence, the unpaid public service and the patronage of the arts which even she had seen obtaining at the Castle? "Prize-fights", "the pictures", and "the telly"—the very names, so completely ignoring their classical origins, betrayed a sordid lowering of the standards which humanity had held in esteem for centuries past.

In spite of these gloomy sociological reflections, she found time to keep an eye on her cousin and the mate of the *Vidago*. Clearly they were going ahead at a rate of knots—and presently Edina threw out, with elaborate casualness, that she had arranged for Mr. Reeder to accompany her as courier for her journey southward in search of camels. She would have to pick up a photographer in Casablanca, but he would probably be some terrible dago, "or a Moor with sheik tendencies". "One must have a man with one in these Moslem countries, Angus says," Edina pronounced seriously—"and Mr. Reeder speaks Spanish. I had enough of Hispanidad at your pub, Julia, to last me for life." Anyhow, she added airily, it would all go to expense account. Julia shot a glance at Reeder; he raised his thick eyebrows at her with a comical look of resignation—happy resignation. "What did I tell you?" those eyebrows signalled—Julia grinned sympathetically in response.

When the launch took the three guests ashore Julia was struck afresh by the calm, natural manner in which Edina sent Mr. Reeder to fetch a taxi; when it came—"I'm taking Julia home," she said. "Where shall we drop you?" Mr. Reeder said he should walk—"Probably look in at Purcell's."

"Give him my love," said Julia.

In the taxi—"Do you like him?" Edina asked, her thumb beginning to jerk in and out.

"Yes, enormously—but do keep your damned joint quiet, Edina! It makes such a sickening noise!"

Edina laughed, and held her right hand in her left.

"It—it seems to be brewing up a bit," she said, with unwonted hesitation, almost shyness.

"Brewing up! Edina, it's practically on the boil! But how do *you* feel?"

"Well, as a matter of fact, I feel an inclination," Edina said, at which Julia laughed loudly.

"J., don't be coarse," her cousin protested.

"Sorry, dearest. I really do like him terribly."

"And this trip," Edina pursued, with more of her usual firm manner, "will give one an idea of what he's like to work with, and—well, of what he's worth."

"Worth in what way?"

"Well, I've absolutely no use for men who try on extra-marital relations; I know it's done, all the time, but I *despise*

290

it. If he 'propositions' me on this trip, which is a business arrangement, he's out."

Julia pondered.

"A test, in fact?" Edina nodded. "Rather a stiff one, isn't it?"

"I want it to be stiff!" Edina said—there were centuries of Presbyterian ancestors in her voice.

The taxi drew up at the Pension.

"Come in and sit with me while I get into bed—we'll have a cuentra," Julia coaxed.

"Isn't it rather late?"

"Eleven?—they'll only just be sitting down to dinner," said Julia. "We keep *horas espagnolas* here!"

Upstairs—"But Edina, if you marry, what about your job?" Julia asked, peeling off her clothes and flinging on a night-gown. "Golly, how good it is to be in a bed again!" she exclaimed as she lay back on the pillows.

"Weren't you in bed last night?" her cousin asked in surprise.

"No—in a flea-bag in that tomb! Push the bell, Edina." Natividad appeared on the instant—undoubtedly she had been hovering outside. "Cuentra, Nati—*prontito. La fiasca.*"

"Julia, you're utterly mad! You said you had to leave Philip's party early last night because you were tired."

"Well one has to say something. Anyhow bother me and the tomb—what *about* your job? Ah, *muchas gracias*, Nati. Pour out, Edina, like a kind creature—Thanks. Now go on—your job."

"Being married and having lots of children is an infinitely better job than fooling people into buying things they don't really need," Edina pronounced vigorously. "And besides"— she paused for a moment—"it might be a sort of double job. He—Philip—knows everything there is to know about running a place like Glentoran; so if we can't find Colin, or he won't come home if we do, he could do it perfectly—and what's more I believe he'd like to. Which would put paid to *that* worry. Oh, by the way," she went on, with a rapid and (Julia

291

guessed) deliberate switch of subject, "Angus has a story that you thought you spotted Colin in Marrakesh just before the bomb."

Julia hesitated for a moment. No, until Colin was willing to meet Edina she ought not to say anything about him.

"Well, yes, actually I thought I did, but just then I got blown up," she said. They both laughed. "So now I'm a bit concussed about it all."

Next day a note arrived from Lady Tracy, bidding Julia to a sherry-party two days hence. "The *Frivolity* party are all coming, and Angus Ross-shire tells me you have a most lovely girl cousin staying with you—do please bring her too. Pray ask her to excuse me for not writing to her, but I have stupidly forgotten her name. Hugh will be there, so you will meet him at last—I am so glad! And he says he is bringing a charming young friend of his, who goes with him on his botanical trips." There was a P.S. "I do hope you are *resting*. Don't let Clémentine work you too hard in her enthusiasm—enthusiasts have no mercy."

In fact Julia was resting that day. She found herself surprisingly tired after her broken night in the grave, and all the driving to and fro on top of it; the coffins were safe in the Museum, and she spent most of the day lying on her bed and writing to Mrs. Hathaway. She had told Edina not to come in the evening, so as to leave the field free for Colin, but he turned up about five. This second meeting was calm and easy; but presently Julia asked why Astridite had marks like the bark of a tree on it?

"How do you know that?" Colin asked.

For answer Julia drew her precious lump, which she had recovered from Paddy Lynch, out of her handbag.

"I say, you oughtn't to cart it round like that! It's radioactive, you know. How long have you had it?"

"Since we met the caravan."

"Oh, only about a fortnight. All the same I shouldn't." He

took it from her and tossed it out of the window, where it landed in a bed of freesias under a palm.

"Are you going to leave it there?"

"No—better not." He ran downstairs and Julia saw him stamp it into the freesias with his heel.

"I'm not an expert, but it's stuff to be handled fairly carefully," he said on his return. "I expect that's too small to do any harm, and it was in your bag anyway."

"Oh, dear, I did like it! But Colin, if it's bad for me, what about the camels?—and the boat?"

"The camels only carry it for a few days, and it's always taken off them at night—and on board it's stowed well away from the living-quarters. We only handle it at longish intervals, too."

"Still you haven't told me why it had marks on it like the bark of a tree," Julia said.

"Persistent creature, aren't you? Because it *is* a tree—fossilised. They get something like it in America too, a uranium phosphate, found in sandstones and near phosphate deposits —of course this country is stiff with phosphates."

"But does it look like a tree when it's in the ground?"

"Not very, though you do find a bit of fossil bark now and again. No, it looks more like soft sandstone, so soft that one can chop it out in chunks; usually we bag it because it's so friable —and we bag the rich sand too."

"What fell on the road in the Djebelet wasn't bagged," Julia observed.

"No—the damn bags got mislaid on that trip."

"How did you get the trousseau-coffers down from Fez to Ouarzazate or Tinerhir or wherever you were going? Surely you couldn't get enough into the camionnette, along with the shirts and nylons—after all, you had to have something to sell."

He stared at her.

"How on earth do you know that we were in Ouarzazate and Tinerhir?"

"Well, that was Affaires Indigènes, actually."

"And they told you about selling shirts and so forth, I suppose?"

"Did they? Oh, yes, M. Nussbaumer! But I'd heard that before, in Fez." She explained about the ex-*cantinier* at her hotel there. "Perfect cover, of course, and taking you right into the area of the mines. Only what I'm still not clear about is how you get the coffers down from Fez, and where you keep them while you're grubbing out your fossil chunks."

"Generally we send them down by lorry direct from Fez to a French *cantinier* who's in the thing."

"Ah, and then pick up one or two at a time and cart them out to your little diggings, hidden under the gents' wear?"

"That's it. Oh Julia, I wish you could see all those places! —it's terrific country. Sometimes you come on huge gorges nearly a thousand feet deep, with a great river raging through, and the little thread of road looking as if it was disappearing into Hell's mouth! And scrambling slowly about among the scrubby herbs and bushes—most of them smell so sweet in the sun!—with the Geiger-counter—at right angles to the strike of the rocks, of course—till you think you've picked up another deposit; and then working round plotting it on a one-metre or five-metre grid to make sure. You'd love it."

"Goodness, yes. But Colin, when you've bagged your ore, and crated it in the coffers, where do you assemble it for the caravan? Surely you can't keep a mass of it at a cantine?"

"Lord, no—there are far too many snoopers—like your Jew. No, that can be a problem. If there's a handy cave—often there is—we use that; if not we use our wits! One can't use the same place twice of course, though old St John's camel-men are very trustworthy as a rule—they'll do anything for him."

"Did he tell you I was a spy?" Julia asked.

"Well he told Torrens so, but he gave your name, and of course I guessed then that you were just after me, and said so. But this job is so secret that it was damned disconcerting to have anyone know as much as you'd obviously found out, you wretch!"

"But where can young Bathyadis stow trunks and trunksful of the stuff, till some ship comes in? His shop didn't look very big, and there were at least thirty camels in that caravan, with two trunks apiece, I suppose?"

"Yes, that has been another of the rather tricky things," he agreed. "We try to arrange only to send it down when we know that a suitable ship is due—but ships aren't always very punctual."

"You're telling *me*," said Julia with feeling. "Are camels any better?"

"No—worse! But—you saw his shop?"

"Yes—just under the wall of the Old Medina, nice and handy to the harbour."

"Exactly. And he's had a great hole scooped out in the thickness of that wall where he can stow the trunks quite safely, and if, for any reason, like a ship failing to call, we can't use Casa at all, there are always the tombs," he said grinning.

"And the *Finetta*. I see. By the way, did you get this last lot off all right?"

"Yes—worked like a charm. If we're really stuck I take the yacht down to Casa to relieve young Bathyadis. It's a lovely run."

Julia was still thinking it all out. It was wonderful to get the background to the problems which had been obsessing her for the last two months, but there was still more that she wanted to know.

"Why are you doing something illegally here, if you say it's legal in Paris?" she asked.

"You must ask the boss that—I'm not really in a position to say. These small lots that we've been getting out are only for experimental purposes—if the stuff does all the back-room boys hope, I imagine that there will be a proper international agreement, with concessions, all open and above-board. But everything in Morocco is such a mess-up at the moment, with no one knowing whether the ex-Sultan will come back or not, or where the French will stand if he does, that I imagine *they*"—he grinned—"thought it better just to carry on quietly under the rose for a start. Mind you that's only my private guess."

When Colin finally said that he must be getting along—

"When can Edina see you?" Julia asked. "You know what trouble there'll be if she meets you somewhere, and finds I've been keeping you hidden!"

"Why should she meet me anywhere?"

"Why shouldn't she? She goes to Purcell's."

"Yes, but I don't, for the moment."

"She may go up to see the Mendoub, and spot you on the roof of Mr. T.'s house, like I did," said Julia gaily. The young man put down his béret, turned round, and stared at her.

"*Did* you see me there?"

"Yes. That's how I knew you and he were together. It helped a lot, one way and another."

He appeared to reflect.

"That might explain Bathyadis, of course, if you mentioned Torrens to him. Did you?"

"Naturally—at least I described him."

Colin took up his hat again—and then suddenly gave her a boyish hug.

"You must have had a lot of fun!" he said. "Bless you, Julia love. I'll be seeing you. Look after your face."

Lady Tracy's small sherry-party had developed, by the time it took place, into a rather large cocktail-party, as these affairs have a way of doing—if the household is going to be disturbed in any case why not work off as many social debts as possible?—and one can't really leave out the poor So-and-Sos, they would be hurt. So most of Tangier's small *Corps Diplomatique* had been invited, including the young vice-consul who had been nice to Julia; the Bunch, who were

296

residents of long standing, and the English head of the Sûreté branch of the Zone Police, a tall dour Highlander called MacNeill; Mme La Besse and the Professor, the Duke and all the *Frivolity* party, and many more. Arrival by car or taxi was a little complicated, since only one machine at a time could perform the difficult manœuvre of reversing and turning at the edge of the cliff; but it was a fine night, and most people elected to get out some distance down the street on the landward side and walk the rest of the way—Moors in wild dress stood holding lanterns at intervals down the steep cement path to light the feet of the guests. This rather unusual approach to a social function delighted Edina. "*How* Old Testament!" she said, pausing.

"Why?"

"Oh, 'Be Thou a lamp unto my feet and light unto my path'—that really means something here. And besides, look at their clothes!"

"Yes, but come on—I think we're late," said Julia.

They were rather late. When 'Abdeslem ushered them into the big hall it was quite full of people, though the noise was less deafening than at most cocktail-parties because the voices rose up and lost themselves in the vaulted ceiling, above the high Moorish arches. Julia led Edina through the crowds across to where, as she expected, her hostess sat enthroned in her usual chair, under Jane Digby's picture of the Wilder Shores of Love; she introduced her—"This is my cousin Edina Monro, Lady Tracy."

The old woman gave the two young ones her usual gracious greeting—"But now you must meet Hugh. Hugh!"—she waved a copy of *Ebb and Flow*. "That is my signal. Ah, here he is. Hugh, I want you to meet my dear young friend Miss Probyn." Julia turned and found herself face to face with the red-haired man.

Major Torrens' expression at that moment was not lost on Edina Monro.

"How do you do?" Julia said in her slowest tones, holding out a languid hand. "I am delighted to meet you at last—I have been wanting to for quite a long time."

"Er—the pleasure is mutual," he replied rather stiffly—his well-drilled politeness, as Edina said afterwards, recalled the barrack square.

"Really? Do you know, that surprises me," said Julia coolly. "The last time we saw one another you seemed, I heard, to be in rather a hurry to get away."

He flushed up to the roots of his hair—Lady Tracy looked from one to the other, with raised eye-brows.

"But have you met already?" she was beginning, when another guest claimed her attention.

"Good evening, Lady Tracy. A splendid party! And how are *you*?"

"Oh, Captain MacNeill, how nice to see you! Now—Hugh I think you know, but not Miss Probyn"—she indicated Julia—"and her cousin, Miss Monro. Dear Julia, this is Captain MacNeill, of the Sûreté."

This time it was Julia who observed a certain stiffening in the police officer's expression at the name Monro. Edina's likeness to Colin was very marked—the height, the dead-white skin, the black hair and the surprising grey eyes. He shook hands, however, politely enough, and was saying something suitable about hoping they liked Tangier when Edina gave a sudden cry.

"*Colin!*" She darted into the throng and grasped her brother by the arm. "Oh goodness, Colin, you at last! What a place to find you! Come—" she tugged at him—"here's Julia, poor love—all plaster!"

Heads turned at this little scene; the wretched Colin thought it simplest to follow his sister where she led—which was up to the space near Lady Tracy's chair already occupied by Julia, Major Torrens, and the Head of the Sûreté. "Julia, *here's* Colin!" Edina said triumphantly.

"I've seen Julia," said Colin, shaking off his sister's hand from his arm, and glowering at MacNeill.

"But do you know one another already, too?" Lady Tracy said, beaming at the three beautiful young creatures, who indeed made a group of astonishing splendour as they stood together. "This is Hugh's assistant, dear Julia, whom I wanted you to meet."

"Yes, darling Lady T.—but he's also Edina's brother, and my cousin, and the missing man!" As she said this Julia shot a glance of delighted mischief at the Head of the Sûreté, who stood gnawing his moustache and looking sourly from Colin to Torrens and back again. "Don't you remember, you always promised to help me to find him? Colin Monro?—and here he is!"

Lady Tracy looked a little vague. "Ah yes—I do remember now. Monro—that seems to be everybody's name! And all so handsome!" She rounded smartly on her nephew.

"Hugh, do please bring some drinks! Here are all these beautiful young people dying of thirst, and poor Captain MacNeill too." Her tone was one of brisk authority, and to Julia's secret delight Major Torrens obeyed with the alacrity of a curate.

"I'll come and help—" Colin began, but Edina grasped his arm again.

"No you don't—not out of my sight till we've talked a bit!" She turned to her hostess. "Lady Tracy, will you forgive me if I get into a huddle with my prodigal brother? It's so exciting to find him here."

"Oh, yes, of course—if you go through that archway you will find two or three more rooms, and fewer people. But wait till Hugh brings you something to drink. How amusing this rencontre is, isn't it?" she said to Captain MacNeill. "This poor child has been looking for Mr. Monro for *ages*."

"Er—yes—quite so," the police officer replied rather stiffly, as another guest approached Lady Tracy.

"I'm not the only one, am I?" said Julia, a slow mirth spreading in her calm face.

"I beg your pardon?"

"Looking for Colin, I mean. It seems to be quite a local industry in Tangier."

Captain MacNeill stared at her, incredulously—then his face became blank.

"I'm afraid I don't understand."

"Don't you? Do you know, I really thought you did! Oh well, never mind—anyhow you know now, from Lady Tracy's own mouth, that Colin is Major Torrens' assistant; and he has been, for the last ten or eleven months. That's from mine, but you can take it from me, and confirm it at your leisure."

Captain MacNeill bent his dark Highland gaze, like a gloomy searchlight, on Julia.

"I don't think I caught your name," he said. "Might I know it?"

She laughed out loud.

"Oh, you're in the very best tradition! *Quite* splendid. My name is—

"Darling Julia, *here* you are!" The Duke of Ross-shire had come up, and enfolded her in one of his usual expansive hugs. "Evening, MacNeill. How's crime? Nothing but Spanish murders and dull smugglers? I see you are cultivating Miss Probyn as a welcome change—how wise. She is more bombed against than bombing!—I was there; I can vouch for it."

"Angus, have you had your stitches out yet?" Julia asked, rightly considering that the Duke had amply answered Captain MacNeill's last question.

"Yes, dear kind child; this morning. *Agony!*—but all over now, thank God. Ah, and here is Hugh with some drinks—thank God for that too!" He took a glass from the tray held by Major Torrens, handed it to Julia, and took another. "Mac-Neill, how are you? Hugh, I had an idea that I caught a glimpse of you the other day at Marrakesh, in a *highly* improbable moustache, just an instant before Miss Probyn and I were bombed. Or am I wrong?"

"My dear Duke, can even you be wrong sometimes?" Torrens asked—his words were adroit, but his brow was irritable. But both his adroitness and his irritability were lost on Angus Ross-shire, whose glance, straying round, lighted on the two young Monros, standing together in silent and rather angry beauty, waiting for their drinks, as bidden by their hostess.

"Good God! Isn't that young Colin?" he exclaimed. "Torrens, what an *un*-gay deceiver you are, keeping him hidden all this time, and driving our lovely Julia into the jaws of death looking for him—also, I may say, making an almighty quick get-away from those same jaws yourself! I must have a word with him"—and he strode over, glass in hand.

Julia entertained herself with a glance at Captain MacNeill; she found his expression rewarding.

"I find all this rather amusing," she said. "Don't you?"

"It has the merit of the unexpected, if that is a merit," he said slowly, but a little less stiffly.

Major Torrens presently came up to Julia with another drink.

"Oh, thank you. Do you think you and I could talk sometime?"

"Yes, perhaps we had better. Only this crowd—" he looked about him.

"Is there a corner? What about the roof?"

He laughed shortly.

"You seem to know as much about this house as about everything else. Yes, the roof by all means."

Julia led the way up. The air struck cool and sweet on her face as she came out into it; the night was full of stars, the sea was conversing gently with the rocks at the foot of the cliff. Away to one side Tangier threw up a diffused golden glow, set here and there with strings of brilliant lights; on the other, when she went and sat on the parapet, a single very small light shone up from the dark slopes below. "That must be Nilüfer's house," she said, gesturing at it with her cigarette.

"Yes." There was still hostility in the man's tone; slowly, she turned full towards him.

"Look, Major Torrens, I don't think we shall gain anything, either of us, by quarrelling, or even by stalling. I know you are not very pleased with me—but quite frankly, I am not very pleased with you, either."

"Oh, really? Why not?"

"Well, presumably you took the trouble to find out something of my cousin's home background before you roped him in for a job of this sort—or not?"

"Yes, naturally I did."

"Well, if you knew that he was the only son of his mother, and she a widow, don't you think it was rather irresponsible of you, not to say merciless, to prevent him from answering any of the letters urging him to come home—or the advertisements?"

"Did he tell you that I prevented him?" Torrens asked.

"Of course not. But I know him, and now I've met you— and I am perfectly confident that he discussed it with you, in his concern, and was acting on your advice when he didn't reply. Are you prepared to swear that I am wrong?"

"I feel a good deal like swearing, but—no, I am not prepared to swear that. I gave him the advice that in the circumstances seemed to me wisest. When I took him on to work for me he also took on certain obligations—including a considerable obligation of secrecy." He paused. "And I covered up a good deal of disagreeable publicity on his account."

"Oh, I know you did. That—oh, and taking him on at all —was really a work of mercy, and I'm grateful for it. By the way, was it you who got his last letter posted at Ceuta? A cover up, was it?"

Torrens laughed—but this time the laugh sounded genuine, almost friendly.

"How detailed you are! Yes, of course."

"Good-oh. That was one of the things I wanted to know."

"Are there others?"

"Yes. If it's really all right in Paris, why have you been getting out this Astridite stuff so secretly here, and running all these risks?"

"I see Colin has been indiscreet," Torrens said.

"Not about the name—I got that elsewhere," said Julia.

"The devil you did!"

"Yes, but never mind how. Do go on."

He proceeded to explain. One Secret Service might have an agreement with another Secret Service, if it was to the ultimate advantage of both; the French in fact preferred these particular underground activities to be carried on by the British—"We are less subject to leaks—as a rule! This time we haven't been quite so successful as usual."

"Meaning me?" Julia asked.

"In fact, yes."

"Oh, what a worry! Shall you be able to go on?"

He hesitated for a moment before replying, and walked quickly round the roof; no washing encumbered it on this occasion, and it was easy to establish that no one was lurking behind the two chimney-stacks.

"I think it will probably not be necessary," he said when he returned to where she sat on the parapet. "What we have been sending was really for experimental purposes, and I think they have sufficient for that now."

"What, with this last lot from Bathyadis, and the tombs?"

"Yes." She could almost hear that he was smiling.

"So in fact Colin could come home?"

"If it was absolutely vital I suppose he could, if he wanted to. But it would be a great pity."

"Why?"

"Because he is rather a valuable person for this sort of work. He's clever, he's resourceful, he's energetic, and he has a most unusual gift for languages; he has picked up Arabic, which isn't an easy language, in the most amazing way—he can even imitate rustic dialects."

"He always was a good mimic," said Julia happily. "Go on."

"Well, I have been working with him now for nearly a year, and I think I understand his character to some extent; I believe he could make a career for himself in the service in a way he would hardly be likely to do outside it. He hates routine, being in harness—"

"That's true," Julia interjected.

"—And in this job, though there is discipline, there's very little routine. I should have liked to see him find himself in work for which he is quite peculiarly adapted, where he could make a reasonable living, and be of real use to his country. He's young still, of course, and uncertain of himself—and sometimes unwise—" this time the smile was quite audible— "not unnaturally, perhaps, in the circumstances."

"How well you know him," said Julia; there was warmth in her voice.

"I've got fond of the boy. But you think it's his duty to go back to his place and his people?"

"It certainly was at one point—when everyone wrote. But it's just possible that there might be another solution to that problem, now."

"Oh, really? It would be quite excellent if that could be arranged. Are you going to organise it? That would relieve me of all anxiety—if I may say so, you seem to have rather unusual gifts too."

Julia turned from the parapet and swept him a curtsey; the distant glow of Tangier's lights on her black-and-gold frock illuminated the graceful movement.

"*Merci!*" she said.

"Well, Miss Probyn, I have to hand it to you," Torrens said. "Reluctantly, I admit! But though I have been on this job for a longish time, and often up against quite powerful organisations, I've never before been brought to a full stop by a single young woman."

"Oh, splendid!" said Julia, laughing. "You wouldn't have a job for me too, as a sort of Mata Hari, or something?"

"Not till I have young Colin properly run in and thoroughly stabilised—not on your life!" said the Major. "Apply again three years hence. But will you try to get him released to carry on with me?"

"It doesn't really depend on me—but I'll try to foster it. If Colin stays with you, where will it be?"

"God knows! Wherever we're wanted next."

Chapter 17

JULIA and Major Torrens descended from the roof in high good humour, exchanging laughing remarks; at the foot of the stairs they encountered a new arrival coming in from the front door, a very diminutive figure indeed—it was Mr. St John. Hugh greeted him warmly—"Oh, splendid, Sir. I'm so glad you made it; my aunt will be delighted. I believe you know Miss Probyn, don't you?" he added blandly.

"Er—yes, we have met," said Mr. St John stiffly; but he made no movement to shake hands—he stood looking from one to the other with the aspect of an incredulous, resentful, and completely bewildered tortoise. Julia's ready pity awoke.

"Major Torrens and I have made it up," she said gently. "And I have seen Colin at last—in fact he's here tonight! So perhaps you will let me say how sorry I am to have caused you so much anxiety in Fez, when you had been so good to me."

Mr. St John opened his mouth and shut it again two or three times, soundlessly, like a lizard catching flies; then he turned his small reptilian eyes enquiringly to Torrens.

"She's perfectly right, Sir. I'm so glad you're down—we must have a word later on. But I have practically retained Miss Probyn's services as an assistant! I think she may be able to help me very much."

"Miss Probyn's *ability* was never in doubt," the old gentleman enunciated dryly. "Therefore it is almost certainly better to have her as an assistant than as an opponent; and though I confess to surprise at this development, for your sake, Torrens, I welcome it." He turned to Julia, and glanced at the long strip of plaster on her forehead.

"I was sorry to hear of your accident," he said, in his precise tones; "but you may remember that I warned you that your intervention might be dangerous. I hope you are

306

recovered, and that there will be no permanent disfigurement?"

"Oh, I don't expect so, thank you so much. But am I forgiven?"

"If Major Torrens has forgiven you, clearly I may also," the old man said, a little smile at last appearing on his withered lips.

A Moorish servant came up with a tray of drinks—several of these creatures, hardly less wild in appearance than the lantern-bearers outside, constantly moved through the rooms; Julia guessed that they were some of the hangers-on who took their toll of Lady Tracy's peas and eggs. Mr. St John took a glass of sherry; Julia and Major Torrens went on with cocktails.

"Look, Sir," Torrens said, after politely raising his glass to the old man—"Before you come and talk to my aunt, have you any news? You can say anything in front of Miss Probyn," he added rather hastily—"she is practically on the strength!" Julia grinned at this statement.

"Yes," said Mr. St John, with his customary deliberation. "Very interesting news, in fact. Of course you left Marrakesh rather hurriedly, and in any case your contacts are on somewhat different lines to mine." He paused, and sipped his sherry.

"Yes, Sir?" Torrens said, with rather studied patience.

"I hear that the Glaoui is changing his mind," the old gentleman pursued. "He recognises, it seems, that resentment at the deposition of the ex-Sultan is stronger than he had reckoned on, and he is considering the idea of his return."

"Good Lord! You don't say so!" Torrens exclaimed. "But the Glaoui took the main part in throwing him out."

"Quite so. He miscalculated—not a usual Arab mistake. But the broadcasts from Cairo have been intensified considerably since he took that decision, something he could not foresee. Anyhow he is now trimming his sails to suit the prevailing wind—it may not emerge for some time, months, perhaps—but it will happen."

"Will that be a good or a bad thing?" Julia asked, putting in her oar. "You told me before that the ex-Sultan was frightfully recalcitrant, and held up all reforms, so that he really had to go."

Hugh Torrens' eyebrows went up at this statement—Mr. St John gave an unexpectedly genial twinkle.

"You see that you are indeed to be congratulated on your new assistant, Torrens! She has quite a grasp; but then she is a disciple of de Foucauld." He turned to Julia.

"Perhaps the ex-Sultan miscalculated too—and it may be that a disagreeable exile has caused him, also, to modify his attitude. As to that I have no information as yet, though I expect it presently. But you can count on the other development. And now I think I must really pay my respects to my hostess."

Hugh was about to go with him when Julia laid a hand on his arm. "Just *one* second."

"Yes?"

"I forgot to ask you upstairs. If you're closing down partly because Affaires Indigènes have got wise to your goings on, what about the East Germans? As they know now about them too, I mean."

"Why do you suppose that Affaires Indigènes know about them too?"

"Well, don't they?"

He laughed.

"I certainly won't swear that they don't! But how did *you* know?"

"Good contacts. But won't they be cleared up?"

"Probably. It is being discussed, I believe."

"Why not certainly?"

"Oh, because metropolitan France is in such a bloody mess!" said the man, with a sort of cold, weary anger. "Neutralism in high places—the Abomination of Desolation standing where it ought not, in this case in Paris. Has it ever struck you how apocalyptic the world is, today?"

308

"Yes, often," said Julia. "When one was a child and read all those ghastly goings-on in the Old Testament, dashing children's heads against the stones and all that, one thought it just crazy barbarous rubbish, something the world had grown out of—but in this last war it became completely *à la page*, every bit of it."

"How right," he said, turning onto her a deep intense stare which startled Julia. "I see that you recognise our times for what they are. But then you are a disciple of de Foucauld, St John said?"

"Yes—anyhow, a student." But her words were unimportant; what spoke was the interchange between their eyes—his fixed plunging gaze, the half-reluctant compelled response of Julia's dove's eyes.

"God! I should like to have you to work with," he said at last. "All the root of the matter—and *such* natural camouflage!"

Julia laughed, in slight and quite unwonted embarrassment; but she was aware of a strong desire to respond somehow to this rather back-handed praise—it was of a different order to the tributes she was accustomed to receive. Before she had found any words—

"You were so sweet to the old boy," Hugh Torrens went on, "when he'd been all set to do you down."

"Weren't you, too? You were nearly as nasty as he was when we first met, tonight."

"Was I? Perhaps I was. You weren't very friendly yourself, if I remember rightly! Anyhow I should like to take it all back now."

"Julia, sweet!" Colin Monro, coming up, hooked an arm familiarly through hers. "I've got some good news—at least near-news."

"Yes?" said Julia, with a certain lack of enthusiasm—at that precise moment she could have dispensed with the presence even of her dear Colin. Major Torrens made to move away.

"No, half-a-second, Hugh—this concerns you, too, even if it is a bit of a family secret still."

"Well, what *is* it?" Julia asked impatiently, though beginning to guess.

"Well, I might not have to go home after all—I mean conceivably I might not be needed even if I *could* go—because Edina has mopped up a most delightful type—although he has a beard—and Angus says he knows all about sheep and farming, and moreover is very *rich*, believe it or not. So if they were to get married he could prop up Glentoran indefinitely, as well as run it."

Major Torrens threw a glance of amused enquiry at Julia.

"And exactly how do I come into this, Colin?" he asked the eager young man.

"Well, Sir—" belatedly, Colin remembered his official manners in Julia's presence—"you did say something about possibly keeping me on even if our show here has folded up; of course I should like that better than anything, if it didn't mean leaving Mother in the cart, and the place to go down the drain." He paused.

"Yes—so?"

"Well, the position is this: Edina—my sister—has to go South in a day or so on some lunatic business about getting camels photographed for advertisements, and she had laid on this aspirant for her hand," said Colin, with a grin—"to act as courier and so forth, because he speaks Spanish. But she has suggested that I might come along too, as I speak Arabic, to help out with the camel aspect, and—well, to act as chaperone, I suppose. Save any embarrassment, and generally foster the affair. But would that be all right by you?"

"Colin, I think you couldn't be better employed," said Torrens. "Go by all means."

"Thank you very much, Sir. I'll do everything in my power to see that they do get engaged—judicious absences and all

310

that. I'll go and tell Edina it's O.K."—and he moved gracefully away.

"So it is Colin who is to 'foster' this excellent arrangement, not you," said Hugh Torrens to Julia, looking amused. "I should enjoy seeing him acting Cupid. I must say."

"Lunatic child! But you know he will do it beautifully. He's very percipient and quick," said Julia.

"That seems to run in the family! Well, I do hope he brings it off, or it brings itself off. Meanwhile, would you dine with me tonight, when this show is over, or are you entangled with your relations? My aunt I know will go straight to bed—she loves parties, but they exhaust her completely."

"Yes—what a mercy she has someone like Feridah to take care of her."

"Oh, you know Feridah? Of course you would. But did 'Yes' mean that you will dine?"

"Well, I shouldn't think Edina and her 'aspirant' will want an extra, and I daresay Colin will tag along with Angus Ross-shire," said Julia. "Oh, by the way, why do you know him well enough to be called 'Hugh', and Lady T. not know him at all?—Angus, I mean?"

"I was his fag at Winchester, and since he's been in and out of here I have seen him fairly often—my aunt of course lives in a certain isolation, in the sense that she doesn't meet all the casuals. But—forgive my persistence—*are* you going to do me the honour of dining with me?"

"Thank you. Yes, I should like to very much," said Julia. "But not in your house," she added quickly.

He looked at her in surprise.

"It shall be wherever you like, of course. But why not in my house?"

"Because it's the only house in the world where I have given my name, and then had the door shut in my face."

He looked disturbed and astonished. "Please explain," he said.

311

Julia explained.

"Yes, well Hassan was only obeying orders, up to a point—but he was being a little extra smart," Torrens said at the end. "I dislike its having happened, though." Suddenly he began to smile. "So you saw us on the roof? Well!"

"Purcell says he was always warning you not to sit out there," said Julia; "but it was well for me you did, that day, because it gave me my only clue."

"How did that clue help you?"

"Telling Bathyadis that the jeune Monsieur I was seeking worked with a red-haired man," said Julia. Torrens pounced on this.

"Oh, *that* was what made the old Moor blow the gaff! We've all been wondering how on earth you worked that—whether you slipped a Truth Drug tablet into his mint tea, or what. I hope you will tell me every detail tonight—at the Minzah!"

"Chère enfant, *where* have you hidden yourself all the evening? One has not seen you, and now we leave," said Mme La Besse, coming up with the Professor in tow.

"I got here rather late—I'm so sorry," said Julia.

"You come tomorrow? We shall open some more of the coffins in the Museum."

"Yes, assuredly. *Adieu, Chère Madame*—goodbye, Professor."

Other people were beginning to leave; in the mysterious manner normal to the end of cocktail-parties the hall, so recently densely packed, in a matter of minutes was almost empty. "We must go. I wonder where Edina is?—I must find her," said Julia, who with Torrens had begun to make her way over towards her hostess.

"Oh, good evening, Miss Probyn." This was the young vice-consul. "I expect you know already, but your cousin for whom you were enquiring before is here tonight—I met him just now, with the Duke of Ross-shire."

"Oh, thank you so much—yes, he came to see me yesterday. He's been away," said Julia smoothly. "But you have been *so* kind. Goodbye." The young man cast a curious glance at Major Torrens, still at her side, as he moved away.

"*Born* for it!" Hugh exclaimed in delight.

"No, but tell me this—why didn't *he* connect Colin with the *Finetta* business? I went to ask him about that, and though he obviously knew *something*—he wouldn't say what—about the bother with the *Finetta*, he never connected Colin with her."

"That was owing to the efforts of your humble servant."

"At the Consulate-General! They *must* have known."

"Another department," he said blandly.

"Oh, I see. Now there are our lovers, in the far room; would you round them up, while I say Goodbye."

"Dear child, must you go?" the old lady said, as Julia bent and kissed her.

"Darling Lady Tracy, *yes*—we've stayed a shameful time, but it was such a lovely party. Thank you and thank you."

"Did you have any talk with Hugh?" Lady Tracy asked, with a bright glance.

"Yes, a splendid talk—all about Colin."

"Ah, yes—how *amusing* that it is he who has been helping Hugh all this time. If only I had realised!—I could have helped you so much sooner, and you need not have got your face hurt," said the old lady, putting up a hand and stroking Julia's forehead. "But you will always be beautiful—and a scar is so *interesting*."

Julia, though a little puzzled by the beginning of this speech, was still laughing when Major Torrens came up, shepherding Edina and Mr. Reeder. "Now where's my young aide?" he said, looking round.

" 'Here Sir! Here Sir! Here Sir! Here Sir!'—as they say at the opposition shop," said Colin, emerging from a window-recess. They all made their farewells. "Heavens! We're the very last! How awful," said Julia, as they crossed the hall. "Major Torrens, oughtn't someone to send Feridah to your aunt? She must be quite worn out."

"Look," was all he said—glancing back Julia saw that lovely veiled figure bending over her aged mistress, in the familiar caressing attitude.

Out on the windy concrete path, where the lantern-bearers still lingered—Moors always know whether the last guest has left a party or not; they probably count them—Hugh Torrens said—

"Now, who's going where? I have a car."

"I'm meeting Angus at Purcell's before I go on to dine on the yacht," said Colin, after a glance at his sister.

"Purcell's will do for us," said Edina. Colin gave a nip to Julia's arm at the "us". So to Purcell's they went—Torrens told Julia, rather abruptly, to sit beside him in front.

"Plenty of room in Mr. Smith's car, Charles!" she murmured in his ear as they drove away down the steep narrow street—he laughed explosively.

It was very late when they reached the bar; except for the Duke it was empty.

"My friends have gone on board to recuperate," he said to Colin. "We will follow them in due course. But do everyone sit down and have a stirrup-cup first—indicate your particular form of stirrup, all of you."

"The Mongols line their stirrups with cork," said Torrens, sitting down beside Julia.

"Quite appropriate to cups, Hugh, corks. But am I right in assuming that we all go on with cocktails? Right—much wiser. Purcell, could we have six Martinis?" He turned to Julia. "And now that you have found your long-lost cousin—you may remember how cross you were when I suggested, in this very room, that that was what your charming presence here was in aid of—what are your plans? Are you going home, or will you come and cruise with us? My sickly friend is going back, so there is a cabin to spare."

Julia was suddenly and unaccountably aware of a tension, at this question, in the man sitting beside her.

"Neither, Angus," she said in her near-drawl. "I shall stay on for a bit. I can't *plaquer* poor old Mme La Besse just now, while her Cambridge expert is here—and besides I want to see all those coffins opened. I'm hoping to filch a pair of Phoenician ear-rings when no one is looking."

"Devoted girl! I can only applaud, though I found your whiskered female employer *peu séduisante* to a degree. And our lovely Edina is setting out for the South to photograph camels, and make millions out of it, *n'est-ce-pas?*—so she can't come. Colin, are you tired of the sea?—or have you other commitments?"

"It's very good of you, Angus, but I'm going South with Edina."

"But I thought Edina already had an escort," said the Duke.

"Ah, but he can't talk Arabic—I shall cope with the camel-owners for her."

Reeder was saying something inaudible to Edina—she nodded. He cleared his throat.

"I am allowed to say that Miss Monro and I are engaged to be married," he announced. "You might as well all know it now as later."

"No! What a surprise!"

"Angus, you're tight," said Edina bluntly.

"Darling, at least I'm not *quarrelsome* drunk."

Reeder ignored this exchange.

"I realise that a week may seem rather quick work," he pursued, in the very cultivated accents that had first struck Julia on the wet quay-side at the London Docks—"but since it was bound to happen anyhow, it seemed more sensible to settle it at once. It gives me a *locus standi*."

Julia got up, sliding out with some difficulty past Torrens' knees, and gave her cousin a kiss. "Darling, how *lovely*. Bless you," she said. She turned and took Reeder's hand. "It couldn't be nicer."

"What did I tell you, right at the start?" he said.

"Yes, yes—how right you were."

"As head of the family, I should perhaps say that this arrangement has my full approval," Colin pronounced, with a fine display of young male pompousness, as he too shook Reeder by the hand.

"Edina, have you realised that he'll be able to talk Spanish to Olimpia every single day, so you'll always have the most miraculous food at Glentoran?" said Julia gaily.

"Yes. Olimpia is our Spanish cook, and she only functions properly after a dose of her own language," Edina explained to Reeder.

"Oughtn't we to send Aunt Ellen a telegram?" Julia asked presently.

"Do you think so? At once?" Edina said, a little doubtfully.

"Yes, I do. There are she and poor Mrs. H. stewing and worrying away, when Colin's found, and you're engaged, and I'm perfectly fit again—as well as Angus—and the factor problem, I rather gather, is solved—or is it?" She glanced at Reeder.

"Yes. The new factor is engaged," he said, grinning broadly in his beard.

"Well, then!—and here we all sit carousing, while they moulder! We *must*, Edina."

"She's quite right," Reeder said to Edina, with a certain brusque firmness.

"It'll have to be a jolly long telegram," Colin observed.

It was fairly long. They compiled it there and then, with a good deal of laughter; everyone except Torrens signed it, and Reeder undertook to get it sent off that night. "Our agents can always make a signal."

"Well, now that filial piety has done its part, and the electric telegraph is about to give its imprimatur to this happy arrangement, I think it should be drunk to in due form," said the Duke. "Purcell, would you have any champagne?"

Purcell had champagne—moreover when it came to the

table and was poured out it was obvious that it had been in ice for some considerable time. Across her frosted glass Julia glanced towards Reeder—"*Sabe todo*," she murmured. He laughed.

When the health of the pair had been duly drunk she said—

"I should like to propose another toast."

"Whom to, dear? Me?" the Duke asked.

"*No*, Angus. To Mr. Purcell, who seems to me to have been responsible, one way or another, for most of our happy endings."

"I second that," said Torrens.

"And I," said Reeder.

From the first moment that she had set eyes on him Julia had always been fascinated by the play of expression in Purcell's face; but when they all six stood up—Angus Ross-shire and Edina manifestly a little mystified—and raised their glasses to drink his health, that half-negro mask surpassed itself—tears, unbelievably, stood in those surprising grey eyes. He came round from behind the bar, bent over Julia's hand and kissed it, murmuring, "*Con permiso*."

Over dinner at the Minzah Hugh Torrens and Julia had a tremendous clearing-up of what, on either side, lay behind the events of the last two months—always such a highly satisfying process to the participants. Hugh for instance learned how she had originally got onto the fact of the transfer of Colin's account to Casablanca, of Mr. Consett's *volte-face*, and Mr. Panoukian's highly suspicious behaviour; Julia, in fits of mirth, listened to exactly what poor Mr. St John (in code) had written about her. They got it straight, bit by bit, mightily enjoying themselves; but quite at the end Julia, still puzzled by Lady Tracy's enigmatic remarks as she said Goodbye, quoted them. "*Did* she know all along that Colin was working for you? And does she know what you are doing?"

"One never really knows *what* she knows!—almost always more than one thinks."

"But I told her his name at the very beginning, when she promised to help me."

"Ah, yes, but she forgets names—she's ninety-two remember. Did you tell her about the Bank, and all that?"

"Well, no, I didn't." Julia did not feel it necessary to mention the reason for this, her desire to protect Mr. Consett.

"Ah, there you are. I feel pretty sure that if you had told her that it would have rung a bell, and she would have done something about putting you onto Colin, because she's absolutely enchanted with you—not so very surprising!"

"Yes, I'm sure Lady Tracy would always be perfectly straight, if she remembered," said Julia—a little unsteadily under his words and his eyes.

The telegram composed in Purcell's Bar in Tangier reached Glentoran the following afternoon. Mrs. Hathaway and Mrs. Monro had been out calling on old Lady Monteith, and since Forbes was too deaf to hear anything on the telephone, and Olimpia knew no English, the post-mistress flagged the car as it passed through the village, and handed the envelope in at the window. "Grand news for Mistress Monro about Miss Edina," she said, beaming.

Mrs. Monro fingered the envelope, which was unusually fat, as the car turned into the drive.

"Why about Edina? Why not about Colin?" she said, rather fretfully

"Try opening it to see," said Mrs. Hathaway, displaying her usual patience with her poor friend.

"Oh—well, here we are at the house—let's go indoors first," said Mrs. Monro, struggling incompetently to disentangle herself from the rug before the chauffeur could come round to remove it. "Forbes, tea in the morning-room," she said, as the old man appeared on the steps. And indeed it was only in the morning-room, a small apartment next to the dining-room— with faded chintzes and a fire as bad as all the other fires at

318

Glentoran—that at last, putting on her spectacles, she opened the telegram.

"I can't make head or tail of it," she said, still fretfully, having done so. "And why should Angus Ross-shire sign it? You read it, Mary"—and she handed the sheets to Mrs. Hathaway. At last that much-enduring lady read—

COLIN FOUND SAFE WELL HAS GOOD JOB STOP JULIA QUITE RECOVERED SCAR WON'T BE MUCH STOP NEW PERMANENT FACTOR ENGAGED WHO SPEAKS SPANISH NAME PHILIP REEDER STOP EDINA IS ENGAGED TO HIM STOP FIANCES AND JULIA RETURN IN ABOUT A MONTH COLIN'S RETURN INDEFINITE BUT THAT DOESN'T MATTER NOW STOP EVERYTHING PERFECT ALL VERY HAPPY AND ALL WRITING STOP BEST LOVE FROM COLIN EDINA JULIA HUMBLE SALUTATIONS PHILIP REEDER STOP ELLEN I ENTIRELY REPEAT ENTIRELY APPROVE

ROSS-SHIRE.

"Can *you* understand it?" Mrs. Monro asked, as her friend turned back to the beginning again.

"Oh, yes, Ellen."

"But can Edina be going to marry a factor? What an awful idea."

"That's only a joke," said Mrs. Hathaway. "That tiresome old Sir Robert Reeder of Otterglen had a son called Philip who went away to sea; he was a godson of an old aunt of Mollie Ross-shire's and she left him all her money the other day—no doubt that's why Angus approves so much!" Mrs. Hathaway added, with an amused smile.

"But if he's so rich, why should he take a job as factor, Mary?"

"That's just their nonsense—I expect they all drafted it over drinks," said Mrs. Hathaway astutely. "Don't you see, Ellen, if young Reeder marries Edina *he* can run the place—that's all they mean."

"Then they should have said so. But why isn't Colin

coming home? It's him I wanted to see," said poor Mrs. Monro, beginning to hunt in her bag for her handkerchief.

"He's bound to come home for the wedding—he'll have to give Edina away," said Mrs. Hathaway, with compassionate cheerfulness. "And you see they say he has a good job, too. *And* that precious Julia's lovely face won't be spoilt," she added, half to herself. "Look, Ellen, take off your hat and sit down quietly, and let's draft an answer before the Post Office shuts."

"Oh, well, if you think we ought to," said Mrs. Monro, putting away her handkerchief—the two ladies were sitting concocting their telegram when Forbes came in wheeling a trolley, surmounted by a vast silver tray, with the tea.

"Forbes, Miss Edina is engaged to be married," said Mrs. Monro.

"Yes, Mistress Monro, so I heard. To a very rich gentleman, who speaks Spanish. Yon cook is highly delighted," said Forbes with respectful contempt, as he left the room.

Mrs. Hathaway laughed. Then she glanced out of the window. Daffodils in thousands were just coming into flower under the chestnut-trees beyond the rather unkempt lawn, where the ground fell away to the noisy river; great scarlet rhododendrons bloomed above an untidy growth of saplings on the further slope; over all stood the silent outline of the hill. So much beauty, so long neglected—it was good to think that it would be cared for again at last.

She returned, happily, to composing the telegram.